Praise

D1434933

'My heart always soars ~~~ ~~~ Mhairi novel, ~~~ ~~
love her. She's so great at treading the narrow line between
humour and loss. I read this with delight and envy'

MARIAN KEYES

'Gorgeously romantic, as well as a story about friendship and
grief and loss; I never wanted it to end'   BETH O'LEARY

'Funny, charming and smart'   LUCY DIAMOND

'Gorgeous, funny, life-affirming'   JENNY COLGAN

'Funny, poignant, full of insight . . . a triumph' KATIE FFORDE

'A luminous, heart-achingly beautiful love letter to friendship'

JOSIE SILVER

'An effortlessly brilliant read – will have you laughing when
you shouldn't and sobbing when you least expect it'

GIOVANNA FLETCHER

'So funny, so sad in parts, and just so sharp and heartwarming'

LIA LOUIS

'Witty, moving and original. I will read anything Mhairi writes,
she is the master of thought-provoking romantic fiction and
I adore the characters she creates'   SOPHIE COUSENS

Between Us

Sunday Times bestselling author Mhairi McFarlane was born in Scotland in 1976 and her unnecessarily confusing name is pronounced Vah-Ree. After some efforts at journalism, she started writing fiction and her debut, *You Had Me at Hello*, was an instant success. She's since sold over 2 million copies of her books. *Between Us* is her ninth novel and she lives in Nottingham with a man and a cat.

Mhairi McFarlane

Between Us

HarperCollins*Publishers*

HarperCollins*Publishers* Ltd
1 London Bridge Street,
London SE1 9GF
www.harpercollins.co.uk

HarperCollins*Publishers*
Macken House,
39/40 Mayor Street Upper,
Dublin 1
D01 C9W8

First published by HarperCollins*Publishers* 2023
1

ISBN: 978-0-00-841248-7 (PB B-format)
ISBN: 978-0-00-841252-4 (TPB)

Set in Bembo by Palimpsest Book Production Ltd, Falkirk, Stirlingshire

Printed and bound in the UK using 100% Renewable Electricity
at CPI Group (UK) Ltd

For Jeanie
A woman telling great stories

Prologue

2003
Stockport Plaza Theatre

Wythenshawe's No. 1 Psychic! proclaimed a poster on an easel on stage, for tonight's show: a clairvoyant called Queenie Mook. The name was so peculiar, it couldn't be made up.

'You wonder who decides that?' Roisin said. 'It's not like you can get . . . accredited.'

Aged twelve, she was proud of *accredited*.

Her mother looked at her with narrowing eyes, under Lancôme-blacked lashes, sensing sedition.

When Roisin had been permitted to join her girls' night out, it came with a warning.

'Don't bother if you're going to be a smart arse – it's rude to Diana and Kim,' her mum had said. 'Di's dad, Rodney, died of acute pancreatitis last November. She's hoping he'll come through.'

'Oh, right,' Roisin said, thinking that treating Queenie Mook as a switchboard for the Afterlife didn't seem destined for success. Her promotional material showed she mainly worked cruise ships.

'They've been at sixes and sevens since. Rod still ran the financial side of the drain-cleaning business.' Lorraine made it sound as if Diana had a pressing but functional enquiry: *where is the 2001 VAT return*, or similar.

Roisin wanted to attend for two reasons: curiosity about mediums, and because this was a properly exciting jolly. Her mum was drenched in a forcefield of Guerlain Shalimar, a lion's mane of salon-blown hair, satin dress stretched across her hips, sheer tights and patent heels.

It was fun to be in her mother's orbit on such occasions, seeing the heads she turned. Like being PA to someone famous. There was a taxi from Webberley, Lorraine's perfumed coven demanding that Lionel Richie's 'All Night Long' was *TURNED UP, PLEASE.*

Fifteen minutes to curtain up. Thanks to the carafes of pink wine they'd seen off during the pre-show brasserie dinner, there was a flurry of trips to the ladies.

Lorraine went first, then Di and Kim together.

'Don't you need a wee?' said her mum, after a minute of concerted pouting into her make-up compact. Roisin vaguely wondered if Lorraine wanted her out of the way. For the purposes of a surreptitious phone call, perhaps? Her parents kept secrets. Roisin was always caught between wanting to know what they were, and not wanting to know what they were.

'Nah.'

'Hmmm, I think you should go. We're in the middle of a row and those seats will fill up.'

Roisin's conviction that her mother had an ulterior motive deepened. But she knew it was easier to comply, so she stood up and headed to the toilets. All the stall doors were closed. As she plonked down on the cold seat in her cubicle, she heard the acoustics of the other occupants exiting theirs.

Flush. Door bang. Tap gush. Flush. Door bang. Tap gush.

'With the way Lorraine's hitting the Pinot Blush, I assume she's no longer *with child*?' said a disembodied Kim.

For a split second, Roisin thought they meant her.

'Oh no. She got rid. A couple of weeks ago.'

'She never told Glen?'

Glen. Roisin's dad was called Kent. (A pub landlord called Kent. His name was a gift to customers he kicked out.)

'God, no. As she says, what would be the point? He'd not want her to keep it, and two's enough. Who'd go back to night feeds?'

'What about Kent? Did he know?'

'Doubt it, don't you? Don't ask, don't tell.'

'Mmmm. She wants to be more careful.'

'Says she had a dodgy omelette at the Fox & Hounds, threw up her pill. Never thought.'

'You know, I've wondered about the food at the Fox's. I had coleslaw once that tasted like tuna. I'm sure it gave me the shits.'

There was a blast of an air dryer, which obscured the next part, until Roisin could tune back in:

'. . . does what he likes, too. She and Kent are like a couple of carefree teenagers, aren't they?'

'Mmm–hmm. She's free of that particular care now, anyway. Is my skirt seam straight?'

They clattered out.

Roisin sat with her knickers round her knees as she absorbed the fact that her mother had got pregnant by a man she knew as one of her parents' card-playing friends.

This information put the official signature on a disorientating, gruesome experience she'd had a year earlier. On these particular social occasions, involving Texas hold 'em and copious amounts of tequila, her parents issued stern warnings not to come downstairs *under any circumstances*.

Roisin and her brother had long ago developed a technique for sneaking down to spy on Christmas present wrapping, and later to subvert being grounded: the bar in the family pub was high enough that, as a smaller person, you could crouch low and crab-scuttle behind it.

You were in the saloon at the front, which the grown-ups typically inhabited after hours. You could, with the agility of a safe-cracker, carefully unbolt the little door panel at the side and escape into the lounge, and then the pub garden and Webberley beyond.

This Saturday, despite the muffled hubbub below, Roisin had a powerful craving for Dr Pepper. She would look back and wonder if, in fact, her subconscious had a thirst for knowledge, because the appeal of the drink and the potential bollocking in no way balanced out.

Roisin crept downstairs, heart in mouth. Sliding the bottle out of the rack and hooking its medal lid on the opener was made infinitely easier by the raucous, booze-fuelled badinage of her dad and a woman, Glen's wife, Tina, unseen but very close at hand. Cigarette smoke curled in the air and the jukebox played something jazzy. Ice clinked. Laughter exploded.

Mission accomplished, as Roisin gripped the soda pop bottle, yet something compelled her to take the insane, additional risk of opening the side door and poking her head into the lounge bar. In the near distance, at the pool table, two figures were clamped together. She couldn't see the faces of either. Her mother's legs, feet with painted toenails in gold strappy shoes that Roisin coveted, dangled either side of bare male buttocks. Roisin made out foreign, animalistic noises as the dull thud of understanding hit her in the guts. A cry of shock and objection caught in her throat before she withdrew and fled back upstairs to lie awake in bed, awash with sweat and chest pounding, trying to make sense of what she'd seen.

Now, returning to her place in the theatre balcony, Roisin felt similar.

She couldn't help staring at the near imperceptible, shallow curve of her mum's stomach under shiny fabric, inspecting her glossed face for clues. When had she done it, the termination? During a school day?

She'd assimilate tonight's lurid intel entirely by herself: with perhaps one failed attempt to discuss it with her younger brother, Ryan. No matter how many times he made it clear that Roisin's revelations weren't welcome, she lived in hope of him as a confidante.

Roisin became grateful for the distraction of watching

Queenie Mook ply her strange trade, in the multicoloured up-lit, kitsch altverse of the variety theatre.

Queenie was very petite and had a helmet of fluorescent orange hair, a startling synthetic tangerine that recalled Johnny Rotten.

She addressed the throng as 'my loves' and was dressed in a silk blouse with an egg-sized enamel brooch, navy trousers, like the manager of a branch of Vision Express. Roisin was a little disappointed, having envisioned an imperious Sixties matriarch with a chignon, in a beaver fur coat.

The show soon settled into a rhythm – Roisin figured out it was a game of harvesting information from the audience, while weaving the illusion of having supplied it. The phantoms, seen and heard only by Queenie, only ever offered their first name, which was always a plain and common one. None of them gave surnames, which would've resolved identity a lot quicker.

A procession of Teds, Marys and Jacks queued up. Queenie auctioned their presence to the auditorium, along with a few other salient, yet vague details. Perhaps Mary loved music – *everyone would say that about her,* she says – or Jack was motioning a steering wheel? Did he . . . *like cars? Drive tractors for a job? Did he – sorry if this is difficult, my loves – die in a road accident?*

There'd eventually be a gasp of recognition from somewhere in the stalls and Queenie would zero in on a target.

However, whether the message was indeed for the – usually emotional – recipient was conditional. If they corrected

Queenie too many times, she'd snap: 'Sorry my love, this message isn't for you,' and move on briskly.

Lorraine, Kim and Di were rapt throughout, hanging on Queenie's every word, wiping under their eyes when Queenie provided dubious catharsis. Diana's dad, Rodney, did not put in an appearance. *Should've had a more common name,* Roisin thought.

Roisin's composure only faltered in the last twenty minutes, during an interaction with a widow near the front row.

The woman's late husband, Clive, victim of a chronic lung condition, was reportedly on stage with Queenie.

The widow was sobbing. The chicanery of the whole thing had seemed like relatively innocent – if bizarre – fun to Roisin, until that moment. Did Queenie know she was inventing these visitors? Did she really give credence to her own powers? Do liars always know they're lying?

'When he went, it was fast?' Queenie said, once the woman had quietened.

'No. It was slow. He was on oxygen for weeks.'

'But when he went, it was fast?' Queenie paused. 'Clive's telling me it was fast – he's very certain,' she added, to make it clear who the woman was contradicting. 'He keeps gesturing to his chest, as if he's short of breath,' Queenie added, banging her own sternum with a fist, somewhat unnecessarily.

'Uhm . . . well at the end, I suppose it was quick?' the widow said.

'That's what I meant,' Queenie said, nodding. 'He is saying: "it was slow, but fast at the end."'

Roisin barked a small laugh. People glanced over and her mother angrily shushed her.

7

'How can it be slow *and* fast?' Roisin whispered, and Lorraine glared.

'Clive wants you to know you did everything right. He loves you very much. He says it's lovely where he is,' Queenie said.

There was audible weeping, and more expressions of gratitude. Roisin squirmed. Queenie clearly knew it was time to go out on a high.

'Thank you for being here and sharing what I call my *moments of clear seeing* with me,' Queenie said, and the room broke into rapturous applause.

The arc of history was long, and it bent towards sick humour. When Roisin and Joe broke up, twenty years later, Roisin could only think that it was perfectly summarised by the paradox of Queenie Mook.

It was slow, but fast at the end.

1

'Miss, Miss, *MISS*. Miss? Dirty weekend with your boyfriend? Miss!'

Amir gestured at the trolley case standing sentry behind Roisin's desk, which she was poorly concealing by draping with a cagoule. He was in the naughty-yet-good-natured category among her students, and she responded accordingly.

'Very clean actually, Amir. A spa weekend with some of my girlfriends.'

If there was one thing that both her childhood and her career had taught Roisin Walters, it was that lying to kids might not be noble, but generally got the job done.

'A SPA. Like, a sauna?' He chewed his pen and made a cheeky face.

'Back to the text, please. I'm going to collect your papers in . . .' She glanced up at the wall clock, her ever reliable teaching assistant. '. . . five minutes' time!'

'Miss,' Amir persisted, then seeing her under-her-brow look of scepticism: 'No no no – it's about the book!'

Roisin rolled her eyes. 'Go on.'

'Right, everyone thinks *Great Expectations* is good, like. A

9

posh book. Which is why we're studying it in an English Lit lesson.'

'Yes?' Roisin knew a time-waste trolling when one began, and so did Amir's peers, waiting with delighted anticipation for the payoff.

MPs who ran the parliamentary session down with pointless, aimless debate were *filibustering*; online arguments that involved repeated requests for evidence, made with fauxsincerity and excessive civility, was an exhaustion tactic called *sealioning*.

Roisin felt neither *filibusterers* nor *sealioners* could hold a candle to a class of restless Year 10s in a so-called *doss subject* on a sunny Friday afternoon, right at the end of term.

Last week, one of Amir's accomplices, Pauly, had arrived at Roisin's lesson with a breed of tiny, furious-looking dog she was told was called a 'Brussels Griffon' in an old-fashioned white-wheeled pram. Pauly was allegedly 'childminding' this creature 'for his nan'. The canine, known as Sprout and resembling an abandoned Jim Henson project, had caused a disruption akin to the President landing in Air Force One.

'And this Dickens book is well old. 160 years old,' Amir continued, in his quest for enlightenment.

'Correct.'

'So, in another 160 years – that'll be . . . the 3080s,' he said, pretending to count off his fingers. Comic pause. 'Will everyone in here reading *Fifty Shades of Grey*, yeah? It will be a well old proper book.'

The class responded with the required laughter, Amir grinning proudly. Roisin waited it out.

'I doubt it, but that's still a question worth asking, thank you, Amir.'

She judged that with what was left of this lesson, subverting Amir was more fruitful than trying to get everyone back to pondering the motives of Abel Magwitch.

'It's because the worth of literature is not only determined by the passage of time,' Roisin said.

'My mum and my auntie really like it though,' Amir said, to more cackling. 'My auntie reads it on her Kindle . . . in the bath. If you catch my drift.'

This information provoked hyena whooping.

'And they can enjoy it,' Roisin said, her tone making it clear she was ignoring the innuendo. 'Not all books have to be studied for education.'

'Why is *Great Expectations* better than *Fifty Shades*, though? Is it because it's by a dead man, Miss? Isn't that sexism? And . . . alive-ism?' Amir chewed his pen again.

Despite herself, Roisin smiled. He was putting sincere effort into this derailing.

'It's because *Great Expectations* is about class, social mobility and the way we use that social status to judge human worth, and *Fifty Shades* is about a billionaire having sex with a college student.'

Getting the teacher to say the word 'sex' was of course a huge victory in itself, and her Year 10s' last period before the weekend now took on a festival atmosphere.

'Exactly, Miss, so a college student boning, like, Elon Musk, is socially climbing then,' Amir said, pausing for a high five with Pauly, the pensioners' choice of dog-sitter.

'It sounds like you've thought about this, have real insights on this subject,' Roisin said, folding her arms, leaning against her desk. 'Perhaps you should give a presentation on the meanings and themes of *Great Expectations* and their mirroring in *Fifty Shades*?'

'Totally up for that, Miss. I'll need a telly bringing in, though, because I will have to show clips from the films to explain what I mean properly.'

'Sadly, those films are an eighteen certificate, Amir, so not only is it not allowed, but I'm also sure you've not seen them.'

'I totally didn't see them because my auntie doesn't have them all on Blu-ray, Miss.'

'Well done, Auntie.'

The bell rang – a piercing shriek – and the usual scramble to the door ensued while Roisin called, 'Papers on my desk before you go, please!'

'Is your husband's new show on this weekend, Miss?' Amir said, loitering, as he hooked his rucksack over his shoulders.

Roisin was momentarily startled.

'Sorry, *boyfriend*,' Amir said, mistaking the reason she looked taken aback.

Roisin had thought Joe's next project had flown under the radar of the population of Heathwood School. She'd been careful to barely mention it to colleagues, too: forgetting the name of it when they asked. Promising and then failing, on purpose, to tell them when it aired.

But if Amir knew, then everyone knew, or they soon would do.

'Uhm, yes, on late, though. After the watershed for you.' She tried to recover a smile. (Was the watershed even a thing any more?)

'I'll ask my auntie what it's like then,' he said, with a wink and a cackle, as he swaggered out.

Alone in the classroom, Roisin tied up the unruly stack of pages of lined A4 with hot hands and swallowed, hard.

2

Miss Walters, a popular and, at thirty-two, youthful member of the English department, was known for two things.

Firstly – and this was a low bar for fascinating character traits, but that was comprehensive schools in leafy areas like Cheadle for you – she had burgundy hair.

Roisin didn't spend much on her appearance, but her one vanity splurge was her below-shoulder-length mermaid waves. They were a glossy shade of black-claret grape that wasn't so punk that it immediately registered as not natural, but equally didn't exist outside of children's picture books, Marvel films, or Aveda. Joe called it her *warrior space princess* hair.

She usually wore it up in a large crocodile clip for work, which didn't stop admiring female pupils asking for details of prices and treatments involved, and the male ones sometimes wanting to know why she had 'a purple bun'.

The other thing to know about Miss Walters was that her partner, Joe Powell, was a screenwriter.

Three years ago, he'd created and written a drama about Scotland Yard's real life 'super recognisers' squad, people with incredible powers of recall for faces: *SEEN*. (Caps Lock, trendy production company's own.)

Initially, the nature of Joe's job was merely gossip in the staff room, but you no more contained gossip in the staff room at Heathwood than an airborne virus.

She'd not expected Joe's show to become a culturally beloved, 'water cooler', mega ratings hit that millions watched. In her defence, neither had Joe, or the television bosses. Its cast of unknowns were now household names, its plot twists were worthy of tabloid stories, and on the evenings when it was transmitted, Twitter didn't really talk about anything else.

After the season two cliff-hanger finale, Roisin was being asked in every lesson if it was true that its lead character, Harry Orton, was really dead, or if he'd survived being shot and falling into the Thames.

Her by-rote answer: 'I don't know, and if I did, I still couldn't tell you!' (Real answer by Joe: 'I wish he fucking was, the whingeing diva.')

She had been relieved when *SEEN* went on what Americans called *hiatus* before its third series, despite an outcry from the nation.

The career breakthrough for Joe that they'd thought would mean calmer, warmer waters financially was more like a tidal wave that washed away life as they'd known it before. It had left them clinging, bewildered, to a remaining rock. (A very nicely appointed rock: they'd bought a luxury apartment in a converted chapel in West Didsbury. When handed the keys, they'd felt as dazed and fraudulent as if the money had come from a drug deal.)

Joe had blank chequebooks flapped open around him to write whatever he fancied in the rest from *SEEN* and he'd come up with *Hunter*. It was a three-part show about a maverick Manchester detective and sex addict thrill-seeker, Jasper Hunter. 'Much darker and edgier than *SEEN*,' Joe said, proudly.

Having realised she was a powerless passenger on this drunken joyride, Roisin's feelings about *Hunter* were mixed. She didn't know whether to fear failure, or success. Given Roisin didn't like her accidental notoriety at Heathwood as it was, she was sure she'd like being asked about a shagging drama even less. Sex scenes written by your partner – it was going to feel weird, and she didn't even get to feel weird in private.

What could she say to Joe, though? 'Please don't depict frantic carnal couplings and make everyone think about you and your girlfriend of the last nine years'?

It was an intractable problem. It was also what her department head, Wendy Copeland, codenamed as NFI – Not Fucking Ideal.

Roisin opted for the underrated coping strategy called Pretend It Isn't Happening and, without intending to, Amir had made it clear that was an illusion.

She wrestled her suitcase out from behind the desk.

It'd be fine.

This bells-and-whistles minibreak in the Lake District would take the curse off. She'd view the first episode in the bosom of her friendship group and feel a sense of proud ownership. The mocking in her lessons would bounce off her like small stones on a toughened windshield, ripping along at motorway speed.

Roisin knew she was self-soothing, and it'd only really convince her when she had a glass of wine in her hand, and not for long after the point she didn't have a glass of wine in her hand. But fuck it! Otherwise, there was Pretend It Isn't Happening.

This holiday was thanks to their friend Dev, an extrovert, indefatigable social engine and one-time reality-TV star, winning the short-lived, torrid *Flatmates*, almost three years ago. He had hired what looked to be, on the photos in their WhatsApp group, a stately home.

Tonight, they had a dinner party, celebrating Dev and his fiancée, Anita, getting engaged. Tomorrow, there was a party for their friend Gina's recent birthday and afterwards, the mansion's screening room would be deployed for the premiere of *Hunter*.

Roisin was getting a lift up with their friends Gina and Meredith; Joe was heading there already with Dev (what with writers and ex-reality-TV stars keeping much more loosey-goosey schedules than secondary schoolteachers). Their mate Matt was arriving via airport transfer, after some kind of wine tour in Lisbon with his latest woman, because of course he was.

Roisin rolled her wheeled suitcase down the corridor and out through the entrance-exit and into the school car park. It was teeming with departing kids, shouting, kicking balls, anticipating two days of freedom before the last week of the school year.

Gina's classic VW camper van, in orange-and-white colourway, was easy to spot, and indeed had been spotted by curious pupils.

'Ahoy there! Your unobtrusive carriage awaits. Throw that anywhere in Ethel.' Meredith gestured at the slid-open door and Roisin's case. The van, which Gina had won in a raffle last year, had been christened Ethelred the Unready. Given the running costs, the competition organisers had a cheek calling it a prize rather than an adoption.

'Though if you don't wedge it in properly and Gina takes a corner too hard, it will be the last thing to go through your mind. You alright with me in the front, doing the navigating?'

'Damn right I am,' Roisin said, manhandling her belongings into a shape where she was available to lean over and hug Meredith.

She was in a very Meredith outfit of gold Birkenstocks, jeans with roll ups, a t-shirt saying ALEXA PLAY CHER, and a raggy headscarf tied in her fusilli pasta-shaped wild mop of blonde curly hair. A look she called 'Gay Boden mum goes to Latitude festival'. (She referred to herself as an 'out-of-work lesbian', due to an extended period of being single.)

'Actually, I'm going to stretch my legs,' Gina said, appearing round the side of Ethel. 'Hi, Rosh. We've got tins of Pornstar Martini in the Saino's bag under your seat, dig in. I am not digging in yet, obviously.'

Gina, both bosomy and slight, was in a fluttery spring-summer yellow dress and blush ballet slippers. Her shoulder-length brown hair was tied up in a practical scrunchie. This one small concession aside, she looked absolutely nothing like someone about to confidently manhandle a tin bin with a steering wheel the size of a bicycle tyre for an eighty-mile distance. Yet there was no safer or more ballsy driver.

'Miss! MISS! MISS WALTERS?'

They all looked over to see Amir and Pauly, waving.

Amir shouted, 'GET ONE OF THEM MASSAGES WITH OIL!'

3

'This place,' Meredith said, as they began their approach. '*Twelve grand for the weekend*,' she mouthed, with an expression of faux-scandal.

'Are you kidding?!' Roisin said, pulling the tin of metallic-tasting, foamy Pornstar from her lips and grimacing a little. It was like pineapple-flavoured phlegm.

As they hit a loop in the winding path among the trees that offered a clear view of Benbarrow Hall, Roisin actually gasped.

She'd been readying herself for grandeur yet still felt like a Jane Austen heroine, intimidated by the estate of her suitor. It seemed as if the approach should be soundtracked by the clip-clop of hooves and not the complaining rumble of the VW van's engine and Paul Simon's *Graceland*.

Benbarrow Hall sat on a hill, a storybook mansion made of slate-grey Gothic turrets and sand-coloured stone. The late afternoon summer light made its giant arched windows glisten cinematically.

'Fuck my boots!' Meredith said reverently. 'It's *a monster*.'

'It's like a murder mystery place,' Gina said, easing off the accelerator and letting Ethel slide to a near halt so they could admire it fully. 'Like you'd find Colonel Mustard in the study, with the lead piping.'

A contemplative moment passed.

'*Makes you think*,' Meredith said.

'Makes me think it'd be worth the risk,' Gina said. 'Imagine the size of the en-suites.' She rattled the gear stick. 'Come on, be reasonable, Ethel. Relationships are give and take.'

They lurched back into motion.

'I feel properly dirty for letting Dev spend this much,' Roisin said. 'Are we OK to only contribute a groceries delivery? Is this immoral?'

'Oh, Dev is as Dev does. And Dev does a lot,' Meredith said, turning back to the road. 'Seriously though. You know that you no more deter Dev from a tremendous plan than you bring a 747 out of the sky by shaking your fist at it.'

This was true. They surveyed rolling green slopes down to the lake, the surroundings reflected in the still mirror of the water, and collectively continued sighing.

The van grumbled to a stop in a space next to Dev's shiny blue 4x4. After he won seventy thousand pounds from *Flatmates*, he set up a media consultancy and now employed twenty people.

The women in the group still earned entirely normal salaries: Meredith worked for HMRC; Gina did external comms for Manchester University. (They'd bought together in Urmston, a plan by Meredith to get them both on the property ladder early.) Whereas Dev and Joe were now loaded, and Matt, well, he was in sales for a wine merchant, so who knew. But good living was like breathing to Matt, as he was from a fearsomely well-off family. Roisin hoped this increasing disparity in wealth wasn't what would end up dividing them all.

Going on one obscenely spendy trip, based on three special occasions, was one thing. It couldn't set a precedent.

'Which door do you choose?!' Meredith said, as they dragged their luggage towards the building. 'I'd not want to be a Parcelforce driver looking for their safe space, would you?'

Roisin turned her face into the warm breeze and breathed in more countryside than she usually experienced. She left it to Joe to have artistic flights of fancy, yet she sensed being on the verge of *events*. Her gut told her things were about to happen. Perhaps that was the magic of any holiday; it lifted you out of the familiar and gave you a brief aerial view of your life in progress. It made you confront your world's smallness in a vastness of opportunity.

They opted to fumble their way in the back of Benbarrow Hall through a group of outhouses, scented with that unmistakeable farmyard honk, and the intriguing rustling noises of non-human life. The wheels of their cases on rough ground sounded like an angle grinder.

They tried the wrought-iron curly handle on a door that led in to a cavernous, brick-shelved pantry and then through to a stunning kitchen. It was a mix of vast brushed-steel modern appliances, Art Deco pendant lights, cream Aga range and old flagstone floor.

Roisin was a bit nauseous at how much she loved it. Her kitchen *was* great, and now her kitchen was shite.

'Hello!' Meredith called. 'The strippers are here!'

Joe appeared in a doorway, holding a bottle of Camden Hells lager.

'Oh, bloody hell, there's been a mix up! I asked for *stacked slags*, not *knackered hags*!'

Gina hooted in delight. Meredith barked, 'Bad twat!' and Roisin said, 'Pfffft.' He threw his arms around all of them in turn, Roisin last.

Joe looked good, Roisin thought, as she watched him squash his face, eyes squeezed closed in affection, into Gina's slender shoulder.

He'd acquired that subtle yet undeniable burnish of a high-flyer. His writer's pallor had been contoured by Californian sunshine and he was sharper-jawed and leaner-bodied due to sessions at Waterside Leisure Club with an unfeasibly handsome Ghanaian personal trainer called Eric. He needed to please Handsome Eric as desperately as if Handsome Eric was an emotionally inconsistent father.

And the man who once wore the same Pixies t-shirt for days at a time was now clad in understated, well-tailored navy and grey things in soft, thin fabrics, which arrived in matte boxes with logos.

Joe slung an arm around Roisin and absently kissed her on the head, without making eye contact or focusing on her in any way. Gina and Meredith got blasts of warmth; Roisin was furniture.

She asked herself, once again, if the last six months was a rocky patch or a terminal decline. Six months? Eight months. Alright, being honest – a year.

'Fair warning, Dev is at level seven or eight already, out

of a possible ten,' Joe said. 'It's increasingly hard to tell if what we call his "bubbly moods" are in fact some sort of manic upswing. Thank God he's off the booze and chisel.'

Suede's 'Trash' was blaring from a distant zone as they rolled and hefted their luggage into an incredible vaulted hallway. It was decorated with busts of statues on plinths, and a huge stone vase, the size of a small child, held an explosive flower display of white lilies, lime-green hydrangeas, gladioli and snapdragons: the sort you got in hotel lobbies. They gazed up the carved wooden balustrades of the broad stairway, lit by a stained-glass window.

'Those are stairs you descend down for dinner,' Gina said, as they all oohed and aahed.

'And you can. Dinner at seven p.m. With canapes in the drawing room first,' Joe said, ushering them onwards. The deal was, the men cooked tonight, the women tomorrow. It was rather cheesy to split the teams this way, but no one could think of a different rationale.

They found Dev and Anita on stools at the bar. The room was done out with a crystal chandelier, noisy flock wallpaper and a neon sign on the wall that read IT'S MIDDAY SOMEWHERE. It also had a music system, evidently.

Dev jumped down at sight of them. 'GIRLS! Have you seen! We've got fuckin' HENS!' he shouted, doing fist pulls in time with crotch thrusts to the song, facial expression set in an underbite.

'Are you planning on having sex with them?' Roisin said.

Dev continued his gyrations, shouting, 'ALSO DUCKS!' while doing a perturbing ass-slapping mime.

His fiancée, Anita, abandoned what looked like a fishbowl G&T with juniper berries and located the stereo, reducing Suede to a level where they could communicate.

'WHADDYATHINK?' Dev said, in the new quiet, throwing his arms wide. 'Some Bruce Wayne wild shit, no?!'

'Awful, dismal, shabby,' Meredith said. 'Very threadbare, isn't it?'

'Ask for your money back,' Gina agreed. 'So dark! Needs some of those Velux skylights putting in.'

'Honestly, Dev,' Roisin said, free to be sincere now the British part was covered, '*out of this world*. We don't deserve you, or this.'

'No one else I'd rather have here.' He beamed, gathering them all at once in large arms. Anita joined in.

'Wait until you see how many dresses I've brought,' she said, voice muffled.

'We practically needed a trailer,' Dev said.

The voluptuous Anita was a make-up artist – speciality, shades for Asian skin tones – with a huge Instagram following; she and Dev had met exchanging DMs.

The group loved Anita, having got off to a shaky start when she turned up post-fame and pre-rehab. It was a period when they were at maximum suspicion of New Dev Pals and actively trying to rid him of druggy parasites. Being a man who made friends with such ease and openness was terrible for an addict with a recognisable face.

Thus, Dev's old guard were initially near certain she was dating the infamous Dev Doshi for what the kids called *clout*. In fact, she was solid gold and good for him – someone as ebullient as Dev, without the hyperactive edge. She'd stuck by him getting clean and kept him out of places where he might meet unhelpful influences.

They were living in rented digs while they had the family house of their dreams built in Alderley Edge.

When Dev said he'd proposed a few months back, they were able to offer a full-throated and wholehearted HOORAH.

'Oh my life! And finally, it's the gentleman con artist, Mr Staff WiFi!' Joe said, having lifted a swag of drape to peer out of the window.

4

'Staff WiFi' was one of Joe's more recent nicknames for Matt. Whenever they were in a venue with crap coverage on public WiFi, Matt would be merrily messaging away. When asked how come it was possible, he would shrug *oh, I got the password for staff WiFi*, doing a hand flap in the direction of front of house.

There was absolutely no reason why a customer who wanted the staff password should get it, other than the fact the customer looked like a cowboy as imagined by *Cosmopolitan*.

They clustered around the window to see Matt striding up the hill towards them in a Crombie coat, large boots with yellow laces (half unlaced), a canvas duffle bag slung over his shoulder. He'd have a look of a man out of time, who'd clambered through a torn rift in space, apart from the fact he had a pair of headphones clamped round his ears.

'Why's he on foot?' Meredith said.

'Look at this absolute plum,' Joe chortled. 'Like he's auditioning for the next *Doctor Who*.'

'He was getting an airport taxi. He's been in Portugal with . . .' Roisin, in vain, ransacked her mind for the name. 'Cassie?' She held her hands out in hopeful prayer, teeth gritted.

'Hah, Cassie is LONG gone,' Meredith snorted. 'You're *so* April-May.' She tutted. 'This was . . . does it begin with an L . . .'

The trouble was they didn't file Matt's glamorous girl pals by names so much as salient detail for the post-fact analysis.

They were like *Friends* episode titles. The One Whose Grandad Invented Striped Toothpaste. The One Who Kept A Chinchilla Called Shamone. The One Who Naked Video-Called Him At Three A.M.

'Ruby,' Gina supplied, in a calm yet smaller voice.

'Ruby! Of course,' Meredith said. 'The . . . hot yoga enthusiast. Or maybe that was the other one.'

Conversation moved abruptly to who was going to let Matt in. There was often this shift in tone, in unspoken deference to Gina's feelings.

Gina's love for Matt was as powerful and constant as it was unrequited. The group stepped around it delicately while simultaneously not acknowledging its existence. Every so often, they'd try to persuade each other, unconvincingly, that it was long past.

There was nothing to be done. Matt was very fond of Gina. No matter who Gina got involved with – and there was no shortage of men falling at her Barbie-sized feet – they could tell she still yearned fruitlessly for him throughout.

It's toxic hope, isn't it? Meredith had said. *Who knew there was such a thing.*

His carousel of meaningless flings was like artillery fire to

Gina's heart. Yet equally, they dreaded the day when Matt met The One, as it would hurt even worse.

Dev darted off to intercept Matt. After a minute, he presented a similarly awestruck guest.

'This is a bit of alright, eh?! Dev, you've outdone yourself. Hello, everyone.'

'The ensemble is complete! It's like *Peter's Friends* but with even worse people,' Joe said. 'Wait, what is going on with your face?'

At closer range, it seemed Matt, sharp haircut and otherwise clean shaven, was sporting a thin pencil moustache. Matt put his fingers to his top lip.

'Is it bad? Ruby told me it looked good.'

'Ruby is clearly working for your enemies, sorry to say,' Joe said.

'Why have you walked here?' Gina asked.

'I asked the taxi driver to drop me off when we got closer. Looked too nice to drive through. I wanted to take it all in.'

'What a good idea. I might have thought of it if I wasn't so lazy,' Meredith said.

'We did stop the car briefly, which is kind of the same.' Roisin said. 'Lisbon good?'

'Lovely. Sunny. Though the hotel gym was below par. Had to queue for the rowing machine. It was quite dehumanising.'

'Who goes to the gym on holiday?' Roisin said.

'Now you know,' Joe said.

'Given Matt's here – a toast!' Dev said.

Anita had clearly been primed for this moment, already

behind the bar and easing a cork from a bottle of champagne, slopping it into a row of glasses. Dev had a cloudy kombucha.

'To THE BRIAN CLUB!' Dev declared, once they were handed out. They knocked flutes and echoed him, saying, *thebrianclub*! while laughing, and in a split second, Roisin understood what this weekend was really about.

She'd been so busy assessing her and Joe's drift, she hadn't spotted the group possibly becoming looser at the seams, too.

5

The Brian Club title hadn't been used in a long while, though it remained the name of their WhatsApp group.

It was based on a notorious incident a decade ago, not long after they all met, while working at Waterstones Deansgate. Brian was a colossal arsehole who used to busy-body around the shop most days, being obnoxiously difficult and making specious complaints.

One day, after a fight with manager Dev over a mysteriously bespoiled tome about a cricketing legend, Brian dragged one of the shop stepladders into the middle of the Biography & True Stories section. Upon clambering aloft, Brian pointed – *Invasion of the Bodysnatchers* style, with staring eyes and contorted expression – at Dev.

'TWAT!' he shrieked, in the tone usually reserved for '*fire!*', bringing many customers to a dead silent halt.

Then, Brian's eyes alighted on Roisin nearby. 'ANOTHER TWAT!'

'Twat, twat, twat,' he narrated, jabbing fingers in turn at a startled Meredith, Gina and Matt, who had rushed in to see what the commotion was about.

A Saturday part-timer called Lia had also wandered into view and Brian's gimlet gaze fell upon her next.

'You're alright,' he conceded, to everyone's surprise.

Then Brian reeled theatrically at the sight of Joe, who was entering stage left with a stack of hardbacks about Edmund Hillary.

Brian drew breath, extended a trembling forefinger and said, '. . . A CUNT!'

Roisin had wondered why Dev didn't invite more people to Benbarrow Hall – they certainly had the space – and now she knew it was to define who belonged. He was a benevolent patriarch, bringing the wayward sons and daughters together, not letting them forget about the importance of family ties.

'You know, I'm on the fence about the moustache,' Roisin said, looking at Matt appraisingly, after half a flute of Moët. 'It's strangely compelling. You look like the RAF rotter in one tattered photo found hidden in a bureau drawer during a house clearance, who turns out in a family scandal to be the real grandfather.'

'Yes! RAF Rotter Sex Grandpa was the look I was going for! Thanks, Rosh,' Matt said.

Joe rolled his eyes.

'Seeing Ruby again, then?' Gina asked, and everyone's shoulders tensed.

'Therein lies an incredible story. "Ruby" basically catfished me! But it was *a reverse catfish*.'

'What's a reverse catfish?'

'A catfish is when someone's hiding behind a different

identity to their actual one, right? And their actual one tends to be a nasty shock? In *this* case . . .'

'You know what, let's save this for later?' Joe said, interrupting Matt. 'Got the feel of something we need a sweet, floral dessert wine for.'

Matt shrugged and said sure, and the subject changed. Roisin felt a pang at the mannerlessness of it, while understanding Joe was white-knighting Gina. She made a mental note to apologise to Matt and address it with Joe. Joe and Matt had always had a slight friction between them, but Roisin worried it had lately bloomed into a full-blown antipathy on Joe's side. Matt was blissfully unaware, as Matt's life generally was a lot of bliss and unawareness.

A month ago, she'd ticked Joe off for sniping and provoked a rant.

'What irks me about Matt McKenzie is that if he was a woman, you'd hate him. Whereas I merely find him annoying and occasionally . . .' Joe paused to choose his word with the consideration of a word-choosing gourmet, '. . . *dispiriting.* But if he was female? My *God.* You'd judge him so hard and have got rid years ago. So don't judge me.'

'Why?! Because he dates lots of people? Dev gets on with him!'

'Dev won a reality show because he gets on with anyone. *Dates lots of people* is a decorous way of putting it, like he's Michael Caine in the Sixties. Don't forget I know more than you, thanks to lads' talk.'

Roisin shrugged, a concession that this much was true.

33

'He trades relentlessly on his looks and his whole concocted . . .' Joe waved his hands. '. . . light-hearted Casanova persona. But he plays with women like they're catnip toys. He bats them around, until that addictive scent of the *new* is gone. I can't imagine it's very nice for them and it's horrible for Gina.'

'Matt can't help how Gina feels. Or how he doesn't feel.'

'Mmmm, maybe not. I think he can't be with her because it'd have to mean something, and he can't risk that. My guess is he'll ruin both their lives by only realising they should be together when it's far too late. Which is very Matt.'

'If he's so awful, why would he be any good for Gina?'

'He wouldn't. But Gina, I am sorry to say, is never going to be truly happy with anyone else. Sometimes that just happens to a person. They can't move on.'

Roisin thought this was a trifle dramatic. Typical writer.

'Mark my words,' Joe said. 'He'll realise she's his forever love when he turns up on her doorstep, crying over the three kids he's lost access to – now with added drink problem, a mortgage lost to the Crypto crash and a head full of Rogaine. And she'll blow up her good-enough marriage to take him in.'

Roisin had a secret suspicion about what really wound Joe up about Matt, which she wasn't foolhardy enough to tell Joe.

Joe's self-image, if not much of his career, was based on his skill at a barbed observation and sparkling one-liner. *Whisper it*, Matt could do those, too. He just didn't make a deal of it.

He casually chucked away for free what Joe cherished as his currency.

Joe sensed competition, but worse than that, competition from someone who wasn't bothering to compete with him.

When Joe had finished his speech about Matt's criminality, he opened his phone and tapped things he'd said into his Notes app. A move with which Roisin had grown wearily familiar.

6

'Was it really necessary to cut Matt short like that, when he was merely answering a question?' Roisin hissed, at the precise moment she remembered to raise it.

Roisin had exited the bathroom in a towel, one smoky eye made up, kohl pencil in hand, the other eye slightly pink from the hot shower.

Joe was sitting shoeless, smart-trousered and cross-legged atop the quilt in their four poster. Their room was so royally lavish that Roisin felt awed and yet borderline sickened, like it had raised her cholesterol. Was this where the concept of something *making you weak at the knees* came from?

They'd opened the heavy wooden door to the sight of a giant potted fern, Art Nouveau-tiled period fireplace, and a canopied bed, the sort women died in after childbirth. Dark red walls, like a blood clot. It could've been gloomy but the sky-high ceiling prevented it from becoming overbearing. There was a free-standing, roll-top scarlet bath in the marble bathroom, along with a walk-in shower.

Joe, who had been frowning intently into his silver MacBook Air, now looked up with a nonplussed expression.

'You what?'

She was sure Joe knew exactly what she was referring to. It suited him to feign confusion, to make it seem as if Roisin was forensically obsessive – slash – a massive nag.

'When Gina asked Matt about his Lisbon girlfriend. *We need a drink for that, Matt, hush now*? I know we all want to protect Gina, but he's not doing anything wrong, either.'

'Oh – he was clearly about to do some unseemly bragging about sexual athletics that Gina didn't need to hear.'

'He barely began – you didn't know what he was going to say. He's never exactly crude or graphic, either.'

'Ach, come on, you know Matt. Any opportunity to show off. Everything's a horse to his Lady Godiva. And "The Reverse Catfish" sounded sufficiently ominous to me.'

'Well, Gina *asked him* how it went. She may have a crush, but she's not a child.'

'Nor is Matt. Yet here I am, being told off for being less than mildly snippy to him.'

Joe made a palms-up *whodathunk* gesture and smiled, to defuse it. Roisin made a diplomatic head tilt in return. She dropped her voice even lower.

'Look. I feel the pressure that Dev has made a huge gesture. He doesn't want us squabbling and ruining it. This has to be a success, for his sake.'

Or at least seem like one, she thought.

'I agree, no squabbling,' Joe said. 'Like . . . say . . . this.'

Roisin had been outmanoeuvred.

He moved his eyes back to his screen.

37

'Just tryna concentrate on transatlantic publicity schedules here. If that's OK, darling.'

Roisin was accustomed to this gently patronising tone when Joe reminded her he had VIP business to attend to. It had started out as ironic, and was now not particularly, if at all, ironic.

7

Roisin remembered when she used to pay for Joe's train tickets to London and for clothes that weren't faded band tees. She didn't mind, and today Joe could rightly say her investment had been repaid to the tune of many, many thousands. The apartment was in both their names.

She wasn't selfishly nostalgic for Joe being dependent on her, she was sure of that. She just wished it hadn't led *here*.

Once, Joe's career had felt like wholly shared excitement; she had the seat next to him on the fairground ride. *SEEN* started out a moon-shot, an outline written in coffee shops, its plot twists tested on Roisin as the first audience.

So, wait: HE turns out to be the man in the video doorbell footage, too? Wow, no, I wouldn't see that coming. That's really clever, Joe.

Then it became a pilot script in Final Draft software – Roisin had enjoyed reading the lead female character's dialogue aloud for him. She felt robbed when a hair-tossing actress got to say, palms down on desk: 'Harry. I'd bet my life we're dealing with identical twins. And if this play we're making doesn't come off, I HAVE bet my life!'

Thing is, Roisin hadn't only been unprepared for its impact, she'd been complacent. *The great thing about Joe being the writer and not an actor,* she'd blathered to the group, *is he can get creative fulfilment and no hassle down Burton Road.*

When *SEEN* became signed contracts, they bought fish and chips and a £10 bottle of cava and had a picnic date in the park together. It felt like a statement, instead of going to a fancy restaurant. It's going to be Still Us, the way we always were, Plus This.

Joe's diary used to be: get up, drink black coffee, preferably wash, write, stick something in the oven, more writing. Rinse and repeat. Now it became complicated and ablaze with fuss. Roisin learned the lingo of *co pros* and *turnaround* and *punches*.

After a day of high-powered breakfast and lunch meetings in the capital, Joe would get off the train mid-evening at Manchester Piccadilly, and Roisin would meet him for dinner out.

He'd talk too fast, and they'd drink too fast, and she gloried in every last detail of the latest developments. She was so pleased for him and always thought, girlfriend bias aside, he had the talent to make it.

Then the work came so thick and fast it often made sense to stay in London overnight, and Hollywood called, and he was flying back and forth to Los Angeles.

A production company in New York bought the rights to another of his ideas. At some point, Roisin accepted *get past this week and things will calm down a bit* was a coping mechanism lie of adulthood.

Joe being away never bothered Roisin. She enjoyed her own company, liked hearing about his adventures.

Yet somehow, at some point, hectic and mentally occupied became cold and detached.

Roisin learned not to message Joe when he was away, because she rarely got much back. He must be the only man, she thought, to deploy the heart react emoji to WhatsApps as a dismissal.

How'd it go with Fox Searchlight? Heart. *Did the hire car get replaced?* Heart. *Oh my God, that ginger moggy is back soiling our garden! Pooing with his tail vibrating, making unnerving eye contact!* Heart. You heart defecating cats, OK.

She'd not raised it. When someone comes through the door after five days away bearing a duty-free Toblerone, you don't want to greet them with whining.

A thought came to Roisin, and once she'd had the thought she couldn't un-have it: the prolonged absences were doubling as practice for breaking up. Each time he returned, he was a degree more distant than the last time.

Life had fundamentally changed, or maybe more accurately and painfully, Joe had changed. *Can success really change a person, though,* she wondered? *Maybe it only brings elements that were always there to the fore?*

The humour that once bonded them felt like sparring, underscored by resentment. Like an arm-wrestling bout that had to have a winner.

Plans with their friends were an obligation, if not an irritation – Joe always had something slighting to say.

God, that place again? We've become bourgeoise. Soon we'll have Bless This Mess decal stickers on our wheelie bins.

She half wondered if hating on Matt was a way of carving out a convenient exit from the Brian Club. *Sorry, not if he's there – I can't stand him.*

Sex had dwindled, and when it occurred, had the unmistakeable sense of reaching a deadline: . . . *best do it or it'll become a thing we haven't done it.*

When they first met, the spark between them was obvious. Joe had immediately mentioned he had a long-distance girlfriend, Bea, back in his home city, York.

Nothing had happened between Joe and Roisin – nor would it have, if the girlfriend had remained; Roisin wasn't into foul play – but she'd catch Joe looking at her, across tables, at the hour of the night when blood alcohol levels were high and the lights were low.

One Friday afternoon, Joe had found Roisin alone in a corner of the shop, stickering Signed By The Author copies of Terry Pratchett.

'I want you to know. I'm ending it with Bea.'

'OK,' Roisin said.

'When I've done that, I'm going to ask you out.'

'OK,' Roisin said, and tried not to flush sunset red.

He walked away. *Woah.* Quietly spoken Joe, with a love of the graphic novels of Alan Moore and a winning resemblance to young John Cusack, had a streak of real confidence. It was undeniably, hugely attractive.

Those were the days they hung on each other's every word. The times they did nothing but talk: a day off together, walking round parks, browsing record shops, spinning pints of real ale out in old boy's pubs. Everything was interesting if they were together. Oh, to be that young again, when everything felt new.

As the first – and it turned out, only – couple of the group, they became the ones to have everyone back to their flat when they were all too pre-payday skint to go out: Joe on the music and snacks, Roisin on lighting candles and mixing drinks. They were foundation laying and empire building, as a team.

Had someone else now been made a similar promise to the one she got made over *Discworld*? Roisin had gone back and forth over it and concluded:

1. Their origins story showed Joe could be ruthlessly decisive, and a year of near intimacy-free purgatory wasn't that, and 2. He was talking about their getting a dog.

Nearly a decade on, it was as if their love was a neglected, autumn leaf-strewn swimming pool. It technically still existed, yet Joe had drained the water out, inch by inch. If you jumped into it, there was nothing there. You'd break your ankles.

Roisin had started seeing a counsellor, without telling Joe.

Do you think he's being unfaithful?

Hah, no. He'd certainly have a huge scheduling headache if he was.

Can the relationship be fixed?

I don't know.

Do you want to fix it?

I don't know. I think so. I want to be how we were. But I don't know if that's gone for good.

Roisin kept telling herself, get this or that out the way. Get through Dev's Downton Abbey do, get *Hunter* safely launched into the world – and nurse Joe through any bad reviews. Afterwards, there'd be time for a state of the nation.

Frankly, she suspected Joe would ask for one eventually, and dignity demanded she went first.

It made sense to wait, yet Roisin knew a pointless delaying tactic when she invented one. It was the personal life equivalent of Amir querying whether *Fifty Shades* was great literature of the future.

Faking it never really worked.

'ARE YOU DECENT???!' Dev roared on the other side of the door.

Joe, typing, was so startled he almost sent an unfinished email, cursing Dev under his breath.

'Decent!' Roisin said, flinging the door open, striking a pose in her black dress.

'Bloody hell, Sheen. If I wasn't engaged and your boyfriend wasn't a friend, and also just over there, near a brass fire poker.'

'Haha! Thank you.'

'Meredith and Gee are already on it downstairs, go join them. Anita's taking forever, as per. Joe, we're up. You're in a crucial role – you're my head of the butter chicken dept,' Dev said. 'I'm on parathas and raitas. Got Matt manning the bhajis station, with a side line in lassis. Mango lassis.'

'I'd not let Matt near the lassies' mangoes,' Joe said.

Roisin snorted, despite herself, and Dev disappeared off, cackling. Roisin could tell Joe resented the interruption.

Joe doesn't enjoy anything any more, Roisin thought. He didn't enjoy her. Enjoying was happening elsewhere.

'Do I look OK?' she asked, smoothing the dress over her hips and holding her stomach in.

Joe glanced up from his screen. 'Sure.'

'*Sure.* And you a writer.'

'It – looks – really – nice – you – always – look – really – nice,' Joe said, deliberately mechanically. 'That do?'

No, of course not, Roisin thought, but didn't say it. She needed a fight right before this dinner like a hole in the head. One thing she knew for sure: there'd be no showdown on these premises.

'Coming down?'

'Just gonna finish this mail. Go on ahead.'

Are you still in love with him?

What's the test for that?

8

Roisin descended the broad staircase carefully, placing her gold T-bar heels with purpose. Telling kids off for running and tripping in corridors brought with it responsibility. No way was she returning for the last week before the summer holiday in an authority-diminishing orthopaedic fracture boot.

She caught the distant voice of Taylor Swift singing 'Champagne Problems'. It was so apposite; briefly alone and lonely in her evening finery, it was momentarily as if she was starring in a Baz Luhrmann film.

Roisin hesitated on the bottom step, trying to press record on her memories, to take in the otherworldly atmosphere of blank-eyed statues, dusty floors and soaring high space, the chalky sweet smell of the lilies.

It had become a cliché to say your friends were your adopted family, where you felt real belonging – it was no less true for Roisin for being hackneyed. She'd never met people who had stuck to her like this, who made her part of a gang.

The fact that they might not choose each other now – it was hard to see how they'd even encounter each other to do the choosing – made it more special, and vital. They couldn't recapture the clean slates of being in their early twenties. But they could keep hold of each other.

Joe put lower value on it, she supposed, because he could. He had lovely, happily married, supportive parents who middle-class garden-pottered, visited National Trust properties and called him as the credits rolled on every episode of *SEEN*. He still had a circle of school friends back in York, including his *ride or die* best mate, Dom.

The Brian Club was merely a nice-to-have for him; for Roisin, they were everything. They were the point.

She followed the music to the grand sitting room, where Meredith and Gina were both giggling conspiratorially by the fireplace, surrounded by an improbable number of flickering candles.

The music was coming from a lozenge-shaped bluetooth speaker that had been somewhat disrespectfully balanced on the brim of a fireplace statue's hat, as if it was an outsized feather in its band.

If there were curses and ghosts associated with Benbarrow Hall, they were surely going to get them up the wazoo.

Meredith was in a parrot-orange silk top and cerulean blue trousers, while Gina was clad in a sinuous cream dress that clung to her out-in-out mini Marilyn Monroe figure, with a large bow tied at her narrow neck, hair pinned up.

'Oh my God. You both look extraordinary. I look like someone's prom date in 1996.'

Tonight, Roisin had hauled out an old 'posh event' failsafe, which was flattering and easy to wear, if unexciting. It had a full skirt which ended mid-calf, the sort you got on a child's dolly. It had seemed cute in her twenties, but she feared it was a bit gauche in her thirties. When she'd fretted she had nothing to wear for this trip, Joe had encouraged her to go wild with his credit card. Generous, but it was still *his* credit card and she didn't like how that felt.

'You look like the girl *everyone* wanted to take to prom,' said Gina, with her usual sweet sincerity and mild awe. Gina always treated Roisin as if she knew a secret passcode in life that Gina didn't, as if she'd jail broken its phone. Roisin didn't understand why: as far as she could see, she'd never done anything to merit it.

'Notice in the whole time we've known each other, we've never needed to check if we'll be wearing the same thing,' Meredith said, sloshing fizz from an ice bucket into a third glass. 'Don't worry' – she read Roisin's concerned look – 'this is from the supermarket delivery we ordered.'

'And these are pre-canapes – Matt says he adlibbed in case we were hungry,' Gina said, with the customary note of adoration in her voice. 'It's cubes of brie on sour cream Pringles. Slag's canapés.' Gina gestured at a plate balanced on a velvet pouffe.

'Student hors d'oeuvres,' Meredith said.

'Whore-derves!' Gina said, and they high-fived.

'I'm sorry if you thought I wouldn't, but I in fact will,' Roisin said, bending down and carefully conveying one into her mouth between finger and thumb.

'Oh, we've had about ten between us,' Meredith said.

'Here you are, and some actual canapes,' Matt said, entering the room carrying a tray on the flat of his palm, like a waiter.

He was in a white shirt and stupid-handsome, dark brown hair and gilded skin. Like the playboy son of an American tobacco magnate.

It always looked like a lot of fun to have his face. Roisin had never considered that about conspicuous beauty before, that people might want to hang around it simply to see where it led.

But he was without moustache . . . ?

'You had second thoughts?' Roisin said, pointing to her top lip.

'Yeah. If even its fans thought it conveyed a look of irresponsible inseminator . . .'

'It might give too much away?' Roisin finished for him, grinning.

Matt smiled back, a tight smile. 'I'll put these on this side table,' Matt said, crossing the room. 'Mini onion bhajis with a mint and coriander chutney. Surprisingly, caused less angst than the butter chicken.'

'Ah, Joe's area,' Roisin said, tapping her nose.

'No comment.'

'Also, the Pringles are great,' Roisin said indistinctly, through her second. 'Excellent improvisation.'

'Glad you like. Wait until you try my White Russians made with Whiskas Cat Milk.'

Roisin put her hand in front of her full mouth as she laughed.

'Enjoy,' Matt said, heading back to the kitchen.

They dropped the mini bhajis into their mouths, cupping them with the tissue provided.

'Look at us, ladylike, as if we've not just tractored through a load of crisps like wild coyotes,' Roisin said.

'This is the life, eh,' Meredith said, crumpling the paper napkin and gazing at the room. 'Did we ever think, doing our stockroom audits, we'd be here in ten years' time?'

'I didn't think I'd be here ten months ago,' Roisin said.

'I didn't think I'd ever be here,' Gina said.

'Technically we're not *here*-here, I suppose. It's Dev's achievement, Dev's festival. It's Devtonbury,' Meredith said.

'Devload?' Roisin said.

'But we're here, in that we're still together,' Gina said, and Roisin replied with an emphatic 'Yes!' as her stomach constricted.

So, you don't want to finish with your partner, because you think you'd finish the group?

9

She was being ridiculous. It wasn't that fragile, was it – the Brian Club, the old gang? They'd simply reorganise, and the keynote gatherings would be divided up between Roisin and Joe like divorced parents negotiating access. This stuff happened all the time.

What are you afraid of?

The counsellor had to go and drop atomic bomb questions like that, didn't she. Surely that wasn't second session material. Roisin was ashamed of her reply. That ending it with Joe would make no sense to anyone else. And when it's that impossible for anyone else to understand, isn't it a clue that maybe you're doing the wrong thing?

Why do other people's opinions matter?

'I don't know,' Roisin had said, privately thinking: *is a creeping yet unfocused conviction your relationship is a hollow sham sufficient cause to ditch an entire future timeline?* It might turn out that you were in fact self-indulgently pissed off at the realities of being a decade into cohabitation with a workaholic. She could hear her mother's voice. 'There are worse addictions, darling.'

No, that wasn't it, either. She knew the correct answer to that was: 'Yes, it is sufficient, because what you're describing is loveless pragmatism.'

Here it was: the thing that kept her trapped. But somehow being away from home had shaken this revelation loose. Roisin simply didn't know if Joe Now was also Joe Then – if one became the other, overwrote him like old video cassette, or if the former version was still there, available to return to her, if she was patient. Until she'd figured it out, she couldn't make a move.

Roisin caught Meredith looking at her and quickly recovered her features from a worried scowl into pleasure.

Dev had decided to serve their meal in the kitchen, in part to distinguish it from Gina's birthday celebration in the dining room the following day. It was by no means the lesser choice. The sturdy wooden table with black bistro chairs was in a dog's leg around the freestanding Aga. They'd filled the table with a star-studded clutter of tea lights, wherever there was space around plate settings. The white china pendant lamps above had a lambent, firefly glow. The whole look could've been torn straight from an upmarket interiors magazine.

Roisin had forgotten how great a cook Dev was. He had that signature of the truly confident, in that he never tried to do too much.

Tonight, there was a cauldron of butter chicken on the stove, with stacks of paratha and a mound of plain rice the size of a Forest Hog, and a supporting act vat of saag aloo, which their resident vegetarian, Gina, could have as her main.

The table held raitas and something shrimp-pink with beetroot, bowls of chutneys and pickles.

Dev, always a host by temperament, had found a setting worthy of his talents.

Everyone held their phones aloft to record the scene – the modern ritual.

She glanced at Joe for a moment's connection, but he had stationed himself by the butter chicken with a serving ladle.

'We're not going to say grace, so instead let's say thanks, Dev, and a cognac for the chefs,' Roisin said, lifting her glass with a nod to Joe and then Matt, as others followed suit.

'Oh God, do you remember that visiting manager from London who got us to describe "an interesting thing that happened to us recently", at the start of any meeting? Peppy bitch,' Meredith said, with theatrical shudder.

'There is nothing worse on this blue planet than "team building",' Matt said.

'I've got an interesting thing. Last month I was so hungover that my iPhone's Face ID didn't recognise me,' Gina said.

She looked surprised when everyone burst into hysterics.

'That's not possible, surely!' Matt said. 'It's biometrics.'

'It wasn't biometrics, it was mezcal.'

'Ohhhh, was that the same night you called me weeping so hard you couldn't speak, and I thought something terrible had happened . . .' Meredith said.

Gina nodded. 'I said, "I've finally accepted I'm never going to shag Jason Momoa." It was like a bereavement.'

'Woah. I'm still nowhere near ready to accept that,' Matt said.

Once the snorting had subsided, there was a peaceful interlude of shovelling curry, punctuated by murmured *fugging hell this is so good* compliments.

'I'm marrying well, aren't I?' Anita said.

'That reminds me, an announcement,' Dev said, dinging the pepper mill with his fork. 'We've decided on a wedding destination.'

The wedding was next spring: Dev was not much one for delayed gratification. Roisin had vaguely wondered aloud to Joe whether a venue of sufficient majesty would be available to Dev on such a short lead time.

'I can imagine Dev bribing someone to move theirs though, can't you?' Joe had said.

'What, literally paying the whole cost of a venue hire twice, to get another couple to cancel?'

'Yup. He doesn't care about money for itself, only what it can do. Admirable really,' Joe said.

'Mmmm,' Roisin had replied, feeling aghast and basic.

'Destination?' Meredith repeated now, tentatively voicing collective unease.

'*Lake Como*,' Dev said, spreading his palms like a television salesman with incredible reductions for you. 'I'll send you photos of the villa where we're having the ceremony. It's absolutely mind blowing. Honestly, that part of Italy.' Dev made a chef's kiss gesture before returning to tearing his paratha.

'Cypress trees, frescoed walls, Murano chandeliers, faded peeling shutters,' Anita said. 'The whole aesthetic. *I die.*'

'There are rooms available in the villa we're getting married in, but if they're too pricey there's other options nearby. I'll do a WhatsApp,' Dev said, waving a hand. 'Don't worry.'

'Well. This is exciting. I best start sticking more in my ISA,' Meredith said, in an upbeat way.

Roisin's approach to her own finances had been designed by Meredith in their twenties, and she had learned lifelong good habits she'd forever be grateful for.

'Does Lake Como have any Sofitels?' Matt said. 'This year for me is already very staggy.'

'Wait, aren't you loaded?' Joe said.

Roisin tensed.

'My family are loaded, I'm not,' Matt said.

'Very lawyerly distinction,' Joe said, chortling.

'It's not lawyerly, it's true.'

There was a strained pause that Roisin felt obliged to fill. 'I'm imagining the kind of stags you get invited on, Matt,' she said. 'Tell me if I'm warm. Posh lads in straw trilbies, mirrored aviators and pink polo tops, drinking free pour rosé at cabana pool bars in Ibiza?' She smiled at him, hoping to communicate that this was entirely friendly ribbing, unlike Joe.

'Why are you so full of hate, Roisin? Perpetually flooded with rage, aren't you?' Matt said, with a real smile in return. 'You are NOT cleared to board HMS Bants with Bags, Wills and Piggers.'

'No worries, mate! If you can't afford it, I can cover it,' Dev said to Matt.

'Uhm . . .' Matt glanced quickly at other, similarly taut expressions. 'I'd not feel OK about that, but thanks.'

'Don't be daft. All I care about is having you there! And

. . . drum roll . . . as for my stag destination. We're going to . . . MIAMI.'

There was a startled, if not shocked, pause. Any hope that Dev had picked up on the ambivalent response to his Italy reveal was dashed.

'Is there a Miami in Northamptonshire we don't know about, or do you mean Miami-Miami?' Joe said.

'Yeah, hoping there's a Miami nightclub in Bolton,' Matt said to Joe, who ignored him.

'I'm getting the flights,' Dev said, waving a palm. 'Not a thing to concern you, my dudes.'

His dudes made polite noises of disbelief. Meredith skilfully changed the subject by demanding the butter chicken recipe, before Anita could announce a hen do in Australia.

Putting them on this spot, albeit inadvertently, did not feel good. They couldn't really accept Dev's lavish hospitality and push back on newly unveiled obligations to travel Europe and America at the same time. They were compromised and complicit. Taking with one hand and trying to say 'stop' with the other.

Dev had soared into a tax bracket that several of them didn't share and likely never would, and he needed to come back down to earth if he wanted to spend time with them.

How had Roisin not grasped what was going on? She'd fretted this trip was over the top, yes, but in the familiar rhythms and patterns of their socialising in south Manchester, the situation hadn't been so obvious as it was right now.

Had Dev replaced his addiction to narcotic excess with

addiction to this excess: spending money? His Chase Sapphire card no longer chopped out the powder – it *was* the powder?

'While we're doing announcements,' Joe said, 'there's one over this end of the table, too.'

10

In the seconds after Joe spoke, Roisin discovered it was certainly true that faking it never really worked. The group must have sensed that Roisin and Joe were faltering.

If it was still old times, there would've been an excited, expectant gulp-gasp that they were about to hear news of an engagement. (Roisin's willingness to swill Möet putting paid to the other possibility.)

Instead, a fully silent gap followed Joe's declaration, because it turned out they clearly instinctively knew it couldn't be that either of them had proposed. Odd how microscopic pauses could be so decisively revealing.

Roisin had no idea what Joe was referring to, either. She certainly had no expectation of him pushing his chair out and dropping to one knee.

'I've got to leave earlier than planned on Sunday . . . to fly to the States,' Joe said, now he had them all in the palm of his hand. 'I've got a meeting with J.J. Abrams.'

'FOOK OFF!' Dev exclaimed, amid squealing. 'Really?'

'Is he the *Star Trek* guy? Or the *Star Wars* guy?' Gina said.

'Both,' Joe said, basking.

'This is for a film of *SEEN*?' Meredith said.

'Yup. Oh, and consider this information under a verbal agreement NDA. I am NDA-ed up to the gunwales.'

'What's an NDA?' Gina said.

'Non-Disclosure Agreement. A legal way to stop you gossiping,' Joe said. He added, 'Not YOU you. In general, "you".'

'When did you find this out?' Roisin said, though she had a good idea.

'Tonight,' Joe said. 'His people reached out to my people, etc.'

He had known when he was self-importantly banging out emails in their bedroom, then, and told her to go downstairs without him. He had actively chosen to withhold it for a moment with the group than tell his girlfriend, alone.

Nothing was about the two of them, any more. *Champagne problems.*

'Actual Hollywood people. Joe! This is the coolest thing,' Gina said, shaking her head, making a proud mum disbelief face.

'Oh my God – what are you going to *wear*?!' Anita said.

Everyone guffawed at the idea Joe's choice of shirt was crucial and Roisin was grateful for their guilelessness puncturing the lingering tension from Dev's air miles talk.

'What do you actually say, in a meeting like that?' Meredith said.

'To be honest, it's what my agent calls a kind of *let's get a look at you* thing. If they're going to do business developing your idea and involving you to some extent, they want to check you're not intolerable. So not a lot, really. Don't suggestively tongue the cutlery and laugh in the wrong places.'

'Are you having dinner?' Dev said.

'Brunch. But I've already been warned, no one actually eats it.'

'You order something and then look at it? Or you don't order?' Gina said.

'They say, "bring all the things for the table" and everyone ignores it and drinks black coffee.'

'Not called La La Land for nothing,' Dev said, nodding. 'Away with the fairies. Land of the lotus lickers.'

'Fairly sure it's "eaters",' Joe said.

'Destabilise the power dynamic by demanding the Chateau Marmont waiter brings you a large chilled banana milkshake with a half banana garnish,' Matt said. 'It's the kind of place where they'd have to do it.'

'Is it at Chateau Marmont?' Anita said.

'That was a guess,' Matt said.

'Actually, yes,' Joe said, and Roisin could sense Joe's irritation at Matt stealing even one rumble of this thunder.

'What time do you have to go on Sunday?' Roisin said. She knew it was a boring scold's question. A fun girlfriend should be cooing, but she couldn't bring herself.

'Taxi's coming at quarter to seven,' Joe said.

Dev, overhearing, made a pained noise. 'We'll say ta-rah to you on Saturday night if that's OK, mate.'

'Absolutely!' Joe said, addressing the table. 'I don't expect anyone to get up to see me off.'

Anyone? Roisin thought. *What am I, the dog we don't have's mother?*

'I think what you've achieved is so incredible, Joe,' Gina said. 'I remember when we used to donate our fully stamped café loyalty cards to you so you could have a free drink while you worked. Now look at you!'

'Still appreciate it,' Joe said. 'Might be flying business on Virgin Atlantic day after tomorrow but in my heart I'm Diddy B forever.'

'Diddy B!' Gina cried, in warmth at their shared nickname for Didsbury.

Joe gazed back at her with real fondness.

Roisin loved Gina, too. But in that moment, without jealousy, she thought: *Joe, you get on so well with Gina because she is sweetly pretty and built like Jessica Rabbit, and an unabashed Joe fangirl. She worships you and asks nothing of you.*

Maybe Roisin should let herself off the hook regarding Joe losing interest in her – maybe he was always going to do that with any partner who couldn't remodel herself into Joe's adoring foil. He used to like a challenge.

'Is it time yet?' Anita said to Dev. 'For the surprise.'

Dev nodded, and Anita jumped from her chair and scuttled off into the hallway as everyone watched, perplexed.

'Apologies for my fiancée. She has the energy of Satan crossed with a billy goat,' Dev said. 'Yes, I know, and it's me saying that.'

Anita bumped back into the room with hands full, holding a large flat oblong draped in a dust sheet, so large she had to sidestep.

'We've got this for our house, but we'll do more for anyone who wants,' Dev said, getting up.

Joe made a covert comic-grimace in Roisin's direction and she smiled thinly. She wondered why everything had to be smirked and snarked at now. Except, she was pretty sure she knew why. Easier to let go of something you had spoiled.

Dev helped Anita set the object, the size of a flat screen TV, down on the floor. They whipped the sheet away, both of them *TA-DAHing* as they did so.

They all squealed, bar Joe. It was a framed photograph of the six of them, crowded onto a black leather sofa in a Northern Quarter bar. They were under an American road sign, the words DON'T WALK lit up. Waterstones Deansgate Alumni, 2013.

Dev, centre, looked two stone lighter, with a then-characteristic pint and a chaser in front of him on the low table. Roisin, to his left, was grinning. She had her natural dark brown hair separated in low bunches (ugh, what was she thinking?) and a very tight *Muppets* t-shirt that made her look very busty (ugh, what was she *thinking*?). Pepe The King Prawn should not be stretched across a breast.

Her soon-to-become boyfriend, Joe, perched on the sofa arm, raising an eyebrow over the rim of a pint that he was holding up to obscure his face. He was shyer then. Roisin remembered the fascination between them at the time and felt a pang of loss.

Gina was on Dev's right. She had short hair in a pixie cut and a strappy dress with biker boots. She was perched coyly on Meredith's lap. Meredith, mostly obscured in green

Converse, looked like herself. She was always the most herself, from the start.

Matt was crouched on the ground, leaning his head to be sure of being in shot. He looked less chiselled and poised than he did now. More of the keen, gangly young athlete about him, but still boy-band beautiful.

Peering at the past was a strange sensation, Roisin thought, as they oohed and aahed and joked about it. It was an earlier version of themselves they hadn't exactly forgotten, yet it was still a jolt to be confronted with it. Somehow, you always lost the detail.

'I thought we could take another one while we're here; Then and Now.' Dev said. 'Lots of sofas to choose from.'

'You can do one where you're in exactly the same poses,' Anita said, always the art director.

'We can do another in another ten years!' Dev said, looking expansively at them all. 'And ten years after that!'

Much as she loved Dev's idealism, Roisin felt sure that these two portraits would be less of a sequence and more like book ends.

11

'Right, I think we're there . . .' Anita said, standing in front of the fireplace, examining them through her iPhone in its camo shockproof case. It had one of those PopSocket nodules on the back and looked like the serious professional tool kit that it was.

She'd found Dev a prop pint glass and shot glass and filled them with water. Joe was also required to hold a drink at the same level: everything had to be just so.

'Says everything that I didn't score a place on the sofa then and now never will, for *continuity*,' Matt said, making air quote marks, holding his crouching pose.

'Every *Friends* has a Gunther,' Joe said, to much laughter.

'He wasn't one of the main six,' Roisin said, and immediately regretted the lumpen stupidity of making Joe's point.

'Sorry, I weigh a bit more than I did when I was twenty-two,' Gina said to Meredith, who replied, muffled, 'Luckily my knees have got bulkier too.'

'Hold your positions a little longer, please!' Anita commanded, before prodding at her handset. 'OK, I've taken loads, and you can argue over using the one where you look best,' Anita said. 'We'll send copies of both on to all of you after the weekend!'

Dev snapped the overhead light off and the space was one plunged into atmospheric period gloom.

'This is *your* engagement celebration, Dev – we should be making a fuss of you two, not us,' Roisin said, getting up.

'Nothing we'd rather be doing,' Dev said, beaming, and Anita nodded.

'It's true. We were away with my sisters last weekend and Dev's not recovered yet.'

Dev shuddered. 'Chaos demons.'

'Hey. Speaking of demons. This place has to have a ghost, right?' Joe said, pulling his iPhone from his pocket and shaking it lightly, as if it was a deck of cards. 'Who wants to find out if there's a ghost story?'

'Joe . . .' Roisin said, in tone of warning. 'Don't shit us all up.'

'Me, I do!' Gina said.

'Do you?' Roisin said doubtfully.

'If it's not *super* scary,' Gina said.

'Joe, that is heavily qualified consent,' Roisin said.

'Given I don't believe in ghosts, I don't care,' Meredith said.

'I'm agnostic,' Dev said. 'Anita?'

'I believe,' she said, sitting down and reclaiming her fish-bowl G&T. 'But bring it on.'

A split second after she spoke the words *I believe*, the candles on the mantelpiece guttered. Gina and Anita shrieked.

Gina said, 'Matt, do you believe?'

'No. But I keep an open mind,' he said.

'That doesn't make any sense,' Roisin said, laughing, and Matt said, 'Oh chill, Miss Trunchbull,' which made Roisin laugh harder. She'd forgot Matt's comic theme that she was a joyless authoritarian.

'Is that a full house "yes" vote for the story, then?' Joe said impatiently. 'Rosh, you're a sceptic, it can't seriously bother you. You can't fear being haunted by something you don't believe in.'

He had her there.

Joe scrolled his screen. 'Ah, success! Here goes.' Joe adopted the voice of a local TV newsreader. 'Cumbria's ghostly hotspots. The grand Benbarrow Hall is said to be visited by the spirit of a servant girl who drowned herself in the lake in the late 1800s.'

'Oh, for God's sake! Why is it always tragic spurned women or angry men on horseback?'

Roisin realised she was still the bolshie twelve-year-old witnessing Queenie Mook's phantasms. Nevertheless, looking at the candlelight flickering on the walls, she was glad she wasn't going to bed alone.

'They're always "ladies", too,' Roisin said. 'The Lady Of The Something. Tragic, sexy young Ophelias. Someone should do a thesis on the underlying social values exhibited in ghost stories, if they haven't already.'

'Cor, you can tell you're a teacher,' Dev said.

'Forgive my girlfriend's strident feminism,' Joe said. 'It's said the girl was secretly engaged to the son of the family who lived here. When the scandalous liaison with a lowborn woman came to light, he denied her and branded her a liar.'

'Wanker,' Gina, said with feeling. 'Sounds exactly like my ex.'

'Distraught, she ran from her bed and drowned herself by moonlight,' Joe continued. 'Visitors to Benbarrow Hall have reported looking out of the windows and seeing a ghostly figure standing by the lake at night.'

'Argh!' Gina squealed as Meredith jumped to her feet, scuttled to the window and cupped her hands round the glass.

'Don't LOOK, Meredith!'

'What's looking going to do?' Meredith said.

'When you gaze into the abyss, the abyss gazes back!' Gina cried.

'Wasn't that a movie tagline?' Dev said.

'I think it's Nietzsche?' Matt said to Gina.

'I saw it on a poster,' Gina said.

Anita joined Meredith, while Gina performatively chattered her teeth.

'Oh my God, there's someone there!' Meredith said, in a sepulchral hush as she turned to Gina, face stricken. 'She's . . . TWERKING?'

Gina flicked the Vs at Meredith.

'. . . Other visitors report hearing footsteps on the staircases and seeing a young woman in a wet nightgown crossing the gardens at night. She is known in folk legend, due to her sodden hair and distressed appearance, as "The Crying Lady" . . .' Joe said.

'BINGO,' Roisin said. 'A Sad Lady. Told you.'

Joe carried on phone tapping. 'There's a blog here by a local historian, titled "The Curse of Benbarrow Hall" . . .'

'Nooooo, what's the curse?!' Gina said, pulling the satin ribbons from the pussy bow at her neck up to cover her eyes, like bandages.

'It relates specifically to courting couples,' Joe read. 'Every love match made under its roof will end in tragedy. The servant girl's mother put a curse on the house. I bet the wedding venue organisers lobbied hard to keep that out of the official Wikipedia.' He looked up, grinning.

'Ugh, no,' Anita said.

'Wait. What was that?' Joe said, slyly knocking a candle-less candlestick softly onto the rug with his elbow, pretending to startle. Everyone caught their breath, cackled, then heckled.

'Fuck, what if Dev and I are cursed?!' Anita said.

'You're betrothed, not courting. You'll be fine. No courting. Whatever that is. Didn't a frog do it?' Roisin said, mock sternly to each of them.

'You said bring it on!' Joe said to Anita.

'Anita's very bad at predicting how she'll feel a few minutes into the future,' Dev said. 'When we went to California I said, "Do you want to go on a hike through a canyon?" She said, "Yeah, sure," and five minutes into it she says she hates walking, and heat, and heights, and CANYONS. She's in *tears*. Like, what part were you expecting to enjoy?!'

'I had a great denim playsuit for it. That's where my mind goes. What will I wear?' Anita said.

'Can I borrow the denim romper to meet J.J.?' Joe said.

'Yes, sure. I will Febreze the gusset,' Anita said, winking a flicky liquid-eyelinered eye, set in a sweep of copper dust. Her face looked like it was sculpted from precious metals, Roisin thought.

Dev roared. Anita sparkled. They were a good combination. Roisin realised she missed being a good combination.

'Think any of it's true?' Meredith said, taking her seat again, also glancing at the deep shadows in the unoccupied end of the drawing room. 'The servant girl killing herself part, not the ghost resurrection. Though also the ghost resurrection, if you want to make the case.'

'No,' Roisin said. 'On the basis, as said, it sounds like all ghost stories ever.'

'If we are due a haunting, you're absolutely the one who'll get it now,' Matt said. 'The vocal cynic always gets it. You've marked yourself, Rosh.'

'This is true. I'll take my chances,' Roisin said. 'Not least because I know the facetious pretty boy gets it straight after me. You're no way alive at the end. You foolishly have a furtive assignation out by the chicken shed. Then . . .' Roisin made a body thrusting and then a neck slashing gesture.

'*Who is* alive at the end?!' Gina squeaked, as if this was a real prospect she should plan for.

'Resourceful, "main character energy" Meredith, brandishing a tiki torch, in her glitter Birkenstocks,' Roisin said. 'She possibly saves you and Dev, according to the worthy of rescue archetypes. Joe read the ghost story; I derided the ghost story; Matt's, as stated, Matt; and Anita said she was frightened, so she's a goner. We're obvious fodder for the narrative arc.'

There was a pause.

'Do you know, I think I'd have preferred charades,' Matt said.

12

'Why do rich kids always lie about being rich? Is it in the handbook? Do they all get slipped a copy of the rules of having money? Like the way cabbies do The Knowledge?' Joe said, toothbrush hanging from side of mouth, in his Paul Smith ironic striped grandad pyjamas. He was speaking in an exaggerated hush, being quieter than he needed to, no doubt to coax Roisin to join him in the bitching. 'I was waiting for, "we weren't well off, my parents scraped enough to send us private." Every time.'

'Matt?' Roisin was in bed, hair twisted up in a bundle against the pillow, face pale and shiny with moisturiser.

It was incredible they'd been so restrained with the alcohol tonight; perhaps it was the combined whammy of a full day's work (in her case, anyway), heat, travel, curry and being given the willies by ghost stories. One way or another, their plane had taxied on the runway and not taken off. Roisin was glad it left her able to enjoy the thought of tomorrow's walk round the grounds. She'd had visions of sly pukes in wooded copses.

'Yeah. "My parents are wealthy, not me." Oh, please. What

portion of some vast estate in Knutsford is coming Matt's way, along with the private annual income he'll be on?'

'I've never really thought about Matt's financing,' Roisin said.

'Neither has Matt.'

'It's not Matt I'm worried about. It's Dev,' Roisin said.

'He has gone a bit Viv "spend spend spend" Nicholson.'

'Was she the football pools winner in the Sixties who blew it all up the wall?'

'Aye. Ended up bankrupt,' Joe said.

'Shit, don't say that. You don't think he could do that, do you?'

'I dunno – didn't say anything to Dev, but it's fifty-fifty I can come to any of it, including the wedding, anyway. No idea what my schedule will look like then.'

'What? No one's going to expect you to miss a wedding?' Roisin said.

'I think Hollywood people are capable of expecting me to miss births, deaths, weddings, the lot,' Joe said. 'Still. No point telling Dev that until it happens.'

She could've done with Joe breaking it to her gently, and as if it was as much her bad news as Dev's. It wasn't nothing to her to discover he might not be at her side at the occasion of one of their dearest friends tying the knot. He'd never be on the pictures, they'd share no memories of the day? That hadn't mattered?

'Er . . . when were you going to tell me?'

'Well, see above. Not worth getting upset about until it happens.'

Except he had just worried her with it.

She felt as if Joe kept trapping her inside riddles. He might be great at dialogue but a hyper empath, he was not.

Roisin didn't say anything more, as it wasn't the time. But once again, she suspected The Time would not obligingly create itself.

Roisin was jolted awake by the air-tearing sound of a high-pitched scream. She sat up, shaking, trying to orientate herself in the inky proper darkness of the countryside. The scream was followed by the sound of feet thundering across the landing beyond.

She turned to look at Joe, who as usual had wrapped himself in a tight cigar of sheet and remained deeply asleep. Their old flat used to be surrounded by regular high volume, post-kebab shop hoopla, cars backfiring, R'n'B played by neighbours at four a.m. Joe never stirred. It was his super-power.

There followed muffled voices, possibly male or female, or both. There was an odd but powerful dull bang that Roisin couldn't place, although she was at least sure it wasn't a gun shot. It was followed by another, this time bloodcurdling, female scream that sliced through Roisin like a hot knife through cold butter.

She jumped out of bed in a spike of adrenaline and fumbled desperately for the Liberty print kimono that she'd only bought when she knew she was coming on this trip. Roisin wasn't super keen on her friends knowing she often slept in an old pair of cropped leggings and a t-shirt for 'Raccoon

Lodge NYC: A Place Where People Come To Mix And Mex!'

Yes, don't take premenstrual RoshWear on tour, Joe said. *Leave the dressing gown of doom, the Tony Soprano robe, at home. And the slippers that look like Fraggle hooves.*

She bumped along the unfamiliar passageway in the dark and out onto the landing, which contained Dev in vest and joggers and Anita, abundantly braless in silk camisole and big French knickers. Roisin envied the physically confident. Or possibly, the simply semi-conscious in an emergency.

'I told you, I thought she was in trouble,' Matt was saying, beyond them. He was in only boxer shorts, looking sleep-rumpled, peculiarly culpable and, it had to be noted, extremely abdominally honed. *That* was why you went to the gym on holiday.

'I couldn't open the door,' Matt said. 'I was acting, not thinking.'

'Because she'd locked it!' Anita said.

'I know that *now* . . .'

'What's the other explanation for it not opening, though? Did you think the ghost had the other side of the handle?' Dev said, entertained.

'Honestly, I don't know. I panicked . . .'

Matt's sheepish demeanour reminded Roisin of when her brother Ryan, aged seventeen, stoned, had put in the wind-screen of her neighbour's car while climbing on it. He was trying to wave down an alien that had turned out to be a *Minions* balloon.

13

'I thought I was helping,' Matt said, in a defeated voice. 'I didn't mean to upset her . . . Ah, God . . .'

'Knock first, mate! Always knock! Simple as that!' Dev was saying, in the kindly exasperated voice he'd used in emergency situations on the shop floor.

'I know, I know. I'll pay for any damage,' Matt said, looking towards a door which Roisin could now see had splinters at its frame.

'That'll be her therapy bills,' Anita said, and Dev gave his fiancée a hard look.

'Hi. What's happened?' Roisin said.

They turned.

'Gina's had a haunting!' Dev said. 'She's met the ghost.'

'The Crying Lady?' Roisin felt a bit foolish, asking as if it was a real person. Her heart started pounding, nonetheless. 'Really?'

'Yup.' Dev said. 'Or she thinks. She woke up and saw a woman standing at the foot of her bed.'

'That's why she screamed?' Roisin said uncertainly. In the looming silhouettes of the old house, in the early hours of the morning, she felt many degrees less scornful than she had during Joe's online trawl earlier.

'Matt burst into her room when he heard her screaming. He was being a knight in shining . . . pants,' Anita said, looking him up and down and giving a low whistle. Anita, Roisin was learning, could never sustain seriousness for very long.

Matt crossed his arms defensively across his lightly hairy chest. It wasn't their first rodeo – more like second or third – seeing each other in less than full formal attire on holidays, yet Roisin was glad of her layer of outerwear.

Matt looked intensely miserable, and Roisin was definitely missing something here. Hadn't he been helpful? He was somehow as guilty of upsetting Gina as soggy apparitions?

'OK . . . ?' Roisin frowned. 'Your intervention wasn't welcome?'

'Nope,' Matt said.

'Because you broke through the door?'

'He kicked it off its hinges,' Anita said to Roisin.

'Right.' Roisin frowned. That'd take some doing with these two-inch thick wooden doors. 'And now she can't lock her door in case the ghost comes back? It floated through walls anyway, so . . .'

'No. The issue is Gina was . . . *not dressed*,' Anita added.

'*Oh*,' Roisin said. She'd found sleepwear disorientating enough.

Matt clapped a palm over his eyes, as if blaming his having sight. 'I feel like such a creep. It's not as if I was looking for a reason to barge in. I can only keep saying I'm sorry.'

'Shall I go in and talk to her?' Roisin said.

'Yes, good idea,' Dev said. 'She'll want to talk to you.'

Roisin gingerly cranked the handle of a door that had been propped back in place and swung straight open on its damaged hinges. Gina was a tiny, sweatshirt-clad figure wrapped in the sea of blankets in the middle of her four poster, lights low. Meredith was perched awkwardly on the edge of the bed, with consoling arm around her.

At Roisin's entrance, Meredith widened her eyes: a 'Proceed With Caution' look.

'Are you OK, G?' Roisin said, gently.

'Shall I explain . . . ?' Meredith addressed Gina, who shook her head, wiped her nose and raised tear-filled eyes to meet Roisin's. She sniffed, hard.

'I was going to sleep, and I woke up, and I think I might have had that sleep paralysis thing and be still dreaming, you know,' she said, in a tremulous voice. 'I thought I saw someone at the end of the bed. When I turned the light on, it was the wardrobe, but I still screamed.'

Roisin knew it. Her fear evaporated instantly. No spectral floaters – power of suggestion, plus pissed. *Bloody Joe. Joe 'sleeping like a baby while the controversy raged' Powell*. The time to google whether the place was 'haunted' was on departure.

No one better than a teacher – or a submarine captain – to tell him that giving a bunch of people in an enclosed space a crazy idea, was a crazy idea.

'Suddenly Matt was outside the door saying, "Gina, are you OK, what's wrong," and I'd locked the door, and it all happened so fast . . . I jumped out of bed and then he was in the room . . . I was . . . I don't sleep in clothes . . .' She buried her face in her blanketed knees and made a whimpering noise.

'She has been retraumatised by Matt being a heroic bellend,' Meredith concluded.

'It's just . . .' Gina lowered her hand. 'I know he was being nice. But how am I supposed to not want to *fucking die* every time I see him? I keep replaying it in my head!'

Roisin could see that the thing that made this impromptu full frontal not merely embarrassing, but actively quite horrifying, was the 'being in love with Matt' part. No one was saying as much, yet this context was the intangible, oppressive force in the room. More so than The Crying Lady.

No one wants to flash the person they have the bad hots for, Roisin thought.

No one for whom it's not a kink, anyway.

14

Roisin sat down on the other side of the bed. 'I know it doesn't feel enough of a comfort right now but you're going to forget about this much faster than you think, and he will too. The room is half dark and it was a moment.'

'It was quite a few moments, where I was jumping around, and he was like . . .' She mimicked someone staring in boggling, immobile shock. 'Then he turned around, and I was pushing him away in panic and we . . . I . . . sort of slapped against him . . .' She put her palms to her forehead. 'Aaaaargggh. Make it not have happened, Roisin. Every day from now on, this has happened.'

Meredith carried on rubbing her back. Roisin didn't usually refer in any explicit way to Matt's frenetic love life, but needs must.

'Gina, consider this,' she said in an assertive voice. 'Matt is a man of the world. Seeing women naked is his principal hobby. He's seen so many that I promise you he still couldn't pick you out of a line-up after this.'

Gina quietened slightly. 'You think?'

'Yes! Memory is dimming as we speak! Memory-generating

brain cells start dying off age thirteen. Some of my pupils are proof.'

Roisin inclined her head at Meredith, to convey 'help me out'.

'This is very true of men slags. Many women, endless women. Just a blur of boobs,' Meredith said. 'In a long career. Like David Attenborough viewing wildlife. It'd be like asking David Attenborough to recall a specific giant tortoise. Among the . . . *Great Tortoi*. Wait, what's the plural of tortoise?'

'Tortoises,' Roisin said.

'Oh. Makes sense.'

'He's David, and I'm one of tons of Galapagos turtles?' Gina said.

'Yes!' they chorused, emphatically.

''Cos he met so few of them, they had names! All of them died! I saw a documentary with one called "Lonesome George"!'

'Maybe he was just unpopular,' Roisin offered.

Meredith put a hand over her mouth. 'Something more common then. Penguins?' Meredith said.

'Pretty sure David would remember a penguin if it had shaken its double-D tits at him while screaming GEEET OUUUTTTT,' Gina said, palms at her side, doing a little belly dancer mime.

Roisin fought to suppress laughter. Meredith was trembling with the effort of not doing the same.

'Also, if I'd known this was going to happen, I'd have had a wax,' Gina said. 'I've been rewilding to get that Seventies *Hustler* look this summer, I read in *Elle* that the bush is coming back. It's all . . . patchy.' Her voice wavered again. 'Like, I

wouldn't want either of you two to see this. Let alone . . .'
Her face contorted.

'Rewilding?' Roisin said, having to gasp the word out
between her fingers.

Gina nodded sombrely. 'As my beauty therapist says, years
of Brazilians aren't reversed overnight.'

'No need with my rainforest,' Meredith said. 'Nature is
flourishing. Lots of natural grazing habitat.' She didn't quite
make it steadily to the end of the sentence.

Roisin, at last, permitted herself to laugh. 'Perfect for large
herbivores . . . ahahaha . . .'

'No way to describe my ex, but yes.'

'So you're saying you've created a magical haven,' Roisin said.

'Yes, I'm saying that wildlife frolics.'

She and Meredith collapsed.

'Fuck you both!' Gina said, witnessing their honking, but
her heart wasn't in it. She was finally smiling, grudgingly.

Roisin's chest was heaving as laughter subsided. She felt
guilty that Gina's trauma was her first moment of authentic
joy since they arrived.

'Gina, not only is he not going to have noticed the detail,
but I'm absolutely certain you look incredible without your
clothes on. You're leaving out the most important thing here,'
Roisin said, wiping her eyes. 'What will have registered, if
anything, is fitness. Whereas if it had been me, he could've
sued for mental distress. Also . . .' Roisin had to say this without
inviting false hope: 'It shows he cares.'

'Hi. Can I come in?' Matt said, interrupting, from the other
side of the door.

Gina looked to Roisin and Meredith for an answer or reassurance.

'Don't have to talk to him if you don't want to,' Roisin said.

'I'd rather face him with you here,' Gina whispered. She wiped her eyes and rearranged her hair around her shoulders. 'Come in.'

Matt entered, clad in t-shirt as well as boxers. 'I wanted to apologise, again. I've been a total dick. Shoulder-barging locked doors is completely not OK. I'm mortified. Please promise me that you won't forever associate me with this moment of idiocy.'

Roisin wasn't sure if it was emotional intelligence or public school manners that made Matt claim the shame of this encounter; either way, it was astute.

'It's alright. You didn't mean to do it,' Gina said, in a very polite and somewhat recovered voice. Then, 'It's forgotten. I promise.'

'Thank you,' Matt said.

'Night,' they chorused, as he left.

Roisin turned to Gina. 'Gina. This is nothing. It's for Matt to feel awkward, like he said. Be confident in your skin, because if I was in your skin, I certainly would be.'

'I bet you are a lovely teacher,' Gina said. 'You always know what to say.'

Roisin hugged her bare, delicate bones. 'I know how it feels to be held together by sheer bravado and Charlotte Tilbury.'

'What's going on? Where have you been?' Joe said, unexpectedly propped on an elbow, awake, as Roisin gently closed the bedroom door behind her.

81

'Your ghost story scared Gina; she screamed, and Matt broke into her room to rescue her. She was naked and feels very embarrassed.'

'Really? Like, not a stitch?'

'Yup.'

'Lucky bastard, as usual,' Joe mumbled, as he pushed his face into the pillow.

Roisin sighed as she snapped the light off.

15

The next morning, Dev was ladling out fried eggs and bacon in the kitchen with the sang-froid of a man who'd once carried on making full Englishes in *Flatmates* when the police had turned up after a report of common assault by a drag queen, Margaret Snatcher, on a vegan sex toy manufacturer.

The offensive weapon was a bullet vibrator in the shape of a chilli pepper, and the footage of officers inspecting and bagging it saw some of the show's highest ratings.

Everyone was extremely perky at the sight of a breakfast line cook in the stunning kitchen and Anita mixing virgin Bloody Marys – Bloody Shames, as Dev called them. Once again, Roisin felt guilt that the Gina trauma seemed to have cleared something among them: like a rainstorm in a heat wave.

Was it because they'd been on their best behaviour, stilted, and the spell had been broken?

Either way, Roisin was glad of the cheer as she zig-zagged sriracha onto her fried egg, praising Dev's cooking and Meredith's forethought regards the groceries. None of your communal holiday, two miserly allocated Weetabix and off-brand tea bags, UHT milk; she'd thought of every luxury.

(And Dev had insisted on tons of bog roll, with the immortal words: 'I won't play a game of chicken with my own arse.')

They were chatting amiably and discussing the route they'd take exploring the grounds, when Gina appeared in the doorway, wild eyed, looking as dramatic as if she was bursting in for the female solo in a Meatloaf video.

'Matt, what the FUCK?' she said, in a ragged voice, and Matt physically started. Everyone else looked at each other in amazement, too. That Matt could've committed fresh atrocities and be down in the kitchen, freshly showered and crisply shirted by half nine, seemed improbable.

'What have I done?!'

'Your message. Was that meant to be funny?'

'What message?'

'YOU KNOW WHAT MESSAGE! Those texts!'

The collective gaze fastened on Matt, whose mouth was open, his brow knitted. The toast that had been heading towards his mouth was replaced on the plate.

Gina turned her phone towards him and held the screen in his face.

He frowned, silent for a second. 'I didn't send that! Why would I send that?!'

'You tell me. Fourteen times!'

Matt raised his body out of his chair, back straight, so he had pocket space to fumble his phone out.

'I didn't! I don't know what's happening here . . .' Matt

said, tapping at the screen and frantically scrolling to his messages. Another brief and exquisitely taut pause. 'Fuck. It looks like I *did* send them, but I didn't mean to, I promise! It's a bum dial! A pocket dial!'

'What did you send?!' Anita said, unable to contain herself any longer. '*Dick pics?*'

Arm extended fully, Gina marched the length of the table and held her phone up in front of each of them in turn, giving them a second to focus. As if she was a prosecution lawyer, making sure every member of the jury was informed. Roisin squinted. On her iPhone screen was a poo emoji sticker, with hearts for eyes and large grin. A sort of jaunty, laughing turd, a brown Mr Whippy. Unfortunately, Roisin could see how his hearts-for-eyes could be construed as tact-less joy in beholding something.

'Fourteen in a row,' Gina said, in a stage whisper, as if the number had Illuminati significance.

None of them knew what to say as comfort. Roisin guessed Gina must know it was a cock-up but had been trying to decipher the meaning long enough that her jangled nerves had turned it into conspiracy. Every time her phone pinged, she ratcheted up another notch. Jet fuel couldn't melt steel beams and Matt couldn't have missent a coiled pile of anthropomorphic faeces.

'How could it not have been a mistake?' Matt said. 'What message would I have been conveying with those pictures? They're nonsensical!'

'I'm supposed to believe you sent this *to me*, by chance, after what happened last night?! Bit of a coincidence,' Gina scoffed.

'Not exactly a coincidence!' Matt was flushed the colour of beetroot raita. 'I had my phone open to message you earlier. I couldn't think what to say. I didn't send anything. I put my phone away. I must have put it in my pocket unlocked, and then . . . pushed on it.' He gestured with open palms at his trouser area, in his seated position.

'You're making excuses because the joke has misfired! Because I've called you out in front of everyone!'

'I'm not! Why the hell would I send you a picture of laughing shit?!'

'I don't know! YOU TELL ME!' Gina bellowed at the top of her lungs. She ran from the room, making audible noises of distress.

A pall descended.

'I don't know if I should go after her?' Matt said, looking genuinely upset. 'I don't know how to explain if she's going to insist it was intentional?'

Meredith put down her egg and bacon roll and also stood, wiping her hands on a piece of kitchen paper.

'You'll make things worse if you go up to her. I will talk to her and fix it. Gina will be OK for the walk in' – she checked her watch – 'half an hour's time. This is my pledge. But, Matt, while I know you didn't mean any harm, please, no more incidental . . . incidents? Give her a swerve entirely, until she's calmed down. And everyone leave my bap please, I am coming back for it.'

'Thanks, Meredith. Really appreciate it,' said a crestfallen Matt.

Meredith headed off. The convivial atmosphere had dissipated like a needle scratch in a jukebox sound effect.

'Bit of fresh air will sort this out, it'll be over by lunchtime,' Dev said, consolingly, to Matt. 'You know Gina adores you, she's absolutely besotted with you.'

Roisin cringed.

'She can't stay radge for long.'

He toasted Matt with a Bloody Shame, stirring it with the stick of celery and gulping.

Silence fell.

In his 'puppy in the china shop' way, Dev's instinct towards generous overstatement had, on this occasion, merely stated facts. He'd no doubt been trying for a 'thinks the world of you' blandishment, off the cuff, and instead had inadvertently spelled out the thing they never said.

'It's hard to know what to say to her when she thinks I'd hurt her on purpose,' Matt said eventually, sounding slightly hoarse.

'Simply stop attacking Gina's mental health by accident, then,' Joe said.

'Cheers,' Matt said. 'Great to have your positive input, as always. A man who himself has never suffered a tech error, I'm sure.' He raised his eyes to meet Joe's directly, his anger finally breaking the surface of the water. Joe purposely avoided meeting it, mopping up some egg yolk with his crust.

'Well, the unsavoury ogling poo farce is definitely not Gina's fault.'

'Yeah, and you're never slow to point out my faults. I wonder why.'

Joe shrugged. Roisin sensed Joe felt a mixture of satisfaction and apprehension at Matt's hostility. Like a kid pushing their luck, angling for a telling off, and feeling just a little scared at finally getting one.

Matt stood up, abandoning his half-eaten breakfast. He took his plate to the sink in a tense silence.

'I know I messed up last night, but as if I'd harass her when I know she's upset. Is everyone's opinion of me really this bad?'

'No no no, mate, not at all,' Dev said and Anita chorused, 'No!'

Roisin said forcefully, 'Of course not. You'd never be unkind to Gina.'

Joe was pointedly silent.

She felt the truth of Meredith's words, nevertheless. Deliberate or not, Matt had thoroughly used up his honest mistakes quota.

16

True to her word, Meredith had a subdued but cooperative Gina at her side as they assembled by the outhouses for their walk. Roisin was relieved to see her in a better state; she'd had visions of their hearing an engine and leaping up to see Ethelred tearing away towards the horizon. However, Gina was still treating Matt as if he was radioactive. He loitered at a distance.

Dev insisted on going in to say hello to the hens, who were much less interested in saying hi to Dev and crowded into a far corner, clucking irascibly at the intrusion.

'They have a groundskeeper-type guy who pops in twice a day to feed them,' Dev said.

'Can you imagine what he thinks of the absolute nobbers that regularly pile into this place?' Joe said. 'Hopping from the helicopter, busting out the Freixenet and spraying it all over the rooster.'

'No rooster. Sir Drumstick recently passed.' Dev touched his forehead, chest and both shoulders in a cross. 'You'd know about him if he was still with us, I'm told. Screeched the joint down at dawn.'

'Was his death a murder?' Roisin asked.

'*Sir Drumstick*, I love it,' Meredith said.

'Tasteless,' Gina sniffed.

'Why?' Joe said.

'Because it's a cut of meat! Like calling him Lord KFC.'

'Ah yeah, I see what you mean,' Joe said. 'Like prawns don't think of themselves as lollipops.'

He grinned and Gina pushed, ineffectually and coquettishly, at his shoulder.

She alone won a conciliatory, warmer tone from him. All in all, Roisin was grateful that someone did.

'Also, who are you calling nobbers?' Anita said, gesturing at her lilac maribou-trim skirt. Roisin was keen to see her wedding dress: she could only imagine a sort of Tim Burton film level of kitsch drama. A headdress.

'Other nobbers, obviously,' Joe said. 'Nouveau, boozy nobbers who've rolled in from the city. Not classy big house appreciators, like us.'

They set off down to the lake, and Dev's optimism wasn't misplaced: the weak sun and light breeze did feel as if it was blowing fresh air through Roisin's mind and body.

Anita thoughtfully seized on Gina and marched her out ahead, so the Matt issue wasn't an issue. Dev fell lockstep between Joe and Matt, a rose between two thorns, and Meredith and Roisin found themselves at the rear. Actually, Roisin felt Meredith was sticking to her side purposely.

'What do you think to this, then?' Meredith said, after ten minutes or so.

'This?' Roisin cast a look back at the house. 'Minibreak location?'

'No, the weirdness.'

'The weirdness of . . . us? That sounds like the title of the worst romcom ever.'

'The weirdness of the mood since we've arrived. It's as if everyone's pretending. Not me and you, obviously.'

Roisin suspected Meredith meant *apart from the roaring tension between you and Joe.*

'I know what you mean. I felt awful admitting it to myself, but Gina's streaking was the first authentic moment of enjoyment I've had.'

'Same here. Odd, isn't it?'

'Perhaps it's timing. Few pressures coming to a head.'

'Dev and Anita had a huge blow-up last month.'

'*Did* they?' Roisin stopped dead, lowering her voice, even though everyone else was way in front. 'I thought they were on Cloud Nine.'

'I think they are, but Cloud Nine has a ring road traffic jam. I wanted your advice about it, actually. I might not get the chance again. I have a moral quandary.'

'Go on.'

'I was out on a works do last month at The Alchemist, and I see Dev and Anita in a corner. Before I can say hello, I see they're arguing. To the extent that Anita gets up to storm out. I'm thinking, right, I will pretend not to have seen them, but unfortunately, Anita storms right past me. We make eye contact, I make a kind of gesture like this . . .' Meredith stopped and performed a cross hands waving, lip zipping mime to Roisin which she gathered indicated: *no worries, I saw nothing, we don't have to speak.*

91

'OK.'

'So please note, as far as I know, Dev still has no idea I know. Anita then messages me the day after and asks if we can meet for coffee, but *please don't tell Dev*. I'd really rather not, in those circumstances, but what can you do when it's an SOS.'

'Oof. Yes.'

'We go for coffee, and she says the fight was about the fact she wants to come off her pill and try for a baby before the wedding in Italy. She's got background factors that makes her think it might take a while. Dev is implacably opposed to her ending up unable to drink and morning sick at a fifty-grand wedding . . .'

'Fifty grand!' Roisin hissed.

'Oh, and the rest; Anita was probably sparing me the full truth. Over our flat whites, Anita confides in me she's not taking her pill, and is telling Dev she is. *Is that bad, Meredith?* Me – yes, Anita, that is bad.'

'Woah.'

'Mmmhhhm. I said to her, and what will you do if you do get pregnant, tell him you're in the one per cent failure rate? Despite him knowing you wanted to try? She says no, he'll work it out, but once there's a baby he'll be overjoyed and my lying won't matter.'

Roisin looked at Meredith making a grit-teeth gesture. 'This is not the way to embark on parenthood. With lies. Also, Dev not feeling betrayed is a fuck of a gamble.'

'Yep. I told her it wasn't OK. She should take her pill, have the wedding – she's thirty-one, it'll be fine. But knowing

Anita to be somewhat capricious, I don't think there's much chance she'll take it. The advice, or the pill.'

'She's such a party girl, she might actually regret being pregnant on her honeymoon, too. What did Dev say? "Anita's very bad at anticipating how she'll feel a short time in the future"?'

'Oh yeah. Canyons.'

They trudged in quiet for a moment.

'You straight people, you're a mystery to me,' Meredith said. 'Mind you, serious relationships are a mystery to me, so perhaps I should take a seat.'

'Seems to me this is not actually mere conception admin,' Roisin said, frowning. 'This is quite a large and meaningful difference of priorities. If Anita wants a pregnancy more than far-flung weddings she should tell Dev to scale the whole thing down and even consider delaying it until after kids.'

'Ah, I said that; no can do. Her Hindu family are liberal but not that liberal. Marriage before babies or there'd be hell to pay. If she gets pregnant it'll be Gretna Green, accelerator pedal to the floor. A lot of pressure to go against wishes of fiancé *and* family.'

Roisin blew out air. 'If you've told Anita it's wrong, what's your moral quandary?' she said.

'Do I tell Dev she's not on the pill?' Meredith said.

'Good God, NO. Is that even a question?' Roisin said. 'Or am I a self-preserving coward? But no. I see only bad outcomes if you break Anita's confidence. It was unfair of her to burden you with it.'

'Thank you! That's the advice I came for. The thing I wanted to hear anyway,' Meredith laughed.

They stopped to gaze out over the rippled water.

'Lake Como is the problem, you know,' Roisin said, once again speaking quietly, as if it was profane to say it at normal volume. 'It's wonderful Dev's been so successful, but the attitude to money is spiralling out of control. I've realised what it reminds me of – those nights out where we'd be done, and Dev would bang down a tray of shots no one asked for and announce we were "going on somewhere". The rapid escalation.'

'That has occurred to me. That he's going to end up in high-roller rehab next,' Meredith said.

'Alternative approach,' Roisin said. 'Someone talks Dev out of Miami and Lake Como. This then provokes a proper heart to heart with his fiancée about the marriage-babies timetable.'

'*Someone?* Good luck, Rosh!' Meredith said and they laughed. 'I hope you don't mind me burdening you, too. You're such a solid person about these things.'

'Honoured.' Roisin patted her arm.

'You know, looking at that photo of us from way back when,' Meredith said, 'reminded me of what a superstar you are. I've never met anyone who's such a natural leader, always the centre of things, but who has so little ego to go with it. Dev was our manager but you were too, in an unofficial, HR way.'

'Wow,' Roisin said, blushing. 'Really?'

'Uh huh. We all thought Joe had won the lottery, the first time we spied you holding hands.'

'Blimey, Mer, where did all that come from?! But thank you.'

'I get the feeling you're not hearing things like that enough,' Meredith said, with a penetrating look.

Roisin's mouth opened in surprise, and nothing came out.

'GIRLS! You waiting to drown yourselves?! Come the fuck on!' Dev roared in the distance, doing a little Riverdance.

They laughed and moved on, and Roisin was grateful, as she had no idea what she'd have found to say.

17

As the Saturday night meal was in honour of Gina's recent birthday, Gina chose the menu. She was very enthusiastic about this, taking charge of the cooking. Others were less enthusiastic.

'Dreading it, if I'm honest,' Joe had said, a week prior. 'I'm not being funny, but I've seen how much Gina eats, and there'll be no meat either. I'm hiding Yorkies and a family bag of Walkers salt and vinegar in our room for later.'

'Joe!' Roisin had chided. 'She's a great cook.'

'I know. She makes sensational banquets. For a family of MICE.'

'I've been saving *Vogue* and *Tatler* photos of dinner parties for inspo,' Gina had told them. 'No one cooks any more. Basically, everyone fashionable serves a platter of radishes and shrimps with the tail on, with aioli, and big bowls of cherries.'

'A radish, a prawn and some cherries. I'll try not to gorge myself,' Joe said.

Yet when Gina finally unveiled her full three course concept to Meredith, Anita and Roisin in the kitchen that lunchtime,

Roisin did silently ponder that it sounded a trifle on the lean side. Gina must lack the greedy enzyme.

No, wait – you're being infected by Joe! she told herself. *What did Dev teach you?* A few things, properly done, is much better than a nervily assembled mish mash of a dozen.

Gina rehearsed the menu, which included 'dressed red leaves'.

'Is that a salad, when in Urmston and not Umbria?' Meredith said.

'It's chicory! I suppose leaves means no blue cheese or sweetcorn or ranch dressing.'

'Ranch dressing, I could snort it,' Anita said mistily, a woman whose appetite was closer to Meredith or Roisin's.

There was tiramisu for afters.

'The genius of it is, it can pretty much all be done in advance,' Gina said. 'All there is to do before we sit down is frying the arancini balls, then cooking the spaghetti.'

Hunter starting at nine meant an easy breezy approach to it wasn't wise. Gina had timings written on a scrap of paper affixed to the towering fridge: they were having a 'baby's tea' starting at six, to avoid jumpy clock watching.

At half five, Roisin lit the taper candles on the long mahogany table in the grand dining room, surveyed the huge window with its view onto the lake beyond, and sighed. You could serve Joe's old skint writer's dinner of 'Prison Ramen' in here (ramen noodles plus Wotsits) and it'd seem like a feast.

'Reckon you can get Deliveroo to Benbarrow?' Matt said, as they sat down, hurriedly adding, 'Not that I want to!'

Roisin placed the red table plonk at intervals down the

runner in the centre. Gina wasn't present, still putting the finishing touches to their balls.

'Lol. No, of course not,' Joe said. 'Imagine the poor wee fella cranking his bike up the path. Your rider tip would need to be a king's ransom to make them take the job. Everything would be stone cold.'

'We've found the one drawback of owning this place. No takeaways,' Matt said. 'Who knew the super rich can't get takeaways.'

'Your private chef probably takes the sting out of it,' Dev said.

Roisin went back to the kitchen to collect the starter plates and she, Anita, Gina and Meredith entered carrying them, to applause.

'Porcini arancini,' Gina said, as they began.

'Pleasing rhyming,' Matt said, and she smiled at him before remembering she currently hated him, her face twitching and dropping in a comical manner.

'Really nice, G,' Roisin said, after a few mouthfuls. 'I can say this without self-praising because I was only involved tangentially.'

'Really good,' everyone murmured in agreement.

'Great balls of fire!' Dev said, having caught an especially molten lava bit of gruyere, grabbing for his water.

It didn't take very long to consume two of them and Roisin once again regretted not taking an interest in the decisions on scale in the preceding weeks. Her job meant the group WhatsApp often pinged away for an hour before she was able to look at her phone.

'That's left me pleasantly peckish for my main,' Joe said to Roisin, who glowered at him as she cleared the plates.

Meredith and Roisin were thrashing the men at pool, while Anita was off taking 'mood board' photos of the house, until Gina appeared in the doorway of the games room, looking agitated.

'Can I borrow you?' she said to the women.

She led them back towards the kitchen, wailing, 'the spaghetti's not fucking cooking!'

They broke into a trot across the hallway to keep up with her speed.

'It must be, it'll be some posh bronze dyed stuff that needs longer, that's all,' Meredith said.

'Try it!' Gina said, gesturing at the double-handled mega pan on the Aga hob.

Meredith, and Roisin each hook-a-ducked a strand out of the rolling boil and chewed contemplatively, preparing to tell Gina in meltdown mode that it was merely al dente and *exactly how the Italians eat it.*

Ugh. Roisin had to agree, it was like chewing a chalky shoelace. It tasted raw. Hot and raw.

'Another fifteen minutes, it'll be reet,' said Meredith, looking similarly doubtful. 'How long's it had?'

'Half an hour! More than!' Gina screeched.

'Any second now, honestly,' Meredith said. 'Let's have a wine and wait it out.'

She sloshed red into three fresh glasses.

'If it's not cooked in half an hour, I don't see why a bit

longer is any guarantee,' Gina said, and Roisin thought she had a point.

'Let's not panic,' Meredith said, stoutly. 'Here,' she looked at the wall clock. 'Testing again, at dead on half seven. The lads can play another game of pool.'

The alcohol had the required sedative effect as they chatted, and it was closer to quarter to eight when they remembered to try it. They chewed gingerly this time, in foreboding: yep, stubborn ropes of inedible semolina.

'FOR FUCK'S SAKE!' Gina said. 'What are we going to do? Joe's show is on at NINE! Why have they sold me TWAT SPAGHETTI!'

Roisin looked anxiously at the clock. She did not want an agitated Gina trying to ladle out a dinner of twat spaghetti at a whisker to nine p.m., Joe refusing to stay and eat, and another huge fight. Gina's mood felt knife edge as it was.

'OK. I think we have to accept the pasta may not cook, or it may be some strange masochist's variety that is never going to taste cooked,' Roisin said. 'Contingency plan. Meredith, any other options, carbohydrate wise?' Roisin asked.

'Bread. Lots of loaves of bread, and two bags of oven chips,' Meredith said. 'I think Dev used the potatoes up in his saag aloo.'

'How about . . . bruschetta, using the tomato sauce, and a load of chips, and the salad?' Roisin put her hands up. 'Call me a goblin, but I'd eat it.'

'Yes!' Meredith said. 'Also, we have butter and garlic? Garlic bread!'

Roisin made a fist pump gesture.

'What's everyone going to think at me serving them fucking TOAST?!' Gina said.

'Delighted. It's fashionable simplicity, like the radishes,' Roisin said. 'I'll fetch Anita.'

Roisin, Meredith and Anita worked hard to give Gina a sense of Blitz spirit jollity in the food they put out, but Roisin could see Gina was crushed by the dinner bork.

The less said about the profanities she unleashed when they finally gave up, drained and binned the Magical Never-Cook Spaghetti, the better.

'I'm sending that deli the mother of all customer complaint emails!' she stormed. 'They will gaze into my abyss!'

'When you're sober though, yes,' Meredith said. 'I don't want you going domestic terrorist on the only place I can get burrata.'

18

Roisin decided that two of the most beautiful words in the English language were 'make ahead'. She gave real praise to God for the beauty of the safely assembled and refrigerated pudding.

The main course was a tense experience, but the tiramisu at least tasted wonderful. There was nothing like a hefty bowl of fat, cocoa and sugar for reconciling you to your current circumstances. Roisin could feel her calm and stoicism increasing as she took her first mouthfuls.

'This is the best tiramisu I've ever had,' Matt said to Gina, 'And I've had tiramisu everywhere.'

'I bet you have,' Joe said.

'Thank you,' Gina said, without meeting Matt's eye.

'No one's going to talk about Doshi's boring curries after this.' Dev raised his glass of cranberry juice. 'Gina's Italian banquet smashed it. To Gina. Happy belated birthday, beautiful. We love you.'

They raised their glasses and repeated 'we love you' as Gina cast her eyes down, Princess Diana style, and said thank you.

'Ey up, have we got visitors?' Joe said, turning in his seat.

In the encroaching dusk, the panorama afforded by the dining room windows meant they could see the headlights on an approaching vehicle a mile off. 'A mile off' was barely a figure of speech, in fact.

'Is that car coming here?' Anita said, bouncing up from her seat and twitching back a curtain. 'It's a fancy looking Range Rover thing.'

Given the only possible destination was Benbarrow Hall, they were soon crowding the window in curiosity.

'Owner probably does spot checks to get a look at whether you're trashing the place,' Joe said.

'Doubt it,' Dev said. 'They make a right song and dance about leaving you to do your thing in privacy and only having that man here to feed the hens. Made me wonder if they get hired for fetish parties or something.'

'Maybe they're lost?' Gina said.

The Jeep pulled up on the gravel outside and sat idling for a moment, then the engine snapped off.

A man got out of the back, in dark suit, black t-shirt and poseur's sunglasses. He walked the perimeter of the car before opening the other passenger side door. Everyone at the dining room window looked at each other.

'Oh my God, what if they're hit men?' Gina said.

'Hit men hired by who?' Joe said. Then, under his breath, 'Food Standards Agency.'

Roisin craned her head above the group, meerkat-esque, to give Joe a SHUT IT look. Luckily, Gina was concentrating on the unexpected guests.

'Or we could be double booked?' Roisin said.

'Nah,' Joe said. 'They can see lights on and it's Saturday evening. Who hires anywhere from Saturday evening? Dev, level with us. Did you get us adult entertainers?'

'Oh my God, for my birthday! Magic Mike XXL!' Gina screeched, clapping her hands.

An auburn-haired woman, also in sunglasses, emerged from the back seat of the car, clad in white shirt, grey skinny jeans and towering tan platform sandals. Her figure was narrow yet had feminine curves, like a stylised fashion book sketch. She bent down by the open car door and patted her knees at someone unseen, still inside the car.

'Magic Michaela XXL,' Joe said. 'Things are looking up.'

'Oh, fucking hell,' Matt exclaimed loudly, jolting them all to attention. He tore out of the dining room, off into the cavernous hall.

They took a split second to exchange glances and race after him.

On the other side of the arched front door, they saw two men, the second dressed much like the first, standing by the vehicle.

'Come on, Granville. Come on. That's it! Yes!' the red-headed woman was saying, still bending and patting her knees.

A small, low slung and chunky breed of dog disgorged himself from the car, panting hard. The woman gathered him into her arms and finally, turned to look up at them.

'Where's Matthew?' she said, pushing her glasses up onto her head and surveying them. *Not a very charming greeting,* Roisin thought. Regal, almost. Matthew? These were Matt's friends?

'Ah, there you are! Surprise! Granville, wave to Matthew!' She manipulated the dog's paw to waggle up and down. She had a funny accent: clear as a bell, aristocratic English yet with a singy-songy, transatlantic twang.

'What are you doing here?!' Matt said.

Roisin looked over at him to assess his response. He was so pale white, he was tinged with a citrus yellow.

'You know how we were saying I had no time off before Mexico?' the woman said. 'I had this total moment of "lightbulb" – I'll swing by the house party. Have I surprised you?!' She said this not apologetically, but with the delight of someone waiting to be praised.

'Yes, just a bit. How did you even remember what the name of the house was?'

'You looked it up on my phone when you showed me, remember! I found the page was still open. Felt like a sign.'

She rearranged the dog in her arms as if cradling a Baby Jesus. Gosh, she really was beautiful, Roisin thought. Not common-or-garden attractive; an otherworldly creature. Like Galadriel had evanesced out of *The Lord of the Rings* and up the M6.

'Everyone,' Matt said, 'this is Ruby.'

'This is Ruby, from Hinge?' Meredith said, disbelievingly. It wasn't very polite to mention the dating app, but they were knees deep in plonk and in a state of mild shock.

'Yes,' Matt said, in a flat voice. He didn't seem remotely pleased by the cameo, more like he was condemned to trudge to the scaffold.

Ruby turned to the two men. 'Bring my luggage into the hallway, Mark. Drop it anywhere, until we've chosen rooms.'

Luggage? Choosing rooms? Who were the entourage?

It was spectacularly evident that they did not have the full story of Ruby from Hinge, the reverse catfish.

19

'I'll need a bedroom at the back, if there's one on that side of the house,' Ruby said to Matt, as if there were only two of them present, as opposed to eight of them round the dining table, having filed back in for a pudding that had been unfortunately, yet inevitably, abandoned. Plus, their number included a pedigree dog and two men who looked like agents from *The Matrix* roaming somewhere in the bowels of the house beyond.

'Mark and Ted will need rooms, too, but I presume you have plenty of space. Is this everyone?' She surveyed the stupefied gallery of faces.

You presume *quite a lot, huh,* Roisin thought.

Matt went round the table, pointing and reciting their first names, as Ruby stared.

'I can't be around phones, I'm afraid,' Ruby said to Gina, who was toying with her iPhone as a displacement activity. 'If you wouldn't mind, just . . .'

She pointed with both her index fingers, down the length of the table, shaking them lightly, like an air hostess indicating where the aisle lights were.

'What?' Gina said, not unreasonably.

'I can't have phones present, if you don't mind. No cameras. No photos. Easiest to say phones away. People forget.'

Ruby returned to whispering sweet nothings to the bum-faced mutt.

'No, I don't understand. No one's taking photos,' Gina said, and Roisin winced.

'I know you are not taking photographs,' Ruby said with a sort of solemn, exaggerated graciousness. 'You understand, however, it's simpler not to risk it at all.'

'You keep saying I understand why you don't want photos – I really don't?' Gina said, her tone now openly querulous.

'I'm a person with a profile,' Ruby said.

There followed a pause in which everyone wondered how to politely vocalise *what the fuck*.

'A what?' Gina said. 'Anita's got a big following on Instagram too, she doesn't care.'

'I mean I'm a prominent creative.' She flicked her curtain of immaculate cinnamon hair back over her shoulder. 'Oh, Granville, no! Oh, he's shy, bless him,' she said, as the dog abruptly disembarked from her lap and began rhythmically headbutting the door. 'Shy' wasn't how Roisin would characterise his behaviour.

Ruby had a very unusual manner to go with the uncommon accent: sort of Head Girl in a boarding school, combined with the rigidly poised, religiose self-certainty of a West Coast wellness guru. Roisin could imagine her selling you a five grand cucumber juice enema in a way that made it clear you were lucky she'd even speak to someone with a non-salad flavoured arse.

Roisin cast a look at Matt, who looked a queasy stew of both hideously stressed and lightly stunned. Why? A date inserting herself like this was embarrassing, but he seemed exceptionally ill at ease for a man who usually carried himself effortlessly.

'Do you want some wine or tiramisu, Ruby?' Dev said pleasantly, the only one remembering she was a guest, albeit one who'd fallen out of the sky.

'Thank you, I've brought my own food,' she said, as she settled the pedigree dog back on her lap. 'And I don't drink. Trying to persuade Matthew it's the way to go. I'll get there . . .'

She tinkled a laugh, showing a mouthful of exceptionally white, expensive dentistry.

'Wasn't your Lisbon trip a wine tour?' Meredith said.

'I taste and spit,' Ruby said, poker faced, which was absolutely begging for the kind of punchline no one dared supply.

There was something about Ruby that was nagging at Roisin. As she stared at her peculiarly perfect, tiny features, her creamy, shimmering skin, she realised what it was. She could, for some reason, exactly picture her in Forties garb. Pencil-thin eyebrows, dark lipstick drawing a cupid's bow. Curled and pinned hair, a wartime bride's cap-like veil over the top, with the voile flowing from ear level.

Where had she seen Ruby before, and why would it be from that era? Was she the world's most assertive ghost? The Bossy Lady? Had Roisin erased the memory of a fancy dress party?

At once, it came to her: a notion that was absolutely, wildly ludicrous, and at the same time, had the magic slam-dunk click of the right answer. No? Surely, no?

Wine unlocked Roisin's mouth before she could stop herself. 'Uhm. Are you Amelia Lee?'

No one spoke.

Ruby blinked rapidly at Roisin, looking almost affronted, as if she'd been cat-called by a lairy street pedlar in a market.

'Yes? Didn't Matthew say?'

Roisin gulped. Wait. What? Was this really happening? She couldn't be? Roisin had said the daftest thing imaginable, and this woman was agreeing with her?

'I thought your name was Ruby?'

'Pet name. Family name. Due to the hair,' she said, riffling it with her fingertips. She returned to nuzzling Granville.

'Fucking hell,' Meredith said, and if Amelia Lee heard her, she didn't show it.

20

The air pressure in the room dramatically shifted in the way it only can when everyone comprehends that a very, very famous person is present.

It was akin to a plane suddenly plummeting a few thousand feet and the oxygen masks tumbling out.

At least, Roisin *assumed* this was the way it always was: this had never happened to her before, unless you counted the time they saw Mick Hucknall from afar in a Spinningfields pizzeria.

Amelia 'Milly' Lee wasn't reality star or soap opera famous, she was the real deal: cinema-marquee, name-up-in-lights, her-last-alleged-boyfriend-was-Tom-Cruise famous.

She'd recently moved up to lead role status – starring in a film about a World War Two seductress spy that Joe and Roisin had seen on a now-rare date night. Joe had pulled apart its poor plotting – and Roisin, its sexism – in the pub afterwards.

Here she was, a couple of feet away, asking the hired muscle guy in the doorway to 'fetch Granny his organic venison biltong'.

A catfish was a concealed identity? Ohhhh. Roisin yearned to say, *Matt! I know what you meant!* So 'Ruby' was the Hinge pseudonym. She catfished him as a celebrity undercover as a citizen.

'Were you really on Hinge?' Meredith said, asking the question they all wanted to ask, because frankly why the hell not. Roisin felt like she was tripping off her tits.

Amelia threw an appraising look at Matt for his indiscretion. 'Sure,' she said, flintily. 'Why not?'

'Don't they have a dating site for famous people to meet other famouses? No offence, Matt, but you're just . . . Matt,' Meredith said to him.

Matt twinged a smile and Roisin felt for him. Once again, she could see how little of this he'd intended. Once again, it probably wasn't going to save him from the consequences.

'That's Raya. I'm on there too.' She played with Granville's ears and snuffled his head. 'But, let me tell you . . .' She paused, hand outstretched, and Meredith took a beat to suss she was meant to supply her name.

'Meredith.'

'*Meredith* . . . there are some *slimy motherfuckers* . . .' She slipped into full American drawl, for a moment. '. . . out there, who want to date actresses. Star fuckers, you know what I mean?'

She made a face, like she was meaningfully confiding. Meredith replied with a terrified, automatic, 'Yes,' which almost gave Roisin hysterics.

'It was nice meeting real, down to earth, honest guys who wanted to meet Ruby,' Amelia concluded.

'And also, Matt!' Joe said, trying for his first Joe Powellish witticism since her arrival.

Amelia simply stared at him, like he'd guffed.

'Would any of you mind terribly if we closed the curtains?' Amelia said. 'I very much doubt any picture agency would send anyone anywhere this remote, but it'd be such a bore if they did.'

'Yeah, we do mind,' Gina said suddenly, making backs straighten. 'We also mind you telling us we can't use our phones, and which bedrooms you and your bouncers want.'

'Bouncers? Mark is my driver and Ted is my security,' Amelia said, as if this was apparent to anyone who wasn't deficient in faculties.

'Whatever,' Gina said. 'You're not only here visiting your boyfriend, but you've also crashed our weekend. You don't get to tell us what to do.'

Roisin cringed, yet couldn't fault Gina on any point of accuracy. Therefore, intervening seemed impossible. She suspected everyone else had made this calculation, too. On what basis did they stand Gina down? Amelia was, being honest, the original provocateur here.

'Gina,' Matt said, clearing his throat, 'it's alright if Ru— Amelia wants to stay. Right, Dev?'

'Of course!' Dev said.

Gina, flushed, twitched in her seat as if she'd been tasered. 'Says fucking who? You've not asked the rest of us?'

'I've not had a chance, but . . .'

'Are you and Matthew an item of some sort?' Amelia said in dispassionate tone, with her perfect diction.

113

'Er. *Nope*,' Gina said quickly and with a nasty laugh. Roisin gathered Gina was drunker than she'd thought.

'Sorry, what is the problem then? I'm not clear,' Amelia said. One of her anonymous men entered the room and she said, 'Ted, close those curtains, would you? That's right, those ones, thanks.'

'DON'T YOU FUCKING DARE, TED!' Gina screamed, and Amelia's dog fell onto the floor with a plop and started wolf-howling.

'Seriously,' Gina stood up and turned to Matt, 'how dare you? This is my birthday do, and once again, you've fucking ruined it. You've brought this weird nightmare in here . . .' She turned to point at the impassive Oscar nominee. 'Let me guess, Matt, you didn't mean to do it. But you have. I am so sick of you acting like nothing's your fault. SHE is your fault. It's your job to find her somewhere to stay, because she's sure as SHIT not staying here.'

Gina had gone a mottled salmon colour, breathing coming in gasps.

'Alright, it's late,' Matt said, clearly having one of the worst experiences of his life, trying to figure out how to tap dance through the crocodile swamp he'd found himself in. 'How about, if tomorrow—'

Amelia interrupted him, turning a large gold watch round on her child-sized wrist so she could see its face, 'If we can't stay here, it's about what, two hours to Manchester? But there aren't any hotels there.'

Everyone's mouths opened to query this assertion before

they all realised she wasn't saying there were no hotels, but there were no *hotels*.

'Four hours to London?' Amelia continued.

Ted leaned in and said something in her ear.

'Four or five, give or take. Matt, you grab your things and we can be in Soho House by one a.m. I'll drop Nick a text, I'm a member.'

Matt said, 'Uhm . . . ?'

'See you out by the car. Granny, come on! We're not staying! Come on, Granny.' She fished the French Bulldog out from under the chair legs and scooped him up into her arms. They held their breath for her parting shot, but there wasn't one; she simply left the room without further acknowledging their presence.

A silence fell over the party. Even Joe Powell couldn't find the quip to break the astonishment.

'Dev, it's super rude of me to leave with her. I don't know how else to fix this, though. Do you want me to tell her I'm staying?' Matt said. He rubbed at his temple and looked like he was grinding his teeth.

'Yes, it is rude, but we don't want you to stay!' Gina said. Then, checking herself, 'I don't want you to, anyway.'

'Gina! Matt is as much a part of this weekend as any of us,' Roisin said.

'Yes,' Meredith agreed. 'Settle down, G. This isn't Matt's fault.'

'QUELLE SURPRISE!' Gina roared, clamping her wine glass to her face.

'I don't want to spoil things,' Matt said, with a pointed look towards Roisin and Meredith. They grasped its meaning. It was clear Gina and Matt's rift wasn't going to be healed overnight, a second time, and if he remained, the mood was likely fatally poisoned.

'Mate, you do whatever you want!' Dev said. 'No hard feelings. Your gal is a bit of a tornado, hah.'

'Your gal is a bit A LIST FAMOUS. What on earth, Matt?' Meredith said. 'Our minds are fucked, here! A warning would've been nice?' She smiled.

'I was working up to it,' Matt said, rather brokenly. 'I didn't think the big reveal there was time sensitive. Dev, I'm so sorry – I never thought for a moment telling her where we were staying would mean she'd take it as an invite. Her schedule's nuts, I didn't even know she was in the UK.'

'Are you kidding, stop apologising! This is an all-time killer brag.'

'OK. Bye, then,' Matt said, barely meeting their eyes as he left, to muttered farewells.

Roisin wanted to say something supportive, but with Gina on her last nerve, she didn't dare say more than, 'Bye, take care.'

After a beat, they shamelessly reassembled by the window to spectate, the Jeep now with tail-lights on and one door open. Eventually Matt walked into view, dressed like hip *Doctor Who* again, headphones round his neck.

He glanced at the dining room window and raised a palm.

'It's like he's getting into a spaceship,' Anita said. 'With an alien.'

'Goodbye, Matthew McKenzie,' Joe said, waving. 'Your passing leaves a huge hole.'

'Lesson learned,' Dev said. 'Always worth checking exactly who Matt is dating. Next time he says "Kylie", I'm going to be like "Minogue or Jenner?"'

Except, Roisin thought, had Joe not stopped Matt's reverse catfish reveal, they would've known.

And she noticed, save one piece of sass, Joe had been unusually restrained around Amelia Tornado. She guessed it was because his precious career prohibited being sarcastically insulting to very well-known actresses. Game recognised game.

'Did this happen? I'm shaking,' Roisin said, as the car drove away and adrenaline started ebbing back out of her veins. 'Did Amelia Lee turn out to be Matt's latest girlfriend, and Gina told her to go fuck herself? Did I really say: "are you Amelia Lee?" like a total melt? I felt like I'd asked someone in the Mafia if they were in the Mafia. Something you don't ever do.'

'Glad you did, 'cos until then I was going to go with jewel thief,' Anita said. 'I thought she might be on the run. No photos!'

'If it's a hallucination, I must have eaten the same hash cake,' Meredith said, putting her arms round Roisin. 'Oh, Miss Walters, make it make sense.'

Without needing to communicate their next thoughts, they looked at each other in concern, and over at Gina, who was saloon-in-a-western sploshing more wine into her glass, while making a sly face Roisin could only classify as 'Fleabag'.

Much as Gina had chewed Matt out for his felonies, Roisin

felt sure she'd feel even worse than him tomorrow, psychically as well as physically.

'Joe! The time!' Anita said, looking at her phone. '*Hunter* starts in five minutes! Everyone, get your drinks, we're going to the screening room!'

'It's going to feel like something of an anti-climax now, isn't it?' Joe said. 'Talk about a hard act to follow.'

Very recently, Roisin would've said this statement from Joe was false modesty. But frankly, he could be right.

21

Roisin had no detail about *Hunter*, beyond the skeleton of the premise and the casting. She'd been involved in every spit and cough of *SEEN*, but Joe was fully launched now, had a small army of professionals to give him notes. He deserved some space.

In last-minute regret, as they took their seats in Benbarrow's plush screening room, Roisin wondered what she'd thought was charming and relaxed might've in fact been reckless to the point of negligent.

'It's really quite filthy,' Joe said to them, proudly. Roisin felt suddenly sick. *Filthy*? She could really do without her GCSE kids seeing filthy. What if there was some dreadful talking dirty, or Bad Sex Award, purple scene? Why did she feel such a lack of faith? Was she a prude? OK, she'd known it was about a 'sex addict', but it wasn't *porn*, so. She very stupidly at last caught on that there were still several degrees of heat between U-rated and X-rated. The devil was in the detail.

'I hope you like it,' Joe said to the room. 'No pressure!'

'We are guaranteed to love it,' Dev said.

Whatever show was finishing before *Hunter* crackled into

119

life in front of them, in eight-foot-wide HD. Meredith opened chocolate peanuts and Liquorice Allsorts and tried to get a bladdered Gina to have some.

Anita rejoined them, having been projectionist. 'Oh, Joe! I am a bag of ants, so what must you be like!'

Roisin really wished she could share their euphoria for Joe, instead of being eaten up by anxiety.

This must be how the parents of actors felt when their offspring was playing Hamlet. *Stop this,* she told herself. *You're having stage fright by proxy. It's going to be amazing. Breathe.*

She squeezed Joe's arm and smiled at him in the dark. He smiled back, slipped his hot hand into hers and squeezed, let go. It was the tenderest moment they'd had in a long while.

The screen went black. A friendly, youthful, and northern-accented female voice said, in a confidential tone:

Now on BBC2. A new series from the writer-creator of SEEN. *Get ready for the rule-breaking, fourth-wall-breaking, case-cracking* HUNTER. *Please be aware that this programme contains scenes of a sexual nature and strong language from the beginning.*

A 'wahey!' roar went up. Roisin's stomach cramped.

The screen filled with a group of thirty-somethings, laughing over nightcaps in a fashionable restaurant.

'Is that the place in Didsbury?' Dev said. Then, 'Shit, sorry, no talking! I'll save it to the end!'

The camera tightened in on the good-looking lead. The character Jasper Hunter was played by a leonine, much-lusted-after thirty-year-old actor called Rufus Tate, who was hovering at that level of fame between indie darling and prime-time heartthrob.

He had his arm round a doe-eyed girl, a cherubically pretty brunette called Becca. The group were teasing them about recently getting engaged, Jasper being a workaholic misanthrope who'd finally accepted he wanted 'the chocolate Lab and the roses round the door.'

'Or a Nespresso machine with the pods at least,' he said.

'Speaking of which. *Jas.* We should go,' the brown-eyed girlfriend hissed behind a palm. 'They're wiping down the coffee machine parts.'

Roisin gulped hard as the nature of the ensemble emerged. Long-term girlfriend, sweetly steady in nature with an arch turn of phrase. A punkily dressed, forthright lesbian, Victoria; a loud, confident Indian lad, Avi . . . a petite blonde, Gwen, barely laced into a halterneck top, who seemed to be Becca's best friend.

On screen, outside the restaurant, what Roisin thought of as the Fictional Brian Club group clambered into a taxi.

Moments later, Jasper leaned forward and called to the driver, 'Can you let me out here, please?'

'Fuck it. Forgot my scarf,' he said to the other occupants. 'I'll go back.'

'Are you sure? Looks like it might rain,' said Becca.

'Nah, honestly. You go on. I'd like the time to sober up.'

He grinned and banged the door shut, watching the taxi round the corner. Hands thrust in pockets, he walked back to the restaurant.

The series in general looked lustrous, Roisin noted: Manchester shot to look like New York. It was dark and rainy, in a *Bladerunner* way.

On arrival at the restaurant, Jasper sees the lights are dim and the doors are locked. He cups his eyes to peer through the glass and raps on the door. Then he tries the handle: it's not locked.

He steps inside.

The place is deserted but for a strikingly attractive waitress with a sharply cut, Louise Brooks bleached bob, who was glimpsed bringing their espressos earlier.

She stops moving at the sight of him, her hands holding a broom. The camera lasciviously zeros in on her slender fingers with dark red manicure, gripping and unfurling round the broom handle. It cuts between Jasper's face and hers.

'Hi,' he says, polite-reticent. 'I . . . think I left my scarf behind? Ah. There it is.'

He draws it out from the back of a chair, puts it on. She cocks her head to one side, watching him.

'I'm not sure blue's your colour, to be honest,' the waitress says, in a feline voice.

'Really?'

'Yeah.'

'I also saw you take that scarf off and leave it on purpose.'

'That'd be a strange thing to do.'

'Wouldn't it.'

A jump cut: to the sound of grunting and gasping, the camera pans over the top of a bathroom stall, where Jasper and the waitress are going at it like knives. The bird's-eye angle ogles his chest and her push-up bra.

'What does this mean?' Jasper gasps, putting his hand on a

tattoo on her shoulder. It has a series of numbers, next to a tiny crescent moon and a tiny sun.

'Private joke,' she says, catching her breath and smiling.

Jasper grins wolfishly and kisses her.

In the next cut, he's alone in the restaurant toilet, looking at himself in the mirror over the sink.

'I know what you're thinking,' He says to his reflection, to the camera. 'Why? Well, not why, you know *why*.' He rips a paper towel from a dispenser. 'The heart likes commitment, and the libido likes novelty. What you're really thinking is how. *How* could you. There are two things to know about me.' Jasper pulls open the door and turns to look directly at the camera. 'I don't feel guilt. And I'll do it again.'

22

The screening room once again erupted in excitement and Roisin could feel Joe crackling with pleasure at the reception.

Roisin was conscious of her frozen position in her seat, not wanting to twitch or move an inch in case it betrayed her feelings. Which were: tumultuous. *The voice was so unmistakeably Joe's,* she thought. The attitude.

Underneath her hair, at the nape of her neck, she was damp with sweat.

Grey daytime. Jasper's voiceover:

Manchester, at the start of the twenty-first century. Capital of the north. Banish your preconceptions. It's not just feral youth, spice casualties and old prams in canals . . . My job is pretty much all that, though. Welcome to detective work in the Manchester Met.

Laughter in the screening room.

'Oh Joe, you're not going to be able to drink anywhere by the end of this, are you?' Dev said. 'Sorry, shhh shhh.'

Jasper walks along the city streets back to his car, speaking to the camera again, in a heightened reality where none of the ordinary people streaming past him can hear him.

'Why do I cheat? It's interesting we call it "cheating", isn't it. It's called cheating because it's not observing the rules of a game that we're forced to play. Or if not forced, heavily coerced. If society makes honesty near impossible, people will choose deceit. You don't change human nature, only its avenues of expression. It's always been this way.'

What an arseholes manifesto this is, Roisin thought. Was she too close to the writer to judge it fairly? She didn't know. Possibly more like too distant from the writer.

Jasper told the camera that your partner always has that one sexy friend who is, even for a man of his loose morals, completely off limits. Jesus. *Thanks, Joe.* Roisin wanted to die.

She glanced at the back of Gina's head in front of her. She wondered what she was thinking; though to be fair, Gina was in no fit state to be viewing anything, much less interpreting it.

The whole show, Roisin thought, was meant to be so cerebral, erotic and knowing, and came off to her like Horny Ferris Bueller.

While taking notes about the last corpse, Jasper sees, to his shock, that the dead girl has a distinctive tattoo on her shoulder . . .

The episode ended with young Jasper in flashback. He creeps down for a glass of milk in the night and sees his father dancing with a woman by the stereo, but as he follows other noises, sees his mum is in a clinch with a man on the kitchen table, feet in high heels dangling . . .

Roisin sat bolt upright in her seat. What? *WHAT?*

Her flesh was prickling and damp with sweat.

Over the sight of child-Jasper's face, the opening chords

of Metallica's 'Enter Sandman' boomed out via the speakers in the cushioned space.

The group, bar Roisin, erupted into cheers and air-punching.

'Seriously?! "Enter Sandman"?!' Dev bellowed. 'How much did that cost, you absolute baller?!'

'They made it clear it was quite a treat,' Joe said, almost delirious with the fuss he was receiving. 'Did you like it?'

'C'mere, I've got to hug you. Incredible, mate. Can't believe it. You smashed it.'

Roisin clapped weakly, with clammy palms.

It was for the best that other people were here to give Joe the praise he sought. Roisin couldn't have managed a word of it.

23

Roisin stared at the bed's canopy in the thin dawn light, as the minutes ticked by.

Eventually she grasped for her phone on the nightstand and looked at the time. 4.58 a.m. Half an hour before Joe's alarm. She was incontrovertibly conscious. The kind of brain-abuzz state that makes it clear to you that if you try to fight it, you'll only lie sweating, mind racing.

She had woken up with perfect clarity about what had to happen. Roisin had been fretting and second-guessing and what if-ing and it had come to a head. She had confused loyalty and forbearance with a determination to stay stuck in the past, rather than confront the present.

She slid noiselessly from the sheets, grasped for the robe. Joe was snoring: he was a sound sleeper anyway and he'd put away a hell of a lot to drink the night before.

Roisin couldn't recall a single thing that was said between the end of *Hunter* and her going to bed, beyond general back-slapping. She'd gone up to the room before Joe, keen to be asleep or feigning sleep so they weren't ever alone.

She tiptoed downstairs in the deserted house, flicked the

kettle on in the kitchen and made herself a steadying cup of tea. She carried it out on to the lawn outside, sitting on a low stone wall and watching the sun rise over the lake. She waited.

Roisin checked her watch for the umpteenth time. Joe must be up and moving about by now, if his alarm had worked. As she thought this, she looked up to see him walking across the grass towards her, also holding a mug.

Roisin's stomach roiled and her heart pounded, in a grisly parody of an encounter from a Regency romance. She was prickly hot under her clothes in the early morning warmth, trying to steady herself for what was to come. Working out the words for this showdown that she wouldn't regret later. She suspected any plan of what to say would go out the window fairly fast.

She reminded herself, again: she had no choice. There wasn't any point in avoiding it, pretending to be asleep longer and spinning out the meagre amount of time until his Addison Lee came crawling up the path.

If Roisin pretended last night hadn't been a problem, she'd lose both her courage and a good chunk of her right to reply. You can't convincingly express being shocked and appalled on an expedient seven-day delay, when someone gets in the door with West Coast-sized jet lag.

There being no correct and appropriate moment to raise any problem was one of the ways the game felt rigged. Pick an otherwise pressured time? She was thoughtlessly adding to it. During a nice evening out? Ruining it. Try to raise it on a quiet day? Ambush.

Roisin inhaled and exhaled and accepted that, the mental cruelty of *Hunter* aside, she'd been pushing this reckoning away for too long. Hoping that in exile, banished from serious possibility, the idea would change or die. That it would sort itself out. In a twisted way, Joe had done her a favour. He'd demonstrated a level of disregard she couldn't ignore.

'Why do I get the feeling you didn't get up early to see me off with a big hug?' Joe said as he reached her, sipping his black coffee. His face was still slept in and puffy from last night's drinking, his hair glistening wet from the shower.

'What do you mean?' she said, testing her voice.

'You've been in a threatening mood all weekend, Roisin. Barely said a word after the show, yesterday. You're stood here alone at dawn with a face on like you're the Benbarrow ghost, risen from her drowning. I'm not stupid. What do you want to say to me?'

Claiming to know she was upset, and taking the piss out of her, didn't exactly match up. A simple *are you OK* would've done. Joe was battle ready.

Deep breath.

'Why did you put my mum and dad in your story?'

Joe paused, mouth to mug. 'In *Hunter*? That wasn't your parents? It was fictional.'

'The kid creeping down and catching the mother on the table? You're telling me that's not from a particular thing I've told you?'

'Yes, sure. Lots of things I write are from lots of things people have told me.'

'"People"!' Roisin exclaimed, her temper breaking faster

than she expected. The plans were already out the window. 'I'm your *girlfriend*. Don't give me a "how stories work" spiel like I'm the public at a Q&A, asking where you get your ideas.'

'What do you want me to say, I just admitted it? Yes, some of that was inspired by things you told me. As it goes on, you'll see tha—'

'You betrayed my trust?' Roisin said.

Joe grimaced, in an exaggerated performance of disbelief. 'That's wildly misrepresenting what happens when you draw on things around you and the people who are close to you. Am I supposed to run everything I write through a sources and similarities check?'

'It's a bit fucking specific for that paper-thin defence, isn't it, Joe? How many people do you know who saw their mum with other men?'

'As I said, yes, you'd be the trigger for it.'

'*Trigger.* By depicting it? In the same way the sinking of the ship *Titanic* was the trigger for the film *Titanic*.'

'It was a few seconds on screen, not the whole subject. It's not possible to do what I do and not be influenced by elements of real life.'

She was almost relieved to find how livid she still was, and how pathetic and glib his excuses were. It made it simpler.

'You're pretending not to understand the difference between using anecdotes in general and ripping off traumatic, private things direct from your girlfriend's past? Things told to you in strict confidence. Why didn't you give me a warning about it? Is there anything else I should prepare for?'

The thought of the abortion being used made her insides turn into a mini earthquake.

'OK, I'm sorry about that. I didn't think. No, nothing else. I didn't realise it was still this upsetting to you. You've probably forgotten, but you thought it was kind of . . . darkly, bleakly funny, when you first told me.'

This was so sly and unfair that Roisin authentically hated him, for a second. Maybe she had been playing it partly for laughs on the first telling. That was drunken youthful dates, trying to be fascinating and bold and own your family's dysfunction as part of your fabulous rainbow, for you. Things said between two people newly sleeping together were not to be held up for daylight inspection. If you were perceptive enough about human nature to write about it, you were perceptive enough to know what was off limits.

'You're blessed with perfect memory for the tone of conversations we had ten years ago, but completely at a loss over why you didn't think to consult me when you were writing it, a few months ago?' Roisin said.

'I see, this is one of those fights where anything I say gets me in bigger trouble.'

'Are you serious?'

Joe screwed his eyes closed and paused. It was a stagey device, to make it clear that this was unnecessary. That she was what her pupils called *extra*. He necked the last of his coffee and set his cup down on the step.

'I intended to mention it. But in the hugely long-winded process of writing and rewriting and going into production, it fell by the wayside. As I said, I'm really sorry. It wasn't intended to be such a clear reference that you'd find it this emotional. In my mind, it had become Jasper's origins and part of something totally different. Obviously, as someone not involved in the process, I should've realised it'd be more of a shock to you.'

Roisin wasn't sure what she'd expected, but nevertheless, she was aghast at this smooth horseshit. There was a level of honesty she needed before she could contemplate supplying her understanding or forgiveness. Even now, Joe wouldn't be forced into offering it. She could only assume he didn't need either her understanding or forgiveness. It felt more than dismissive. The word *contempt* floated into her mind.

'You know, Joe, this is ruthless. Worthy of a sweaty corrupt politician on *Newsnight*. You're not being remotely truthful with me about what happened here. What's even more worrying is that I don't think you've even asked yourself why you did it. It doesn't interest you.'

God, that was it. In a nutshell. Joe hadn't wondered, in light of his girlfriend's distress, why *did* I think this was OK? She'd not seen him wrongfooted or concerned, whatsoever. He'd gone straight into damage limitation 'fob her off with a glib apology' mode. It didn't bother him enough to check his conscience. It didn't apparently occur to him to check it.

'In what way am I being dishonest?' he said.

'The real version of this, Joe, goes — you knew it was theft and you knew it was sensitive. If you'd told me, I'd object and you'd have to take it out. So you went ahead and chanced it, thinking, if you got away with it, cool. If it went wrong and I kicked off, it was a price worth paying to keep it in the script. Even when you knew I'd watch it here, with our friends around us, it didn't change the stakes enough for you to come clean before you put me through that. Because why gift me an opportunity to be a nuisance? None of this fall-out means anything, because my pain over this is absolutely nothing to you. Not compared to your career. This is merely an inconvenient difficulty to be managed, before you get to the real business of some brunch meeting with men in designer sunglasses in Los Angeles where no one eats the food.'

When she finished speaking, Roisin saw that Joe looked embattled, but also faintly – and uncharacteristically – impressed. She had his attention. Roisin's fury was obviously the first time he'd listened to her in a while.

She wondered if he was filing it away to use in the future. She wondered if any privacy was now an illusion.

Between us meant nothing.

24

Roisin wasn't going to break the silence that followed.

'Right, we're on the clock because of my flight,' Joe said, after a while. 'Before we both crank up any more levels, can I suggest we keep it for when I get back? It's a lot right now. Especially when we're here.' He nodded back at the house.

'Ah, the Calm Down, Crazy Woman gambit.'

'No, more about the fact we have no time and a lot of company. It's Dev's special weekend.'

'I'd have preferred this not to happen in front of them, too.'

'Look, I haven't actually exposed any secret. No one but us would know that moment came from your childhood.'

This said more about Joe than he realised. Image was everything, and he'd not damaged hers. That the fact that only she could perceive the treacherous plagiarism meant it as good as didn't matter. Because, once again, she didn't.

'Even if that was the point here, my mum might recognise it, don't you think?' Her voice wavered. She couldn't bear the thought of it.

'She won't see it. She stopped watching *SEEN*, didn't she?'

Joe resented his mother-in-law for her indifference to his work. Lorraine, of course, hadn't bothered with the social nicety of pretence: 'not my cup of tea'. Jesus, was Joe also taking oblique revenge?

'Who knows, but it's far from guaranteed that she won't, isn't it? What do I say if she asks me about it?'

'You'd think she wouldn't, though, eh,' Joe said, raising an eyebrow.

'Meaning what?'

'It's quite delicate. For her.'

This was so much hypocrisy, Roisin felt she might choke. 'Wow, *now* you're aware of how intensely taboo it might be? Better late than never, huh. Oh wait, no, late has exactly the same value as never, here.'

'You know what I mean! She's not going to go there.'

'Yes, I do know what you mean, having never suffered from your curiously useful brain fog about this. I know it would be completely agonising for my mum to ask me if I discovered things about her open marriage by accident, twenty years ago. That I'd obviously told my partner, and he put it on television, and she recognised herself.'

Joe shook his head. 'I wish I'd thought this through, I really do. I'd not have gone near it.'

Fuck you, Roisin thought. *You are a liar. The only regret here is discovering how strongly I'll defend myself.*

'Given I know the last thirty seconds came from my life, can I ask if the taxi bit at the start was something that happened, too?'

'What?'

'Leaving your scarf at a restaurant and walking back when we got a cab. Getting in late. That was two summers ago, right? The Italian place, Sesso? In fact, it'd be exactly two years – I think it was Gina's birthday.'

'What's the question here? Did I sneak back that night and bone a waitress?' Joe said.

'Yes, that's the question.'

'Amazing. Do I get to be offended you would even ask that, or is that not how this works?'

'Did you not think by using an actual scenario I recognised that I might be a bit disorientated or worried by that?'

In the context of their monogamy, using their real life as a set felt so tacky. It spoke of a great hinterland of laddish wish fulfilment. Did he really not realise she'd be affected by it? It was like Joe had had a radical surgical resection of his empathy when he signed his first contract.

'No, because I thought you understood we were firmly in the realm of fiction. If it needs spelling out, then yes, that's made up, Rosh,' Joe said. He was drawing himself up to full height, trying on some indignance for size. 'I'm not a chronically unfaithful danger shagger like my anti-hero. Nor in the past have I ever headed up an elite squad of police with extraordinary powers of visual recognition.'

'I think it was reasonable to ask,' Roisin said. 'The girl-friend's hot friend sub plot was somewhat gross, too. How is Gina meant to feel about that?'

'Gina's not meant to feel anything because that wasn't Gina. Or me. Or any of us. Wow. Starting to wish I'd got a gig writing *Emmerdale*. You could demand to know who the sheep were based on.'

'Nice. Loving being your straight woman in the teeth of my humiliation.'

'These questions are ridiculous, so they'll only get ridiculous answers. It's pretty shit for me to have my work pulled apart by my girlfriend like this. Do you not think it hurts, that you didn't like it?'

This was so self-absorbed, Roisin could only gasp.

'You know what you really don't like,' Joe continued. 'You don't like losing the spotlight.'

'What?!'

'For a long time, you had the upper hand; we both know that. I was always punching. Fit, funny, confident Roisin, great at her job, centre of attention . . . How did that skint, sarky wannabe writer guy in the corner pull her? Now *I'm* the one getting the fuss. The balance of power has shifted, and you don't like it, so you're projecting other reasons.'

Some accusations, from someone you knew well, were like being shivved under the ribs, an attack by an expert assassin who knew exactly how to puncture a vital organ in one economical move. You felt it because you knew it was true. Others were out of the blue, from nowhere: like a frisbee arcing through the air, straight at you.

This was a frisbee.

'That is completely mad and also insulting. I'm really proud of what you've achieved.'

'That's why you've been off with me since we got here? You say you're upset by *Hunter*, but you've barely met my eye since you arrived. It's as if you were looking for a reason.'

'It's not jealousy, Joe. It's because our relationship has evaporated. It's like you've packed your bags and moved out. You don't even seem to notice me, most of the time.'

'You mean during this insane time for me – for us – where I've built us some financial security, I haven't focused enough on you? I've not made enough of a fuss of you?'

She wondered how long it'd take for the wealth to be raised up. She wasn't going to use her support of him for all those years as a weapon. Love was not meant to be balance transfers.

'The fact you're calling it "making a fuss", as if I'm a brat, rather than being concerned I'm unhappy, is exactly what I mean.'

'Fuck me. This argument, which you've clearly prepped for, and I haven't, is a set of bear traps. What am I meant to do then, agree with you that I'm a cold bastard?' He ploughed on before she could respond. 'I really don't need your drama, Roisin. I'm about to spend ten hours on a plane and then face some of the most daunting meetings of my life, ones that could change my life. Our lives. I'm starting that journey with this? Seriously? It couldn't have waited until I got back?'

There it was. Joe couldn't even see that complaining she was interfering with his work might be a bad look in a fight about how she was insignificant compared to his work.

'If I'd waited, you'd say I couldn't be that bothered and must have been inventing grudges while you were away. Your total unavailability to me is iron clad, Joe.'

'OK, well, regardless of what I might or might not have said or done, in alternative universes,' Joe said, once again not missing a beat to think, checking his watch, 'my cab will get here soon and I'm going to write a thank you note for Dev. Can we bring this to an end?'

Roisin said, blood rushing in her ears, 'I want to end things entirely, Joe.'

He paused. 'You want to break up?'

'Yes.'

The summer air hung heavy around them.

'You don't love me any more?'

'I don't think I know you any more, to love you,' Roisin said, holding in tears in the tight wall of her chest.

'Hah. Good dodge.'

Joe wouldn't do anything as lame as look surprised, yet, to her surprise, she sensed he was. Why did he not consider that's where this could be going?

Yes, they'd been together almost a decade. But they were still young, they weren't married, they had no kids, and the tenor of this fight, with no concessions or gentleness on either side, felt explicitly terminal to Roisin. If it wasn't the end, it was certainly signposting the way. Hadn't Joe been working up to this? Had he not accepted it himself yet? Did he want to go first?

Ah, wait, the money, she thought. Joe wasn't particularly materialistic or macho about it, but nevertheless, that was the quiet part out loud – no one really thinks a not-rich person will split up with someone who is. By forty, he'd have a fortune, and Roisin was opting out.

That he currently felt undumpable actually made quite a lot of sense.

'I don't have the bandwidth for this. I had no idea that you were going to wake up this morning and decide we were over,' Joe said.

'I think we've been over for a while,' Roisin said. 'I'm just the one to say it.'

She was braced for some spiky comeback, a stinging contradiction, but Joe only looked at her, with those dark eyes she'd once seen so much depth in.

Could she fall back in love with him? Not without his help.

'I can't do this now. Can we talk again when I'm back from the States?' he said eventually. 'I'll be back in a week. Ten days, max.'

Roisin nodded yes. It wasn't as if they could avoid that anyway.

Joe blew air out of his cheeks and picked up his mug. Roisin felt a wave of guilt at what she'd done and once again told herself: *you didn't choose this timing or location. You didn't force this conflict into being.*

'I don't want to run into anyone in the house, together. Can you give me ten minutes' head start?'

'Sure,' Roisin said.

'I'll message you when I land,' Joe said.

'Thanks,' she said stiffly.

He leaned over and gave her a quick hug that was more like a second's grip, giving her no time to respond, and walked away.

She watched Joe cross the lawn to the house and didn't know how to classify her feelings.

Glad the declaration was over with. Torn up, and sad. Devastated that it had happened at all and immediately, despite everything, self-doubting whether it had to happen.

In the distance, he closed the door behind him. Roisin let her shoulders drop an inch and tried to absorb this altered reality.

What was this other sensation, one she couldn't instantly name? Wait – spooked. Spooked to the point of creeped out, even more so than she'd been in the screening room. Why?

She got a message, direct from her gut, so shocking and surreal that her brain immediately rejected it. Her gut nevertheless stubbornly clung onto its instinct.

The night he walked back from Sesso, Joe had had a shower when he got in. He never showered before bed, and she'd registered it as odd at the time. When she mumbled a question as he climbed under the covers, he said he'd got rained on. Except it hadn't rained, unless Burton Road was in the most micro of microclimates: Roisin loved sleeping with an open window. The night had been still.

And it was somewhat contradictory that this evening had both inspired the opening scenes of a story and had been completely uneventful. At the very least, he'd thought about it, hadn't he?

Roisin strained in vain to recall any specific waitress.

Though she had asked if the cheating was autobiographical, she'd never seriously considered that it could be. She felt she was entitled to make the point that others might think it was.

What if it was? Was she going mad? Before last night, she'd have scoffed at the idea, said it was impossible. He wasn't the type. Lacked the chances, anyway, as she told her counsellor. Even if she could conceive of Joe doing those things, why rub her face in it and risk his neck like this?

Except . . . look at what he'd done with her past. He couldn't care less. He thought a hollow *mea culpa* was enough, once caught red-handed. He'd played the odds.

A huge wave of nausea rolled up, so strong that Roisin felt it might knock her off her feet.

What if the failure to check his conscience was because Joe didn't have one?

What if the greatest betrayal here wasn't the one she thought it was? What if Joe *was* Jasper?

Two things to know about me. I don't feel guilt. And I'll do it again.

25

'Here she is! Seen the papers?!' Dev sing-songed, doling out a bacon sandwich to Roisin while the bluetooth speaker blasted Wet Leg's 'Chaise Longue'.

Anita was at the kitchen table, halfway into something egg-based and heavily sauced. That she loved to eat, and Dev loved to cook, was another way they were well suited. Roisin hoped they sorted out the procreating priority snafu.

The Brian Club were otherwise two men down, one in London, one en route to Los Angeles, and the two remaining were apparently yet to emerge.

What had become of Matt, after he climbed into that kidnapper-looking car? Roisin imagined him on all fours in a wet room in Soho House, ball gag in his mouth, as Amelia Lee barked orders and Granville, with venison biltong, looked on.

'No?' Roisin said to Dev, pasting on a neutrally curious yet psychologically robust kind of smile.

She had no intention of ruining the last hours of Dev's grand trip with any hint she and Joe had fought. Yet she feared she'd have Recent Disaster written all over her face.

She dreaded one of those moments when people cry, 'Oh God, what's wrong?!' at the sight of someone who imagined they looked normal.

Roisin couldn't convincingly mimic over-the-top high spirits, and it'd feel morally gross, so the acting job was mundane-cheerful.

As it turned out, Roisin needn't have worried about what the focus would be.

'Hoh, you need to hear the reviews!' Dev said, hopping about once more at the sight of her in the kitchen. It hit her as insensitive, yet he wasn't being. Why *wouldn't* Dev expect Roisin to be overjoyed at Joe's accomplishment?

She was gaslit by the fact that only she seemed to find the echoes of their lives in *Hunter* disturbing. Was Joe right – *had* she wildly overreacted?

Had her unhappiness in the relationship completely warped her judgement? Had it nuclear-fusion powered her response?

Dev dusted his fingers of toast crumbs, then put one hand on his hip as he authoritatively scrolled his phone.

'Here we go . . . Sheen, it's total five-star raves across the board. Only the *Telegraph* was sniffy. Listen to this . . .' Dev muted Wet Leg.

Roisin sipped coffee and looked at a bacon sanger on sourdough that would feel like chewing a sofa cushion smeared with HP.

The world was laughing at her.

'Right . . . right. OK, so, someone called Niall Thingy in the *Observer*,' Dev said, drawing breath. ' *"I compartmentalise, that's all. We all compartmentalise. Everyone has separate parts of their lives they divide and wall off from the others. Mine are simply a little more interesting than yours." So says Jasper Hunter, the titular star (an indecently charismatic Rufus Tate) to camera. It looks like he's the only detective on the force who's going to be able to figure out who's behind a spate of gruesome murders of fashionable young women. The victims' only connection: they're barmaids and waitresses. "Someone hates 'sharing plates' even more than I do," quips Jasper's morose, chauvinistic boss, Nev, played with evident glee by the Happy Mondays' Shaun Ryder. (This is a show happy to provide in jokes aplenty.) Jasper meanwhile is engaged, ecstatically happy with fiancée Becca: his one secret weakness is risky sex with strangers. "The only people who'd ask me what the appeal is," says Hunter, after a graphic coupling with an improbably gorgeous receptionist in a car park, "are the ones who've never tried it."'*

Roisin was hoping Dev might stop, but he was on a roll.

'*. . . In less experienced hands than writer Joe Powell, of SEEN fame, Hunter would be a standard "maverick detective with private life in disarray" cliché. Yet Jasper has (I'm sorry) all his balls in the air. Hunter poses a bigger philosophical question. Does infidelity truly matter if you successfully keep it to yourself? The best mobster dramas force you to question your own complicity in the seductions of the lifestyle, your vicarious enjoyment of some of their most abominable transgressions . . .*'

Dev looked up: 'Abominable transgressions, I like that.'

Roisin gave a very taut smile.

'*. . . Similarly, Jasper's exhilarating amorality towards casual sex draws you in. You start out shocked and even repulsed by his promiscuous duplicity. Monogamy, Jasper argues, is the price society asks us to pay for a settled life with a soulmate, and it's too high* *for some. Certainly, after an hour of such pulse-racing, stylish tele-vision, plenty of us will be unhealthily addicted to Jasper Hunter.'*

Dev looked up. 'What about that, then?'

'Incredible,' Roisin said, though in her head the sentence continued: *Dismal male fantasies really get a pass, don't they. Let me help you, Niall Thingy: yes, it does matter if you hide your shagging around. Where are 'Becca's' rights not to be shagged on? It's not about what society asks of him, it's what he promised her.*

Becca. Roisin felt vomitous. She needed time and space to sort through what she'd learned about Joe. There was a spectrum of possible revelation here. It ran from: Joe showing considerable insensitivity in not priming her for sensitive content, especially when he was robbing detail from real life. To: the whole thing was a deranged form of confessional, the most *hidden in plain sight* insult imaginable. Even Roisin had to admit, the latter was a large proposition, possibly too huge to be plausible. He wasn't, as he'd said, drawing from life in *SEEN.*

The shower, though. After that night after Sesso.

Had he simply needed a cold shower, after his mind had been racing? Ugh. That had to be it.

The alternative, to borrow a beloved phrase of her moth-er's, didn't bear thinking about. Yet she was.

26

Roisin heard a noise and turned to see Meredith who had been listening, arms folded, to the review. She was wearing a pale blue sweater with cartoon clouds on it, like *The Simpsons*' titles. On Roisin, it would look insufferably twee, but on Meredith, it made her seem like fresh air in human form.

'Now Dev has done the good news, I best break the bad,' Meredith said, picking up a jug on the table and pouring a glass of orange juice. She popped two ibuprofen from a blister pack, threw them to the back of her throat and washed them down with a glug of Tropicana Original With Bits, in a practised movement. Once she'd swallowed, she said, 'Our driver is in no fit state. I even question if she's still pissed, given the number of units imbibed. We don't want to be three Princess Dis in a Paris tunnel.'

'Oh no!' said Roisin, though once again, sinfully grateful that Gina's indisposition was providing diversion.

'Is Gina really minging?' Anita said. 'I did wonder how bad she was when she was saying we had to play swim-up blackjack at Caesar's Palace in Vegas for my hen.'

'And was calling it Pisa's Salad. She doesn't remember much of the evening,' Meredith said. 'Which . . . might be something of a blessing.' She made a face.

'You know what, when I dried out, I didn't realise just how much I was gonna love never having hangovers,' Dev said. 'The days I spent feeling like I'd been attacked with the pointy end of a Polonium umbrella.'

'I'm not too clever myself; I might take my bacon sandwich to go,' Meredith said, nodding towards Dev's spatula.

'Sure thing.'

'Please come view her in the Chapel of Rest,' Meredith said to Roisin.

She led Roisin through the soaring hallway towards the drawing room. 'Now, I must warn you, I've done my best. But Gina may not look how you remember her. The embalming process takes its toll.'

'I CAN HEAR YOU!' Gina croak-roared, out of sight.

'She sounds the same though,' Meredith said.

Roisin laughed.

Gina was in a saggy t-shirt and football-length soft cotton shorts, doll-sized and horizontal on one of the giant sofas. She looked like a trendy art installation where they skew the scale. Her complexion resembled candlewax, hair slicked back from her face.

'I fear she does not have long,' Meredith said.

'Honestly, worst hangover ever,' Gina said to Roisin. 'Never drinking again. I woke up at four a.m. and didn't know where I was. I caught the belt of my dressing gown on a door handle, couldn't move and thought I was having a stroke.'

Roisin hooted.

'Concentrate on recovering. Roisin and I can share the drive back,' Meredith said.

Roisin nodded agreement, while inwardly shrivelling. She had in no way prepared herself, in her state of inner turmoil, for the prospect of manhandling a temperamental vintage coach down a motorway. How do you overtake in that thing? Buy it flowers and ask it nicely?

'No, Ethelred won't like a stranger touching her. It has to be me,' Gina said. 'I'll be OK. Another hour.'

'Does Sunny von Bülow want another drink?'

'Who's that? No, thank you – I threw the Fanta up.'

'Do I need to rinse the washing-up bowl?'

'I made it to the fireplace.'

'What?!'

'Heh heh.' Gina managed a tiny evil smile. 'Not really – the loo.'

'Oh, if you can do humour then you're recovering,' Meredith said. 'Why am I bedpan nurse?!'

Her eyes narrowed and she pursed her lips, like a mum who has been told their child's stomach bug is suspiciously impervious to tortilla chips.

'No, Mer. I feel awful,' Gina said, 'In every way. I can't even remember a lot. I can't remember Joe's show!'

'It'll be on iPlayer,' Roisin said, hoping she sounded less terse than she felt.

Gina dropped her voice. 'Was I really *really* horrible to Matt?'

'No! You were . . . robust,' Meredith said. 'You were quite horrible to his girlfriend, though, haha.'

'The girl who looked like Amelia Lee,' Gina said, eyes closed. She was maintaining the perfect immobility of someone who knew if she moved, she'd puke.

Meredith and Roisin exchanged glances.

'Er . . . she was . . .' Meredith began.

'Was what?' Gina said.

'Yeah, she acted like a VIP,' Roisin said. 'Total diva. I'd not worry about offending her.'

Roisin, already holding her phone, hurriedly WhatsApped Meredith.

If she's forgotten that bit, let's go with it! Wait until we're safely home/Gina is out of her intensive care x

You make a very good point.

They left Gina to her convalescence, found a croquet set in a cupboard and passed the last hour playing a game on the front lawn.

Eventually Gina appeared, dressed, packed, headscarf on, and said, 'Girls, I feel good to go, but it has to be now before my stomach or bum change their minds.'

They scarpered into the house to grab their luggage and it made the farewells with Dev and Anita mercifully brief. Roisin didn't want to perjure herself, but, stumbling through effusive thanks, she had to.

'You are, as always, the store manager of our hearts,' Roisin said, planting a kiss on Dev's cheek.

'Yes, Bolton's Rose. No thank yous could do this justice,' Meredith said, helping out.

'Ah, shut up. Only you lot could have made it this incredible. Insane and incredible.'

Roisin realised it was in fact a blessing that Dev had loved *Hunter*. She had been selfish.

'No music,' Gina said, as she started the engine. 'I must have calm and near-silence.'

She rattled the gear stick and coaxed the van into reluctant action. They waved at Dev and Anita.

'Goodbye, Benbarrow,' Meredith said, twisting in her seat to face the road again. 'Until next time.'

It wasn't often you said those words and they were fully untrue: unlike a holiday island, or a rental villa, or any of the many places you might feasibly return, Benbarrow Hall was pretty clearly a once-in-a-lifetime deal.

Roisin turned again to gaze up at its architectural magnificence as they retreated down the hill, trying to absorb the finality of the farewell.

How would they remember this weekend, in another ten years? She knew what it'd mean to her.

What was the curse: *all lovers that court here* – whatever that meant – *are doomed*?

Roisin thought of her and Joe splitting, of Matt and Gina's barney, Ruby's appearance . . . she'd have said Dev and Anita were fine, until she spoke to Meredith. She tried not to shiver.

Did people honestly get wed on its lawns, without looking that up? Not that it would've necessarily bothered her. But

151

you know, they lived in a world where hotels didn't have thirteenth floors.

She opened her phone and, with a few mistypes as the VW bumped over uneven road surfaces, googled *Benbarrow Hall Curse*. Here was a strange thing – she couldn't find any blog using that phrase.

27

As they passed Preston, their phones pinged simultaneously, which typically meant a Brian Club WhatsApp.

Roisin looked at the notification.

Matt McKenzie left the group: BRIAN CLUB

She involuntarily sucked in air and looked up at Meredith.

Gina said, 'What? What's it say?' glancing at her phone in its holder on the dashboard.

'Nothing,' Meredith said. 'Just Dev saying bye.'

'Why does Roisin look so worried, then?' Gina said, observing her in the rear-view mirror. *Damn my face,* Roisin thought.

'OK, it's that Matt's left. It's a flounce, he'll be back,' Meredith said.

'Left Brian Club?' Gina said, in a tone of real surprise.

The VW pulled sharply to the left, threatening to stray from its lane. Meredith winced and said, 'Yeah,' in a forced-casual way.

'Don't let the door hit you on the arse, Matt,' Gina said

after a pause, in unexpected defiance. Clearly she was doubling down. Neither Roisin nor Meredith said anything, not wanting to antagonise their driver in her delicate state.

'No doubt firing all his old friends off on orders of *that woman*. Says a lot about Matt that he's going along with it.'

Given Gina had forgotten Ruby's identity reveal, this might be truer than she realised. He might well have been told to put some distance with a bunch of often-pissed, indiscreet and variously hostile friends, for the duration of their liaison.

But leaving the WhatsApp group?

The thought Matt might be going for good was very painful. Until this moment, Roisin hadn't doubted the fracture could be mended. This falling-out had taken on the feel of something initially mundane that they'd complacently let slip out of control. A runaway golf buggy you thought you could easily catch up with if you broke into a run, which was now going to intersect with a freight train before you reached it.

Roisin felt traitorous to the sisterhood, however, she didn't think Matt had deserved his ignominy, either. Had Gina been in a nightie, he'd no doubt be her hero for the very same behaviour. And everyone had done a pocket dial in their time. Subtract Gina's intense self-consciousness, and the poo picture confetti would've been hilarious to her.

Yes, the timing of his girlfriend's arrival was unfortunate. Yet if Matt had asked to bring her, Dev would've said sure. So where was the crime, really? Not anticipating the capricious whims of, and limitless chauffeuring available to, *prominent creatives*? Roisin suspected it felt a bigger gaffe than it was because they'd subconsciously absorbed the expectation

Matt should keep his girlfriends out of the Brian Club activities to protect Gina's feelings, and that wasn't at all fair.

As she'd realised, he'd tried to tell them about Ruby from Hinge – Joe's discourtesy, and Matt's frankly impressive lack of interest in bragging, were why they weren't forewarned.

She could hear Joe scoffing: *tell me, what is it about the good-looking man that's won you over?*

Roisin had come to a conclusion on that, too. Joe's distaste for Matt as a conceited attention seeker was to cover for the fact he actually hated that attention sought Matt.

Maybe there was a deeper truth, a bigger problem that this series of minor calamities had poked at. Maybe, as Joe had implied, spending a lot of time around someone you are in love with and can't have will come to grief, eventually.

Roisin still really disapproved of Matt's timing, though. It didn't feel like him – she knew he'd not want to offend Dev that Benbarrow had torpedoed relations.

He must be very hurt then, to make it this explicit? She remembered Dev saying it was alright for him to leave with Ruby, and none of them asking him to stay.

As they reached the outskirts of Manchester, Roisin's phone lit up again. This time, no else's did.

Hi R. I've already spoken to Dev, but I wanted to explain to you individually: I'm going to take some time away from the group. I feel really bad about fucking up this weekend and think this rest for you all is overdue, frankly ☺ I'll stay in touch, obviously. FYI Dev is insisting on meeting up to talk me out of it. While I know it comes from absolutely brilliant intentions, I really don't want that – my mind's made up. I'm not angling to be made a fuss of and persuaded back. I'm not trying to create drama, I thought it best to draw a clear line. Take care, Matt x

Roisin wasn't fooled: if Matt was merely having a rest, he'd simply have muted the group or found the leave silently function, and they'd be none the wiser. He didn't want to chat to them any more, he didn't want to be asked to go on evenings out. This was a more profound goodbye, which was trying to take the stinger out of the bee.

'Hope you don't mind if I don't get out,' Gina said, as they drew up at the smart stone urns flanking the steps up to the Grade Two–listed chapel that housed Joe and Roisin's apartment. *Let's do the quirky choice before suburbia proper, eh?* Joe had said, after the viewing. Given it was mainly his money, Roisin thought it was his call anyway.

Even glancing at it, Roisin felt like a grimy, compromised charlatan. Her home, bought with her boyfriend's money, which he got for writing about her mum's sex life. *And his . . . ?*

'Are you kidding, you got us home!' Roisin said, forcing herself into one last push on the fake cheerfulness front. 'You deserve The George Cross. They should rename it The Georgina Cross.'

'Thanks, Rosh,' Gina said, looking at her tiredly from under her headscarf. 'The hot bath, sheet mask and Uber Eats McDonalds is going to feel good, I can't lie.'

Meredith got out of her seat, slid the door open and helped Roisin pull herself and her case out of the vehicle.

'Did you get the Matt explanation, too?' Meredith said, in a very low voice, deliberately speaking with her back to the van as they walked towards the house.

'Yes! This has spiralled out of control.'

'We need to reassure him,' Meredith said. 'He's imagined we're as raging as . . .' She inclined her head towards Gina. 'Love her as I do, she needs to calm down where McKenzie's concerned.'

'*Yes*,' Roisin said, in relief. 'He's refusing to be talked round, though?'

'Mmmm.'

Roisin paused, house keys in palm, as she gathered that Meredith was hesitating.

'Come over,' Meredith said eventually. 'Next Friday. For dinner. For a proper chat. Without Joe. When's he back?'

'Next week. I will. Thanks . . . ?' Roisin said. *Without Joe* had never been uttered in their friendship before. Joe as a permanently welcome addition was always a given.

'Good. Go easy on yourself.'

She grabbed Roisin in a tight hug. As Roisin absorbed the meaning of their exchange, she tried not to burst into tears on her shoulder then and there. She hadn't realised how broken she was, until someone acknowledged it.

28

She held her emotion behind a broad yet tight smile as she waved them off with energetic vigour.

Meredith knew, and she had known all along. Not the full details, of course. Not Roisin's decision. That's what going round for tea was for.

Roisin was in the funny state of being relieved someone else had perceived Joe's cool, careless behaviour, and also being ashamed of it. Come to think of it, she couldn't recall Meredith saying much after *Hunter*.

She pushed the door open and screamed as it met the resistance of a large man in a sweatshirt on the other side.

'IT'S ME! IT'S ME! DON'T CALL THE COPS!' said the man, who revealed himself to be Cormac, the sparkie who they'd agreed could have the keys to finish up the rewiring job while they were away.

'Sorry, sorry,' said Roisin as her spike of terror subsided.

'I've only got another hour or so to do,' Cormac said. 'Nice trip?'

'Yeah, thank you, not bad.'

'Fella not with you?'

'No, already in the air,' Roisin said apologetically. 'Hollywood calls.'

'Amazing. Just amazing.'

Cormac was a huge fan of *SEEN* and had importuned Joe for a good forty-five minutes about it when he'd come round to spec the job.

Ordinarily Joe might've been irritated at the unprompted *Radio Times* interview, but Cormac's fandom was so sincere and thoroughly informed that he ended up revelling in it.

Roisin wished she could say the same about the lack of privacy in her home right now.

'I've secured that good and tight, 'cos you don't want to be wearing it as a necklace,' Cormac said, gesturing up at the colossal wheel of modern chandelier that Joe had lobbied to have hung over the dining table.

'Haha. Too right,' Roisin said.

She dumped her luggage inside the doorway in the open-plan space, muttering brightly about 'leaving you to it', and fled upstairs to the bedroom, where the door could be safely closed.

Roisin sank down on the bed, holding her phone, staring morosely at the wall.

She'd thought agreeing to workmen in on a Sunday, paying time and a half, was stupid when Joe had set Cormac on, but Joe relished being Lord of the Manor and insisted they embark on a programme of renovations.

There was a framed photograph of them on the bedside table, next to a Boston fern. Like all photos of the candid and very flattering genre, it both caught a real moment and canonised a glamorised, aspirational one. A truth and a lie at the same time.

They'd been at a wedding of a school friend of Joe's in York a year ago and the photographer had supplied hundreds of images after the event, roaming around capturing the guests unawares. The couple, Jim and Liddy, had sent this one on. *You look like a pair of movie stars!* They were listening to the speeches, Joe's elbows balanced on the back of his chair in relaxed pose, his mouth half open, laughing at something being said, the expression lifting his cheekbones and making his eyes crinkle. Roisin looked beatific-angelic with a halo of Grecian braid. She was in fact mid-evening tired-pissed, leaning her head for support on Joe's shoulder rather than, as it looked, in devotion.

The day for them hadn't been a roaring success, despite the dice-throw luck of creating such a portrait. Joe was surly at being around 'back in the day' people 'he no longer felt he had much in common with'.

She remembered Joe doing up his tie in the hotel room, quoting *The Sopranos*: '"Remember when" is the lowest form of conversation.'

Roisin wanted to turn the picture to face the wall to stop it laughing at her, yet she didn't dare. She'd forget she'd done it and Joe would walk in from the red eye, see it, and think it was a pointed act of aggression.

Roisin thought of Meredith's hug. She wanted to howl, explode into tears, and yet, thanks to Joe's arrangements, which now felt like a clever form of oppression, she couldn't risk it. She couldn't emerge with puffy face, sniffing, when Cormac knocked on the door to say he was leaving.

Roisin unlocked her phone as mindless reflex. She listlessly scrolled to the flight tracker app that she used to feel connected with Joe as he crisscrossed the world. It told her he was currently somewhere over northern Canada.

He'd not messaged her from the airport waiting lounge, she noticed. But then they'd moved beyond casual interactions; anything he said now would bear the weight of history. She could see why he'd opted for nothing.

Nevertheless, she couldn't help herself. Roisin scrolled to his name in her contacts list and saw:

Last seen today at 10:48

Several hours after they parted on the Benbarrow House lawn, then, there were others to talk to. He'd been messaging right up until boarding his eleven a.m. flight. Who? Work? Probably. Could it be personal? Would he have conceivably got himself a business-class complimentary drink and rung his best mate, Dom, to tell him she'd broken up with him? Joe's pride wouldn't let him, she felt fairly sure. Not while it was raw.

Or . . . what if he was contacting another woman? Roisin had a sensation like she had stepped onto a moving walkway and misjudged its speed. She was being whipped along, trying to keep pace.

Roisin wasn't used to feeling like this. She could honestly say that, as far as she knew, Joe had never given her cause to be jealous. Part of the reason his admiration of Gina was so unthreatening was because Roisin had never felt it crossed a line or hinted at inappropriate interest.

Yet your partner always has *that one friend* . . .

She wasn't sure the thought of Joe entangled with a mystery woman made her feel jealous, exactly, either. It was more like fear of the unknown and disorientation of uncertainty. Perhaps these were the preliminary stages required before you could get jealous.

Or, had splitting up with her boyfriend of nine years on the same weekend his sex series aired sent her a little crazy? That sounded likely.

She exhaled: poor Dev, trying to celebrate the Brian Club's ten-year anniversary and, for a cool twelve grand, throwing its wake. She'd hold back the news about her and Joe for as long as possible, put some blue water between it and Benbarrow.

They could hardly prevent him from noticing it was their last joint public appearance.

Roisin scrolled from P in her contacts book up to M.

Going back over Matt's message, every serious reply she could imagine fell flat. A silly idea came to her and eventually she thought, *fuck it, do it*. She swiped until she found a poo emoji with heart eyes, and sent it.

She immediately received a one-character reply.

x

29

'I know it feels as if your exams are a way off yet, but I can promise you, they aren't,' Roisin said, to a gallery of catatonically blank Year 10 faces.

She remembered such threats being made to her once, with similar lack of impact.

'I know it's hard . . .'

There was a low-key outbreak of wheezing and spluttering at the word hard, that she waited out.

'. . . to concentrate, but put in this last push . . .'

More sniggering.

'. . . and it'll pay off next year.'

'Would you say we will *come good*, Miss,' said Amir, to shoving and *OH NO YOU DITTENT!* from his sidekick, Pauly.

Roisin put her head on one side and gave Amir the patented teacher Paddington stare. It was designed to allow time to let the air go out of the balloon without the need for further discussion.

When she was a green, keen newbie, Roisin told herself she'd never deploy such tired methods. She was full of *Dead*

Poets Society fervour. She was going to transform and inspire with the ingenuity of her lessons, and they'd be so transported, they'd discipline *themselves*. Hahahahaha.

Once she was battle-hardened by the reality of the daily grind, Roisin discovered why the teacher clichés ever became ones in the first place. The only real goals were to get them to: 1. shut up and 2. pay attention. Anything on top of that was major high achieving.

It was the last lesson of the day, last week of term. Investment in outcomes was low, restlessness was high. Staying in charge was like trying to steer a shopping trolley with one wonky wheel along a narrow bridge over a shark pond.

'I'd like your thoughts on Pip in this chapter, Pauly. As Pip becomes more conscious of social class, he becomes more embarrassed of Joe's behaviour. Do you think Pip's response to Joe is snobbish, or . . .'

Incredibly, Roisin only registered the risk in her line of enquiry seconds too late.

'Miss, isn't your husband called Joe? *Boyfriend,*' Amir said. 'I saw his name on the credits. *Of that show.*'

Roisin's heart rate spiked. She'd got through today without *Hunter* even being raised in the staff room at lunchtime. She figured she was lucky that this was the frantic, tie-ends-up final days and not the mid-term lull.

'That's none of your business,' Roisin snapped.

Amir made an under-his-breath *wooooooh* noise that caused a ripple. Roisin instantly knew she'd mishandled it, revealing it had got to her. She'd put a bounty on a disruptor trying again. Never show them they've got to you.

'Pip versus Joe . . .' Roisin repeated, aiming for a confident tone. She paused. 'Whose phone is that?'

Her eyes swivelled to the intimidatingly self-assured prom queen, Caitlin Merry.

Some kids were embryonic, outline-in-principle versions of their adult selves – Roisin was once in this category. She was sort of a mousy, feather-pencil sketch of a Future Roisin. She did a butterfly from chrysalis around aged twenty and had blossomed into her confident, lairy phase by the time she met Joe.

Others were somehow completely and totally their fully formed identities in their mid-teens. Caitlin Merry was one of the latter. Roisin could absolutely see her in middle-age already; she was fourteen going on forty-seven.

She dripped with languid scorn for her teachers and yet, Roisin was certain, would be one of the ones who would call her over in the supermarket to say a wildly enthusiastic hello in a few short years, her eyes full of affectionate wonder for times that had unexpectedly flown past, and a slight hint of sorrow she'd been such an arsewipe. Funny how patterns repeated.

'My phone isn't on! Airplane mode in lessons, always. It's the rules, isn't it, Miss,' Caitlin said, as if she was explaining trig to someone thick.

'Why can I hear Adele from roughly where you're sitting, then, Caitlin?' Roisin said politely.

'You love her Prosecco Mumrock so much she's playing in your head all the time, probably?' Caitlin drawled, to laughter.

'Haha. Turn it off, please.'

Caitlin, chewing gum and eye-rolling extravagantly, opened her bag. She found the phone, in a case adorned with a photo of her own heavily filtered face, cuddled up to a scowling older lad. She turned the screen towards her teacher.

'See? Not mine. Can I have an apology, Miss?'

'Who's is it then?' Roisin said.

A silence opened up, albeit one that contained a tinny version of 'Set Fire to the Rain' trickling out in the background.

Amir started quietly singing along.

'Right, either the person playing it turns it off or everyone gets detention, how's that?'

The room erupted into the sort of jeering howls and boos of objection that were heard when a wild claim was made by an MP at PMQs.

It wasn't much of a threat: they were too close to the summer break to go through the rigmarole of letters home, punishing non-attendance. Feasibility always counted less than attitude, however. Hold your nerve.

As one of her morbidly pessimistic colleagues, Andy, once observed: persuading up to thirty people that one person stood in front of them was more powerful than them was a sort of mind trick, anyway.

'The short arse mob could kill you if they wanted,' Andy said, cheerfully.

'Then go to prison for a long time,' Roisin said.

'Under the age of responsibility, with lawyers for each to spread the blame around thinly? They'd do less time than I've got booked away in Crete.'

'Thank God our Cheadle kids simply have too much conscience to go *Lord of the Flies* on us.'

'There speaks someone who hasn't taught 10E yet.'

It wasn't a good moment for Roisin to recall that conversation, as her management of 10E disintegrated like wet tissue.

'Last chance. Is anyone going to admit to Adele, or does everyone get in trouble?' she said, hand on hip.

'Miss. Miss!' Amir said. 'What song was that at the end of your fella's show, Miss . . . ? Was it Metallica?'

'When he was with that waitress, behind his girlfriend's back . . .' Pauly supplied, knowing his role was to keep it going. 'What was that about, Miss?'

Amir and Pauly didn't usually upset Roisin. She struggled to find a different gear for them, now 'rueful chiding' wasn't sufficient and outright losing it would expose how sensitive she was.

The Adele song mysteriously shut off, and with a bilious lurch, Roisin intuited it wasn't a good sign.

30

Zoe Farmer said, 'Oh my GODS, it was SO DIRTY,' mock-affronted. 'Like, ewwww. Old people having sex, lol.'

'The bit in the toilet,' said Logan Hughes, snickering. Oh no. Roisin had forgotten he was there. He'd not been in her class but last month he'd been regrettably transferred from another form, after fighting or having sex with pretty much everyone else in it. His tutor ended up on beta blockers.

He was what Wendy Copeland codenamed 'FCCC': Future Crown Court Case.

Amir said, 'Miss, you know how you said Charles Dickens wrote about his life? Has your boyfriend done loads of the things in that show?'

Roisin should know what to say to shut this down; she didn't. She had not war-gamed how it would feel for fourteen-year-olds to ask her about her partner's sexual fantasies, or how she should respond. Pretend It Isn't Happening had hit a wall and was about to burst into flames.

That was the thing about losing control of a class: it was a build of momentum, and you either stopped it in time or you didn't. They emboldened each other, not least because it became progressively harder to nick anyone for the crime if everyone got involved.

Roisin turned away, on the pretext of writing something on the white board. Her hands were visibly shaking and she had to abandon that idea.

That was the moment she tasted disaster.

'Right,' she said, in a wobbling voice, and when she turned back to the class, their faces were expressions of amazement, fascination and malicious glee.

They had her.

Logan pulled out his iPhone and started playing a clip of the show, audible grunting and huffing coming from his handset. He whacked the volume up sharply, so the classroom was filled with the disembodied voice of Jasper commanding, *'You like that? Tell me you like that!'*

Roisin could recognise Joe's voice in their intimate moments. She'd blocked the memory of those few seconds of homage out since the screening: there'd been so much that was difficult to think about, no wonder some of it had escaped her.

Roisin struggled to breathe. Shooting pains ran up and down her arms, her legs feeling like they were going to give way underneath her. She started dissociating, the classroom becoming scenery. She didn't care how she looked any more, she was merely trying to survive. Roisin gripped her desk and recognised she was having a panic attack. It was her second: her first had been when she was sixteen years old and saw her brother Ryan running down the street towards her. A police car was parked outside the pub behind him.

'Miss, are you going to be sick? Miss Walters!' she heard someone male ask.

'Is she, like, literally having a heart attack?' a female voice said dispassionately.

Roisin gave up bracing herself on the desk and sat down on the cold, hard floor. *Concentrate on what's real. The floor is real.*

She heard Amir saying, 'Pauly, get Mrs Copeland!'

'No, I'm alright,' Roisin said, unconvincingly, in a voice that sounded like an echo down a long hall.

Within a minute, Wendy Copeland was in the doorway. Her shrewd gaze took in Roisin's position on the floor and the toadish smirks and otherwise avoidance of her gaze from the members of 10E.

The bell that signalled the end of the day rang in a piercing shriek. The pupils started throwing their bags over their shoulders and piling towards the doors, moving extra fast in the hope of avoiding consequences.

Roisin got unsteadily to her feet.

'Excuse me, everyone!' Wendy bellowed.

They froze as if in a game of musical statues. Mrs Copeland was not to be, and did not get, fucked with.

'I'd like to remind you that phones in lessons are *strictly forbidden*. If I hear of any making an appearance again, they'll be confiscated and locked in a drawer in my office for as long as I see fit. You won't get another warning. Use it, and lose it. Understood?'

They muttered assent.

'Good. Go.'

Wendy knew what had happened: Pauly had briefed her on the way. Roisin moved into a new zone of shame.

'Let's go to my room,' Wendy said, once the last pupil had left.

Wendy's office always felt like a diplomatically protected embassy, while civil war raged around its walls. A Tamara de Lempicka print of the green Bugatti hung on one wall, some Aztec-print cushions arranged on chairs beneath.

Wendy Copeland was in her late fifties, with swishy, bobbed bronze hair, beautifully cut clothes, and an air about her that said she should be running MI5, or perhaps just the country. She was a caring and supportive manager, while brooking not an inch of idiocy from anyone. Roisin revered her, tried to emulate her, and craved her approval, above most things.

'Talk to me, Miss Walters,' Wendy said, after gesturing for her to sit. 'What's up?'

Roisin gulped. '. . . I think I've got food poisoning. You'd think I'd learn not to reheat Chinese takeaways for breakfast aged thirty-two, but . . .' Roisin made a comic grimace.

Wendy nodded and let a silence stretch between them that was more eloquent than any verbal contradiction.

31

'You are one of my most buoyant, capable, unflappable members of staff, Roisin. You *brim* with Can Do attitude and *joie de vivre*. Heathwood is very lucky to have you. I feel sure that if a Kung Pao Chicken with Cashew Nuts was on its way back towards civilisation, you'd have told the toerags to read quietly while you ran to the lavs,' Wendy said.

Roisin nodded, because if she spoke, she'd cry. Kindness was pushing her over the edge.

'I understand they were doing some teasing regarding your partner's television series? The one that was on last weekend?'

Roisin swallowed a throat lump the size of a hamster and nodded again.

'Your personal life entering the classroom is a deeply unpleasant feeling, and no one can really prepare you for it,' Wendy said.

'It's just . . .' Roisin tested her voice, which sounded hoarse, and hoped she'd not need the box of tissues discreetly placed near Wendy's left elbow. 'I had so little say. Over the content of my partner's show, I mean. Obviously, it's great

Joe's had the success he's had, but . . .' She trailed off.

'It's a poor fit with your line of work?' Wendy said.

'Exactly,' Roisin said, with gratitude. 'They brought it up, and I'd not anticipated . . .' She had to pause to gather herself. '. . . how it'd feel.' Her voice wavered, dangerously.

'Smart phones don't help, but let me tell you, there's nothing new under the sun. This has always happened, and always will,' Wendy said, to rescue her.

Roisin cleared her throat. 'Yes. I think I'd have handled it better if I'd been prepared. I stupidly didn't expect my partner's job to be that interesting to them.'

'Oh, they're seagulls with chips,' Wendy said. 'Indiscriminate yet ceaseless scavengers. The word-of-mouth wildfire never fails to amaze me. Last year they discovered Pamela Mellen in Physical Ed had an oophorectomy. They're accessing *medical notes* now.'

Roisin had forgotten about that. Like the American gossip site, TMZ, it turned out the student body had contacts working inside hospitals.

'Needless to say, I traced the source to Jagger Riley in Year 8. His aunt works at The Christie. Yet I couldn't prove anything. I must say I will be relieved when the last of their ludicrously monikered dynasty make their way through our system. I hope to retire before the next wave arrive.'

'Ohhhh . . . is that why Madonna Riley was a Madonna?' Roisin said. 'I didn't know if it was pop or Catholicism.'

'Mmm-hmm. I hear tell of an exhilaratingly revolting Miley Riley on her way towards us, in primary.'

Roisin laughed.

'However, this is no reason to skip your smear,' Wendy added.

Roisin laughed again. Her boss was dry-as-a-bone funny. She was also very grateful right now that she was a woman. Roisin had a feeling a male manager, with less class, could be approaching this problem in a way that made it considerably worse. *Your man is what they call 'Sex Positive' now, then, eh?*

Wendy moved a stapler to one side and clasped her hands on her desk. 'Let me tell you a story. In my first teaching job in Hampshire, I was foolishly having a fling with a married member of the Geography department. Neil Hartley. In my innocence, it was as though he bestrode that grammar school like a balding colossus. His classroom presence was that of a baboon. Made love like one, too.'

Roisin let go of a surprised snort.

'It was unfathomably stupid on a personal and professional level. I was twenty-five and awash with lovesick hormones. Jesus, did not, as they say, have the wheel.'

She took a sip from a water bottle on her desk. 'We revelled in the clandestine nature of it. Sneaking around is rather exciting and becomes a bit of an art, even more so before the internet. It was very much part of what made it electrifying. We drove miles and met at pubs and restaurants in the middle of nowhere, so we'd not be spotted. Of course, if you play the odds, sooner or later, you lose.'

Roisin felt something surging up inside her again, a self-doubt like severe vertigo.

'One evening, we were what my parents would've called "necking" in a car park at this little village in the New Forest called, I'm not making this up, Buckler's Hard. Who should saunter past but one of the most insidious, slippery bullies in lower sixth, who we were looking into expelling. You know, precisely the bastard you'd least want to have the Gotcha.'

She drew breath. 'We knew we were sunk. By the time I came to take my first lesson on Monday, it had done the rounds so many times, they'd practically hung bunting out. I was called in by the head and read the riot act. I could do nothing but sob, confess and promise it was over. Which of course, in my heart, it was absolutely not.'

'Oh God,' Roisin said. 'I'm cringing for you even thinking about it.'

'It was dreadful. Every lesson involved being heckled about my ruinously stupid love life. Luckily, soon after, Neil got offered a headship at a school in Worcester. I say luckily; at the time I was devastated, as I felt sure we were going to be together. Just as soon as his father-in-law had recovered from his non-specific but debilitating illness that impacted his wife, as his carer.' Wendy pulled her black-rimmed spectacles down her nose to peer directly at Roisin. 'Need I tell you the plot twist there?'

She sighed heavily.

Roisin thought of Wendy as a force-of-nature, self-assured and invulnerable, yet she felt the old hurt bubble up, even at one remove.

'Neil left. The news cycle moved on. Another intake of

kids turned up. And another. And another. I met my husband-to-be. It became very old news, passing into folklore. The affair was forgotten by everyone. It's actually difficult to be terribly interested in gossip if you only know one of the parties involved. Bear that in mind.'

Roisin said, 'I will.'

'This isn't anything like as bad as my indiscretion,' Wendy said. 'You're blameless. You've not been caught with your tongue down the throat of a man who wore nubuck action sandals.'

Roisin actually guffawed.

'Some advice from an older owl. You need to go on the offensive. Make it clear that discussion of this programme, let alone waving phones around, will mean they're sent straight to me. I know you wield authority with a light touch but sometimes, I'm afraid, discipline has to be a big stick.'

'I feel as if I do that, I'll admit it's getting to me.'

'They will briefly thrill to the announcement, for that reason. But then it's over. My general point is in the eye of the storm – and this isn't a storm, believe me – it feels impossible it'll ever lose its sting. But it will, and faster than you think.'

'Thank you, Wendy,' Roisin said. 'That helps.'

'OK. Take the rest of the week off. I have a supply in Humanities here who was at a loose end anyway—' She raised her palm as Roisin's mouth opened in amazement and objection. 'No, it *won't* be an admission of defeat. You know as well as I do, this last week is febrile. It's more like being riot police than an educator. They've tasted blood in the water. Unfortunately, you're not going to be the one to get their mind on the set texts.'

Roisin was mortified. She'd not thought this was heading in the direction of her being unfit.

32

'This really isn't necessary . . . Honestly, it'll blow over, like you said.'

'*Roisin*,' Wendy said, in an emollient tone, 'this isn't a vote of No Confidence in you. It's valuing my staff's wellbeing. I don't want you to have a harder time than is necessary. It's four days. Go enjoy yourself.' She leaned back and waved her hand. 'Plus, your partner's show is on again, when? That ending was a cliff-hanger, wasn't it?'

Roisin inwardly recoiled at the casual reveal that Wendy had seen it. She'd been so ridiculously naive. *SEEN* had generated catchphrases and memes. Sometimes, modesty was just a posh form of stupidity.

'Next Saturday.'

'There may be trailers and suchlike? Are they still called trailers? TikTok is a foreign land to me.'

'When I come back next year, won't it be a thing that I walked out?'

'They're fourteen. They were raised on social media. I can promise you that in September, the discussion points of July will be like recalling The Wars of the Roses to them.'

Roisin was not wholly convinced. But it was not wise or tactful to argue with a boss being nice to her, who had obviously made up her mind.

'OK then. Thank you.'

'Have a lovely six-week break,' Wendy said, standing, and Roisin followed suit. 'Going away at all?'

'Ah, no plans yet. Was going to paint the sitting room but couldn't agree on a colour,' Roisin said. They'd talked of getting a last-minute dot com deal to somewhere in Europe. Now it would be The Summer She And Joe Split.

'Sounds relaxing. See friends, eat and drink outdoors as much as you can, paint that sitting room, and we'll hit the ground running in the autumn,' Wendy said.

'Wendy,' Roisin said, as she showed her out, 'Were you still able to expel the pupil? The one who saw you and Neil together?'

'No,' she said. 'The devious little shit got so very lucky. It would've looked too much like revenge, and he had the kind of vocal parents who would've been straight on to the local rag. Guess where he is now?'

'Prison?'

'A rising-star Tory MP.'

Roisin groaned.

She hoped she'd convincingly feigned being both grateful and emotionally stable as she thanked Wendy and returned to her classroom to collect her things. She carefully made no eye contact with anyone in the corridors but felt numerous sidelong glances.

Oh God; the stories that would be doing the rounds, that they showed Miss Walters a clip of her bloke's sex show, and she fainted. It caused a whiplash of embarrassment so strong that Roisin almost wailed aloud, recalling it.

Short of the students getting hold of nudes, she struggled to imagine what could feel more exposing. The only way it would have been survivable, dignity-wise, was if she'd played *Hunter* off as nothing. That option was not open to her any more.

In her abandoned classroom, Roisin saw a folded piece of lined A4 on her desk. She unfolded it with trepidation, to see crude blue biro art of a spurting cock and balls with YOUR BOYFREIND (sic) written underneath it.

Roisin balled it, threw it into the bin, and aggressively stuffed her bucket bag with the necessary bits from her cupboard and drawers. She hoisted her ruby pink-streaked Calathea into her arms, its leaves partly obscuring her face in a useful way. *It was the only fucking thing thriving around here,* she thought.

Chin up, she marched out to her car. If anyone dared speak to her, they were liable to get twatted with a tropical plant.

Outside the school building, she strapped the Calathea into the passenger seat like a small child made of foliage, before getting in the driver side. Roisin momentarily stared in disbelief through the windscreen of her Fiat while she processed what had happened.

Compassionate leave. Wow. Mr *I Don't Need Your Drama, Roisin* had written a drama that officially publicly humiliated her: nothing notional about it now.

Here she was, in a car park, four days before the end of term, unable to function as a secondary schoolteacher in an era where kids had computers in their pockets.

There was a tap at the window and Roisin startled. Amir. She lowered the window.

'Don't you think you've done enough for one fucking day?' she said. The swear word was purposely intended to shock and intimidate him. It looked like it had worked; he was momentarily wide-eyed and speechless. They were more or less off school property here, and Roisin was a long way from caring.

'I wanted to say sorry, Miss,' he said, appearing genuinely quite stricken. 'I was only being funny. I didn't mean for it to get to you like that.' He paused and said, solicitously, 'I hope you are alright.'

Roisin appreciated the sentiment, though Amir was unintentionally rubbing it in. It was necessary but difficult to accept a sincere apology when the distress caused wildly outweighed the offence. She had an insight into how Gina had felt after StarkersGate.

She swallowed hard and summoned up her most altruistic teacherly qualities.

'Thank you, Amir. It's very good of you to apologise. You have to be aware that when you're winding me up, you're encouraging others, who may behave much worse.'

That was reasonable code for, *giving Logan Hughes that cue was like handing a chimp a shotgun*, she thought.

'I know. I'm gonna apologise in front of the class tomorrow, too,' he said. 'You'll see.'

Roisin wouldn't see, but on balance, she decided not to warn Amir of that. His punishment was how guilty he'd feel at being told they were getting a supply in the morning. It was unfair, but it was worlds easier to punish any pupil with a conscience.

'Thank you,' Roisin said.

'I really love your lessons, Miss.'

He stuck a hand through the window for Roisin to shake, a sweetly comical moment.

Sneaking around is rather exciting and becomes a bit of an art. It was very much part of what made it electrifying.

It was only as Roisin was sat gridlocked near Congleton, staring morosely at a bubble-gum pink BMW Z4 with a *100% THAT BITCH* bumper sticker, replaying the conversation, that the thought came to Roisin.

Was there more than one reason why Wendy Copeland told her that story?

Of course, if you play the odds, sooner or later, you lose.

33

Roisin was browsing the fruit-forward and complex whites of the Loire Valley when she felt her iPhone buzzing in her bag. She pulled it out to see: *MUM (MOB)*.

The caps lock suited Lorraine. Joe once called his mother-in-law *a human push notification*.

She'd not told her mum about her and Joe. She'd had plenty of time in the dreadful, listless four days off work. Roisin had hated time alone with her thoughts and dragged the stepladders and dust sheets out and painted the spare room in a neutral shade. A true 'fiddle while Rome burns', using Farrow & Ball Estate Eggshell in Mole's Breath.

She also slept in the spare room, where she'd stay. Roisin put her head round the door of Joe's writing study, stared balefully at the mid-century modern desk with the hairpin legs, where he churned out his evil. There was no computer, Joe preferring to be a 'digital nomad' with a laptop. Nevertheless, it was as if she expected it to contain answers.

In holding back from her mother, Roisin wasn't being purely avoidant, for once. Starting to put word round the parents before she and Joe agreed a comms strategy wasn't really on. Lorraine had phone numbers for Joe's parents, social media made things even more porous – discretion couldn't be guaranteed.

Given *Hunter* was almost a week old, Roisin hoped against hope that Lorraine either hadn't seen it, or if she had, wasn't going to raise it.

Joe had been in touch intermittently since they parted on the lawn. He sent carefully business-like, neutral WhatsApps that informed her how his meetings had gone (good), what it was like getting connections at LAX for JFK (bad), and when he'd be back (next Tuesday evening).

He signed off with one small kiss, which signified respectful affection but not coupley warmth. Roisin was glad, and returned the courtesy.

Want me to bring anything back, sweetheart? X was the only slightly peculiar one, received at one a.m., which she put down to delayed flight boredom and gin-pissedness.

Yes, please, a large bottle of Elizabeth Arden 5th Avenue, a tin of Bailey's fudge and your interest in me. (Instead, she went for: *No, thanks, I still have lots of Toblerone left!*)

Standing in Reserve Wines on Burton Road, Roisin felt the usual foreboding at having a bracing, mood-altering inter- action with her mother. There was no way of knowing if she was in Lorraine's good books – Roisin's popularity ratings rose and fell in her absence, without her needing to have done anything to affect them.

She slid the bar to Accept Call before the heavy reluctance could overtake her.

'Hi, Mum.'

'Hi. Is it a bad time?'

'No . . . ?'

'Oh. You were using that voice.'

'What voice?'

'The *HI MUM* tense one, in a high register,' Lorraine said. 'I can call back. Don't want to be a *nuisance* to my children.' *And we're off.*

'It's fine,' Roisin said, jaw muscles already locked. 'I'm buying some booze to take to Meredith and Gina's tonight for dinner.'

'That's nice. Girls' night? Joe's away?'

'Yes, Joe's away in America again. Back Tuesday.'

'Ahhh. I've not watched his new thing yet, sorry. I've recorded it. Terence said it's very blue!'

Roisin's stomach swirled with acid; she wanted to unscrew the wine and start swigging it before she'd paid for it.

'How is Terence?' she said, something she'd never asked with such desperate eagerness before. Terence was her mother's daytime barman of fifteen years standing. A stranger fit with the so-called 'hospitality' industry you'd never find.

'You know. *Terency.* I put salami sandwiches on the menu this week and he accused me of trying to turn it into "one of those gastric pubs".'

Roisin was grateful to laugh.

'Actually, the pub is why I'm calling . . .'

Here it is: The Thing You Want. They never ever had a *how are you* catch-up without an angle. Although, if she made this complaint, Lorraine would say Roisin didn't want those chats either, which was true.

185

'. . . I've had a staff walk out. I'm down to just me in the evenings until I find someone, and the agency's slim pickings are absolutely shocking, honestly. Since Brexit, no one's around who wants the work.'

'OK . . . ?' Roisin said, extremely apprehensive about where this was heading.

'I wondered if you could pop in and help me. Only until I hire someone.'

'Mum, I've started my six-week break . . . today,' Roisin said, with a careful amend.

'I know! It's ideal for you to come and help your mother when she's in a pickle. You've not been back for ages. It'll be fun.'

Fun. Rinsing drip trays, pouring pints of mild, parrying flirtatious remarks from sixty-seven-year-olds, and scraping leftover food into the pig bin. The emotional blackmail section had commenced, natch. Roisin cursed herself for answering.

'You're seriously asking me to move to Webberley to work a summer job, the moment I've got a holiday from my very pressuring actual job?'

Roisin recalled the panic attack for the hundredth time, and wanted to curl up and die.

'Not move! You can drive home every night if you want.'

'Gee, thanks.'

'Your room is ready for you if you do want to stay.'

'As enticing as this is, Mum, it's a nope. No thank you.'

Roisin sounded like a chippily defiant teenager. In fact,

she was waterlogged with guilt, as was the way of familial bonds. As was the way when your widowed mother was putting the squeeze on you. It was the equivalent of tapping your kneecap with a little hammer, and your leg involuntarily jerking.

'Alright then. I was going to tell you this in person, because I didn't want to worry you. I've also had a little scare. A breast lump scare.'

'A scare?' Roisin said, stepping away from other customers. 'What happened?'

'I had a lump and the GP checked it out and said it was likely nothing. It was a little frightening.'

'They knew it was nothing, from that check-up?'

'No . . . I've had a biopsy.'

Roisin's stomach plummeted. 'A biopsy? When did you have that? When are the results?'

'They'll let me know later today, they said. I *have* felt quite tired but put it down to overwork. You know, with doing it all by myself here.'

Roisin ignored this. 'Have you told Ryan?'

It was totally within the realms of possibility that she had told her brother, and Ryan hadn't contacted Roisin. Ryan had moved to Toronto seven years ago. As far as Roisin was concerned, emotionally, Ryan had always lived in Toronto. Her mum was closer to Ryan, and Ryan could do no wrong.

'No. I'll call him after this.'

'OK.' Roisin was surprised to be prioritised, but clearly, needs must.

'Please note I put the request first and health news second, so you couldn't say I was using it.'

'Except . . . this still amounts to using it, Mum.'

'Oh, for goodness' sake, Roisin, I can't win! So I shouldn't have told you?'

'I don't think you can ask your offspring to be your relief staff.'

'You can in a family business. You know how it is. It's not like other jobs. I can't sign off sick – would that I could. And if The Mallory goes under, I lose my home.'

This was a keynote speech of Roisin's youth and partly why she hated the place. The Mallory: millstone, HQ of drama, a home that any stranger could walk into. Helmed by a marriage that other people could walk into . . . God, no wonder Joe throwing their life on the screen had traumatised her.

Yet she knew, as no doubt Lorraine had expected, that she'd not be able to live with herself if the biopsy results were bad and her mum was working a solo shift. In that event, she'd be visiting tomorrow anyway. Even if the news was good, she should visit.

'Alright, look.' She pulled a face that her mother couldn't see. 'I'll help out tomorrow. But, Mum, you *have* to look for someone as a matter of urgency. This is a one-off.'

'Yes, absolutely! Completely understood.'

'Will you text me the result?'

'Of what?'

'The biopsy?' Roisin said.

'Oh yes! Of course.'

Eesh. She knew an optimistic outlook was to be commended, but there was optimistic, and then there was Lorraine.

34

'You got us nice wine! You can stay! We're dining al fresco,' Meredith said, taking Roisin's offerings as she stepped into the hall. Nice smells and Chvrches drifted out of the kitchen beyond.

Roisin loved coming to their house. Meredith had spotted a doer-upper, and do it up they had.

A large gold disco ball hung between the snowy scrolls of coving in the narrow hallway, and a rainbow-striped carpet ran up the black glossed stairs in front.

'Patterned is BACK, baby,' Meredith had insisted to a doubtful Joe.

The wall to their left was covered in framed photos of the lives of Meredith and Gina. Many, many Brian Club nights out were immortalised in the chosen imagery.

As she put her bag down, Roisin's eyes unfortunately happened to fasten on one featuring the distinctive cheekbones of Matt McKenzie, laughing as Gina jumped on his back and got him in a headlock. Roisin would miss their friendship. It couldn't be forever; this had to be a wrinkle. They were all too important to each other.

Gina was lighting candles on the table in the little split-level outdoor space on the other side of the kitchen, which had the *urban oasis for entertaining* look: nursery blue and pink hydrangeas, wisteria-clad walls and strings of novelty shaped solar lights.

It was known as The Hanging Garden, given the number of times that five-hour-long dinners here had left them hanging out of their arses.

They played with breadsticks and hummus until the dinner appeared. Meredith had taken charge of the cooking, serving a Jamie Oliver Greek lamb recipe with a side dish of fennel, baked with tomatoes and olives. Gina declared herself totally happy with the latter and a Quorn vegetarian 'gammon steak'.

Roisin could hear Joe's ghostly mockery. *Your partner always has that one friend* . . . What if that kind of joshing was to conceal a genuinely ferocious crush that Roisin knew nothing about?

As lovely as the company, the food and the surroundings were tonight, Roisin knew it was a preamble until she broached the topic.

As they sat sipping tumblers of wine in the fading light, over the rubble of the main course, Gina, the only one unaware there was a particular purpose to the evening, unwittingly broached it herself.

'Rosh, I meant to say: I watched *Hunter*! Sober! It was *so good*. It was as good as American things! You must be *so proud*.'

'Not really,' Roisin said, smiling. She was glad she had sorted an order of service out in her head beforehand. She'd planned the best logical order in which to make the reveals, as there was much to get through.

'But I will pass your praise on, G. I have news. I've split up with Joe,' she said. Telling the parents required timing and diplomacy, but rights to speak to the girls belonged to her.

Grenade thrown, she watched as Gina's face contorted into total incredulity. Meredith blinked several times in surprise, then raised one eyebrow, nodded, and topped Roisin's glass up.

'No! Oh my God! What? Are you serious? Why?!' Gina said.

'It's been shit for ages. Since Joe's career took off. I didn't want to say anything, because his career had taken off. I thought it was going to change back, that it was a phase. If I had to guess—' She drew breath. 'And I *do* have to guess, because I can't get him to drop the swaglord act and be honest with me – I'd say he checked out of the relationship almost by mistake, at first. He got suckered in by this exciting new world, forgot about me. Now he can't be arsed to climb down and remember. I pretty much knew we were done before Benbarrow. Then I saw *Hunter* . . .'

Here was the hard part. It was tricky to explain how badly Joe had treated her without discussing her family. She'd decided on a partial disclosure.

'. . . Apart from the things that looked exactly like our lives on there, trust me when I say there were other things, private things, he'd used that I told him, that I really objected to. I'd go so far as to call it betrayal.'

Roisin looked at her friends' transfixed faces over the table candlelight and thought she was lucky neither of them were gossips by nature. There'd be no guessing game between them later as to what Roisin meant. They might work it out individually. If so, so be it.

'I'll probably discuss it, one day. Right now, I hate Joe too much for forcing my hand.'

'We get it, don't worry,' Meredith said firmly. 'For what it's worth, I was only going to dare slag it off if you did, but I found *Hunter* a fairly disturbing experience. Doing take-offs of us all, without warning us, was weird. Then his main character is a Joe-alike, cheating on a Roisin-alike. It was trashy, to be honest.'

'*Were* they us?' Gina said. 'I thought he'd robbed the odd thing here and there, but they weren't us, really?'

Roisin didn't know what to say. If it was based on them, then it strongly implied Joe had letched over Gina.

Roisin would have to vague it out.

'Well, when I challenged Joe, I got *this is my big art, you don't understand how art works* stuff. Maybe not, Joe. I know how relationships and trust and decency are meant to work, though.'

'That's cold,' Meredith said. 'I'm so sorry, Roisin. How long's it been, almost ten years? We care about you both. I know how pushed you must've been to do this.'

'Thanks. Needless to say, I'm only going to watch tomorrow's episode whenever I can steel myself.'

Gina looked agonised: she always felt others' pain deeply and was probably avoiding speaking in case she sobbed. She'd hit a badger once while driving and had to go to counselling. (Again, Joe had found this hilarious, crooning *Badger in the Wind* to the tune of Elton John's hit, pounding imaginary piano keys.)

Roisin understood that tearing Joe down was hurtful to Gina, and she hated doing it. But what choice did she have? She pressed a finger under each eye to staunch any water-works. She could cry anytime; she wanted this evening to be used for other things.

'. . . It gets worse. Or my feelings get worse; whether this is objectively worse, I can't say . . .'

Meredith and Gina looked so rapt, they almost weren't breathing.

'When we had the fight over *Hunter*, he didn't flinch. He didn't have any guilt or remorse at all. I had this overwhelming instinct . . .' She paused. 'It was something in the way he lied to me, as if it was nothing to him. I could tell he'd had shit-loads of practice. I think he's done it himself. I think Joe's cheated on me. Lots.'

35

'No!' Gina exclaimed, in a tone of bare denial. Then, 'No?'

'I know it sounds unhinged. I can't shake it. It's like I flipped the telescope round and I'm seeing everything differently. The restaurant, the scarf, in the episode? Not only did Joe do that – at Sesso, two years ago, your birthday if you remember, Gina? He went back on foot to get it, then walked home. He had a shower when he got in. He never showers before bed. That night he dreamed up the first scene of cheating sex drama *Hunter*, and yet nothing like that actually happened?'

No one knew what to say, which was understandable.

'Rosh, I am absolutely dying for a wee, I've got to go to the loo, but promise me nothing major can be discussed until I get back,' Gina said eventually.

'Promise,' Roisin laughed, as Gina pushed out her chair.

'Did you ever get this feeling about Joe before *Hunter*?' Meredith asked.

'No, never, to be fair.'

'That suggests it's more likely you're seeing Television Joe humping lots of actresses, at a time he's upset you, and it's affected you?'

As ever, Meredith was too deft to say: 'affected your judgement.'

'I know that's the obvious conclusion. I stand on the outside of this, and I think I'm being ridiculous. Then my gut carries on stubbornly saying: *he's done it himself, and this is the cockiest move in the history of cocky moves.* The lines about how monogamy is an imposition, and he doesn't feel any guilt. How he and "Becca" have a great relationship and it makes no odds to her because he's not got feelings for these women. How it's ethical infidelity. Meredith, I can imagine Joe saying those things.'

'*Can* you? I always thought of him as a one-woman man, not someone with a wandering eye at all.'

'Mmmm. Yeah. Always judgemental of Matt's lifestyle, I suppose.'

'Exactly.'

'Jasper Hunter presents as a one-woman man to the world, doesn't he?' Roisin persisted. 'In fact, the whole point is he insists he IS one. He's in love with Becca — he doesn't see that love is contingent on not having sex with other people.'

'But . . . it's make believe . . . ?' Meredith gritted her teeth. 'I don't know.'

'I wouldn't have seen the similarities if I hadn't confronted Joe. He was a barrage of cutting remarks and dismissals, no shame. I'm scared that Joe lies fluently and constantly, without breaking a sweat. Which is terrifying, frankly. Who have I gone out with, all these years? How did I miss it?'

Gina returned, scraping her wrought-iron chair back across paving slabs, and said, 'Joe wouldn't do that to you, I don't think. I can't see it. If you knew for sure he hadn't, would you stay together? Are you two completely, definitely, done?'

It was a good question. Roisin had expected it and still didn't have an answer.

'I think so. I don't know. When I told him it was over, I hadn't formed my shagger suspicions. I only knew he has turned into someone quite ruthless and remote . . .'

Roisin had to stop talking as her voice caught. He'd been the body on the other side of her bed since she was twenty-three. Ending it felt huge.

'. . . It's only afterwards that this idea of his secret rampant infidelity has been eating away at me. I have to know if I'm right.'

'. . . Do you?' Meredith said gently. 'If you think it's over, even if he hasn't cheated, does it matter? I mean, obviously, it matters. But it won't change anything?'

From their concerned faces, Roisin could see Meredith and Gina, in a very caring way, thought she'd temporarily lost her mind. Perhaps she had.

'It matters, full stop,' Roisin said. 'I have to know if my life wasn't the life I thought it was. I have to know if I've been made an idiot. I have to know who Joe is.'

'You think there's a way to make him confess?' Gina said.

'Hah – I don't think there's a way to get Joe to do anything. But Hunter's a detective, right? Why don't I *Hunter* the clues I've been given? Starting with the smoking scarf.'

Gina paused. 'Ask them in Sesso if Joe came in two years ago and had sex with one of the waitresses?'

'No! Well. I guess sort of, yes?'

A silence settled over them.

'A few questions . . .' Meredith said, in the voice of timid officialdom, and they met each other's eyes and started laughing. 'Why would a waitress who's slept with a customer's boyfriend tell you she had done it? I see lots of downsides, from her perspective,' Meredith said.

'She wouldn't,' Roisin said, taking a swig of wine. 'I've not got as far as strategy. Give a girl a chance.'

'Can I ask a stupid question?' Gina said.

'It almost certainly isn't stupid,' Roisin said.

'Why would Joe do this? If he is messing around, surely the last thing he'd do is write about it and put it on the TV for all of us to see?'

Meredith nodded. 'That's what I can't get past.'

'The mad titillation of parading it and hiding it, at the same time?' Roisin said. 'Why does anyone go bet their whole monthly earnings at Paddy Power? Much like the sex he's writing about, the whole high is in the risk of being caught. I mean, the blatant nature of it is the mindfuck here, isn't it? If you say: "He can't have done it because he wrote about it", then you're also confirming that writing about it is a rock-solid alibi. Which is exactly the kind of trap Joe loves designing.'

'I see that,' Meredith said slowly, 'while still thinking it's a huge reach that turns Joe into a crazed super villain. I think he has behaved very badly, but the crime isn't playing away.'

'Yes. I've never got "cheater" from Joe at all,' Gina said, face propped on palm.

'Plus, bluntly, before he miraculously pulled you, I never thought of him as very confident with women?' Meredith said. 'He was always quite shy at Waterstones.'

'That's true,' Roisin said, remembering the flash of self-assurance in his asking her out. 'But maybe the reason I never sensed it is because I think of affairs as perfume on his collar, texts to a secretary kind of cliché. An affair with an *interpersonal* dimension. If it's random bangs in bog stalls, how would I know? He's had years of working from home and teachers have totally inflexible hours.'

'Wow. I need to clear the plates and get the cheesecake, but I need my mind to stop being blown first,' Meredith said.

'I'll do it, Mer, you cooked. Oh God . . .' Gina said, as she stood up. 'I know how you could find out things about behind the scenes at Sesso.'

'Do you?'

'Yeah. What did Joe call Matt? Mr Staff WiFi? Send Matt to talk to the waitresses. You'd probably have the code to the safe by the end of the evening.'

Roisin's skin tingled. Gina was on to something. Roisin had come out tonight with a gaudy suspicion and no way to implement an investigation. But here was Gina, dropping an obvious first step in her lap.

Also, the spectre of Matt McKenzie had been raised and both Roisin and Meredith fell quiet, deferring to Gina to either continue, or drop it.

In the glittering late twilight, a couple of bats scudded about in the blue-dark above them, and they waited.

Gina abandoned the crockery and sat down again. She sighed heavily, raised her eyes to meet theirs. 'Do you know there's a word in Papua New Guinea –*Mokita*?'

There was a beat of silence, after which Roisin and Meredith howled with laughter.

'Never, ever change, Gina,' Meredith said, when she could get her breath back, and Gina looked confused but pleased.

36

'*Mokita* means "a truth we all know but nobody speaks",' Gina said. 'I learned it at work the other day from some international students.'

Meredith and Roisin said nothing.

'My being in love with Matt is *mokita* . . .' She looked at them both in turn. 'You don't have to pretend you didn't know. Everyone knows, and I know that they know. Being in love with Matt . . . when I'm feeling strong, it can be liveable with. Even fun, sometimes. When I have a down day, or he starts seeing someone – I worry it's going to become serious. That I'm going to have to be *friends* with her. Those times, it's like someone is punching me from the inside.'

Meredith put a hand on Gina's arm.

'For the longest time – well, the whole time – I thought being one of his best friends was the next best thing. That the worst thing would be to not see him. Now I think it's the only thing I can do.'

'Oh, Gina,' Roisin said.

'I know that's selfish, by the way. I hate breaking up the

group and hurting you two, or Dev, and Joe, or even Matt. I never, ever wanted to make it "me or him". But that's probably the way it is.'

Meredith opened her mouth to say something, and Gina shook her head to indicate, 'I need to finish.' She cleared her throat.

'I have this test. I have him hidden on social media. He doesn't know – I go in and like random things regularly enough that he can't tell. I have him hidden, because seeing a photo of him with a girl can ruin my day. I have a physical response to it. I actually feel sick. In the good times when I think, oh, perhaps I'm getting over him at last, I check his Instagram. I find any photo of him with anyone and see if I can stand it. I never can. Imagine how it'll be if he stays with a famous actress? I'll have to avoid the news! It takes the piss!'

'Actually, you can cross that worry off the list,' Meredith said. 'I've got a dirty habit of reading American gossip magazines. She's been linked to Jon Hamm. I messaged Matt to ask if it was true and he said, "God knows, but she's no longer seeing me." So, there you are.'

'Oh. Right,' Gina said, processing this. 'But Matt's never going to date a normal person, is he?'

Meredith and Roisin nodded in understanding of what 'normal' meant in this specific context.

'. . . It's like loving him is a chronic condition. It's been ten years, and I don't think I'm ever going to be cured.'

'What if, if you met someone really great . . .' Meredith said cautiously.

'This is it. I can't meet someone, because of my thing about him! A guy at work asked me on a date, and he seems really nice but . . .'

'He's not Matt,' Meredith finished, for her.

'I know I was mental at Benbarrow Hall. I know he didn't do anything wrong. I feel naked around him anyway, so once he'd literally seen me naked, it was more than I could tolerate. There's no point me promising to be nice. It's like I'm being low-key tormented. Matt is my tormentor, and he doesn't want to torment me, and I don't want him to torment me. Neither of us chose the way things are. It just *is*.'

As Gina finished speaking, tears rolled down her face and she said hastily, 'I'm fine, I'm fine. Fuck, it feels good to admit it. My nude episode, it wasn't for nothing if it means I move on. I don't want to move on, but then I think my whole problem has been waiting until I want to move on. I know it's what has to happen, so I have to do it. Even if it's giving me nothing but pain right now. If that makes sense.'

Actually, to Roisin, having failed to explain her position on Joe, even to herself, it made staggering amounts of sense. Roisin and Meredith were both shiny of eye, too. They'd not grasped the extent of Gina's suffering.

Roisin had feared Matt had been peremptory and graceless in his departure from their group; perhaps it was wise foresight. He was going, before Gina had to.

A thought occurred.

'Did he message you? Before the Brian Club message to us all?'

Gina looked sheepish. 'Yeah. I picked it up when we stopped at the services. He asked if it was best if he went and I said yeah. I was still angry then. Now I'm sad. Do you both blame me for being such a child that I've ruined the Brian Club?'

'No,' Roisin said. 'You haven't been a child and you haven't ruined it. It will simply take different forms now.'

'Yeah, I want you to see him! He's not banned,' Gina said.

'Same with Joe. It's not a bitter divorce,' Roisin said, before she could think. It was only as she spoke she realised, in light of all she'd said, how strange she sounded. She supposed what she meant was, it's not a bitter divorce, *yet*.

As she travelled from Urmston to West Didsbury in her taxi, Roisin suddenly realised she'd had nothing from her mum. She fumbled for her iPhone.

Did you get the biopsy result? X

Thankfully, two blue ticks appeared instantly.

MUM (MOB) is typing

MUM (MOB) is typing

MUM (MOB) is typing

MUM (MOB) is typing

Too much typing for good news. Roisin started playing the

lottery of prospects in her head, bargaining. She did that with her dad, before she'd even reached the patrol car. *If it's X, we can cope with that, if it's Y, we will deal. Please, please don't let it be Z.*

She felt the animalistic terror you can only feel when mortality appears on the horizon.

Yes! Is fine. A relief. Looking forward to seeing you tomorrow. Half 5 would be ideal 😊

Phew, but also, what? She'd had that phone call from the clinic and not thought to let her kids know right away?

There had been *something*: Lorraine wasn't so malevolent as to pluck it from the air. But she wouldn't be above getting an all clear before she'd spoken to her daughter, and putting it to use by delaying it, either.

Before Roisin could decide how much of her mother's account she believed, she decided she was going to let it go.

Catching out one liar in her life was quite enough, for the time being.

37

Roisin indicated left and audibly exhaled over the 6 Music presenter as she turned the corner of the familiar, picturesque road. Window down in the heat, she passed a flotilla of chattering girls in bridal veils teamed with equestrian gear, Jilly Cooper novel cosplay. She predicted she was heading into another of Lorraine's tirades about the scourge of Airbnbs.

Families who kept their Webberley mansions as one of two homes had started renting them out for spendy stags and hens.

You'd think it'd at least give me some trade, but no, they're in The Bulls with its horse brasses and shitty shoe scraper because it looks more rustic, said Lorraine. She was always furious when people exercised their freeborn right to dispose of their disposable income elsewhere.

The Mallory had been a coaching inn with rooms at the time Roisin's parents took it over in the early Nineties. Having one child, Roisin, and another on the way, Kent and Lorraine had decided to use the space upstairs as a family home.

It was named after the village's most famous alumnus, a mountaineer who'd died first in a semi-famous expedition.

As a sullen teenager, Roisin had decided that was typical of the place. She called The Mallory 'The Malaise'.

The Walters were an anomaly, owning bricks and mortar in an increasingly wealthy area without, as publicans, being wealthy.

They'd bought it with a giant mortgage which was now down to something more manageable, yet it still didn't mean much left over every month. Lorraine wasn't able to sell The Mallory and make sufficient profit that she was content to retire on it as pension, Roisin's late father being a *screw it, let's do it* kind of guy when it came to spending.

Roisin suspected it was more than financial hubris: this was the place she'd raised her kids, lost her husband, found her principal sense of identity and worth as the siren landlady. Webberley was home.

Once sold, she'd have to move away. She'd not be able to find much for her money in footballer's Cheshire, and it'd mean she'd not only be exiled, but to what Lorraine considered genteel poverty. The rich man she'd expected to remarry had stubbornly failed to materialise – no doubt, she'd told her children, because he didn't want to take them on, too.

So here she was, staking out the last shabby premises in a prosperously pleased-with-itself dormitory village of Manchester, and yet imagining herself its Queen Victoria.

The fashionable pub, The Burnt Stump, sprayed its gable end wall cornflower blue and stencilled its name in huge font on the side, gathering crowds under its white awnings in the summer. The Bull's Head went Good Food Guide-listed, with its crackling fires, hop bine, and exceptional pies.

The Mallory remained the crap one, which, the older stalwart locals said approvingly, 'hadn't changed for the tourists and townies.' As if not changing was a virtue, when you'd started out not being very good in the first place.

Roisin parked up on the gravel outside and crunched towards the familiar arched brick porch doorway, the mouth of the Mock Tudor beast. It was always smaller than in memory.

'My DAUGHTER!' Lorraine whooped, emerging through it. She was in a dress with a palm-leaf print, gathered high about her neck like it was a beach sarong, her thick, dark brown hair in a river of ponytail like a horse's mane. She'd had eyelash extensions since Roisin last saw her, like crushed flies: they had a sultry impact that stopped just short of surprised sex doll.

'Hi, Mum. You look incredible.' Roisin leaned in for a kiss.

'Ah well, thanks. Broiler chicken dressed as poussin, that's me,' she sparkled. 'I do like your hair that lovely deep Ribena shade, I might copy.'

She always forgot: the thing about Lorraine was, she was *good in the room*, as Joe said of certain writers. Roisin gathered it meant effervescent company and quick of wit, which compensated for other shortcomings.

Lorraine was fabulous, right up until the moment you needed anything from her.

Right now, of course, her mum needed *her*.

Roisin dumped her bags in her old bedroom and headed straight down to the bar, before she could become reflective. It was filling up steadily as Saturday evening got going.

She knew this space so well, from the time when her head was on a level with the drip trays. The grubby speckled tan linoleum, the deep basin-shaped bins on wheels, the gummy bottles of lime and lemon cordial with pourer caps, the row of optics for the spirits and the cardboard sheet you ripped bags of peanuts and Scampi Fries from.

As a teenager, she'd been very popular for her ability to serve under-agers, and having the fun parents.

Roisin rolled her sleeves up and said, like slipping into a native language, 'Hi there, what can I get you? Two Harvest Pales, coming up,' as she reached for a pint glass on the webbed rubber matting on the shelf above her head.

Mariah Carey's 'Fantasy' pealed from the jukebox in the corner, the selection last updated in about 2005.

Lorraine swung her hips and sway-bopped as she sang along, word perfect while serving, waving her hand and closing her eyes during the high notes, as if she was Mariah. It was distilled Lorraine: half ironic-humorous, half completely committed showing off. An audience of several enchanted men were hanging around to watch, as per.

'Got the band back together – my daughter Roisin's with me tonight,' she said, as if she was George Michael introducing Elton John, pointing with both fingers at her, over her head, to a smattering of applause and ripple of interest on the other side of the bar.

'Can see where you get your looks from,' leered an old boy in a golf sweater, and Roisin thought, *yep, I'm back on guest vocals in The Mallory supergroup alright.*

38

'Your mum says your fella makes *SEEN*, is that true?' said a thirty-something man in coloured ski glasses like an oil spill rainbow.

'Yeah,' Roisin said guardedly. '£19.98, please.'

'Is Harry Orton dead?' he said, flapping his card on contact-less.

Roisin remembered that was a secret she was keeping for Joe, and Joe's approach to her secrets.

'You really want to know?' she said. 'You want to be spoiled?'

'Yes!'

'No, they fish him out of the Thames alive and the bullet miraculously missed any major organs. He's signed up for another two series at least, so don't expect them to kill him off anytime soon.'

'Woah, thank you!'

Roisin watched him return to a large table to delightedly report his classified intel.

Another episode of *Hunter* aired tonight. Roisin dreaded it and its potential revelations. 'Becca' probably decided to do a PGCE and dye her hair mauve. She was extremely glad this shift would keep her and her mother busy, amply covering its time of transmission.

What about Sesso, and Gina's point that Matt could sleuth it for her?

In the sober light of another day, Roisin hesitated at involving a blameless third party.

Then she pictured seeing Joe in a couple of days' time. Caught once again in his verbal conjuring tricks and scathing brand of gaslighting. The only reason she'd called him out so hard on the lawn that morning was because she knew for sure he'd committed at least one crime. It had taken grit and mental dexterity to pin him to the wall for it, and she still wasn't sure she'd succeeded. Once you knew someone could betray you over something that serious and try to bluff their way out of it, how could you trust a word out of their mouth about anything else?

Perhaps, in one respect, Roisin had become like Joe. She had to prove he was lying, because now she had to win.

She slid her phone out of her bag, underneath the bar.

Hi Matt! Don't send me a heartsick turd emoji for this – unless you really want to – but, with dubious timing, I need to ask you a favour. A considerable favour, which you have every right to decline. It comes with a complicated context that I will have to give you over a pint. Can I tempt you to hear me out, if I buy the pints? R x

PS I don't need sperm

211

When she checked her handset while pulling a pint of lager shandy, fifteen minutes later, she had a response.

> *Hi R! YOU WANT MY SPERM, EH. This is all fine, except is this some bait & switch about rejoining Brian C? The lady is not for turning, on that. Mx*

Roisin let her mother serve the next customers and typed back.

> *No, absolutely not, and we can make that a forbidden topic if you want. I'm helping out at my mum's short-staffed pub in Webberley tonight, driving back tomorrow. Shall I shout you in Manchester sometime next week?*

> *Hmmm . . . or I could come out to Webberley tomorrow? I fancy some fresh air. Arrive late morning, say 10.30, you drive me back? We could do a Sunday yomp, whatever one of those is. X*

> *PS please find Tupperware with a lid that fits for the sperm*

Roisin hadn't expected this request. Her instinct was to deter him, as she never invited her friends out here. Yet she couldn't think of a single decent reason to say no, and she was about to ask quite a lot of Matt.

Sure, if you really fancy the sticks? Here's the link to my mum's pub. Ring the doorbell. Please warn me if you'll be with one of People *magazine's 100 Most Beautiful and I'll at least brush my hair x*

Just me, one of Amateur Potato Grower *magazine's Most Beautiful. See you then! Mx*

Roisin pondered Matt's unexpected interest in the countryside. Was he, despite what he told Meredith, worried about paparazzi?

She idly googled: *Amelia Lee Boyfriend.*

The latest hits showed Amelia in recent days browsing Santa Barbara shops with her new love, Jon Hamm: both of them in aviator glasses. 'The lovebirds met on the set of their new film, an adaptation of *The Beautiful and Damned.*' For fuck's actual sake! Roisin started snort-giggling to herself about how Ruby wanted to date an ordinary guy.

Oh, Matthew, you soar like Icarus: too close to the sun, and at the mercy of your own jawline. She hoped he was beautiful and not damned.

Roisin was trying not to think about the fact he wouldn't be lighting up any Brian Clubbing for the foreseeable. She hoped Gina found someone great and healed, and it could be reconvened. But by then, it'd be different. And Joeless? What more did he want to say when he got back from America? Was it a 'let's keep talking' professional banality he'd ported into his private life? She stared into the middle distance, while her stomach mixed cement.

A stranger's voice interrupted her reverie.

'Can I get a pint of Harvest Pale, love, or is it self-service?'

39

The doorbell shrilled at 10.30 a.m. on the dot and her mother said, 'That'll be the Schweppes.'

'No, it's my mate, remember?' Roisin said. 'I might remove the decoration, but it's up to you.'

Lorraine was in a stunning oyster Japanese-print robe. Roisin was referring to the fluffy unicorn sleep mask pushed up on her mum's head. The grey fabric horn was pointing to the sky, a pair of huge stylised plastic googly eyes beneath. (Lorraine had stayed up later than Roisin, watching *And Just Like That* with a vodka and soda.)

Roisin had forgotten her mother's love of mixing high-end apparel with 'humorous' merchandise.

Roisin bounded down the narrow staircase, out past the bar and through to open the door, the hefty bunch of jangling gaoler's keys sitting in the lock.

She'd prepared her mum for Matt's visit, saying an old bookshop pal in the area was calling on her. Roisin was mercifully marked safe from Lorraine tagging along on the walk: her mother saw no point in ambulatory movement unless there was Selfridges and a French 75 at the other end of it.

It had rained heavily overnight, and the sky was a threatening canopy of grey-beige, like a cup of tea that someone had used to wash a paint brush. Despite the clammy late-summer temperature, she'd need a waterproof.

'Morning!' Roisin said, at the sight of a smiling Matt. He was in a buttoned-up dark denim jacket over black trousers and those battered brown boots with canary-yellow laces. Roisin almost hooted at the way he'd dressed for Sunday In The Countryside, as if he was in a broadsheet supplement fashion feature. He just needed to be laughing at something out of view, one foot up on a sawn log.

'Mornin'. This is where you grew up? It's a bit of a cool place to grow up, isn't it? How big's that garden?' He cast his eyes up at the building, then leaned back, hands in pockets, inspecting the rear.

'It was full of pissheads, but it had to do,' Roisin said. 'Come meet my mum and then we'll head out. I've designed us an actual route and everything.'

She led Matt into the pub, where Lorraine was downstairs, cashing up from the night before.

'Oh my God,' Lorraine said, whisking the mask off her head in a microsecond as she sized her guest up. 'Who ordered young Harrison Ford?'

'Harrison Ford if you ordered him from Wish,' Matt said, not missing a beat.

They both exploded into laughter and Roisin couldn't decide if their first encounter was going really well or very badly. She did not desire their forming a mutual fan club.

'This is Matt, Matt, my mother, Lorraine,' she said, as Matt reached over the till to shake hands.

'She's kept you well hidden,' her mum said, her face suddenly aglow, as welcoming as an open sunflower. Good-looking men prepared to banter with her were her absolute favourite.

Roisin hustled Matt off on their walk before Lorraine could decide he *must stay for lunch*.

They set off, heading out of the village by picking their way along the uneven verge, in that strangely unexpected complete quiet of a country road. Ancient trees knitted leaves together, over their heads, giving the daylight an emerald-green tint.

'Wouldn't have predicted you'd like walking and walks,' Roisin said to Matt, glancing at him in gratitude for being such easy company. Even for such an old friend, it could feel ever so slightly awkward, their being here together, out of context, but it didn't.

'Hard to get anywhere without walking,' Matt said. 'I'm not a totally urban creature, you know! We went to Center Parcs once, remember.'

Roisin grinned. She realised she relished being in Webberley too, which was also unexpected. The pub was full of ghosts, but the landscape around the village had no such negative associations. She had temporarily escaped the claustrophobia of West Didsbury and the mind games of Joe Powell.

'Rained-on bracken! You don't know how much you've become a city git until you realise you never see bracken,' Roisin said, pointing.

'Yes, look at us, present, enjoying the moment. Not a Marmalade Negroni in sight,' Matt said. 'I usually only see bracken in television shows with police tape.'

'Hah, we were saying this about Benbarrow Hall. Why are all our reference points for grand things related to murder?' It occurred to Roisin this could segue into *Hunter* chat, and she wasn't ready.

'Not seeing Amelia any more? What happened there?' she added.

'Ugh. Don't.'

'Sorry! I didn't know how serious you were.'

'Completely unserious, but she still managed to get me sacked from my job before we ended things after two dates, so . . .' Matt paused. 'Actually, no, I got myself sacked, with her help. What's that saying, "meet one asshole, you met an asshole; meet them all day, you're the asshole"? Last weekend taught me that when catastrophe follows you everywhere, you *are* the catastrophe.'

'Sacked from work? You're out of a job?'

'Yep, on gardening leave for six weeks.'

'Gardening leave?' Roisin waited until they'd passed some other walkers, making the mumbled nod-smile hello. 'Does your line of work have that? I thought it was a corporate thing. Not that I'm slyly running it down! I'm ignorant.'

'You're never slyly running me down. Unlike some people we won't mention.' Matt threw her a smile that she returned uncomfortably.

'That jaunt to Lisbon was a work trip. It came with the strings that I had to take a friend or a girlfriend and post content featuring both of us. I'm chatting to this mysterious redhead on Hinge and late night, she says, *why don't we have a first date in Lisbon. I'll meet you there.* I thought, cool, yes, why not. Embrace the spontaneity. Her photos are super lifestyley, she's very modelly, so it never occurs to me she'd mind taking selfies clinking brandy balloons . . .'

'Did you really not spot who she was?'

'No, she'd been clever. Amelia was always in a face mask, at a distance pulling a yoga pose, or half obscured by that dog. She'd only matched with me a week before and to be honest, I'd not paid hugely close attention.'

Plus ça change re: Matt and lady friends, Roisin thought, but didn't say.

'I see. Then she meets you in Lisbon and says, *no photographs?*'

Roisin stopped, poked both her hands out of her cagoule and shook her index fingers up and down, as if she was indicating plane cabin lights.

Matt laughed and groaned.

'Weirdly like Ryanair pre-take-off, wasn't it?' Roisin said. '*Should the cabin lose pressure, an oxygen mask will drop from the overhead area.*'

'I needed an oxygen mask by the end of that, let me tell you.'

'Hahahaha.'

'Yeah, so. She arrives. I find out who she is. I think it's the most incredible publicity for the vineyard imaginable, and then realise it's utterly useless. She won't let me so much as have her hand in shot. What do I do? Tell her to go? Draft someone else in? Call my boss and say, "I'm very sorry, I invited a woman I never met before? It turns out she's so famous she's brought a bodyguard who's ex-Special Forces, and I'll not be providing any evidence of this claim?"'

Roisin put a hand over her mouth and laughed. 'Sorry.'

'It's alright. I know it's ridiculous. Much like me. I return with no pictures, and this deeply bullshit-sounding story. I run our online content, to make it worse. The MD's son has recently taken over the business and he's been gunning to get rid of me from the start. The old MD loved me and paid me well, so I'm a sore thumb on the wages bill. The son uses this fuck-up as a reason to let me go. He had me in on Monday and gave me the speech. "No hard feelings, go quietly and we'll see you right. Take us through a tribunal and even if you win, we'll make the North West scorched earth for you." Also, imagine the tribunal. I'd have to argue, how should I know my date was an A-lister? Can you imagine the story in the *Manchester Evening News*?'

Roisin started hiccup-giggling again. 'I mean, that'd make the nationals. Unfairly dismissed for accidentally dating Amelia Lee.'

'Quite. Plus the payoff is very generous. I get gardening leave as I was about to close a deal with a small chain of restaurants up here and it was a large contract. They don't want me mud larking about while the contracts are sorted.'

'You'll get another job, easy,' Roisin said. 'You're you.'

'Yeah,' Matt sighed. 'I'm me.'

40

A moment passed with only the stamp-stamp of their boots and the whisking noise, back and forth, of stout fabrics rubbing as they strode forward.

'I suppose I should cough to the crazy favour,' Roisin said. 'I need to give you context first. What I'm about to tell you is *absolutely confidential*, and otherwise known only by Gina and Meredith.'

She launched into an account of *Hunter*, of break-up fights, and mounting suspicions. She concluded, nervously, with her idea that Sesso might hold a clue.

Matt listened to it all in silence.

'You mean one of the wait staff at Sesso might have had an assignation with Joe?' Matt said.

'Yes,' Roisin said.

'OK. What's the favour?'

She noticed he did not declare this unlikely, let alone impossible, but then, there was a fair bit of pre-existing enmity.

'You could, with your networking ability and general waitress-whispering skills . . . ask them?'

Roisin was glad they were side by side, as she'd be embarrassed to look him in the face. They were passing the church, which had probably not heard anything this stupid since it had been built in the 1200s.

'Sesso's servers are young. I doubt anyone who was there two years ago will be there now.'

'That's a good point.' Roisin wasn't going to haggle. She wondered if this was indeed certifiable behaviour, as Gina and Meredith had tried to tell her. She was almost relieved to be told this wasn't viable.

'However, their front of house, Rick, has been there donkeys, and I need to be working my contacts at the moment anyway. I'll have a drink with him and do some subtle fishing.'

'Oh! OK. Thanks.'

'Thing is, Rosh. While we're being frank, and given Joe is your ex . . . ?' Matt glanced at her for corroboration, and she nodded. 'I didn't only leave the Brian Club because of tension with Gina. Gina was eighty-five per cent of it. Joe was at least the other fifteen.'

'I'm . . . not surprised.'

'I don't know what I did to upset him, but at some point, he decided I was the enemy. I thought him revelling in the blow-up between me and Gina was really low.'

'Yeah, I agree.'

'If I wasn't doing such a good job of making myself unpopular in the group, I'd even wonder if he wanted to push me out.'

'Funny you say that; I thought it was a tactic to give Joe cause to leave.'

'Not left, though, has he?'

'Mmmm, not yet. Fair point.'

'This makes helping you easier and more complicated at the same time. I don't really fear potentially ruining a friendship that doesn't really exist any more. That's the easy part.'

'I see that.'

'But it's harder for me to say I'm not partly motivated by spite. I'm not wrestling with my conscience.'

'You know what, Matt, I shouldn't have asked you.'

'No.' Matt stopped walking to look at her, a fine mist of almost-rain clinging to his face and hair like dew. 'I don't mean to make you feel bad. I want to be totally honest, that's all. I'm not neutral here and I think that's better said out loud, even if only between us.'

'I see what you mean. Thank you.' Roisin sounded steady but she felt deeply uneven.

She felt like she'd hired a hitman. Her initial shock and anger at *Hunter* having dissipated, the fog had cleared and she could see the size of the ask. Not only in implicating Matt – in what she was doing, full stop. If she went behind Joe's back to try to catch him out, enlisting friends as P.I.s, then trust was gone. Good faith was gone. A chunk of the moral high ground had gone.

After the Benbarrow confrontation, it was an eye for an eye, Biblical fury. Now she was less sure she wanted to get down and roll in the dirt. Joe could justifiably be livid. But Joe had stolen one of her most intimate secrets, her parents' open marriage, and televised it. She didn't go to war; he did.

'Do you think I shouldn't do this?' Roisin said.

Matt paused. 'It's not about what I think. What do your instincts tell you?'

'My instincts tell me . . .' Roisin took a deep breath. 'There's something big about Joe I don't know. When our life together worked, I couldn't see it. In that fight over *Hunter*, everything started to look different. This is probably the only opportunity I'll have to check up on him. I don't want to wonder what the truth of my twenties was, for the rest of my life.' She looked over at Matt. 'You know when an idea is reckless and stupid, but you know in your bones, from the very first moment you have it, you're going to act on it? Any time spent debating it is pointless. It's merely therapeutic. It won't stop you.'

'I do know those ideas,' Matt said, with a broad smile. 'I might specialise in them. Right then. And if there's nothing to find, this doesn't matter, Rosh. If there *is* something to find, then his feelings don't matter.'

'There's the terrible third option: there's nothing to find, but he finds out we were trying.'

'I can't give you one hundred per cent assurances, but I'll be super discreet. I work in the plonk business after all, I have reason to be in a bar. Also, in that worst-case scenario, I'd be fine with being the fall guy. We could leave you out of it entirely and say I was digging.'

'No. I'd never do that to you,' Roisin said. 'I asked you to do it – it's on me.'

'It's a joint enterprise,' Matt said. 'We better shake. A moment to live on in infamy, witnessed only by some squirrels.'

He presented a hand and Roisin put hers into it.

As they trudged on, Roisin asked herself – and she couldn't believe she was only asking herself this now – how she'd feel if Matt returned with solid evidence that Joe had played away.

Deep down, she still thought it was impossible. Counter intuitively, her search made her look like she believed the worst of Joe. In actual fact, she needed it proven for the opposite reason. She couldn't really believe it until there was proof.

What if he had done it? How would she confront him? How do pathological liars behave when the searchlight finally catches them fully square in its glare, and there's nowhere to hide?

41

The circular route Roisin chose around the fields and along the ramblers' paths, by the brook where she threw stones with her dad as a kid, was nearly three miles in total. They felt hearty and vibrant as they stamped back down the shallow slope towards The Mallory.

'You're lucky to have grown up here,' Matt said, and Roisin smiled and nodded, because that was too much of a conversation.

As they crunched across the gravel, Lorraine came barrelling out of the pub, dressed to the nines in a billowing, translucent smocked blouse, tucked into claret-coloured narrow trousers and Louboutins, hair wound up on her head in a loose bun. Roisin almost laughed out loud. The look was: *when you've got a Sunday lunch shift at midday and serving the crab dip on a billionaire's yacht at three.*

'I need to intercept you,' Lorraine said, gesturing for Matt and Roisin to gather round, 'to warn you that Terence has had plugs. Keep a straight face, he's very sensitive. Some of the regulars have been putting "Wig Wam Bam" on the jukebox to . . . what do you call it? I want to say GNOME him, but that's not right. When you're trying to upset someone else on a computer, on purpose?'

'Troll him?' Matt said.

'That's it!'

'He's had plugs?' Roisin said. 'As in a hair transplant? Terence is my mum's longstanding barman for the day shifts,' she explained to Matt.

'A weave,' Lorraine said. 'It's not well judged. He's over-done it. He's gone from a hairline like an old tennis ball to a thatch that looks like it'd come running if you shook a packet of Dreamies.'

Matt burst into laughter and Roisin couldn't help joining in, much as she knew her mother was performing for the visitor.

'*Act casual*,' Lorraine said in a hoarse whisper, beckoning them back into the pub. Roisin could feel how thoroughly beguiled Matt was. Lorraine hadn't lost it.

'Matt, let me get you a pint before you go. Can't visit a pub and not have a drink,' her mum added, as they walked in.

'Given I'm not driving, thanks, Lorraine – if Roisin doesn't mind?' Matt said.

'ONE,' Roisin said, mock-stern.

Lorraine poured Matt a Carlsberg and made Roisin a Diet Coke, flinging ice into a tall glass from the bucket with tiny tongs. The jukebox was thundering away with The Verve's 'Sonnet'.

Her mum's only menu was sandwiches with chips (her

nonchalant manhandling of the baskets in the deep-fat fryer had frightened Roisin for decades now), so it was relatively quiet. Even the hardened drinker Mallory fanbase would only get going by mid-afternoon.

'The wanderer returns! Finally found your way back,' Terence said, appearing from the back, holding a crate.

'Hi, Terry,' she said, in friendliness with a tiny top note of weariness. She made sure she kept her eyes on his, with no drift upwards to the new mane. 'This is my friend, Matt.'

Terence was *harmless*, her mum always said, in that way British people used harmless to mean often annoying but not actively malicious. He was also, and this was a crucial virtue that many lacked, able to rub along with her mum. This, despite Terence's wife Julie always agitating for another pay rise due to his outstanding contribution, as if Terence was an underappreciated VP to the CEO of a City trading firm with massive turnover.

'Ahhh, good to see you,' he said, hulking the crate down and appraising her. 'You never look any different to when you were a sulky teenager doing your A-levels. Still the same hair, the jumper, the boots. Remember when you went at your clumpy shoes with Tippex, like a lunatic?'

Terence had never encountered a youthful fashion trend that didn't baffle him.

'Daisies on my Doc Martens,' Roisin clarified to Matt.

'Plus those hieroglyphics.'

'CND symbols and yin-yang symbol,' Roisin said, to an amused Matt.

'And names of boys!'

'MH in a heart, because the hot lad in my year was called Mike Hennessey,' Roisin explained, glad she was no longer as embarrassable as she had been at seventeen.

'Oh, *that* bastard,' Matt said, and she laughed.

They settled at a corner table, under the sepia photo of the village's tragic explorer of Mount Everest. He had often stared down in withering judgement upon Roisin's youthful hangovers.

'This place is an absolute belter. I love it,' Matt said, gazing around. 'It must be popular?'

Roisin looked at him as he sipped his lager, levelly, and was surprised to detect zero sarcasm. She'd perhaps spent too long around Joe.

'Not really,' she said, quietly so as to not be overheard. 'This village has the Bib Gourmand food pub, the trendy Espresso Martinis pub, and The Mallory.'

'That's exactly it's charm though, right? It's what it is, proper boozer of its era. It's not trying to be what it thinks will impress well-heeled clientele. No off-black walls, wanker's art of Wonder Woman as Joan of Arc, menus on brown paper on clipboards. Cocktails with a dehydrated fruit slice and half a shrub sticking out of it.'

Roisin smiled. 'Yeah, it's definitely not that.'

After they'd finished their drinks, she grabbed her bag from her room and tried to make a hasty farewell to her mother and Terence. Unfortunately and inevitably, Lorraine suddenly needed to walk her daughter out to her car.

'Can I really not persuade you to do a few more shifts? Everyone loves you,' Lorraine pouted. 'Dennis said it was like a show you loved returning! Like the *Friends* reunion. Honestly, I'm on my arse here.'

'*Show* is about right,' Roisin muttered.

'You really struggling?' Matt said.

'I'll see what I can do,' Roisin interrupted. 'Bye, Mum, see you soon!'

Her mum shaded her eyes against the afternoon sun and said, 'She's awful to me, Matt, what can I tell you? Give my love to Joe, won't you. When's he back, Tuesday? SO nice to meet you, Matt.'

Roisin tensed as her mother leaned in for a peck on the cheek with her and then Matt.

As she pulled out of the car park, Matt said, 'Tell me to piss off by all means, but . . . you've not told your mum? About you and Joe?'

Near six feet of him was folded into her passenger seat so it wouldn't have been easy to tell him to piss off, not that she wanted to.

'No, because he flew straight to California after the fight. We've not agreed on how and when to announce the news.'

Matt said nothing and a silence developed. Because he was usually good at putting people at ease, Roisin sussed it was an unvoiced thought.

'You think I shouldn't wait?' Roisin said.

'I think . . . be clear in your own mind what you want. Or Joe will be clear in his mind what you want.'

'Thanks, but I've reached a level of cynicism where

nothing's going to work on me.' Roisin indicated at a junction and pulled out. 'Which is just as well, 'cos nothing's what he's giving me.'

42

There was a lot of full-throated advice and encouragement out there about big, headline-making relationship decisions, Roisin thought, but nothing much about the minute-by-minute management of those choices. A lot of t-shirts exhorting *DUMP HIM!* and songs with rabble-rousing choruses, designed to be paired with salty margs and red lippie. But far fewer things said about the tone to adopt when his loving parents, Kenneth and Fay, unexpectedly called you on a Sunday afternoon for a speakerphone chat about the progress of the flat's communal garden they were helping you with. Roisin had gone for the same jolly, bland normalcy she'd deployed with Lorraine. It still felt unpleasantly deceitful. She had to pitch it so she was neither OTT fake-perky or ominously and even discourteously flat.

Gloria Gaynor had nothing for her there; when it came to the moments between the moments, the awkward segues, the grey areas for protocol and the conversations that no longer flowed, you were on your own.

Thus, on the Tuesday evening Joe was due to return, Roisin found herself caught in another miniscule but agonising fix: jump up to go to the door when she heard him arrive? Or remain on the sofa and wait for Joe to make his entrance? The former felt eager and peculiar – to say what? She'd made it clear she wasn't much fussed how his trip had gone. (*News: J.J. Abrams 'Bad Robot' prod co want to make* SEEN, *nothing signed yet* had been fired off mid-trip, to which she'd replied, *Great news! You must be floating.* Effusive but drab. Like he was a colleague.)

Standing by the entrance, almost as if in a challenge, felt weird. But the latter felt needlessly belligerent.

After half a glass of red, she twitchily WhatsApped Gina and Meredith to ask their advice about the world's most pathetic micro-dilemma.

Meredith:
Lock yourself in the loo and shout through the door that you're having a massive Tom Tit.

Gina:
What if Joe thinks that means another man

Meredith:
OK then 'a Brad Pitt'

Roisin:
Thank you this has been invaluable

It felt pressured because this was the first moment, albeit in private, that they were a former couple. How Joe acted now would forecast the weather to come while they financially, practically, socially, and emotionally disentangled. He had a lot of power in deciding how the next two months of Roisin's life played out.

Their breaking up, after so long, it was one of those things that happened all the time – but when it happened to you, it was unfeasibly gigantic. Roisin remembered thinking that the words, *my dad died*, were far too mundane and ordinary a statement, regarding its seismic impact and otherworldly strangeness. This, after nearly ten years together, had some of the same feel.

Roisin settled to a home renovation show where she could try to lose herself in the tricky choice of tiles for the pantry instead. The second episode of *Hunter* sat stubbornly unwatched: it was deeply inconvenient that iPlayer revealed that fact. Roisin guessed Joe wouldn't have the neck to complain she'd not bothered.

She did not yet have the stomach for its content.

In the end, as was so often the way, the decision about getting the door was made for her. She heard a car loiter, then Joe bump up the steps and curse as he clearly failed to find his keys. She stuck the television on mute and went to answer.

'Hi,' Roisin said, opening the door, heart overclocking. 'Too much luggage and too many pockets?'

'Hello. Yep, thanks.'

Joe looked up, his sun-kissed skin again incongruous under Manchester skies. He must have made use of those rooftop bars.

He hoisted his ridged silver trolley case through the door and looked around. 'Place looks immaculate? Cormac's stint go OK?'

'Oh. Yeah. Fine. I kept busy. Had extra days off work,' Roisin said, in a stupid blurt. She wasn't ready to talk about that.

'Oh, really?'

'Yeah.'

Joe obviously intuited they weren't the good sort of days off and sensibly asked no more.

'I'm going to have a shower and change, and then can we have a chat?' Joe said.

Roisin felt numb. 'If you have the energy,' Roisin said.

'No time like the present.'

Roisin couldn't read his tone. She got herself more red wine, and after a moment's thought, fetched the bottle and put an empty glass on the other side of the coffee table.

Joe reappeared with wet hair, in a clean t-shirt and joggers, sat down and poured himself a Shiraz.

'It's good to be home,' he said, after a mouthful. He gazed far more intently at Roisin than he had in a long time. 'You're in the spare room?'

Roisin nodded. She didn't want to seem mulish but had no idea what to say, until Joe showed his hand.

'About last Sunday. I'm sorry for not . . . I'm trying to find a less speech-making sounding phrase than *meeting the moment*. I'm sorry for not knowing what to say. I was blind-sided. I was about to fly to America for a huge meeting and my head was elsewhere. I'm sorry I didn't listen to you.'

Roisin said nothing, glad he was being conciliatory yet still feeling intensely apprehensive. He wrote Cool Things To Say for a living, so she'd wait until she felt a truth.

'. . . I'm also very sorry I put a painful chapter of your childhood memories into my programme and didn't anticipate how upsetting that would be for you. I had a discussion with you on my mental to-do list at the time. Then it was Dom's stag do weekend, if you remember that? Three nights in Budapest.'

'Yeah. You went up to York the night before. You can remember this now?'

'I've had a lot of time to think. I've gone from "no time to think", to "fourteen hours of staring out of a porthole window at clouds" amount of time. I went into ultra-defensive arse-hole mode when we spoke. I was gearing up to face terrifying moguls and execs who bark BORED at you in the middle of a sentence.'

He drew breath. 'By the time I came back from Dom's stag, I'd got a raft of notes and the *seeking permission* necessity slipped from my mind. The way I write, I memory hole things very fast and move on to the next bit. I thought it was my superpower for productivity; I never considered how much it could hurt you, Rosh. I must stress I'm not defending how I've acted or reacted, as it's plainly not OK. I just want to be fully honest about how it happened.'

'Did you think I'd say, *yeah sure, use it* if you asked me?'

'Uhm . . .' Joe's brow creased. 'I thought you'd allow it eventually but bombard me with lots of – justified – questions about how it fitted into what I was writing, and I wasn't ready to talk about *Hunter.* That was the very selfish inhibition at the heart of it. I didn't even ask myself if it was a good enough reason. I was a marathon runner who could only focus on the finish tape. Then it was all in the can; I couldn't change it if you wanted me to. The denial and avoidance deepened. I'm like a fucking armadillo in Japanese trainers, these days.'

Roisin couldn't smile. She hadn't anticipated any of this.

'About *Hunter* as a whole,' Joe continued. 'After *SEEN*, my agent said, "Now is the time to push the envelope – you'll never be in a stronger position to write something really bold." Agent-speak for, *you have a pass to fuck up on this go, so take a risk.* I thought about the men I know, from the super uxorious ones like Dom, still with Victoria from college, to the absolute bed hopper, lawless scoundrels who've done Mick Jagger numbers, like our pal, Matt, to dull serial monogamists like me. Among other things, I wanted to write about how straight men treat women.'

Roisin's muscles tensed during this description.

'Our pal'? Did Joe even realise how badly he'd alienated Matt? Did he care? Was there a glimmer of a possibility that Matt was, as Joe had said, a very attractive façade on a much darker place than she realised?

'I already knew I was writing another detective, which felt a little ho-hum. I thought the more *real* I can make this feel, the more potent it will be. So, I set it here. I didn't for a second stop to think that it might make you make connections with our life that aren't there. Which is idiotic, and makes me realise I've been on a luxury cruise up my own colon.'

Roisin still said nothing.

'. . . It's supposed to have themes about *the crisis in masculinity*. What I wanted to say on Sunday was, you have to see all three episodes to realise Hunter's behaviour isn't glamorised. It doesn't pay off; he's really humbled by the end. But you can imagine that saying, "No, Roisin, you'll calm down if you watch MORE" wasn't advisable last weekend.'

'What about the Gina character?'

'That's not Gina. I think Gina is a very attractive girl but she's like a little sister to me. Can I tell you something in complete confidence?'

'Go ahead,' Roisin said. Pretty rich to be boasting about his discretion.

'I don't ever break male codes of honour. Which is why I've never pulled down Matt's statue and have let you ladies think he's charm personified. What's discussed over the single malt stays over the single malt. But it came out on the stag do that Dom has had a long-term crush on Vic's best mate, Amber. He'd never, ever do anything about it. He hates himself for it. I wrote that in. I was so arrogant I thought I could casually implicate myself all I wanted, as I had the world's most chill girlfriend. And the world's most boring private life, locked in that study all the time.'

Joe looked like a man who wouldn't fear a polygraph, his gaze meeting hers, steady and unblinking. His previous rationales for what he'd done had been torturous excuses and PR gloss, but this admission of careless ego rang entirely true. Roisin finally believed him.

She didn't dislike what he'd done any less, but she had

the peace of mind of at least following how the person who was meant to love her had treated her this way.

And she no longer thought he could've done those things himself. Perspective had returned. She had been so shaken up, knowing he wasn't giving her the truth, she'd leaped to two plus two makes seven.

Was it too late to call Matt's investigation off?

43

'I see now how *Hunter* happened,' Roisin said. 'I still don't understand where you've been mentally for the last year or so. It's as if I didn't exist. When I was ranting at you at the Lakes, you looked directly at me for the first time in a very long time.'

As he was doing now.

'I know. I realise I've spent a lot of time thinking that because we don't have kids yet, I could disappear into work-aholism. Make these the empire-building years, for both our sakes. It wasn't fair not to explain that, to put your life on hold. It wasn't OK to not be a partner.'

Ominous 'yet', after 'kids' there, Roisin thought. Ominous to the point of strange and presumptuous, given they were separated. *Be clear in your own mind what you want, or Joe will be clear for you.*

'Roisin. My question to you is, is there no way back now? Because I love you, and I love our life together. I want to have this adventure with you. That was the whole point from the start. I got side-tracked and let you think you were irrelevant, rather than the reason. You are . . . undemanding. That sounds a bad word and yet I mean it as the highest praise. You've never been needy, and lately it meant I took the piss.'

'What happened to "you can't bear me to hog the lime-light"?' Roisin said.

'I was a cock. That was an awful thing to say. Of course it wasn't ever that.'

'Why say it then?'

'Because when someone's punching you, however much you deserve it, you put your fists up, too. That's all.'

Joe finished his wine and poured another, offering the bottle to Roisin first. She shook her head.

It was slightly absurd; however, Roisin hadn't prepared for Joe announcing, 'I don't want us to end,' accompanied by a proper apology, couched in the terms of utmost persuasion.

She had no answer.

'If you wanted – as a hard reset – we could try relationship counselling,' Joe added.

'I thought that was *snake oil for couples who won't read the writing on the wall*,' Roisin smiled, quoting a Joe-ism from a very different, untroubled era. Ah, the haughtiness of youth.

'Haha! Damn your smart mouth, Past Me. Yeah, I'm unsure, but I want to show you I will take accountability.'

Eesh, that wasn't Joe from York; it was very Californian-sounding. Who was he becoming?

'Also, something else. The sums of money being bandied about during this trip: they are genuinely nonsensical, and if any of my things go into production it gets sillier still. Whether we are over or not, Rosh – I want you to have my half of this place, outright.

241

I'm going to sign it over to you. Then it's yours, sorted, whatever you decide.'

'Joe, thanks, but I can't possibly . . .' Roisin started.

'No, I absolutely mean it. You're a teacher, what you do is harder than what I do, yet you're never going to be paid millions. You put a roof over my head and bought my dinner for five years. None of what's happening to me, now, would be possible without you, then. If we do go our separate ways, my half is your gift in return. A memento of our relationship. I'm overdue showing you some gratitude.'

'Thank you, but that's mad. I can't accept that.'

'You'd still be taking the consolation prize. You'd be giving up Santa Monica and going to the Golden Globes with me,' Joe said, with a rueful smirk-smile.

'You're thinking of moving out there?'

Joe shrugged. 'It's on the table. If I'm single, I might. Or we can do Los Angeles. Sky's the limit, Walters.'

He'd not used her surname this way since he used to flirt with her in the staff room.

Single. Joe being single. Their not belonging to each other any more. Roisin was being confronted with the simple reality of what she'd decided.

She didn't know how to feel about this huge shift in gears with Joe: the largesse, the humility, the dangling of carrots. After the unrepentant attitude and acid thrown around outside Benbarrow Hall, it was almost dizzying.

'Can I think about this? Everything you've said is a lot.'

'Sure.'

'I'm going to be back and forth from Webberley a bit in the coming weeks. Mum's managed to leave herself without bar staff in the evenings so I said I'd help out.'

Roisin had no idea she was going to say this until she opened her mouth.

It suddenly made perfect sense. Use The Mallory as a bolthole to get some space from Joe, and Cormac's visits, and their situationship. The nice walk with Matt and the freeing escape into the countryside had warmed her up to the idea.

'Oh, wow. Lorraine has clashed like a Titan with a twenty-two-year-old pot washer again, has she?'

'Something like that.'

You don't have the latitude to mock my mother at the moment, she thought.

'That reminds me. I was going to suggest . . .' Joe said, dark eyes looking up from under his brow. A look that used to turn her stomach over when they were first dating. 'We keep our troubles from our parents, for now. I want to tell them something definite.'

'OK.'

Roisin didn't offer that she'd told Matt, Gina and Meredith – fifty per cent of the Brian Club total – and she was slightly surprised he didn't ask. Did he think nothing on their WhatsApp meant nothing had been said?

She was forced to conclude later, lying looking at the ceiling rose in the spare room, that when it came to their friends knowing, Joe didn't care much either way.

243

44

Roisin had wondered if her abrupt change of heart regarding her mother's personnel resources issue would register as odd to Lorraine. She had forgotten that not only was her mum not a woman to look a gift horse in the mouth, but she also wasn't a woman to ask for the gift horse's backstory or motivations in any way.

'Thank God, I thought I was going to have to put a mop up my arse,' Lorraine said when Roisin called to say that she'd move back for a bit, returning for social-life engagements in Manchester. 'It's not as if it's easy to do a busy shift with two, even.'

'You mispronounced "thank you",' Roisin said.

'*Thank you!* I'll grovel if that's what you want.'

Roisin rung off and sighed. It was relatively easy to flee.

Joe, now full of lavish apologies for it, was once again cloistered in his study, wearing a headset mic as if he was giving a Ted talk, taking part in meetings about the meetings.

'I'd bin these off so we could go to dinner tonight but there's no binning these people unless you're in intensive care. Even then, they'd probably ask what the hospital WiFi's like.'

Roisin grimaced a smile, like she'd not heard that spiel before. She said, 'Sure, it's fine,' and that she was going anyway.

On her drive out to Webberley, she asked herself again and again: *Do you still love Joe? Is this a love of many years, on pause during a rough patch? Or is it former love?*

Why does he want *to mend this?* Every last person she knew would reply, 'Because he loves you! Why wouldn't he?'

During service that evening, she saw she had a missed call: Matt. She'd never felt dismayed to see his name before.

Roisin didn't want to ring him back, but she also knew she'd be completely distracted until she did.

She chose a quiet moment to step outside the front. The Mallory was mostly gravel and space for parked cars outside, only four tables for customers, which were inevitably monopolised by smokers. The August air was balmy and blowsy, in that last gasp of summer way.

'Hi, Matt,' she said, tucking the phone under her chin as she picked up two foam-clouded pint glasses from the flower bed.

'Hello! I went for a drink with Rick.'

'That was fast!' Roisin said, adjusting her phone again. 'Thanks.'

'Gardening leave means I have the time. I even watched *Hunter* as my homework. I don't want to do any gameshow host ticking clock suspense here, so I would describe my findings as something and nothing, but ninety per cent nothing.'

Ten per cent of something startled Roisin. She'd declared

it possible and now, on the brink of it, she couldn't allow that it was possible.

'. . . Scarves being left behind rang no bells for Rick, and he didn't recognise Joe.'

'You showed him a picture?'

'Yeah. I kind of had to. Did you not want me to?'

'No, I . . . hadn't thought what your inquiry would entail.'

That was exactly it. Adrenaline surged. *Joe will never find out, it's fine. Not gonna happen.* If he did find out, could she justify it as payback for *Hunter*? Point out how much turmoil she had to be in, to check up on him like this? She could try, but distrusting your partner this deeply wasn't something you could easily come back from. It would change things between them. Did it not change things if she kept it to herself?

'However,' Matt said, as Roisin's stomach pancake-flipped, 'around two years ago, Rick tells me they employed this flaky Croatian girl called Petra. She'd disappear for long smoking breaks whenever she fancied – notorious for it. Apparently she got the nickname *Fagatha Christie* for such disappearances. She told other waitresses she was seeing an older, married guy. They thought it was BS because she had no photos with him. She said she didn't even know his real name to look him up. He was very low profile because of his job. You'd think "the wife" was more likely the reason, but . . .'

Roisin blew air out of her mouth. So it was a colourful ten per cent. 'He'd originally been a customer?'

'Yup, she said so. His job was in the military police. He

said his secrecy protocols were so strict, he couldn't be in any house with an Alexa.'

'An Alexa? Who's she?'

'An *Alexa*. You know, your speaker that's a virtual assistant-cum-listening device that you pay Amazon to install in your home.'

'Oh! *Alexa, Play Cher!* Right. That much doesn't sound like Joe.' Roisin's nerves started climbing down from the roof.

'Nope, it doesn't. Anyway, Sesso finally let her go after she went for a smoking break during a closing up and didn't return until her shift the following day. That was high summer, he remembered. I asked what she looked like. He found an old photo of a staff night out on his phone. She had bobbed hair. She looked reasonably like the actress.'

'Right,' Roisin said dully. Her nerves, currently shinning down the drainpipe, hesitated.

'There's no getting in touch with Petra, either. She used a fake surname on her payslips. I quote Rick: *the type of girl who's a tax ghost, a social media ghost, the lot. Probably has different-coloured hair now, working a bar in Dubrovnik and dating Jason Bourne.*'

'Hah.'

'All we have is the coincidence of a popular haircut and a shady private life, which is many waitresses I've met. I wouldn't convict on this much evidence.'

In the absence of anything conclusive, he was patching this up, making it right. Given there was no love lost between him and Joe, it was honourable. It put Roisin first.

'I wondered if I could ask you a favour of sorts in return,' Matt said. 'I have nothing to do, and I can't get a job yet. I took a real shine to your mum's pub and you say she's short-handed. Could I help out?'

'Oh NO!' Roisin squealed in self-consciousness and genuine amusement. 'Seriously? You want to pull Carlsbergs at The Mall? It's a village. There's nothing here for a gentleman like you. Apart from the hen dos, I suppose . . .'

Matt laughed. 'I won't push if you'd find it weird. I'm longing to feel like I'm any good for anybody or anything at the moment, that's all.'

There was such a note of authentic sadness in that statement that Roisin couldn't possibly refuse.

'Alright. Thank you. My mum will flirt with you relentlessly. Please bear it with good humour but absolutely DO NOT succumb and sleep with her. I don't want my stepdad coming this much out of left field.'

'Roisin!' Matt exclaimed, in an un-Mattlike way, genuinely shocked. 'What on EARTH? How much of an Uncle Disgusting do you seriously think I am?'

Roisin laughed and felt a little grief-stricken that she couldn't confidently answer that.

45

'Get out!' Lorraine cried, at the sight of Roisin and Matt in the doorway on Saturday afternoon.

'Wobbly start,' Matt said.

'Sorry, not you, Matthew – that stray,' Lorraine said, pointing in the area of their ankles. 'MEATBALL, GEDDOUT!'

They glanced down to see that a cat had taken advantage of their entering the pub to 'plus one' himself onto the premises.

'Aw, hello, Meatball,' Matt said, stooping to pet the black and white animal of considerable circumference. His facial markings gave him a pleasing look of a piebald highway bandit.

'*Meatball*?' Roisin said.

'That's his name, I'm told,' Lorraine said. 'You can see why. Loafs around the place uninvited and bothers people for their chips.'

'A cat that eats chips?!' Matt said.

'Oh, a cat that eats anything he can hoodwink people into giving him. Shoo!' Lorraine said, as Meatball steadfastly ignored her.

'Is he really a stray?' Roisin said, joining in the fussing, noticing how she and Matt could brush hands and it not be odd. She was lucky to have a male friend like this. She trusted him to spend time here and not use any information he gleaned to embarrass her. Matt was a man absent of spite.

'Well, he's strayed from somewhere 'cos he's in here all the time,' Lorraine said, snapping her fingers and pointing at an indifferent Meatball, who waddled off in the direction of the saloon bar.

Roisin and Ryan had never been allowed pets, notionally because a public house was an inhospitable environment.

('They will only up and die and upset you,' Lorraine had said.

'Everything dies!' said an adolescent Roisin. '*The price of love is grief.*'

'Yes, well, I'm not having the grief of changing a guinea pig's straw when you lose interest.')

For tonight's Saturday shift, Roisin had arranged to settle Matt in, go for dinner in Manchester with what was left of the Brian Club, and drive back here later. It looked, on the face of it, a considerable sacrifice. In actuality, she was glad of the excuse not to drink, and to spend time on the road and in her own head.

Leaving Matt and Lorraine to interact unsupervised for around four hours made Roisin slightly uneasy, given her mother's loose cannoning, but perhaps a baptism of fire was best. She couldn't be here to supervise the whole time.

Matt was going to get a taxi back to his flat in the city until Lorraine – unsurprisingly – said he absolutely must crash in Ryan's old room. At least her parents were into privacy in one way: each room had an en suite, so as Roisin got ready to go out she had no fear of doing an impromptu first-floor landing tango with Matt, both of them clad in slipping towels.

Roisin would've shown Matt round the till, but Lorraine was super keen to play tutor. Reminding herself that Matt had wanted this and that she shouldn't feel anxious for him, after changing, Roisin bid them farewell and promised to return around closing up.

'Nice dress, by the way,' Matt said.

In her near-week of purgatory, Roisin had gone to & Other Stories and bought herself a pouffy-sleeved black dress with a sweetheart neckline.

'Yes, it's great to see your waist for once,' Lorraine added supportively.

Tonight's dinner out was the first post–Benbarrow catch-up. Roisin fully endorsed Meredith's reply to Dev's original venue suggestion.

Meredith
Sorry can we not bother with places serving reindeer moss and any menu with the word 'nixtamalized' on it? I want to see you all and consume melted cheese and cheap liquor, not pretend to be interested in an espresso-cupful of jizz and a tray of mossy pebbles

Dev
I depend on women pretending to be interested in my cupful of jizz and mossy pebbles

By an elimination process of things being booked out on a Saturday and Dev's name still meaning something, they'd landed on San Carlo, a central pizza-pasta place full of rowdy, glamorous, high-cosmetic-maintenance twenty-something Manchester.

Roisin wound her way to the table in the buzz, ten minutes late after forgetting city centre parking was a bastard, and saw it had an unexpected occupant.

'Joe? You made it?' Roisin said, thinking thank God she'd WhatsApped Gina and Meredith and given them a full update on Joe's offer, Sesso being what Americans called a 'nothing burger', and their current status.

(Meredith's reply had been pure wisdom: *I think you half wanted to find out he'd been unfaithful so the decision was made for you. This way you'll know you were in control of your choice.*)

Joe had been too busy tonight preparing material for next week's meetings – except now, as he sat beaming, sandwiched between Dev and Gina, apparently, he wasn't.

'Ah, Dev called me and persuaded me to knock it on the head for an evening. Messaged you.' He nodded to Roisin's phone, which she'd not seen while driving.

Roisin tried not to seethe on this turn of events. If Joe had told her he was going, she'd have stepped away.

It was lying to their friends. Well, lying to Dev to be precise, and making the women awkward. When she said she wanted time to think, she didn't mean, 'while we attend social outings as a couple.'

Her frayed nerves made it harder to judge, but, watching

Joe dunk a piece of bread in oil, this surprise cameo smacked of a power play.

Minutes later, she checked her phone discreetly and saw:

Hey R: I'm hitting brick walls and bleeding all over Final Draft tonight & Dev called, saying to sod it off and come out. I won't if you'd find it tricky. LMK. J x

Immaculate housekeeping. Forty-five minutes old: sent too late for her to prevent it, yet providing Joe with complete comprehensive cover.

When he'd come through the door earlier this week, drenched in contrition, why hadn't she simply stuck to her guns and said no, they were done?

Because she was caught off guard. Because she'd not, at that point, got the feedback from Matt going to Sesso and sated a thirst for evidence. Because she thought nine years deserved a second chance. None of these reasons, on inspection, were good reasons.

Nothing that mattered had changed. She'd go home tomorrow and say she had finished thinking, they were definitely done. It wasn't a good moment to finally have this conviction, at the start of an hour and a half of being friendly and social in Joe's company.

'Cor, if lip fillers were sticks of dynamite, we'd be blown sky high here, right?' Joe said, under his breath, glancing around.

'I've left Matt working a shift with my mother in Webberley,' Roisin said to the table, to keep her mind occupied.

MHAIRI MCFARLANE

At least Joe looked wrongfooted now, instead of her.

She'd checked Matt was alright with her telling the Brians and he'd shrugged, *sure, why not*. She was impressed he didn't care about status.

'*Lol, what*? Matt? A barman for your mum? Is this his most ambitious seduction attempt yet?' Joe said.

Roisin looked at Joe, levelly. To everyone else, that was a standard risqué jibe at Matt. With what he knew of her family, it was crasser than that.

'*Nice*. He's on a sabbatical from work and keeping busy,' Roisin said, deciding to sidestep Matt's sacking for his dignity. 'It's a lifesaver for my mum.'

'Let me get this straight: Matt is dating a Hollywood star and his job is making bitter shandies for old boys playing darts? If I pitched this in a Hallmark movie, I'd be told it was a step too far,' Joe said.

'Not any more,' Roisin said. 'He and Amelia have gone their separate ways.'

'What a shame, she was so nice,' Gina said, snapping a breadstick. 'They could've had such beautiful, rude babies.'

'No Anita?' Roisin said to Dev, glancing around.

'Nah, she's poorly. Tummy bug. Left her watching *The Real Housewives of Beverly Hills* in her clown trousers. Honestly, the one way we're incompatible is TV. She says I only like things with people in snowstorms saying, "We must keep moving! We need to get to the camp by nightfall, before It awakens!"'

'Have you had a chance to look at the menu, guys?' a waitress interrupted, and they guiltily tasked themselves to making choices.

Roisin saw she had a message from Meredith and read it carefully, holding her phone inside her bag.

I bloody hope it's not morning sickness.

46

'You've got a second series, though, right?' Dev whooped as Joe nodded.

'They're announcing it over the final credits. God knows when, mind you. Rufus has got a pilot for something with Michael Keaton and a role in the *Stranger Things* spin-off. That goes no further, obviously,' he said, looking at a group of people without a hotline to the news desk of *Variety*.

Roisin had been able to withstand ten minutes of Dev on the genius of episode two of *Hunter* because Gina had gamely protected her with, 'No spoilers, Dev! I've not seen it yet!' which reduced him to detail-free superlatives.

'Got the last one recording!' Dev said. Of course. Tonight was the finale. They were missing it.

Joe looked at Roisin from under his brow, twiddling his fork. He'd be unsure if she'd seen it yet and he also knew raising that question was a kamikaze mission.

Only when Dev got on to his stag do and wedding again, did Roisin push her ravioli around her plate in quiet agony. An event that Joe Powell across the table might well be attending with his next girlfriend. That'd be fun.

If he turned up at all, of course.

Was the other reason Roisin had agreed to 'think about it' earlier this week purely a result of the base motive of flattery? She'd spent a year thinking she was going to be let go of, by someone with options. It was obvious Joe was a considerable catch. His declaring her worth to *him* had been too gratifying.

Dev was extolling the benefits of hopping over to Palm Beach in a hired Chevy truck when Roisin spoke up, unable to take the dissonance any more.

'Heads up that I don't think, with his work situation, Matt can afford Miami,' Roisin said, hoping to both do Matt a favour and start the process of conveying: *we are all disquieted by the price tags lately. Team No Reindeer Moss.*

'What are you, his mum?' Joe shot back, trying to be flip and landing hard.

'Yeah, I was going to say,' Meredith said, both rescuing and ignoring Joe, 'I'll probably need to see the total cost of Lake Como before I commit. Our boiler's gone kaput.' She looked at Gina. 'She dresses well to hide it though, hahahahaha.'

'Vicious witch,' Gina said, craning to see a waiter. 'I might have another Aperol. Oh yeah, the boiler. I have some emergency savings I could dip into for that.'

Roisin saw that the necessity of emergency savings dipping had registered with Dev.

'I can cover flights to take the cost down. It's no trouble,' Dev said.

Roisin took a deep breath. 'Dev, you are the most generous

soul alive, but we can't accept being paid for as a solution. No one wants to mooch off you and live beyond their budget. *Can't do it* has to mean *can't do it*, or you feel trapped.'

'The girl with the good hair has a point,' Meredith said. 'Hey, why not have TWO stags? Miami and Manchester.'

'Actually,' Dev said, shaking the ice in his lime and soda, 'you may have hit on something, Rosh. Anita's gone cool on the Lake Como plan, too.'

'Really?' Roisin said, realising it was a stroke of luck to have the freedom to discuss it without her present.

'Yeah. Some of her family have kicked off about the expense and the travelling, and she thinks it's too complicated. Not least as Hindu wedding guest lists are *large*.'

'Would you consider the UK?' Roisin said.

'Yeah, totally but . . . you only do it once, hopefully. I don't want her to regret it later.'

'Honestly, cypress trees won't end up mattering to you,' Meredith said. 'Having a huge tear-up and going home happy are the only things that count. Don't cause endless politics with your cousins – stay here.'

Dev nodded and Roisin could sense him reading the room at last. There was a distinct absence of their exhorting him to stick to Italy, or Miami, and that in itself was surely telling him something.

'Would you all like it if it was here? My Bolton lot would probably be relieved, too.'

'We'd *love* it,' Gina said. 'Also, I could afford all sorts of add-ons. Like a contouring spray tan. There's this guy who's meant to be like the Picasso of mobile spray tans.'

'Oh, hark at Lady Gaga,' Joe said. 'Is that like when I drew better abs on my Action Man with a felt tip?'

They fell into their affectionate bickering and Roisin was glad they'd dealt with it light-heartedly. It helped that Dev was a man near-incapable of taking offence.

'Oh, by the way, I'm off to York tomorrow,' Joe said to Roisin, as the group parted outside. 'Going to see Mum and Dad for a couple of nights, then London for one, back Thursday.'

Thursday it is then, Roisin thought. It'd be better. Rip the plaster off. An improvement on this limbo, as daunting as it was.

'OK,' Roisin said. 'Have fun.'

'Ships passing in the night, you two, aren't you?' Dev said, chortling, and no one knew where to look.

Roisin came through the door into the lights-dimmed pub, saw Matt and her mother, and screeched.

'It's like' – Roisin had to lean on the wall to get her breath back – 'like walking into a Cold War Steve artwork or something.'

'Coldplay who?' her mum said.

Lorraine was sitting at a table, hair gathered up into a green casino croupier's visor, a vape stick jammed in the corner of her mouth, counting what looked like raffle tickets. The jukebox was serving Bryan Ferry: 'Slave to Love'.

Matt was behind the bar, Meatball the cat balanced on his shoulder, straining dark liquid from a steel shaker into coupe glasses.

'How on earth did you get that much cat onto your shoulder?!' Roisin said.

'Years of practice,' Matt said. 'Want a Manhattan with us? McKenzie secret recipe.'

'Ooh, yes please.' Roisin shrugged her jacket off. 'Mum, you're allowing this insolence from Meatball?'

'Keeps the horrible thing off my floor,' Lorraine said.

'How did the shift go?'

'Amazing. They LOVE him,' Lorraine said, casting a look of pure adoration up at Matt.

Third drink made, Matt lifted Meatball down from his shoulder. The cat walked round the bar, straight to the door and batted it with a paw to be let out.

Roisin leaned over and opened it for him.

'Yes, off you go, you ungrateful swine, to whoever's fool enough to keep you the rest of the time,' Lorraine said.

'That was how she always said goodbye to me,' Roisin said to Matt, who laughed as he set both their Manhattans down.

'Same time tomorrow, Mr Ball!' Matt called.

'Oh, it's that shitting fête and the annual humiliation next Sunday. A week tomorrow,' Lorraine said to Roisin. 'Please say you'll be here for that, Rosie. Grace Peters has got Imogen visiting, so if my daughter's not present, it'll be another thing to lord over me.'

'Shitting fête?' Matt said.

'My mother was convent-educated,' Roisin said. 'The annual village fête for a nominated charity. All three pubs decorate their gardens and serve Pimms, and there are games

260

and so on. Mum hates it, as we tend to make less than everyone else.'

'Oh, I *love* a challenge like this. We'll smash it,' Matt said. 'What about a guess-Meatball's-weight game? Little pair of scales?'

'You're not even joking, are you?' Roisin said. 'Oh, and Grace Peters: Grace is a very attractive divorcee about town, and Mum's principal village frenemy. Has a lovely big cottage up on the high street.'

'Came into her looks late, like Carol Vorderman,' Lorraine said to an entertained Matt. 'Goes on girls' holidays constantly with her huge alimony payout and tags it GALIMONY,' Lorraine said. 'Rubbing my face in the fact that Kent left me potless.'

'Narrator: Grace was not, in fact, thinking about Mum at all,' Roisin said, and Matt grinned. 'Imogen is her daughter, same age as me, qualified GP. I'm a teacher, so right now we're even, unless one of us gets married and pulls ahead, in this game that only exists in my mother's head.'

'No, you're not even. Imogen's single and my son-in-law is famous, so Grace can chew on that,' Lorraine said.

Roisin and Matt shared a look.

47

Matt stood at the back doors of The Mallory with a cup of coffee and said, 'This garden is huge. It's got tons of potential. Reckon your mum would consider changing the décor, a little? For the fête?'

Once again, she scanned for satire, finding none. Roisin would never have predicted that Matt would be excited by her mother's pub in the sticks. It was like a rich kid loving the dictionary they got for Christmas.

She gazed out, standing shoulder to shoulder with Matt.

The lawn, surrounded by a neat privet perimeter hedge, was punctuated by half-a-dozen circular wooden picnic tables, still in decent nick. There was nothing wrong with it and nothing to get excited about. Matt was right: it had potential and a serious deficit of love.

'I'd say no, then I remember if it's you asking, she'd probably install one of those striped helter-skelters. I was coming to ask if you fancied doing last week's walk again?'

'Now? Yes, why not! That was good scenery.' He lowered his voice. 'How'd it go yesterday? Did *Hunter* come up?'

Roisin had already decided her decision in San Carlo last

night would stay secret until she'd told Joe. Whatever else had happened between them, he didn't deserve someone else finding out their relationship was definitively over before he did. Plus, as far as Matt knew, she'd never wavered.

'Since your inquiries, I've discounted that *Hunter* stuff entirely. I feel pretty embarrassed, actually,' Roisin said, checking her mother was definitely upstairs. 'I've not watched the rest of yet, in case I go loopy again. Meredith and Gina tried to tell me I sounded insane. I wouldn't listen. Now I'm cringing so hard I'm wearing my bum hole as a scrunchie, as Lorraine would say.'

'For what it's worth, I didn't think it was insane,' he said. 'Not likely, but not insane either.'

Roisin said she appreciated that, while wondering if both he and Joe were engaged in a Battleships game of subtly undermining each other with her.

They got their jackets and headed out.

'Joe doesn't want to split up,' Roisin said, as they got a safe distance from The Mallory. 'He's offering me life in Los Angeles and going to the Golden Globes. Or a house in West Didsbury if I walk away. Like *Who Wants to Be a Millionaire?*'

'L.A.? Are you going to go?' Matt said.

'No. What would I do out there? Listen to Joe's Zooms? I'm just amazed he's trying to save the relationship.'

'Are you? Why?'

'I honestly thought he'd checked out of it.'

They walked uphill in silence for a moment.

'You talk about you and Joe in terms of what he wants

and what he might be doing or thinking or feeling all the time, but say very little about yourself.'

'Hah, yes. He said I was "undemanding",' Roisin shot back, though she knew she was replying quickly to mask her discomfort. She needed to do better than that. '. . . Something shifted, in the last year. It was confirmed for me in the fight we had. I always liked how intelligent and sharp and witty he was, but I've come to see Joe as— I see him differently. I worry that he's got a very hard, pitiless streak.'

Matt did a double-take.

'What?'

'That . . . is new?'

'New to me. Is that stupid of me?'

Matt hesitated, so Roisin assumed the answer to that was: *yes*.

'I always assumed you liked that.'

'What?'

'That he's a Mean Boy.' He looked at her with an awkward expression. The uncertain, apologetic face someone pulls when they know a conversation has strayed beyond the limits that your conversations usually keep and can't predict the reaction.

Roisin didn't know what to say. Even allowing for the fact that Matt was pissed at Joe, he said it so simply, so starkly. As if it wasn't subjective. It was the conversational equivalent of accidentally seeing yourself in the front-facing phone camera.

Joe was mean – and Roisin 'liked it'?

She supposed she had. She thought he was clever. What

did it say about Roisin, that she had chosen mean? How did you explain having fallen in love with someone who wasn't nice?

It wasn't a very sympathetic error.

'I don't want you to think I'd stay in a bad relationship for bribes,' she said, not knowing what else to say.

'I don't think that,' Matt said. 'Not for a second.'

'It's been nearly ten years. I thought he might've been having monkey sex behind my back. I need to get my head together before next steps.'

'Sure.'

Roisin needed to be alone to dwell on what Matt had said and she needed conversation about something else. She opted for Matt's employment.

'I'm going to be careful with my payoff, as I expect the raw terror of "no one else will hire me" will bear down suddenly in the middle of the night like the shrieking ghost in *The Woman in Black*,' he said.

'If you were really up against it, could your family not tide you over? You know I'm not saying that in the way Joe would.'

'Hah. Nope. I'm sure I was disinherited years ago.'

'Seriously?' Roisin said, stopping dead for a second in surprise.

'Yeah,' Matt said, balled hands thrust in denim jacket pockets. 'I mean, I assume I was. I've not seen my parents or my brother in four years, so I guess so. It's a fair assumption.'

'I'm so sorry. I had no idea.'

Matt lived in a city apartment at Deansgate Square with its own lift, a mezzanine bedroom with floating staircase and a herringbone parquet floor. Joe called it *fur coat AND fur knickers wealth*, but she supposed it could all be on tick.

'No, I've not made it known. Please don't tell anyone, either.'

'Of course. But . . . you go home at Christmas?' Roisin said, frowning, running sums in her head. 'I thought I saw photos?'

'I stay at some nice chintzy hotel and take a few pictures. Sometimes people take that to be my parents' home. Or think that's my family tradition. I never correct them. That's all.'

'Why don't you want people – us – to know?'

He was a black sheep, and not a golden boy? Roisin was already perceiving him differently, and maybe that was why.

Matt gave her a sidelong glance. 'I'd not want to single one person out, swear them to secrecy and put that burden on them.'

That was a nice way of saying that he didn't trust it to circulate, whomever he chose.

'. . . I didn't tell you all because, firstly, I don't want to get into why I'm estranged from them. Secondly, because some people would probably gloat.'

'I'd not have suspected this at all. I'm really surprised.' Roisin tried not to be just slightly hurt, working it out. He didn't want Joe specifically to know. Whomever he'd told would think Roisin was safe as confidante, and Roisin couldn't be trusted around Joe. Mrs Mean Boy.

'I know why you'd not suspect it.'

'Why?'

Matt pulled himself over a stile with easy agility and, once on the other side, offered a helping hand to Roisin, which she accepted.

When they resumed walking, Matt said, 'Because I seem superficial and shallow, so my life must be a cinch. Guess what: superficial, shallow people can have shit happen to them, too.'

He threw her a smile to defuse this, and she couldn't return it. She could hear how hurt he was.

'No, you seem to handle things so effortlessly and have such a sunny disposition, that's why. From the outside, your life seems *well joyful*, to use a phrase of my pupil Amir's.'

'When you put it like that. Thank you.' He smiled. 'I've cultivated the frivolous image enough, so who am I to complain. It was easier.'

'If it helps, I've never discussed the complexities of my family background with the Brians either,' Roisin said. 'Which feels so surprising, given how close I am to the girls especially. I'd trust them with anything. I just can't. It worries me that, at thirty-two years old, I must think it's my shame and disgrace also. Why else keep it secret?'

'Can I ask more about it?' Matt said. 'Are we playing "you show me your dysfunction and I'll show you mine", out here in the woods, or are we being way more elegant than that?' They broke the mounting tension with laughter.

'I was leaving that up to you,' Roisin said. 'Plus, you've got to go back and act normal around my mother.'

'OK, you go first, because mine is worse, and you won't want to say much after it.'

That might be bullishly overconfident, Roisin thought.

48

Roisin breathed in and out and looked at the swirling eddies of the river as their path brought it in sight. She remembered coming out here to sit on the bank and drink cans of cider in her youth.

It felt easier to be open, in this seclusion. Still difficult, but easier.

'Long story short is, my parents were what you'd call swingers. The thing about your parents getting up to that kind of rum shit is, no one tells you what's going on. Your responsible adults are the ones responsible. It's not like anyone sits you down and says, "So there's the birds, the bees, and also your mum and dad, who are a whole petting zoo." You work it out, bit by bit. That process of figuring it out alone is what messed me up the most, really. The whispering and the locked drawers and the snogging they thought we didn't see. The drastic warnings that my brother and I had about leaving our bedrooms after lights out when they had "parties", even if we had nightmares.'

Roisin looked at Matt. Just recounting it, she felt queasy.

'You see why this is unbroachable? Most people are like,

ugh I don't want to think I have a sibling so my parents did it TWICE.'

Matt smiled.

'You know that bit in *Hunter*, where he sees his mum with another man, round the corner from Dad with another man's wife? That was Lorraine. I told Joe about it. He ripped that off, didn't ask me permission. So I saw that old wound unexpectedly reopened in the screening room.'

'Seriously? He didn't tell you he was using it? *Wow.'*

It was grimly satisfying to see Matt's amazement.

'My dad died of a massive stroke when I was sixteen. He was lying unclothed underneath one of my mother's best friends, Kimberley, at the time. Who was also married. As much as my mum knew the deal in general, I don't think she knew that particular deal. I think with Kim it was just good old-fashioned cheating, with someone off limits. I overheard the phone calls after he died. That's the lie of the open relationship, I think. It's never going to hurt anyone, until it does. It's not as if I've ever asked, though.'

Matt nodded.

'There had to be an inquest, so it all came out. Massive village scandal. It'd be bad enough if your dad's affair was made public at a time like that, but rumours were flying that it was much more than that, with Mr and Mrs Walters. It was fun going to school after that, I can tell you.'

Roisin sighed. 'The Mallory got graffitied with PERVERTS PUBE. Was it a misspelling of pub? We'll never know. Maybe why I can't talk about this is that it sounds funny, but it was the opposite of funny. We have to make a joke of it to cope with it, right? I try, and I can't. I end up feeling like I am the joke.'

'It doesn't sound a funny thing to experience, at all,' Matt said supportively. 'You need your mum and dad to be your mum and dad.'

Roisin picked up a stone and threw it into the river, watching it glance off the water before disappearing under the surface.

'Our lives were in tatters and my mother was there in her black dress and birdcage veil at the wake, like Jackie Kennedy, crying to me and Ryan, "What *am I* going to do now?" It was her tragedy alone. As it turned out, what she was gonna do was have flings with a string of unsuitable men and get an even worse reputation.' Roisin looked over at him. 'There's a background reason she can't get staff, Matt. Women in this place don't talk to her much, and they don't let their husbands spend their money in her pub either. It was sixteen years ago, but in a village, that's sixteen minutes.'

Matt's eyes widened slightly. 'I see.'

Roisin was sorry if she'd soured the easy rapport he had with Lorraine. Equally, she was tired of sharing her mother's burdens.

'Were you close to your dad?' Matt asked. He chose the correct turn left, remembering the route from last time.

'I was when I was a kid. I was the apple of his eye and Ryan was my mum's favourite. I thought that was normal at the time, but I look back and realise, like everything else about my childhood, it wasn't, really. It was accepted that they sort of sponsored a child each and ignored the other one. My dad adored me when I was tiny with bunches and cute and his angel, then around thirteen, fourteen, when I became a hormonal, lumpy teenager with my own private life, he rejected me. I'll never know why now or if it would have improved. That's life's mystery, isn't it? You're left with best guesses. Oh my God.' Roisin paused.

'What?'

'That's what I've been doing, with Joe? A man has stopped loving me, and all my focus is on why and what I did wrong. Solving the mystery. Fuck,' Roisin said. 'Are you some kind of incredibly stealthy therapist in expensive boots?'

'I have been called a healer, yes,' Matt said, slipping back into the Matt McKenzie mode she was familiar with. 'And the boots are value per wear.'

'What about you? Why did you fall out with your family?' Roisin said.

'Oh . . . well.' He rubbed at his hair as he plucked up the courage. 'The context is that I was never very popular. My older brother Charlie was the heir, and I was the spare. He loved our school, went and got the high-flying job in the City they wanted for us. I hated school, was the disappointment, the problem. The unpromising one. Jesus, why am I telling you this, like it excuses me . . .' He broke off. 'Here's what happened, Roisin. My dad's brother was possibly, we thought, interfering with his teenage daughter, my cousin. There were hints and she told me coded things once. She didn't tell me I couldn't tell anyone, so I told my parents. It was discussed in hushed *well, what can you do* tones.

No one was going to do anything. Family comes first. Or, more accurately, *our reputation* comes first. So I reported it anonymously. I thought that the authorities would intervene, get her some help. Get her out of that house.'

'. . . You did the right thing?'

'I didn't,' Matt said.

They fell silent as they approached and passed some ramblers with sticks.

'I didn't consider the impact or the repercussions, at all. I revealed she'd said something. I made her life a living hell.'

'Your family were angry you'd done it? Did you tell them it was you?'

'When my uncle rang up in a rage, accusing me, they figured out it pretty fast. He denied everything, and my cousin did, too. She insisted it was malicious invention on my part. There was no charge, obviously, because without her testimony they had nothing. Who knows if it was true; I have to accept it might not have been. She had mental health issues, but given what could have happened to her, that's a chicken and egg situation, isn't it?'

Matt exhaled. His voice sounded different. 'Either way, she hasn't spoken to me since. I possibly falsely accused my uncle of the worst crime and tried to blow their family unit apart. She was fragile, and I wrecked her head. They all loathe me and want nothing to do with me, obviously, so I can't go to any family events. And as time went on, my own parents and brother started to miss me out of things. It started off as easier, and then, I guess . . .' Matt fell silent.

Roisin swallowed hard. She didn't want to say something trite she'd regret.

'So, yeah. That's who I am. Excommunicated. Self-important bad actor, to the point of destroying families.'

'You're the bad actor of this piece? *You?* I don't see it?'

'There's about nine other people who do.'

49

'Why are you terrible for trying to help someone?' Roisin said.

'Because I was thinking of myself and my self-image. Thinking I was a crusader for what was right, my juvenile ego. Rather than the consequences that she would bear. I was very "fuck this toxic conspiracy of silence!" The debate over whether or not it was the right thing to do, Rosh, has been proven by the fall-out. Positive outcomes: zero. Damage: huge.'

'You can't possibly know what would've happened if you'd not tried to do something. You'd have hated yourself.'

'The twist: I still hate myself,' Matt said, kicking a stone out of the way.

'The blame lies with your uncle and frankly, the bystanders, if they had suspicions and did nothing. You're the only innocent.'

'Thanks. I've tried those rationalisations, too. Then I think about what my uncle must have been like to live with after the visit from the police, and . . .' Matt shook his head. 'Plus, I didn't warn her.' His voice wavered and he was quiet for a moment while he got control back. 'I didn't warn her,' he said, with effort, 'which you're supposed to do. Believe me, I could recite all the guidance now for you off by heart. I didn't ask her. If I'd asked her, she'd have told me not to do it. Which is why I didn't, of course. I thought I knew better. I was going to *save* her. A twenty-three-year-old twat.'

'Have you seen her at all, since?'

'Nope,' Matt said. 'I wasn't going to make life worse for her by seeking her out.'

'Well,' Roisin said, 'If your mortal sin was taking action when no one else would, I can tell you it wasn't one. It wasn't your fault. Your family are wrong, and blaming you for what happened is genuinely horrific. I've said this to Joe many times, but I think that, if you grew up in a normal, happy family, you just can't fully imagine the mad ones. They're like trying to stay upright on a trampoline which everyone else is bouncing up and down on, as hard as they can.'

Matt said nothing.

'What was your family's reason for cutting you off?' Roisin said.

'It was more a deterioration. It became obvious it'd be better for everyone if I removed myself from the situation. We creaked through my brother's wedding day for appearances' sake, me somehow avoiding my uncle all night like *Mission Impossible*. After that I thought, *OK, if my presence only makes everyone uncomfortable, why bother?*'

'I'm so sorry. You don't deserve this at all,' Roisin said, and Matt gave her a grateful but resigned shrug of the shoulders.

They walked in silence for a minute.

'I've never told anyone this, even Joe,' Roisin said, not sure why she was telling anyone now. 'I didn't think it was really boyfriend-friendly. While we're unburdening. I slept with people I wish I hadn't, in the first few years after my dad died.' Roisin couldn't look at Matt when she said this, as confiding in a male friend about this felt tricky. '. . . People who I didn't like and didn't want. The brief period where I thought I was a femme fatale. I dressed up as Rita Hayworth in *Gilda* for a sixth-form fancy dress party and suddenly, overnight, I was popular. I thought, ah right, this is why Lorraine trades on it. So I had a string of boyfriends and tried to impersonate someone everyone loved, while hating myself. It took university and working at the bookshop to find my people.'

'Ah, the self-loathing hook-ups. Yes. Why do you think I never date anyone I might end up liking?' Matt said, terse but smiling. 'Any photos of you as Gilda? For reference.'

Roisin laughed. This was turning out to be three miles of epiphanies.

'When we set out on this walk, I thought we were two fun, laidback people,' Roisin said, patting Matt on the arm. 'In fact, we're a pair of fuck-ups. Harrowing.'

'Let's never do any soul-searching again,' Matt said.

'Agreed,' Roisin said. They found easy subjects to tide them over until The Mallory was once again in sight.

Roisin paused. She'd had time to think. She wanted to find a better part of herself for Matt, someone who wasn't bedazzled by Mean Boys.

'That was a good walk. I feel lighter,' Roisin said, brushing her hair out of her face to look at him properly.

'Yeah, actually, to my surprise, so do I. The importance of your 10k steps,' he said.

'Matt. My dad once said you often regret cowardice, but you never regret bravery.'

'It wasn't bravery, is the problem.'

'Can I ask you something – do you still think he did it? Your uncle?'

Matt looked perturbed. She wondered if he regretted telling her.

'. . . Yeah. I do.'

'Then you had no choice.'

'I did have a choice.'

'You made the right one, which was to do *something*.'

Matt looked at the ground. 'I could've done something, better.'

'An imperfect attempt to help is better than a self-protective nothing. I know that. Your family pushed you away because they know that. They hate themselves for it, and you remind them of it. Deep down, you know that. Or you will, one day.'

To prevent Matt feeling he had to reply, she hugged him. Roisin hoped her mother wasn't looking out the window.

She felt her phone buzz as she pulled her jacket off and found a WhatsApp from Joe's mum.

Roisin could you take me a photo of the magnolia tree? I'm trying to remember how far it is from the fence! Thank you XX

She typed back:

*Sorry Fay I'm actually out at my mum's at the moment!
Will sort pic as soon as I'm home. Rx*

*No problem, I'll discuss with my son when he arrives tomorrow.
Lots of love. XX*

Tomorrow? Roisin thought. Didn't Joe say he was going to York *today*? She could send a phishing text to confirm or deny, but she couldn't think what that would be, and it would make her feel unclean. Before *Hunter*, Roisin would have barely noticed this contradiction.

Was Joe, in fact, still in Manchester?

That was high risk if so, with Roisin only eleven miles away?

Sneaking around is rather exciting and becomes a bit of an art. It was very much part of what made it electrifying.

50

Getting along with her mother, when he sent her hormones aflutter, was one thing, but somehow McKenzie brought Terence on board, too. Roisin began to think of Matt as a sorcerer.

Such a stark irony, to be shunned by his own family and so effortlessly beloved by other people's.

Ostensibly, there was nothing about Matt that would be appealing to Terence. He was inherently suspicious of those who resided in the metropolis, tossing about with their e-scooters and braised chicory.

Yet through a winning combination of Matt seeking Terence's advice, chatting to him easily on topics of Terence interest, and a willingness to roll his sleeves up and clean up a dramatic spill from the exploding keg of guest ale, Terence was won round.

Enough to say to Roisin, 'How long's the pretty boy staying?' and when she said, 'Oh, only a few weeks,' he nodded contemplatively and said, 'Certainly a vast improvement on Ring Tone Brandon.'

Roisin knew better than to ask who Ring Tone Brandon was.

Watching Matt seduce everybody in his path made the rift with his own family all the stranger. That had played on Roisin's mind a lot since he'd told her. She thought about why his cousin might've sought Matt out to tell him. Whether she'd wanted him to report it, then recanted. Given he was older than his cousin, and the opposite sex, it seemed quite a tribute to him, to have chosen Matt to confide in. Roisin asked herself what she would've done.

She thought about how he had concealed it, and those strange Christmases; what the dismissal from Benbarrow Hall must have felt like as a result.

She thought about how he didn't date anyone he might end up liking, because he didn't like himself.

I think he can't be with Gina because it'd have to mean something, and he can't risk that.

Mid-week, Matt announced he had to head back to 'the Big Apple' – Manchester, for Webberley parochials – for a few days.

'My former employer wants to talk to me. No idea what's going on – maybe they want the gardening leave cash back. I'll hear them out at least, I guess, and the plants in my flat need watering,' Matt said. 'Don't worry, I'll be back in good time for the fête.'

Roisin suspected Matt might also have man-about-town dating business to attend to, but didn't pry. It wasn't as if there was much else to do on the evenings in Webberley other than scroll the apps. Who knew which movie stars were lurking behind false monikers on Hinge.

Lorraine had finally found a couple of bar staff to trial: a forty-year-old woman called Amy and a twenty-year-old lad called, somewhat surprisingly, Ernest. ('Must be coming back in,' Lorraine said.) Roisin agreed to make herself scarce rather than have them fighting for the soda gun with the landlady's daughter. She still didn't want to face the flat.

Therefore, early on Thursday evening, Roisin was rather ashamed to say, out of pure loose-endyness more than anything else, she decided to confront the final two episodes of *Hunter*.

Watching it on an iPad, headphones in, was a far lower-stakes experience than the Benbarrow screening room. Her mum's iPlayer history showed she'd still not watched the first episode: thank God.

It faded in with The Stone Roses' 'Fools Gold' and a sleeping Jasper Hunter. In the darkened bedroom, his girlfriend, Becca, waves his iPhone handset in front of Jasper Hunter's sleeping face and with Face ID, it ripples open.

His eyelids flicker as she scrolls and, as quietly as possible, replaces the phone in the charger on the nightstand.

Cut to Jasper rubbing his face of suds in the shower.

'I know what you're thinking, and you're wrong,' Jasper says to camera. 'I collect evidence, I don't create it myself. There's nothing on my phone, because only idiots get caught like that.'

There was procedural investigation, quips from Shaun Ryder, the murder of a nightclub hostess in Ancoats, and more frenzied rumping in Jasper's car, bare buttocks pressed against the glass. Roisin realised the greatest threat was to her attention span, not her nerves. She paused it to check how long it had left for episode two. Twelve minutes. Alright: she'd get through that and then go have a beer.

She was zoning out when Jasper was stood in the briefing room, discussing the dead waitress he'd had sex with in a toilet stall, while pointing at a whiteboard.

Another detective flopped open a notebook and read aloud: 'Hard to track down anything about her, something of a mystery and had no records. She's Croatian, from Split. Tangled love life. She was seeing a married man in the military police. We don't have a name for him . . .'

Roisin raised both hands as if she was a passenger in a crashing car, leaping off the sofa as if it was aflame. She'd always thought that 'jumped out of my seat' was a figure of speech.

She hit pause on the chatter on the iPad, hands trembling. Roisin replayed the words in her head. She dragged the arrow at the bottom of the monitor backwards and let the scene play again.

Hard to track down anything about her. She's Croatian, from Split. Tangled love life. She was seeing a married man in the military police. We don't have a name for him . . .

Roisin's teeth were chattering as if she'd walked into a meat locker. That was her – that was the waitress from Sesso, the night Joe said didn't matter, and nothing happened?

Roisin added up the points in her head: Croatia. (That was enough on its own, really. What were the odds on that coincidence?) The affair with a military policeman. Her lack of digital footprint. Oh, and her appearance, which Roisin thought must in fact be significant.

Here it was. The proof. Joe had sex with this girl? No, surely not? But how else was the Sesso waitress so clearly the inspiration for this character, someone he supposedly didn't know?

She messaged Joe.

When are you back today?

Just now! I was going to ask if you were free for dinner.

On my way

Roisin made a garbled explanation to her preoccupied mother and jumped into her car, scrunching gravel as she departed Webberley like a bat out of hell, a bat who nevertheless didn't want a speeding fine. Her thoughts were in a tumble throughout a journey that hit rush hour and dragged.

She was going to reveal she'd checked up on Joe, and yet it would surely pale into insignificance compared to what she was about to expose.

Her mind ran on and on with possibilities: was it a one-off, or was this something he did habitually? The thought of it, the thought that she had been sharing her bed with someone she didn't know . . .

Joe opened the door as she stood outside, keys poised. He looked dressed to go out, in a Fred Perry polo shirt.

'Hi, I reserved . . .'

'Hi.' Roisin stepped past him, to encourage him to shut the door again, which he did. 'I've got a question about episode two of *Hunter*.'

'Er. OK?'

'Can you explain to me how a waitress, Petra, who worked at Sesso, two years ago – and so was there when we went for Gina's birthday – was Croatian and had a secret married lover in the military police? And a character in your show, who looked like her, had the exact same biography?' She drew breath. 'Art mirroring life, to an uncanny degree?'

Joe looked at Roisin, eyes narrowed, apparently neither at ease nor startled. 'How do you know all this?' he said.

His voice was steady and calm. He was unruffled and composed. He was either a borderline psychopath or . . . he was innocent? Roisin didn't see how he could be.

'Let's work out how this coincidence happened, first?' she said, fronting considerably more bolshiness than she felt. 'You got home later than me that night, having left your scarf behind, collected it, and walked home. You showered when you got in, which was unusual. You obviously knew this girl. I'd like to hear the super-articulate explanation. Or am I being "ridiculous" again?'

'Oof, OK. I'm starting to go mad, I think . . .'

'YOU'RE starting to go mad? YOU?'

51

'There is an explanation for it, Rosh, yes. It's not that I had sex with anyone in a toilet stall. If that's what you're implying, and I'm pretty sure you are.'

'I'm listening.'

'I left my scarf behind that night. By accident, not intentionally. I walked back to get it, as you know. When I reached the restaurant, I saw it was round the neck of a waitress who was smoking outside. She was upset, she'd had a fight with her boyfriend. She offered me a cigarette. I thought it was a kindness to keep her company. I could also sense there was probably material in it.'

Roisin's eyes widened.

'Yeah, I know that sounds grubby, which is why I didn't disclose it at the time. There we are. I can't write about a man who stays in, looking into a laptop screen in the suburbs every night. Taking an interest in other people's lives and being a nosy bastard goes with the territory.'

Roisin wasn't going to encourage another soliloquy about screenwriting, so stayed silent.

'I hung around, chatted with her and smoked with her for

fifteen, twenty minutes. She told me the boyfriend was a married guy. I offered her some meagre advice she wasn't going to take, wished her luck. I walked home and showered, as I knew getting into bed next to you reeking of Parliament Lights, eight years after I quit, was not a great idea.'

'Yet by the time you came to write it, the way it played out was that you and Petra were climbing each other, yanking each other's hair?'

'Jasper Hunter and a character *inspired by Petra* did those things. Is this really what you think of me?'

'Have you seen your own show?! It's pretty hard to believe that a completely innocent chat became that sequence on screen. And that despite the encounter being innocent, you're only admitting to it now.'

Joe looked incredulous. 'OK, OK – if I'd done it myself, what are the logistics, here? We've established you were awake when I got home, right?'

Roisin gave the most miniscule of shrugs.

'Firstly, we have to believe a twenty-two-year-old wanted to shag a then-thirty-year-old, despite me seeming like Gandalf to her, I'm sure. I'm no Rufus Tate and I don't have any cinematic licence to clear a restaurant. Based on three minutes of chatting her up she's suddenly game, then we've got, what, fifteen minutes left at the absolute most to have a knee-trembler behind some bottle bins?'

Roisin said nothing.

'That wouldn't have appealed to me when I was a randy teenager. Let alone when I had a lovely home and a nice girlfriend to go home to,' Joe added.

Roisin had to admit that Joe's steadiness suggested he had nothing to hide.

'Sure you didn't take Petra's number? Arrange something else for another time? Then fail to mention it to me, for that reason?'

'Yes, I'm very sure. For one thing, I'm not a predatory creep towards distressed young women. Feel free to check my phone if you need to.'

(Except: only idiots leave evidence on phones, right?)

'After the lies you've told me, why should I believe this revised version where *yes, OK, you met her*?' Roisin said.

Yet she was chicken scratching, and she knew it. This fitted all the facts. If there was a hole to pick, she couldn't see it right now.

'The lies I've told you?! I didn't handle the confrontation at the country house well. I admitted that. I didn't lie to you?'

'You didn't mention fag breaks with heartbroken girls from Split, did you?'

'It wasn't relevant! You only wanted to know if I'd slept with her! Why would I get into this, given it didn't matter and sounds weird?'

'Thank you! At least you concede it sounds weird.'

'But having a brief and entirely clothed chat with someone of the opposite sex isn't being unfaithful, last I checked.'

Roisin's pounding heart started slowing, and she remembered that she had revealed more about herself than Joe. Clearly he did, too.

'Your turn. You still haven't told me. How do you know this, about Petra?'

Roisin swallowed. Sweat bloomed under her clothes. 'I went to Sesso for dinner, sat at the bar. Got chatting to the front of house and he told me.'

'*He?* A guy? You went and propped up a bar alone, and got into conversation? To check up on me?' Joe said.

'Yes.' Roisin felt, and looked, crappy.

'That doesn't sound like you at all.'

'I was pretty shaken up by *Hunter*, Joe. You know and I know that it contained at least one scene from real life. I got given the last week off from term because the kids were harassing me relentlessly about it, about whether it was real. Eventually I felt I had to find out.'

It was a manipulative moment to reveal this, yet it was an emergency for her dignity.

Joe's brow knitted. 'Right, because a bunch of thirteen-year-olds know me better than you do. Sorry, I can't get past you going to Sesso to chat to the front of house. What's he called?'

Was Joe jealous? Roisin hadn't much experience of this, yet she supposed she'd never given him cause.

'Rick.'

'You went out for dinner alone and acted like you were interested in the stories of some guy working there?'

'Yes.'

'I think the chances of that bloke getting the wrong end of the stick, using it as an opportunity and hitting on you, are pretty high. Which is why you'd never do it. It's wholly out of character.'

'I'd never do it, and yet I did,' Roisin said. It felt vile, being this brazen. Brazen, and hypocritical.

'Did you?' Joe said. 'On your mother's life?'

'Yup,' Roisin said, flinching hard at the lie and telling herself it was absolutely necessary, to keep Matt out of it. 'He didn't hit on me.'

'You honestly thought me shagging waitresses was so likely, you turned private investigator?'

'I didn't know what to think.'

'I think I'm entitled to feel pretty upset, don't you? I apologised for the scene with your mum, it was out of order. I don't think it justifies the suspicion I'm full scumbag. This is where we are, is it?'

Roisin didn't know how to respond. 'By the way, what day did you go to York, to your parents?' she said.

'Sunday.'

'Your mum said you were arriving Monday.'

Joe blinked, looked momentarily blank. 'Yeah. I kipped over at Dom's on Sunday. I knew we'd get pissed having a catch-up and I didn't want to get in late and wake my parents up. I said York – I didn't think you cared about my itinerary. Why would I tell you the wrong day?'

'I didn't know, that's why I asked.'

'Oh, so I can lurk around here with waitresses?'

'I have no—'

'Tell you what,' Joe said, interrupting, angry now, fumbling his phone out of his pocket and scrolling. 'Here. Proof. Most recent photos on my camera roll.' He turned the screen to face Roisin. He, Dom and his wife, Vic, sat on garden decking, a selfie, cheersing for the camera. 'It makes total sense I'd use my parents as a cover story given you talk to them directly all the time. Fuck's sake.'

Roisin said nothing.

'Why do I feel as if you almost want an excuse, here?' Joe said. 'If you want to finish with me, Roisin, do it. Stop all this casting around for a reason you can raise up that makes you the injured party.'

Roisin said, 'I wanted to know the truth. That's all.'

'I guess at least we've done this at home for free, instead of paying Relate to listen to it. What a way to discover your real opinion of me.'

Unlike their first two face-offs, Joe was on the moral high ground for this third round. He wasn't going to let Roisin off lightly. *Fair enough, really,* she thought. It wasn't as if she'd gone gentle on him.

She cleared her throat. She was going to have to confirm her decision to end things having made a flurry of false accusations. It was indeed what Wendy Copeland had code-named NFI.

'I think we should split up, Joe. Something's broken for me that can't be fixed. I think if we went to counselling, it'd delay the inevitable and waste your time, and I don't want to do that.'

'Wow,' Joe said, regarding her. She couldn't tell what percentage of his righteous indignation was fury and what was hurt. She was busy trying to keep control herself.

He stepped backwards and sat down on the arm of the sofa. 'Fucking *wow*. Ten years together, and you throw it in my face that we're over five minutes before I go to Los Angeles. Now you repeat it, after going behind my back to check up on me and accusing me of fucking around. So it didn't matter whether I was guilty or not? You're still doing this?'

'I'm sorry,' Roisin said stupidly. It sounded awful, because it was.

'Right, well,' Joe said, after an agonising pause. 'The paperwork on the apartment is done – I sent it back today. I'll start looking for flats and packing my things up.'

'I don't want you to give me your share of this apartment. It's insanely generous, but it's too much.'

'I gave you my word and I keep my word. It also means we don't have to drag this out and get involved in interminable back and forth over selling it, solicitors, all that shit. I don't want any of it. I want to go.'

'OK.'

'Well, I don't *want* to go, at all. But.'

He gave Roisin a penetrating, sullen look. It should look like pure loathing, yet it was somehow a Rhett Butler stare that she feared could equally precede shouting or trying to kiss her. Like their initial showdown, it was as if Joe was finally interested.

A thought came to Roisin: that clear bell voice of her subconscious. *Now he can't have you, he really wants you.* A tired love had become a sharp hunger again.

'I'll stay on at my mum's to give you space,' Roisin said.

'Great.'

There was nothing to say as comfort that Joe wouldn't throw

back in her face. It was too soon, and quite possibly the only times that would ever be available were too soon and too late.

Roisin went to let herself out, feeling sick and foolish with how badly it had gone thanks to her rash accusations. It was as if she'd crashed into someone's parked car when arriving to break news of a death.

Play stupid games, win stupid prizes.

'Is there anyone else?' Joe said, as she opened the door.

'What?' Roisin said.

'Oh, sorry, is this mistrust a one-way street? Is there anyone else you haven't told me about?'

'No, of course not.'

There was nothing else to be said.

She got into her driver's seat with the lightheaded feeling of having made history, and not a good chapter. She'd known this day was coming now for a long time, but it was no less weird. Like the shock of a death after a protracted illness. *It was slow, but fast at the end.*

Like Ernest Hemingway said of going bankrupt, in two ways: gradually, then suddenly.

On a drive back in biblically torrential rain, Roisin asked herself how she'd travelled from the girl laughingly shrugging off the suggestion of infidelity to that counsellor months before, to the one covertly researching her partner. Perhaps Meredith was right; the decision to end was sufficiently momentous that she wanted objective proof that she should.

She pushed herself to find the deeper answer as she sat, engine idling in the early evening traffic, quiet tears running down her face as the windscreen wipers hypnotically, mechanically swipe-swiped. What was it about *Hunter* that had changed everything? Apart from the mere fact it involved sex and betrayal?

It was because by watching Joe's onscreen alter ego, she'd become seized by the certainty that there were different versions of him, and she'd been living with only one of them.

52

Roisin didn't tell Lorraine what had happened in the days following, nor did she receive anything from Joe's parents or friends to demonstrate that he had. Roisin felt sure that Fay would've called her within an hour.

Joe had one brother, Grant, who was perma-single: Fay had always treated Roisin as her substitute daughter.

When she checked something on the iPad, she saw *Hunter* episode two still there, minutes to the end, last instalment unwatched. It was pathetically hilarious, how little she trusted herself to view it. Knowing she'd overreacted once, and predicting she might again, had still not created enough self-awareness to stop it happening. She had beclowned herself.

Also, her mother was in enough of a tizzy with the forth-coming fête. Roisin didn't much fancy broaching her singlehood from her high-achieving boyfriend while anxiety about social status already ran high.

Lorraine would, as ever, put her own feelings first in her reaction. *What about Roisin being on the shelf at thirty-two, what if she didn't meet anyone as good as Joe, what about grand-children, and, oh no, Grace and Imogen would crow!* (If that sort of consideration was raised, Roisin couldn't be sure she'd keep her temper.) Roisin would find herself reassuring her mother.

She needed her heart to heal a little before she exposed herself to all that noise. She *did* tell Meredith and Gina, wondering if they were tiring of the *one leg in, one leg out* hokey-cokey of this separation, and explaining they were currently the only ones informed.

Meredith
So sorry. It's sad, but it clearly needed doing and you've done it now. You can't stay with someone just cos you might go to the Oscars. Xx

Gina
Absolutely, though I probably would. Hope you are both ok. Should we message Joe? Xx

Roisin
Yes I'm sure he'd appreciate that xx

It was probably for the best for Joe to know she'd shared the news. Could she delegate his breaking it to Dev and Anita? That was the one she resisted the most. He'd had no preparation, making it a longer conversation that Roisin didn't anticipate with pleasure. She was announcing the effective end of the Brians format to the person who held the Brians dearest.

Roisin then got a one-to-one communique from Meredith, which put telling Dev on temporary hold.

I bring glad tidings of Anita's uterus. Her stomach bug wasn't morning sickness, but the prospect spooked her enough to do a test. In the time it took to turn negative, she realised she absolutely didn't want to be breaking the surprise news to Dev and her family this many months out from a wedding. She's back on the pill and she and Dev have scrapped Italy. No word on Miami, but hopefully your tactful intervention has caused deeper thought there. They've gone on a break to Sóller to thrash out the details.

ALSO, having finally banished the spectre of McKenzie, Gina's going on a date with a fella in her office called Aaron. She'd mentioned him a lot in the last year & I'd wondered if anything could happen there, and I think now it finally can.

So, corners being turned, tides turning, leaves turning. I am still getting absolutely none, mind you. Hope Matt shaped up well as an employee. I miss him. Hopefully one day Gina will find herself indifferent to his WASPy erotic power and we can have him back. <3 M xx

Matt reappeared in The Mallory before opening, late Saturday morning, looking so good in an blue Oxford shirt that Gina would likely not have been indifferent to his WASPy erotic power, had she seen him. He was carrying a couple of boxes.

'What happened with work?!' Roisin asked.

'Oh,' he said, looking oddly gratified she remembered. 'It's quite a bizarre reversal of fortune. Former CEO found out his son sacked me. Went bananas. Has reinstated me, saying I can keep my gardening leave as a bonus and take the rest of August off. I'd have said no, because who wants to be where they're not welcome, right? But the son persuaded me he'd come to see it his dad's way. I think it helped that the restaurant chain I had brought on board kept asking where I was.'

'That's incredible! Well done.'

'It is a bit. Given your mum's insisted on paying me, I'm going to give my wages to a worthy charity. The worthy charity of the Webberley fête. I'm running a bar in the garden, stocked with some wholesale I've ordered, that should be arriving' – he checked his watch – 'in an hour, if you're OK to sign for it?'

'Yes, of course. Matt, this is Superman stuff. What's in your boxes?'

'Fripperies,' Matt said. 'We're going to make the beer garden a magic grotto. These will form a starlight canopy. If the necessary iron poles get here later today, that is.'

He set the boxes down and pulled out reams of festoon lights, Edison bulbs on a black wire.

'Ooh, nice.'

'That's not all, young lady,' Matt said. 'I had these made.'

He unshouldered and unzipped his duffle bag, producing a stack of leaflets. They advertised The Mallory's fête efforts: BBQ, garden cocktails and games.

'Haha! Did Lorraine sign all this off?'

'Oh yes. "Knock yourself out, it can't go any bloody worse," was the direct quote.'

Roisin laughed and thought what how transformative Matt was to this place. His enthusiasm for The Mallory had gone some way to detoxifying it, for her. He turned the flyer over.

Guess Meatball's Weight! was printed next to a photo of the scowling, portly cat.

'Lucky find on my camera roll,' Matt said, tapping his nose. 'Decided to go for it.'

'What if Meatball doesn't turn up?'

'I know celebrities can be temperamental, but I suspect the smell of sausage fat hitting sizzling charcoal briquettes will lure Webberley's greatest networker out to mingle with his constituents.'

Roisin was properly laughing now. 'Listening to the concerns of ordinary people, nicking their chips.'

'Exactly. I'm off to glad hand the high street, if you're alright to hold the fort?'

'Yep.' She beamed. 'Good luck.'

Lorraine appeared from the back of the bar, looking harassed.

'Was that Matt?'

'Yeah. Seen this?' Roisin held out the flyer.

Lorraine inspected it, her expression softening with delight in a way that Roisin had rarely, if ever, witnessed.

'He's a sweetie, isn't he? Such a shame for womanhood that he's gay.'

'What? Matt's not gay.'

Lorraine's mouth fell open. 'He's too beautiful to be straight, surely? What about his clothes?!'

Roisin started laughing.

'He's got that nice Kelly-green jacket! He's NOT GAY? Oh my God. Rosie, *keep Imogen away from him*. And Grace! She's had a jawline rejuvenation at the Harley and her audacity is at an all-time high.'

Roisin's laughter became helpless.

Lorraine turned the leaflet over and saw Meatball. 'Hmph, sly little fucker. Still, rather him than me. I've packed on six pounds eating Jaffa Cakes with the stress of all this.'

Roisin rolled her eyes as she got her mirth under control. Such intermittent and unnecessary self-flagellation was sadly a hallmark of Lorraine's relationship with her body.

'Don't start with your *diets don't work* spiel,' Lorraine added. 'If diets don't work, how come everyone's gotten thinner when they're rescued after shipwrecks.'

Infallible logic, and a case Roisin had heard many times, despite her mother never being in possession of the BMI of any survivors of nautical disasters.

53

'You've said the barbecue will have vegetarian options?' Lorraine said, a fist pressing into one nicely tailored cream woollen hip, the other hand grasping Matt's flyer. *Say what you like about my mum,* Roisin thought, *she can seriously wear a pencil skirt.* Her dry-cleaning bills must be eye-watering. 'You're not leaving Terence in charge of that bit, are you?'

'Nope. It's going to be a job lot of corn cobs and meat-free hot dogs,' Matt said. 'I've assigned Roisin to that stand. I'm cocktails. Terry is meat. You're front of house.'

'Thank goodness! I would describe Terence's idea of vegetarian food as *macabre*,' Lorraine said. 'He once tried to feed them discs of processed burger cheese with a slice of beef tomato pressed into it, slipped into a pitta pocket.'

'Oof. That's probably how the BTK Killer got started. Sent them to taunt the detective,' Matt said, and Roisin spat some of her post-closing time G&T.

Their reward for a day of fête prep and bar service was a takeaway from the Golden Dragon in Knutsford, the foil-lidded cartons now covering the largest table by the window in the saloon bar.

'You've done this because you know I'm on a diet, haven't you?' Lorraine said, before placing two spring rolls on a saucer, and after a moment's reflection, a third.

'There's plenty spare, Mum, have what you want,' Roisin said.

'How dare you!' Lorraine said. 'I'll have some of that chicken and a bit of egg fried rice, leave you two kids to it. See you tomorrow.'

'Night, Lozza!' Matt said, making a *who, me?* gesture when Roisin did an exaggerated double-take.

Once Lozza had safely ascended the stairs beyond the bar, Roisin told Matt about the second episode of *Hunter* and her failed interrogation of Joe. She stressed she'd said she alone had been to Sesso.

'Being fair,' Matt said, digging a fork into crispy beef, 'I'd have drawn the same conclusions that you did. Joe's created a lot of drama around his drama by shutting you out of his creative process, huh. You're not someone who'd lose it if he'd simply said, *hi honey I'm home, got my scarf, had a crafty cigarette with the waitress, might make a plot line, off for a shower.*'

'That's true.' That was *very* true. Joe had started fetishing unnecessary secrecy. Nevertheless, Roisin hadn't put herself in a great position to make that case. '. . . But I'm resigning with immediate effect from the prying,' Roisin said. 'It was a pretty awful prelude to "I am definitely sure we're over, bye."'

'Really?' Matt said. He gave her a direct look and Roisin was grieved to read disbelief within it. She clearly hadn't come across as very decisive.

'Yes. Don't tell my mum yet. But I need to do something to prove it, clearly. Something highly distasteful, that involves collecting my tights from a hedgerow.'

'Speaking of which, I have an actual social event in a week's time. There's a soft launch of a sister bar to a place I supply, new one is in Ancoats. The front of house invited me, and I thought, ack, why not. She seems nice.'

'*She.* Oh aye. In the same way you said to an unknown lady, *join me in Lisbon on a work trip? Why not!*' Roisin made a thumbs-up.

'Fuck youuuuu,' Matt said, tipping beer bottle to lips.

'Imagine, if you cop off with anyone next week, the last person in your bed was Amelia Lee. Don't tell her that until afterwards – it's terrifying. Also might make you sound like a dangerous fantasist.'

'I didn't sleep with Amelia,' Matt said, snapping a piece of prawn toast in half and biting it with good teeth. 'Or even kiss her, come to think of it.'

'What? You went to Portugal with her? Then to London in the middle of the night?'

'The whole thing was like a chaste, extended audition for the role of Civilian Boyfriend, and I didn't pass it. I don't think she ever had a serious intention of getting involved with a normal. She was like a giantess playing with a box of Lego.'

'Oh.'

'Being fair, I think she was also aware of the bragging rights attached to bedding her, and that made her very fussy and careful too.'

Roisin pondered: Joe had always said Matt was a dissolute rogue, yet if so, where were his victims? None of his capers seemed to have victims, only lively and willing participants.

Roisin speared a piece of green pepper. 'Have you ever had a serious girlfriend? I've only known you being a . . . er, roving bachelor.'

'Translation: have I always been this emotionally frigid dogboy?'

'DOGBOY! Hahahahaha. No, I suppose I meant – have you ever been in love?'

'Yeah, I was, once. Well, still am. That any hope of her was lost a long time ago doesn't stop me being in love. Oh God. What a twat. That sounds like a John Mayer lyric.'

'What happened?'

Matt brushed prawn toast dust from his hands. 'I confided how I felt about her to a friend, who I thought I could trust. He wasn't even single, so I didn't think he was any threat. He immediately made a move on her and they've been together ever since. They emigrated to the other side of the world a couple of years ago; I've hidden her on social media to avoid the inevitable baby announcement. I've come to terms with my loss, in some respects. That's the one thing I can't face. *Scroll scroll* your auntie's angry about a rude cashier in ASDA, *scroll scroll* funny raccoons, *scroll scroll* the love of your life is WITH HIS CHILD.' Matt made a 'brrr' face.

This was an eerie mirror of Gina's processes with Matt, and yet Roisin wasn't going to break her confidence by telling him this.

'Oh no,' Roisin said. 'No one since measures up?'

'I've never again had that simple, complete and over-whelming certainty that someone was the one for me, no. Though, being fair, I don't know how much chance I've given anyone else.'

Oof. Once again, he and Gina perfectly understood each other. Divided by a common language.

'Sometimes, in dating, I feel like I ace the interview because I don't really want the job,' Matt said. 'Does that sound REALLY big-headed?'

'Lol, yes it does,' Roisin said. 'Do you think this woman would have gone out with you, if you'd asked in time?'

Matt shrugged. 'No, probably not. My romantic "gazumping" is an ego-saving myth. It wasn't first come, first served. I think I was invisible to her.'

'It's hard to imagine you being invisible,' Roisin said, adding a tactical gurn, to make it clear she wasn't buttering his muffin.

'Depends what you're looking for,' Matt said, mildly.

54

'What are you wearing? For the fête?' Lorraine asked Roisin.

Roisin, by way of answer when she was eating a piece of toast and reading the morning papers, simply lifted her leg in black polka-dot tights, in the style of a dog cocking it over undergrowth.

'Oh NO! Rosie! That's rank madness! You look like one of the teenagers who drink scrumpy by the post office.'

Matt barked with laughter and Roisin flicked the Vs at him.

'You *must* wear a dress!'

'This is a dress,' Roisin said, motioning towards her cord pinafore.

'It's like a school uniform dress. It's a sturdy bag. Borrow one of mine,' Lorraine said.

'Ugh, no! It's a charity fete, not *Strictly Come Dancing*,' Roisin said, the sort of idle parent-baiting that qualified as a leisure activity.

'Charming,' Lorraine said, as if she'd not criticised Roisin's clothing.

Since being home, Roisin had unintentionally sartorially reverted to her early twenties: stretchy dark cotton dresses with spaghetti straps, sturdy lace-up boots, flannel shirts thrown over the top. Hair up, in a bundle. Grungey, in essence. She was still wearing plenty of make-up, so she didn't think her mother had much to complain about.

Lorraine's strenuous efforts to maintain her glamour and beauty were to be admired, yet Roisin wondered if her mother would ever allow herself to be old, one day. If she even wanted to. Whether there was an off ramp, in the business of being pleasing to the male gaze.

For her fortieth birthday, Lorraine wore a bottle-green fishtail velvet gown with raspberry tulle trim, exploding in a waterfall at mid-calf height, which was so tight she had to be fastened into it with a glue gun. She'd sang The Supremes' 'Baby Love' down a microphone to Roisin's father in a packed room at The Stanneylands in Wilmslow. Her parents still had status, the good sort, at the time. Teenage Roisin had been two parts mortification to one part awe.

'I'll be changing, to be clear,' Matt said, by the door in a t-shirt and shorts, off for his morning run round the village. Webberley was not blessed with a gym.

'You'll look *fine*,' Lorraine said.

'Oh, indeed. Male privilege,' Roisin said.

After Matt had left, Lorraine said, 'Spoke to your brother last night.'

'Ah, right.' There was an evident *and* to this statement that Roisin ignored.

'I told him you and Matt were helping me out.'

'OK.'

'Ryan said to be . . . cautious. He's worried in case Matt

307

gets his feet under the table and suggests taking over a portion of the pub. I told him not to worry, but . . .'

'What do you mean? Take over how?'

'As in, suggests co-ownership with me. Legally.'

'*What*?!' Roisin said, outraged. Old furies came rushing in, like opening a submerged car window under water. 'Are you on drugs? Matt's doing you a huge favour by working for peanuts – he's not after anything!'

'Calm down! You know Ryan – he's a long way away, and he's being overcautious.'

'He's a selfish shit, worrying about his inheritance and wrapping it up in concern for you, more like.'

'You always leap to the worst possible conclusion.'

'Sorry, what is the good conclusion in, "Perhaps Roisin's friend is conniving to defraud you"?'

'He was merely asking whether Matt had longer-term intentions regarding The Mall!'

'Why on earth would anyone see this bang average place and think "hoh, a goldmine"? It's been a millstone round your neck for years.' Roisin was being insulting and didn't care.

'Yes, but Ryan doesn't know Matt and doesn't know how nice he is. He heard a man was sorting everything out and he wanted to be sure I kept control of the pub. He was protecting my interests. That was all.'

'You always do this. Whatever Ryan does, you turn it into virtue. If Ryan had genuine concerns about Matt, why not bring them to me? You know, the person who knows Matt and vouched for him?'

'I'm sure he would if you ever called him, Roisin! You don't exactly make yourself available to your family.'

'IS THIS NOT AVAILABLE?!' Roisin bellowed, flailing her arms to indicate her presence in front of her mother.

'Honestly, if I'd known you'd fly off the handle, I'd not have said anything . . .'

'No good turn goes unpunished, eh? Slagging my friends off as potential thieves is next level. As if I'd put you at risk! Did he even address that part?'

Lorraine didn't answer, and was making an *I will have to suffer my daughter's terrible temper as best I can* long-suffering face, arms crossed and eyes to ceiling.

'Also, Matt's been given his job back. He's employed. He *could* simply enjoy his break before he starts again; instead, he's putting in hours here.'

'Knock knock! Bit of pre-match nerves, is it? Haha!'

Terence let himself in, arms full of cellophane packets of catering pack floured baps.

Roisin was too annoyed to feel embarrassed and said, 'Something like that. I'll leave you to talk through the plans with Terry. Give me a shout when McKenzie, aka The Talented Mr Ripley, wants to start decorating the garden and stealing fivers from the till.'

'What's up with her?' she heard Terry say, and her mother replied in a stage-whisper, 'It's *Ladies Day At Ascot* on the calendar today, if you know what I mean. Pay it no heed.'

Roisin stomped upstairs, lay on her bed – unseeing eyes boring into the drum-shaped lampshade – and boiled on what had been said. She considered firing off a *what did you say that for, please?* at Ryan, yet dismissed it within seconds. She knew exactly what she'd get back: a bloodless, curt dismissal. *I simply wasn't clear what his interest in The Mallory might be* followed by a *how are you?* which wasn't a *how are you* as much as it was a *that's as much time as I'm giving your tantrum.*

Fallings-out weren't best conducted on encrypted messaging platforms, across oceans, anyway.

Thing was, it wasn't Ryan she was angry with, not really. Yes, he could be an arsehole, but she knew that. A 3,500-miles-away arsehole.

It was her mother she was mad at. Matt's natural brightness and Lorraine's current reliance on their help had made her forget what she was really like, why she gave her mum a wide berth most of the time.

Lorraine took what she needed, then took some more, yet when Roisin needed some giving back – like, say, her mother putting Ryan politely in his place when he was undermining his sister – Lorraine went AWOL, playacted dumb. Support was something she sought but never bestowed.

Why even tell Roisin that Matt had been misspoken? Because Ryan was always higher in the pecking order. Even as Matt and her daughter saved her fête and saved her face, Lorraine couldn't resist subtly reasserting that her son was CEO of the company. That his was the five-star standard of care. She rewarded words and took actions for granted.

Four years after her dad died, her mother was seeing a man with terrible moccasin shoes called Gary, who drove an uninsured car and flirted with Roisin. Roisin knew Gary had very bad word of mouth among the womenfolk of Webberley, and that sort of grapevine was rarely wrong.

She tried to get her mother to see sense. Ryan told Lorraine she should do whatever made her happy. He resisted Roisin's entreaties to raise doubts, though she knew he had them. Ryan never made an intervention that could cost him popularity or even minor difficulty. Lorraine became engaged to Gary. She then discovered he was already married and had a petty criminal record.

Both of her offspring were at university, yet Roisin was required – with the emotional equivalent of a gun at her temple – to miss nearly two months of her course to come home and nurse her mother through a mini-breakdown and keep the pub running.

Her mother's legend recorded that her recovery was magicked into being the day that Ryan had scraped enough from his student budget to send her an incredible bouquet. She still repeated the emetic message on the card about how *his mother was a queen who deserved nothing less than a king*.

Moccasins Gary had been expunged from the record, and Lorraine instead recalled only that Roisin was so much of a daddy's girl, she'd scared Lorraine's suitors away.

55

Roisin marched into Lorraine's bedroom and threw open the wardrobe doors as if it was a rifle cabinet. The dazzling rainbow of silky fabrics demonstrated where The Mallory's refurb budget was going. Quite a few things still had their cardboard tags dangling.

She selected a black metallic evening dress that looked like it was made of strips of precious bin liners. It was maxi-length and would encircle her legs in a way that made it not the most practical for mobility, but what the hell.

Back in her room, Roisin had to pull and tug at the zip somewhat, having a similar genetic blueprint to her mother but with a more generous chest and hips. When it finally fastened, it gave her a pleasing hourglass shape: a beguiling mixture of everything covered and provocative slink.

Roisin tied a striped butcher's apron over the top and laced her boots back on. She was delighted with herself and felt a pubescent-level roar of rebellion. She looked like an It Girl heiress at Glastonbury.

The sensation was only improved minutes later by sashaying

her sparkled-black shiny bottom past her mother on the front bar.

She garnered a shout of 'Ooh la la!' and a full set of turned heads from the grotty men cabal. And a, 'WHAT THE! That's Hervé Léger and it's NEW!' from Lorraine.

'Harvey Leg said it was fine,' Roisin said, blowing her a kiss.

Outside, taking up her stand, Roisin had completely the opposite problem to the one she feared. She wasn't standing like a nelly, clacking her BBQ tongs like castanets: she was overrun.

Within an hour of opening, customers poured into The Mallory's garden, now canopied with vintage bulb fairy lights and ringed with wooden planters full of flowers, thanks to Matt's efforts. The throng were definitely not The Mall's usual crowd: shoals of girls with peach-coloured and peroxide hair, fairy wings and heart-shaped deely boppers.

Roisin guessed Matt's smooth talking on the high street had decontaminated the pub's rep as one only for the stolid old guard.

Roisin's meat-free offer proved extremely popular with a village that now contained many more vegans, flexitarians and clean eaters than it used to. Although clean eating didn't seem to preclude ingesting a river of white rum.

She and Terence were out of produce within two hours.

'Locusts!' Terence said. 'Scenes of unbridled gannetry.'

He had Lorraine's attitude to people of the world either accepting or declining to spend their money at The Mallory: either way, it was an impertinence.

Matt was busiest of all, with his 'Five Classic Cocktails, Each A Fiver' stand, hurriedly hacking limes to pieces and chopping mint whenever he got a spare moment.

'Want a hand?' Roisin said, and Matt handed her his ice bucket. 'Refill that if you would, ta.'

Roisin made a salute.

Terence went inside to help her mother, so Roisin stayed garden side, to roam for empties and play supporting act to Matt. As his platonic friend, she was careful not to reflect or swoon in any way at how he looked with shirt sleeves rolled up, concentrating, a light sweat on his brow.

'Hiiiiiiiiii, Roisin!' Grace and Imogen chimed in unison as they lighted upon her.

'Hello! Very nice of you to come.'

'Oh we'd not have missed it,' Grace said, swooping in for a double kiss, Imogen following suit. 'Not seen you in an age, Roisin.'

Grace and Imogen were always easy and pleasant company, contrary to her mother's dark mutterings. Roisin supposed Lorraine had long felt banished from genteel society and had made Grace and Imogen erroneously representative of that rejection, as they were also a solo mother and daughter of the same ages. It was as if Lorraine and Roisin were the Slutty Halloween Costume versions of them.

'This place is *heaving*. Never seen The Mallory so busy. Love the little spruce you've given it. Top *sprucing*,' Imogen said, precisely the kind of remark Roisin was glad her mother wasn't here to bristle at.

Everything was a slight if you were determined to find one.

Despite being only Roisin's age, Imogen was in a padded headband, blazer and loafers. She was rather gorgeous in a Ralph Lauren Polo sort of way. Everything about her was either the colour of caramel or the minky-pink of a worn ballet dancer's shoe. Her mother had the highlighted, layered hair of someone who made weekly salon trips, and a navy dress with a corsage at the waist and a knife-pleat skirt. She twitched at Roisin's apron and said, 'Is there some sort of marvellous gown under that? Take it off, let us see!'

'Oh . . . I was protecting it from corn cob splatter . . .'

Roisin unlaced her apron, pulled it away and made a little 'gameshow hostess girl' curtsy.

'Oh my goodness! We don't often get to see you dolled-up – you look like a real vamp!' Grace said, approvingly, as Roisin stood slightly sheepishly in her robbed finery.

'Love those body-con bandage dresses,' Imogen agreed. 'People said they were of their time, but they're a classic now. You've absolutely got the curves for it. I'd look like a plastic safety-wrapped suitcase.'

Roisin laughed and felt relieved that Lorraine wasn't here to fume at any of that.

'That guy over there. He works here?' Imogen said, looking over at Matt.

'Oh, Matt's my friend,' Roisin said. 'Helping out.'

Despite Lorraine's terrors of their predatory nature around

the menfolk, she'd not actually expected this to come to pass.

'He's *frightfully* good-looking, isn't he?' Imogen said.

'Oh, if I was twenty years younger!' Grace said. 'I do my Kegels. Immo got a Gwyneth Jade Egg!'

'Mum!' Imogen barked. 'How's Joe?'

She was still looking at Matt, and Roisin caught the implication easy enough.

'Fine!' she said brightly.

'We loooooooved *SEEN*,' Grace said. 'Immo and I were glued to it, weren't we? We never guessed the courier had cosmetic surgery! Very clever chap, your man. Any chance of making your mother the happiest woman in Cheshire and doing a bit of DUM DUM DE DUM, DUM DUM DE DUM . . .' Grace glanced around – 'Look at the space here!' – and winked.

'I'm not ready to get married yet, Grace. I've not sown enough wild oats,' Roisin said, as she knew Grace did 'bawdy'.

'Oh! Heavens above!' she shrieked.

'She thinks I'm joking,' Roisin said to Imogen, who also screeched.

'You are the funniest, Sheena,' Imogen said. 'I always say that to Mum.'

Grace and Imogen were exactly the kind of people to produce a nickname for you out of nowhere and apply it liberally.

They moved on to circulate, and half an hour later, Roisin glanced over and saw Imogen almost bent double with laughter at something Matt had said. She straightened up, put the back of her hand to her mouth and the other on the small of his back, and Roisin felt a sharp stab of an unexpected, unnamed emotion.

She looked at Matt, and he saw her. His eyes travelled down to her dress, and suddenly it felt two sizes tighter and considerably more revealing than it had done before.

Terence tapped her on the shoulder. 'Have you seen that fat cat? I'm due to clock off but some American tourists want a photo with it. They seem to think it's a celebrity, God help us. Has Elvis left the building? He's a candidate for dying in the same way, that's for sure.'

'Meatball was under that picnic table last I saw,' Roisin said, pointing. 'Want me to retrieve him?'

'Much obliged.'

Terence liked cats even less than her mum.

Imogen grabbed Roisin as she passed her on the way into the pub, halfway through her mission.

'Heading off now – wonderful day, thank you! We MUST go for some bubbles back in Manchester soon, give me some dates.' Then, leaning in, she said, 'Can you do me a favour and forward your pal Matt's number? He's cute as hell, isn't he?'

'Hah, sure,' Roisin smiled, over Meatball's bulk, knowing full well that Imogen only spontaneously craved Proseccos with raspberries in order to pump her for information about McKenzie.

'Thank you!' Imogen said, making a heart shape with her hands, fingertips pressed together, which almost made Roisin change her mind.

56

As darkness fell, she went to find Matt.

'OK, wasn't it?' he said to her, arms folded, surveying the thinning hordes with satisfaction. 'We made a metric ton for the charity, way beyond the target, and your mum is calling her takings a 'gold rush'. That's good fêteing.'

Roisin slung her arm around his waist. 'OK? Utterly amazing. *Look what you did.* You are a prince among men. You have shifted the paradigm.'

Whether Lorraine maintained the momentum Matt had found was yet to be seen, but he'd forever proven it could be done. He'd lifted a sixteen-year-old curse.

'Glad to have helped,' Matt said. 'It's given me an inner glow.'

'Hope that's not Terry's burger relish. I saw Del Monte fruit cocktail going into it.'

She and Matt laughed like Beavis and Butthead. Roisin saw a sixty-something woman seated at a picnic table shoot them both an adoring look, obviously taking them for a couple.

Roisin beamed back. Matt saw the woman too, and glanced appraisingly at Roisin.

318

In a split second, she became acutely self-conscious. Her arm, chucked around Matt's middle, demonstrating how easy she was with him, was suddenly heavy as lead. She could sense every inch of her limb making contact with his midriff, feel the heat of his skin through his shirt. What had been so thoughtlessly done was charged with electricity.

Was her arm even positioned normally? Roisin couldn't tell. She was as stiff-jointed as a shop mannequin. Someone else had cranked her elbow hinge, curled her fingers, and she could only maintain the pose.

Matt put his hand over hers and moved her arm down to her side, and her breathing stopped. A clear indication that Roisin had overstepped, and that he felt awkward too. But . . . he didn't let go of her hand? They stood looking out over the garden, their palms clasped together.

In a little invisible game of raising the stakes, Roisin adjusted her hand inside his grip, interlocking their fingers. Matt responded by squeezing her hand. She squeezed back. *What was going on?* She felt incredible tension in parts of her body that were not her hand.

Lorraine burst into the garden, ringing the bell for last orders like a town crier, and she and Matt sprang apart like foxes who'd had water thrown over them.

Roisin obsessed about the surreptitious handholding, and what it meant, for the rest of the shift. Probably nothing; she was out of practice at courting rituals.

In this burgeoning attraction to Matthew McKenzie, was she the world's biggest hypocrite? She'd tried in vain to get a charge to stick with Joe, and yet, 'heavy flirting with one of our best mates, a New York minute after we split up', was hardly acceptable.

Joe didn't need to know. He'd never know. Nor did Matt, for that matter. Or not explicitly.

'Kids, I'm going to turn in, I'm beat,' Lorraine said, once all chores were finished, towels thrown over beer taps, drip trays up-ended.

'You do look tired,' Roisin said, then, in case it sounded like a dig, added, 'Very well-earned exhaustion, too. What a fête! Meatball was a star turn!'

'Don't pander to that grotesque beast. You're like Neville Chamberlain with Hitler. Thank you, both of you. I've had compliments about how our efforts were the best of the village all day.'

'Pleasure,' Matt said kindly as she left them.

Roisin sensed her mother might've been chastened by Roisin's outburst over Ryan, and that was no bad thing.

'Right then, Roisin Walters,' Matt said, picking up two glasses upside down by their stems and setting them down on the bar top. 'Manhattan?'

'Hell, yeah,' she said, getting a shiver at the prospect of their being alone together.

57

Roisin was experiencing a surge of pleasure such as she'd not known in a long while. She'd warmed to The Mallory: no longer was it a prison with frilly pelmets. She saw it as Matt did; it enveloped her instead of oppressing her. The glow of sconce lights on the red walls, the dark wood, the leather stud-back booths and tartan stools, the rumble of the dishwashers: soothing. As was the velvet quiet of the countryside beyond the windows.

She'd always found the noise of the city relatively comforting and the silence of the countryside spooky. Times were changing.

The Manhattan was helping.

'I believe I have to pass your phone number on to Imogen,' Roisin said. 'Tireless work.'

'Which one was Imogen again? Did she have the head thing, that royal children wear?'

'*Which one* – phew. Though today of all days I can't complain about your allure. I'm so grateful to you acting as a lighthouse to today's mermaids.'

'Don't say that, thanks.' Matt frowned.

'Why not?'

'It's not complimentary.'

'How could that not be complimentary?' Roisin said, puzzled.

'When it means a puddle-deep peacock of a man, slutting about. Sneaky denigration. You sound like Joe.'

'Ouch,' Roisin said, though he was right. It was admiration wrapped in needless mockery.

She thought on it. If Matt was intimidating to Joe or anyone else, it was through no intention of his own. Being pretty *and* smart was simply what he was. Easing their discomfort about this overachievement with ridicule was a price he was expected to pay, like a toll booth he had to pass. She could see why, sometimes, he lost patience with it.

'I suppose if you're told you're hot often enough, it loses its lustre,' she said, tongue inside of cheek, deciding to steer the ship to calmer waters.

'So now I'm conceited?'

'No! I honestly never thought being called fit insulted anyone.'

'That's not what you said, and you know it. You meant I'm a letch, who exploited it today to general economic advantage. Being a successful letch is still a letch.'

'Alright, I apologise for any suggestion you are attractive to women. I withdraw my wholly unfounded and defamatory accusation. Satisfied?'

They both laughed.

'Matt. We'll both feel nauseous if I try sincerity, but I wasn't running your efforts down,' Roisin said. 'The way you've sorted this place out has blown me away, to be honest.'

He smiled warmly. The jukebox had struck up 'Slave to Love'.

'Another?' He stood up.

'Yes, please. Bloody hell, I need to tell Mum to pay for the upgrade, don't I? This thing loops the Eighties and Nineties. It's like a late-night minicab.'

'Some of us like familiarity! You're such a grinch,' Matt said. One hand outstretched for her hand, he mouthed, *Tell her I'll be waiting . . .*

With a groan and feigned reluctance, Roisin accepted the invitation, put her hand in his. She got to her feet and let Matt waltz her around the lounge bar.

She rested her head on his chest. After the handholding, she wasn't sure if this was wise, but it felt too good to stop. Such close contact was a strange mixture of fireworks and security. *That* was it – that was what Roisin had noticed during the handholding. It was completely natural, and yet wildly exotic at the same time. Exhilaratingly new and already familiar. He was a safe place, full of danger.

She toyed with her own feelings, imagining how it would feel if they crossed lines. If they . . . belonged to one another.

Imagine if this was real.

Matt was completely out of her price range, surely? Or she was slumming it, for him.

When Roisin glanced up, to her surprise, Matt was looking down at her with an intense seriousness. She'd almost call it pained. It was utterly unlike him. She realised they had been catapulted into A Moment Before Another Moment – this couldn't be played off as horsing around when they'd gazed at each other with such obvious intensity.

What did she do, or say, next? The answer was simple, and Roisin couldn't believe she acted on it: she leaned up and kissed him.

Their mouths connected and her heart lurched. She wanted this, and wanted him, and as much as it was a huge surprise, there was no point denying it. The kiss was tentative; she felt Matt was responding in shock as much as anything. But he did respond. Time stood still.

Her feelings for Matthew McKenzie had arrived in two ways: gradually, then suddenly. Slow, but fast at the end.

'Wait,' Matt said, pulling back, frowning. 'If you're trying to upset Joe, I can't deny I'm the killer choice. But I don't want to be a nuke.'

He gave her that troubled look again. She felt she was seeing a side of him he always kept hidden. It was slightly disorientating.

'Oh, OK,' Roisin said, flustered and flushed, unsure what she was supposed to say. She'd not expected to kiss him.

'The etiquette is to at least vaguely try to deny that's what you were doing, though!' Matt said, now sounding both amused and offended. Normal Matt had returned. But while his tone of voice was steady, he was flushed, too. She had affected him.

'I do deny it,' Roisin said. 'Completely. I'd never tell Joe.'

Tell Joe what, exactly?

'I don't think you need to tell him for it to be revenge,' Matt said quietly.

The jukebox decided to be a silent wanker, clicking through to the next track with agonising sluggishness. It left them stood in an unbearable silence until Simple Minds' 'Alive And Kicking' came on. It wasn't helpful to have *YOU TURN ME ON* boom out, either, if Roisin was honest.

'I just . . .' She just what? Was experiencing an over-whelming carnal pull towards Matt, and it felt like her heart was along for the ride? How the hell did you say that, out of the blue, after ten years? 'It felt right in the moment,' she finished lamely.

'Nothing to do with that "distasteful" thing you needed to do, to prove you and Joe were over?'

Roisin's jaw dropped. 'Oh God! That wasn't . . . this isn't *that* . . .'

Nevertheless, she saw Matt's point.

'Hmmm. OK. No offence, but I don't want to be a source of regret to you,' Matt said. 'I don't want my body to be the equivalent of the empty bottle of apple schnapps.'

'You'd never be that,' she said, with feeling. How could he ever imagine himself as disposable?

Simple Minds echoed through the dimly lit room, as unsaid things whirled around them.

'Uhm, I'm going to head up to bed,' Matt said eventually.

'Sure,' Roisin replied, a confident monosyllable masking internal chaos. 'Night.'

She was frantically scrabbling to find the words to make

the fact she'd lunged at him normal, or nothing much, or a joke, so they could patch this up, and completely failing.

Once Matt was out of sight, she smoothed her hands down her sausage skin-tight dress and thought, *well. You sure plucked defeat from the jaws of victory there, Walters. Fuck.*

She put a palm over her face. She felt sixteen years old.

Aaaaaargh you tried to get off with Matt and he blew you out! Aaaaaargh! This is the most embarrassing thing to happen, like, ever.

Did he even think the Joe revenge thing, or was it a nimble way of not having to be mauled by her?

Roisin grabbed a trigger bottle of disinfectant and began wiping the tables to Spandau Ballet's 'True' with an amount of force the task didn't require. She tried not to think about how unbearably awkward tomorrow's 'good morning' would be.

She'd have to mumble stuff about being wasted, and both of them would know it was balls. Their whole dynamic was based on Roisin being a woman immune to his charms, and she feared that was permanently shot. She cringed so hard it was as if she'd sprain her stomach.

She heard a noise and turned to see Matt on the other side of the room again, looking at her. Before she could say anything, he walked towards her, pulled her into his arms and kissed her like it was the last scene in a movie. It was nothing like their halting first attempt: passionate, deep and pushy, their hips clashing. Roisin still had Dettol in one hand and a J-cloth in the other but reciprocated as best she could. *Tongues*, woah.

'What happened to apple schnapps?!' she said, when they came up for air.

Matt brushed her hair from her face, smoothing it behind her ear, and smiled. 'I thought if it was a one-off, it needed to be a better memory than that.' He paused. 'Sorry if I was uncool. I panicked.'

This was officially a head wreck: was he kissing her that well to show off? Did he fancy her or not? That kiss felt a lot like the opposite of not.

Before she could begin to process it, Roisin had a thought so violently upsetting she wriggled out of his embrace and almost pushed him away with open palms.

'Oh NO,' she said.

'What?'

'*GINA.*'

'. . . I'm not involved with Gina?'

'No, I know, but *Matt*. She's my best friend. One of my best friends. She'd be utterly shattered by us . . .' Roisin didn't want to look presumptuous. 'By us. You're right – this absolutely cannot happen! What the hell was I thinking? I hate myself right now.'

'Ah, there you go. There's the regret you ordered,' Matt said, in a very flat voice. 'That arrived faster than even I predicted. Amazing.'

'You see the problem though?' Roisin said.

'Yes, I do. I never thought something I didn't do could cost me this much. You know I've never, ever taken advantage of that situation, right? Nothing's ever happened, nor would it?'

'Yes, of course! I didn't think it had.'

Roisin realised that Matt was deeply pissed off, and he had

a right to be. Coming on to someone and then remembering you couldn't because your friend liked them was fifth-form stuff.

'I'm sorry,' Roisin said. 'Really sorry.'

'Probably for the best,' Matt said. He walked off without saying goodnight.

Roisin was left in a state of disarray.

58

'Matt's gone, he said to say bye,' Lorraine said, doing a little shimmy to Girls Aloud's 'Can't Speak French' on the jukebox as she multi-tasked swilling down black coffee and restocking the mini ginger ales.

'What? Where?' Roisin said, her dread at seeing him converting immediately into panic that she wouldn't.

Her mum nodded to the front of pub. 'There. Look.'

Roisin darted out the door and caught up with Matt, who had his duffel bag on his shoulder. He looked, with bloodshot eyes, as if he'd had a sleepless night, or maybe she was projecting her own. He also looked heartbreakingly good, and she wished she could still be indifferent to that.

'Where are you going?'

'Ah, I was going to message you. Home.'

'For good?'

'Yeah. I think now the fête's sorted and your mum's setting those new hires on, it's a good time to go,' he said. 'Plus, got to go back to my actual job sometime.'

'Not because . . . of me?'

He smiled a sad, apologetic smile. 'Also because of you, yes.'

Roisin opened her mouth and closed it again. 'Please,' she said, 'don't go. We'll go for a walk, talk about this . . .'

'There really isn't anything to talk about, is there,' he said, politely; a statement, not a question. Roisin couldn't argue with that, though she was still going to try.

She almost jumped out of her skin to see that while they'd been talking, Joe had been standing right behind them.

'Morning. Hi, guys. Oh dear. Hope I'm not interrupting, sounds intense,' he said.

'What are you doing here?' Roisin said, in bare horror.

'Not the warmest of welcomes. Taking my new car out for a spin.' He nodded back at something small, black and sporty in the otherwise near-empty Mallory car park. 'Forgot you owned the Fiat, so thought I'd splash out.'

'I'll leave you two to it,' Matt said, adjusting the bag on his shoulder.

'Oh no, I want to talk to you as well!' Joe said, with a performative vivacity that signalled real menace. 'First of all, I came to give you this in person.'

He handed a small box with a large red satin bow to Roisin. 'It's my key. For the apartment. I'm all moved out. It's yours.'

'Thank you,' Roisin said, stiffly, feeling exactly as uncomfortable as Joe had intended.

'Secondly, I did some gumshoe stuff myself.' He looked

from Matt to Roisin and back again. 'We should set up a little agency. Powell, McKenzie & Walters. Got a ring to it, haha.'

'I really think I should give you some pri—'

'Remember when I asked you, straight up, *several times*, if you'd personally gone to Sesso and asked about me, and you said you had?' Joe continued, cutting across Matt to Roisin. 'I thought that sounded really unlikely, but you swore on your mum's life that it was true?'

Roisin internally writhed.

'Well, guess what. I met up with Rick, too, and he didn't know who you were. He did recall Matt McKenzie here coming in and asking a bunch of questions about a waitress who might've got involved with a customer. Imagine my surprise!'

Roisin folded her arms.

'You're not usually such a bare-faced liar, Roisin. I have to assume you really *really* wanted to protect him. I wondered why? THEN the answer arrived. Doh! Joe! *They are having regular sexual intercourse.* The whole "trying to find me cheating on you" thing was a way of legitimising this.' He gestured at them both in turn.

'No, we're not,' Roisin said.

'Mmmm. Sure. Looks like it,' said Joe. 'Very normal vibes here.' He made a swirling hand gesture. 'The vibes are feeling highly normal. Just two pals, having a heated emotional exchange, *needing to talk about something*, the morning after the night before, outside your mum's place.' He looked up at The Mallory. 'Do you need me to rip the Care Bears duvet off your wriggling bodies before you admit it?'

Roisin saw now that underneath the superior scorn, Joe was boiling with jealousy. She opened her mouth, but Matt spoke first.

'I helped Roisin because she's my friend. I didn't care about the effect on you, because you're not my friend. Simple really.' Matt didn't sound the slightest bit intimidated and having been agonised he was a witness to this, Roisin found herself grateful he was there.

He pulled his punches with Joe, but he wasn't scared of him.

'Your dear friend, sure. Finally found your moment to shine, haven't you?' Joe looked from Matt to Roisin. 'You keep trying to catch me out, missing the deception going on right here, Roisin. There's a technique that committed shaggers use that you may be unaware of. They pose as sympathetic shoulders to cry on about other men, while spoon-feeding you more negativity about those men. Eventually, you become so sure they're the safe haven and protector, you take your clothes off and fall into bed with them. The "Not Like The Rest Of Them" device. It's a grift, Rosh. You're just this month's mark.'

'Seriously, Joe. Stop . . . you're way out of order,' Roisin said.

'I'm going to go,' Matt said curtly to Roisin. 'Will you be OK?'

'Oh GOD, like I'm unsafe,' Joe said.

'Sure,' Roisin said, gratefully, and Matt walked off.

'You know I know you're lying, right?' Joe said. 'It's written all over both of your faces.'

'You can believe what you want, Joe,' Roisin said, with more confidence than she felt. 'Nothing's happened.'

Joe looked to the box in her hand. 'Enjoy your apart-ment. I should've put a curse on it for when he crosses the threshold. I just want you to own this moment. You were so desperate for a version of our break-up where I was revealed as the bad guy, and here you are, boffing Matt before the ink is dry on the divorce papers. You are the bad guy, Roisin. *You*. As for him, he's something even worse.'

Roisin didn't bother to disabuse Joe further, accepting there was no denial he'd listen to. She let him go. Joe didn't suggest saying hello to her mother and nor, to be fair, did she want him to.

Lorraine emerged from the pub door as Joe accelerated out of the car park in his expensive new toy.

'Was that Joe?'

'Yeah.'

Roisin felt the extreme rudeness of his not having acknowl-edged her, and was left with no option but to say, 'I've ended things with him. Been working up to telling you.'

'Oh dear! I did wonder that you hadn't mentioned him much,' Lorraine said. 'But . . . you're alright?'

'I'm fine. We haven't got along for a while; we'd been growing apart. Needed doing.' She waved her beribboned box. 'He's given me his half of the apartment as a parting gift. Not at all sure I should've accepted, but he insisted.'

'As long as you're alright.' Lorraine squeezed her arm. Then, looking over her shoulder, 'Oh, there's Terence!'

Lorraine had always been a proponent of Roisin sticking with Joe, and that went triple once he started coining it in. Roisin was extremely surprised at the lack of enquiry and voluble objection. Something was up.

Roisin found out what the 'up' was likely to be, within an hour, when she decided – out of a need to draw a line, and a lack of available distractions – to watch the last *Hunter*.

She turned iPlayer on and, with a jolt of what felt like travel sickness, saw it had been watched. Lorraine had seen the whole series. Roisin paused, absorbed this shock. Any hopes her mum had missed the significance of the table sex scene were dashed by remembering how unexpectedly peremptory she had been when discussing Joe.

Roisin stuck the programme on and felt like adopting a brace position.

More procedural detective stuff, a reveal that the killer was the father of one of the waitresses, lots more sex, a promotion . . . once again, Roisin found herself surprised to be bored.

The final cliff-hanger arrived. Becca's best friend Gwen came on to Jasper, and with magnificent restraint, he refused. But thanks to a very ill-timed bum dial, hot Gwen had found out Jasper was shagging around and was blackmailing him to succumb to her charms, or she would tell Becca. Gwen, who was not Gina, but Amber?

The credits rolled to Jasper walking down a Manchester

street, bumping shoulders with passers-by in the style of a music video, to a valedictory burst of 'Knights Of Cydonia' by Muse.

As Joe had said, the voice-over promised more *Hunter*.

She switched the television off with relief and confusion.

Roisin cast her mind back to Joe freshly back from Los Angeles, and his speech to win her round, to persuade her to give them another go.

You have to see all three episodes to realise Hunter's behaviour isn't glamorised. It doesn't pay off; he's really humbled by the end.

Huh? *Humbled?* That was Joe's idea of a comeuppance?

Roisin was completely flummoxed, and then she sat up straight. Her subconscious had picked up the telephone to her conscious again.

This is what he does. He's a liar. A liar who lies in the moment, who says whatever will spring him from the trap. If you pick him up on inconsistencies later, the story will adapt and change shape. He scripts things to produce an effect in his audience. Personally, and professionally.

Joe Powell is not a fixed set of beliefs and behaviours. He is a chameleon with a vocabulary and a major hard-on for pulling the wool. He feels no guilt, and he'll do it again. Do liars always know they're lying? If Joe knows, he doesn't care.

Joe was still right about her culpability regarding Matt, even if he'd got the extent of it wrong. Roisin couldn't feel guilty, even if she should. He prized only survival, the upper hand.

She realised she didn't trust a word he said, and that trust couldn't be restored.

She said aloud, 'Fuck him.'

Roisin couldn't fix Joe Powell or figure him out, but she was done living inside his world.

59

Hair the colour of liquid blackberry required upkeep and expense, and after an aimless, doubt-wracked week, Roisin had to tackle her inch of cocoa-coloured roots.

She made her way to a city salon to sit in foils, avoiding her usual one so she didn't have to provide an account of herself to her stylist, Marco, who watched *SEEN*. In short, she didn't want to be seen. Roisin was now avoiding looking in the mirror at her stupid face for two hours. Every time she let her mind wander, she was back in The Mallory, being passionately seized and snogged over a table in the half dark, accompanied by the sound of Spandau Ballet. Before she made a double-dipped McNugget of herself.

Ugh, ugh.

She was still working at the pub, now as much in avoidance of her empty pad in Didsbury as to help her mother. Champagne problems, but Roisin was sure that stripped of Joe's possessions, the premises would be radiating silent resentment from every room. *What now?* Thank God they never got that dog.

Roisin had booked her hair appointment for last thing

Friday so she could meet Meredith and Gina for drinks after. They met at the Gina-nominated Ivy, and within three sips of a something-Tini and five minutes of their company, Roisin felt as if she'd had weeks of therapy.

Once again, she'd come mentally prepared as what to reveal and what to conceal about recent events. It was a dance of the veils.

She updated them on Joe and Matt's stand-off outside the pub, and Joe's lurid allegations about her and Matt, based on his visit to Sesso. She felt intense discomfort at their dumb-struck shock that he could say such a thing, given Joe had some right on his side.

'I appreciate he's devastated to lose you, but Joseph sounds like he's lost his mind, too,' Meredith said, stabbing at the ice in her drink with her straw.

Roisin squirmed. She had their support under false pretences. This wouldn't do, this partial disclosure.

Roisin thought about how, despite the Gwen-Gina character and Joe's soft spot, she'd never thought for a second that Gina had fooled around with Joe. That wasn't a tribute to Joe, but to Gina. It was unconscionable that she, Meredith or Gina would ever double-cross each other or break these bonds.

Given that what had occurred between her and Matt was unlikely to ever be repeated or ever matter, the expedient thing was obviously to not tell Gina.

But looking at them both, Roisin knew she had to, or it would forever hang over them. These women mattered to her more than anyone, and she couldn't dupe them by withholding this sorry episode. She couldn't stand for their friendship to feel tainted. If she had to withstand a tirade from Gina, so be it.

'Gina,' Roisin said, with a distinct sense of bungee-jumping and hoping the rope between them held out. 'I did something stupid and awful and I can't keep it to myself. I kissed Matt. It was over very quickly but I absolutely despise myself. Joe was completely out of order in the extent of his suspicions, though.'

'Woah,' said Meredith. 'Didn't see that coming.'

'Oh my God!' Gina cried.

Roisin's tense expression fully collapsed.

'No. *Oh my God,*' Gina repeated, putting one hand on Roisin and laying the other over her chest. 'As in, I didn't see that coming either, but also, *oh my God?*' she said with the rising intonation of a question, holding up an index finger. 'I think . . . I'm OK with it? I'd wondered if finally admitting I had to drop him would cure me, and it has. It's like I said it aloud and broke the spell. Like in *Labyrinth.* "You have no power over me." The Goblin King, remember?'

'The Goblin . . . OK no, go back,' Meredith said.

'Really?!' Roisin said, in complete mystification.

'Yes. Did you discuss his feelings for you, at last?' Gina added.

Meredith raised an eyebrow. Roisin's mouth opened. They stared at each other as Gina drained her Spinningfields Sangria.

'I could go for another of these,' she murmured absently.

Gina was supposed to be blindsided, and yet she was by far the most composed.

'His . . . what?' Roisin said.

Roisin looked at Meredith, who made a *no idea what she's talking about* disclaimer face.

'Seriously. Just me?! I thought I was the one out of the three of us who *wasn't* super perceptive!'

Roisin and Meredith shared yet another nonplussed look.

Gina smoothed her hair. She'd pulled it into a French plait and, Roisin noticed now, was quite radiant.

'*Derp*. Matt has always had a huge thing for Roisin. A major, major thing. Would fight on a horse for her with one of those long poking implements. You know the ones I mean?' She made a jousting move.

'. . . A sword?' Meredith said.

'No, like a spear.'

'I think that's a lance?' Meredith said.

'To return to the point,' Roisin said, hardly daring to trust Gina's apparent equanimity. 'Did Matt tell you this?'

Gina turned to Roisin with the look of a kindly caregiver to infant. 'No, course not, but you don't have a doomed obsession with someone for as long as I have and not sniff out a few things about them. Trust me, Matt McKenzie has yearned hopelessly for you since forever. YEARNED. I would go so far as "pined".'

60

'News to me,' Meredith assured Roisin, who said, 'And definitely me.'

'You never mentioned it?' Roisin said to Gina.

She fiddled with a stud earring. 'Well . . . I thought you knew and were too classy to let on. Plus, you were with Joe. It was mischief. I knew Matt would never do anything about it. He's pure chivalry.'

'How did this knowledge come to you?' Meredith said.

'Oh, it's so obvious!'

'Evidently not . . .' Meredith said.

'OK, so remember that time Dev made us go to Center Parcs?'

'Ugh, yes,' Roisin said. He'd been up to his activities for a while. (That was a point: where *was* Dev? Roisin had tried to call him for a state of the nation where she finally broke the news that she and Joe were exes, thinking he was back from Sóller. The length of time it took to connect, and then the connection dropping, made her feel he was further afield than Spain.)

'Matt wouldn't swim and spent all his time with his eyes

boring into one of those *Wolf Hall* books, blushing. Wouldn't glance within three feet of Roisin in a swimsuit.'

Roisin squinted. '. . . He prefers Thomas Cromwell to log flumes?'

'No! He had such major hots for you that he was insanely self-conscious when you were partially undressed! When you've thought about someone naked a million times, you can't act casual when there's skin on show. I should know.'

'I've got to say, as evidence goes, I probably wouldn't build a case on it at the High Court,' Meredith said, indicating to the waiter whose eye she'd caught with circling forefinger in mid-air, and then thumbs up that *yes, they'd like the same again*.

'Yeah. "Doesn't have any interest in my patchy bikini line" feels short of conclusive,' Roisin said, starting to laugh slightly hysterically, as much in relief as anything. 'Given that applies to pretty much everyone sane on earth.'

'Oh, he does.' Gina nodded, sagely. 'He really does. I could find you other examples, but that's the one that comes to me. You *never* see Matt look shy.'

'It was either that or the visual impact of Dev's flamingo swim shorts,' Meredith said.

'Why didn't I notice this?' Roisin said.

'You're modest and not ever looking for it, and Matt has a scarily good poker face,' Gina said. 'He's more of an enigma than we realise. I don't get the impression he's very close to his family, for example.'

Hmmm, she'd got that right, though Roisin wasn't at liberty to confirm it.

'I could never hate you for it, Rosh. I've always thought you were a goddess, too,' Gina said.

'I can't believe I was caught in this web of sexual psychodrama the whole time,' Meredith said.

'Well, either way with Matt, I can't believe you've been so understanding about my lunacy,' Roisin said to Gina. 'Thank you.'

Gina put her head on one side. 'I know you'd never sell me out, but more than that, I *am* weirdly alright with it. More than I ever thought I could be. I have to thank you, in fact. Without this information, I wouldn't have known for sure.'

'But, how?!' Roisin said, scarcely believing.

'The Aaron Effect!' Meredith said, making a praying gesture.

'Yeah that. And also, after Matt went off that night with Amelia, something snapped in me. Or maybe died in me. I stopped my hankering, almost overnight. I didn't expect the effect to be so instant. I think by the end, I was sick and tired of myself more than I was actually in love, you know?'

Meredith and Roisin didn't, exactly, but they nodded.

'You know something, too? Aaron really wanted to go on a date. *Really* wanted to; he was so shy his hand was trembling when we said cheers after I got to the pub. I realised that I want that. I want to be wanted. Matt can't give me that.'

Roisin and Meredith both nodded again.

'I said I couldn't bear to try to be friends with whoever Matt found, but if she's my friend already, that problem is solved?' Gina concluded.

Roisin was taken aback at this and blurted, 'Honestly it was nothing, it lasted seconds before I screamed *what are we doing*. He's off to a sort of date tomorrow night at some bar launch. Normal McKenzie business has resumed.'

Their round arrived and they paused while their empty glasses were whisked away and replaced with full ones.

'Mmmm,' Gina said, giving Roisin a penetrating look. 'If you aren't going to pursue it, please don't make it on my account. I don't want to do any more damage to Matt. He deserves to be happy.'

'Does this mean he's allowed back to the Brians?' Meredith said.

'Sure,' Gina said.

'I think you have to be the one to tell him that,' Meredith said, and Gina nodded. 'Now. That's sorted. Can we *please* try to pass the Bechdel test here,' Meredith said.

'What's that?' Gina said.

'It's whether a film is sexist: do women, when together, ever discuss a subject that isn't a man.'

'We'd pass it easily if you dated someone for us to gossip about,' Gina said, and Meredith gasped while Roisin cackled.

The conversation moved on, and Roisin was left pretending to listen while she was consumed by what Gina had said.

Matt had feelings for her? Longstanding ones? Big, serious ones? She resisted something so seductive and extraordinary being true. It also forced her to ask herself what her interests were here.

She'd revealed what she had with the aim of being

completely honest with her friends, but she feared what it had shown her was that she hadn't been completely honest, at all. With them, with Matt, or with herself.

61

Roisin was experiencing every symptom, while stubbornly denying she had the sickness. His name appearing on her phone was as if someone had stabbed her chest with a syringe of adrenaline.

The following day after her night out with Gina and Meredith, she unlocked the message from Matt McKenzie so fast her fingers were a blur. Roisin had been in agonies at the meaning for his silence and then had to allow she'd not been in contact with him, either. It was hard to know what to say. She'd been hoping Meatball would visit the pub and give her an excuse to send a photo, but rumour had it he was romancing the staff at the village chippy.

Sorry for leaving you with Joe last weekend. I thought my being there was only going to make him worse. How did it go? x

She typed back:

He didn't improve but hopefully that's the end of it. How are you? Is it the Ancoats bar launch tonight? x

Well remembered! Yes it is, 'festa'. (No capital letters here obvs.) I'll report back as to whether the Marmalade Negronis are any good. Give my love to your mum, Terence, and especially Meatball. I left a packet of those chews he likes in my room, if you'd not mind dispensing them. X

Hmmm, large kiss. Emphatically positive, but also a full stop. Also, are they possibly easier to send to people you don't fancy?

Analysing text kiss sizes was another symptom.

Oh God, she missed him. The Mallory was drab without the sound of Matt's laughter and, to be candid, the way his arms looked when he was hefting heavy crates.

Without Gina's encouragement, Roisin wouldn't have had the nerve to hope, but her words circled round and round her head. Was Gina merely a romantic, suffering a long tail with McKenzie Derangement Syndrome, or was she right? She *was* right about his family.

Fuck's sake, what could Roisin DO with all these feelings she was feeling?

'I've got Amy and Ernie on tonight,' Lorraine said, as if she could pick up on Roisin's anxiety. 'Why don't you go out, do something nice?'

'I could, I suppose . . .' Roisin said.

Did she dare? Or did she wait for this madness to subside? What if . . . *What if the love of Matt's life is out there in Ancoats, and tonight is the night they meet,* she asked herself. Then they were forever united as one, on an inexorable track to marriage and babies, and Roisin had to always wonder what would've happened if she'd only had the guts?

That bitch needed stopping.

A plan started to form. A completely crackers plan.

He'd told her the name, *festa*, and that was a hint he wanted her to turn up, right? Right! No. That was the kind of thing that stalkers believed.

Roisin put on the black & Other Stories dress he'd once said he liked and booked a cab, reasoning that if it went well, she'd want a drink, and if it went badly, she'd need a drink.

She nervously pulled out a compact en route to check she didn't have lipstick on her teeth, and the driver saw her.

'First date, is it?'

'Something like that!'

'If you're nervous, imagine him naked.'

'I can't think of anything more likely to make me nervous,' Roisin said.

Given it was a special occasion, Manchester obliged with a rainstorm so heavy that Roisin had to dash into the bar holding her handbag over her head. *festa* was a long, high-ceilinged room full of exposed ventilation pipes and dangling bare lightbulbs on looped cords, which always made Terence say, 'Why does no one finish the electrics any more? The containment is terrible!' He liked everyone to remember he was CORGI-registered to do gas and electrics before he was a barman.

Roisin picked her way through the well-dressed crowd inside and started to think, *he's not here. He's not here.* Did she risk texting him; what would she even say?

Then she saw him against a far wall of plastic green leaves:

an unmissable jawline. Her heart went boom. Her palms went damp.

He looked over as she drew near, and exclaimed, in real shock, 'Roisin?!'

So the name of the bar wasn't a hint. Nope. She noticed then that the woman he was chatting to had a high ponytail and strappy heels like Virginia creeper wound up her endless bare legs. She was breathtaking. If she was the future love, Roisin had brought piss to a shit fight.

Roisin almost said, 'Wrong bar!' while backing away, hearing 'Yakety Sax' in her head.

'Why are you here?' Matt said, putting down his drink and walking over to her.

'Hello. Can I have a word?' she said.

'Er . . . yeah?'

'In private? Outside?' Roisin said.

'Does it have to be outside? It's shitting it down!' Matt said, not unreasonably.

'I don't want to shout.'

There was nowhere in here she wouldn't feel the weight of stares upon them; she couldn't say this with people clustered around. Or over the music: New Order's 'Age Of Consent' was giving them an ear boxing.

She and a baffled-looking Matt emerged into the street and Matt pointed at a shop awning a hundred yards away.

They darted under it, the water pouring from its edge in sheets.

'I'm going to stress-test my dad's thing about how you "never regret bravery", to its absolute limit.'

'OK?' Matt said, wiping rainwater from his brow.

'I really like you.'

Matt looked perplexed, yet impassive. She worried he would even be annoyed at being dragged out of his evening for this crap.

Roisin had rehearsed a more ambitious version of this speech, and she immediately junked it. It turned out life was not like romantic comedy films. Making grand statements about your passion to an unwary person you knew well was not like that scene at the New Year party in *When Harry Met Sally*: it was excruciating.

It was raining, and she did notice.

'Whatever started the other night. You know. With Bryan Ferry. And Spandau Ballet. I really like you, and I think we should . . . date. If you want to. Gina's totally fine with it.'

'That's what you wanted to say? You got permission?' Matt said, and Roisin wanted to die. She'd have to characterise this incident, in the months and years to come, as 'Joe PTSD'.

'What if Gina had said no? You'd choose Gina?'

Roisin nodded, reluctantly.

'The right decision,' Matt said. *Oof*.

And the very fact Matt wasn't saying *wow, really, me too* and clasping in her arms was as much answer as Roisin needed.

'Thing is . . .' Matt said. 'This may be too much honesty, but I am so weary with not saying what I mean, and not being sure what other people mean. Thing is, I'm not who you think I am.'

62

'How?'

Was this where he admitted he was indeed a remorseless womaniser?

'I think you think I'm this fun party animal, who's going to whirl you around the dancefloor and get you back on your feet after a decade of Joe Powell.'

He drew breath. 'Despite what it looks like . . .' He nodded back at the teeming bar. 'I don't have a lot of people in my life. Ones that matter. I don't see my family; I won't be seeing much of the Brian lot from now on. At times, I feel pretty lonely. I don't know why that feels so hard to admit, but it does. I'm not ashamed, and yet . . . it seems I am.'

Roisin exactly understood that feeling of being ashamed of something you weren't ashamed of.

'You, however, matter. You are one of my oldest friends, and I love you. I'm really flattered you think I'm good for a good time. But I can see us on the other side of that, and I don't want it. I don't want to scale down to the awkward WhatsApps every couple of months. Checking in and being forced-casual and cagey with each other about who we're both seeing. It doesn't work to stay mates with someone you've had those times with.'

Roisin nodded.

'If you need a self-esteem boost, then I can promise you: you are staggeringly lovely. You won't struggle to find someone to say yes. But he can't be me. If it helps, I already hate him.'

'Thank you,' Roisin said. 'For the nicest, *You? No, ta, love* I will ever get.' She pulled a comedy face.

Matt smiled, shook his head, and winced. 'It's not "no, ta." It's, "I like you too much to swap close friends status for being kind-of-exes". However much fun the brief spell in between is.'

Roisin said, 'I get it.' That was that. She decided to claw back some tattered shreds of dignity. 'But I wasn't completely off the mark in thinking you might be up for it. You did kiss me? Before I remembered Gina,' Roisin said.

'I never said I found saying no to you easy,' Matt said, with a devastating smile. 'I'm saying it would be too costly a fling.'

Except . . . she wasn't asking him for a fling. Should she say it? Oh, fuck it. She'd come this far.

'I'm not asking you to have some *dalliance* with me,' Roisin said, a last bid she wasn't at all sure she should make. If not quit while you're ahead, quit while you've not completely humiliated yourself.

'Then what are you saying?' Matt said.

'I'm saying . . .' Roisin petered out at the impossibility of looking him in that spectacular face and uttering the actual foolish words.

'Be extremely blunt and as graphic as you like,' Matt said. 'I think we're beyond nice euphemisms.' He put his arm up to shield them as a gust of rain somehow managed to pelt sideways, under the awning.

Roisin took a deep breath. 'I'm saying, Matt, I'm yours, if you want me. I want you to be mine. I'm saying I think I'm in love with you.'

A stunned beat of silence.

'Since when?' Matt said quietly.

'A few days ago. Which sounds flippant, but it's not. It's just . . . suddenly all there. As if it was there all along.'

Matt stared at her, and she stared back. Nearby, a female voice said, 'Sorry to butt in. Matt, should I get you another drink?'

He looked over. 'No, ta.'

The person retreated.

Roisin wondered if she should say something else, but before she could, Matt stepped forward, wound his hands in her hair, and kissed her.

She put her arms around his neck, thinking, *if this is pure sympathy, I may as well get the most out of it.*

'For clarity, what does that mean?' she said, when they disentangled.

'It means, "you could've led with that," Matt said, his face suffused with a joy she could honestly say she'd never seen. 'Then I could've said, "Well, that's a coincidence. I've been in love with you the whole time."'

★

353

'You know what I'd like to do?' Matt said, as they lay side by side in bed. Matt picked up her hand and put his palm against it.

'Horrify me,' Roisin said, certain she would not be horrified, even if she should be.

Her black dress lay on the floor of his mezzanine bedroom in his frankly daft apartment, and they had embarked on what Roisin hoped was the first of many times they'd fall into this bed. Being naked with someone you'd been friends with for so long could feel strange, and at moments it did, but mainly it just felt very, very good.

'To go on holiday with you. One of those holidays that exists mainly in the imagination and Instagram brags. Games of UNO on tables with tea lights, tumblers of cheap white wine. Lights in the harbour beyond. That sort of thing. Possibly a lobster with fries.'

'Sounds like Greece or Italy. We could do that. Holidays in half terms are punitive though. Drawback of my job. Dev Doshi money. Oh God.' She put a hand to her forehead. 'Not looking forward to going back to work. I had a panic attack in front of a class playing a clip from *Hunter*. Urgh.'

Matt rearranged himself on the pillows to pull her into the crook of his arm, kissing the top of her head. 'You are an absolutely ace teacher, and you will be fine. I have every faith. Stroll back in there with your head held high.'

'Thank you,' Roisin said. She gazed at their opulent surroundings, and she didn't just mean Matt McKenzie. 'How much of this is you? I don't mean what's yours, as in own . . .'

'Aye aye. Assessing if I have enough family silver left?'

'Pffft. I mean. If you say the flash and glamour and man about town stuff was a . . . front.' She didn't want to repeat the word 'lonely', though she still felt it in her gut.

'That's a good question. One I asked myself a lot after I got the sack. It's only half serious, in a weird way. Like I played a role on purpose that people found amusing.'

Concocted Casanova persona. So, Joe's assessment hadn't been entirely off.

'The mask eats the face though, and all that. I can't tell you how idiotic I feel admitting to you, and myself, that my lifestyle was some sort of performance-art joke to get people to like me.'

Roisin thought of Matt uncomplainingly mopping up napalmed spaghetti hoops that Terence had detonated in the microwave at The Mallory, and realised why she'd *caught feelings* for him when she had.

'I don't think you need to hide behind anything to be liked,' Roisin said, warmly.

Matt squeezed her shoulder. 'Having never been a couple, I want to be so very coupley. Would you feel vomitous if I did things like wrote you cards with inspirational messages about my love and put them in your work bag to find?'

Roisin hooted with laughter. 'Saying what? Live, laugh, love?'

'Saying . . . I don't know, you'd have to open it to find out. Declarations that would leave you unable to concentrate for the rest of the day. Or maybe I'd go with a joke.'

'Oh God, nothing blue, please. Knowing my luck, I'd drop it and someone from 10E would open it.'

'I promise. Nothing like, "found the keys to your dildo cabinet."'

Roisin shrieked. 'Have you really been in love with me all along?' she said.

'Yeah. I told you I had been. The woman I was in love with, back in the day? Who I told a friend about and he steamed in ahead of me? That was you. And Joe, of course.'

Roisin sat up slightly. 'What? Really? "She emigrated to the other side of the world"?'

'That was an exaggerated depiction of West Didsbury. I needed a red herring. I feared while speaking that you'd seen right through me, with those *old soul* brown eyes of yours.'

Roisin had to take a few seconds to absorb this. 'Wait. That was me? You *hid* me on social media?'

'Haha! I love that you think that's the most shocking thing, not the secret ten-year obsession. Yeah, sorry. I checked in every so often so you couldn't tell, though, right?'

'In case of a baby announcement?!'

'Yeah. I recently downgraded the threat level of your posting an ultrasound from substantial to moderate, obviously. The chances were low, but never zero.'

'This is amazing. Why didn't you ask me out in the first place?'

Roisin cast her mind back to the Deansgate shop floor years. She remembered an absurdly handsome, personable young lad from a monied background, whom she was surprised wanted the grunt work of retail. She remembered suspecting he'd be a brat, and instead Matthew McKenzie being one of sweetest-natured people she'd ever met. And he looked like he'd been carved from marble. Roisin had assumed he had a vast hinterland of attention from women, the sort who didn't dip twiglets in hummus while reading *Hello!* in the staff room.

'I was going to. I kept trying to finagle the seating plans when we went out after work, so I could talk to you. You may recall, a lot of people wanted to be next to Roisin on those nights. Then, as I said, I lost the moment. You were seeing him.'

She'd never seen Matt look shy before. *(God, Gina, you were right.)*

'Joe asked me out because you'd told him you were going to?'

'Yup. He told me you'd forced the timing, not him. Took me an embarrassingly long amount of time to realise that was bullshit.' Matt paused. 'I shouldn't have mentioned this, should I? He's come between us, again.'

Roisin pushed her hand across his chest, under the sheets. She'd told him she'd been trying to acclimatise to someone having this many muscles, more muscles than she actually knew anyone had.

'I promise you. I'm not thinking about Joe.'

63

There might be more awkward places to receive a phone call from your ex's mum than the sky-high flat of your new lover, the morning after the first night before, but if there was, Roisin didn't care to know about it.

Even worse and more cackhanded, Roisin hadn't intended to answer it, for all the aforementioned reasons, but had been mid-swipe when Fay's name appeared, pressing Accept Call in error.

At least she was alone – Matt's job kept some anti-social hours and he'd had to go to a Sunday morning meeting about his rehiring. He'd left her a key.

'You can keep that,' he said, before another feverish bout of kissing that made him late. Roisin would've happily made him even later.

'Hello, Roisin. I wanted to say how sorry Kenneth and I were to hear about you and Joseph separating.'

'Thank you, Fay,' Roisin said. 'It's really sad, but hopefully it's civilised.'

'You're staying in the flat, Joe says?'

Fay was battling to keep the disapproval out of her voice

and failing. Roisin spotted the exact tenor of neutrally raising something that had been discussed in extremely judgemental terms already.

'Joe insisted that it was only fair, after I supported his writing career for all those years. It's extremely generous of him. I guess he's so successful now it's different rules.'

Fay inhaled. 'Joe also says you're involved with someone you both know? A friend?'

Oh GOD. Scorched earth, Joe, is it? There was no need for this. She could've given Lorraine chapter and verse and opted not to.

'Erm. There were multiple factors in the break-up,' Roisin said, terse. 'It wasn't due to any infidelity.'

'I'd have thought it didn't help! Come on, Roisin.'

'Nothing went on behind Joe's back, Fay.'

Nevertheless, she writhed. Roisin wasn't proud of the fact she'd fallen for one of their mutual friends. The reason she was able to, was because she and Joe had already imploded.

The right and proper way for her romantic life to continue was a respectful six months to a year of singledom, and then seeing someone wholly unconnected to Joe. But life was a chaotic, inconvenient bastard, and there it was. Love was love. Joe certainly couldn't say she had stolen his bosom buddy, with her bosoms.

Fay asked a few more questions about her welfare that had answers she couldn't possibly care about. It became clear that she wasn't issuing an elegant and affectionate farewell; she was so appalled that she couldn't resist hearing Roisin's account for herself. She was forcing Roisin to own her infamous treatment of her son, in the style of an officer reading out the charges. To make it clear *They Knew*.

Roisin was surprised by how upsetting she found it. All those years of scraping carrots for the festive lunch, sending them press clippings about *SEEN* and remembering which small-batch distillery gin Kenneth liked, for nothing. She had been a near-faultless daughter-in-law and it all evaporated after a few choice, butthurt words from Joe. *Mothers and their sons.* She thought about Lorraine and Ryan.

After she ended the call, Roisin saw Dominic, Joe's best friend, was on Call Waiting. Was this a 'Line Up To Kick Rosh's Arse' queue? She very nearly declined. Only the momentum from having faced Fay made her take it. Her blood was up.

'Hi, Dominic!' she said.

'Roisin, darling. How are you?' She found Dom's patrician manner with women the same age as him irksome at the best of times.

'You know what, I *was* OK until Joe's mum rang to insinuate I'm a greedy jezebel. If you're offering anything on that theme, can I ask that we don't? The meeting could be an email, as they say.'

'Oh goodness! Mums! Sorry to hear,' Dom said, emollient.

Roisin had expected him to take offence and fell quiet.

'Vic and I are quite gutted, and we wanted to let you know that, and check you're OK. Also, please keep this between us, but I think young Joseph does himself no favours with the cocksure, invulnerable routine. He's an absolute mess over losing you, whether he shows it or not.'

'Ah,' Roisin said.

'When he talks about you, what always shines out is the immense respect he has for you, Roisin.'

Aye, does it, she thought. She knew there'd be an angle, and here it was. 'Give Joe another chance', as heavy subtext.

'You're the only woman in the world as far as he's concerned. He thinks you're a powerhouse. That's the word he uses.'

Roisin tried to sound appreciative. She knew Dom meant well, and maybe it was his manner that grated. But she was being mansplained on how she should perceive Joe, being mansplained on his true amour for her. Did it not occur to Dominic to ask what Roisin thought? Her break-up had become others' property.

There was no point saying any of this: Dom would merely insist he wanted Roisin to know how cherished she was.

'. . . I'm doing a mercy dash to stay with him tonight so he's not on his own. I expect there will be Tom Waits and whisky. Listen, this is none of my business . . .' Dom said.

You can probably stop there, then? Roisin thought, waspishly.

'Joe mentioned someone you both know putting moves on you. He feels this man is very much not to be trusted. He doesn't have your best interests at heart. Joe was very agitated and worried that you think it's mere possessiveness. He discussed it for some time when he called in the other week.'

It was the tiniest of tiny things, a snagged thread on a table edge. Roisin could easily dismiss it.

But, 'called in'? When Joe had said he'd stayed over?

64

Roisin's mind raced as Dom continued on the nebulous and shadowy evils of a fictionalised version of Matt McKenzie.

If she directly questioned Dom on this 'called in' terminology, he might sense Joe was being caught out and deploy male solidarity emergency mode: bluster to Roisin that Joe's version was right, then question Joe later.

She had to be smarter than to simply say, 'Didn't he stay at yours?'

'I hope he didn't stagger in too drunk from that lads' night and wake his parents, after he *called in* at yours, by the way,' Roisin said, flying a kite.

'When? The other week? Oh no,' Dom said. He paused, and Roisin thought he was about to change the subject. 'He was off by half eight – he was taking them for dinner.'

'Ah, of course! I think he said,' Roisin said smoothly.

When she rang off, the hairs on her arms were standing on end. She'd uncovered, by pure chance, an outright lie. A recent lie. Roisin was sure if she challenged Joe, there'd be bullshit.

He wanted a quiet night to himself, his mental health hadn't been so great, he knew Roisin would want an account of why and he wasn't ready, blah blah.

She wouldn't believe it anyway.

Why would I use my parents as a cover story, when you talk to them? Because you'd gambled that they'd not mention it. It wasn't a perfect solution, Joe, but it was good enough. The roulette wheel spin quite possibly added to the frisson.

So where had he been? Roisin had assumed Manchester, but he had to have stayed in York. He'd told Roisin he was at the family home, and Dom was the explanation for that discrepancy. You don't bother to create an alibi twice over.

Occam's Razor: Joe *was* in York, that Sunday night, and didn't want anyone to know what he was doing or where he was sleeping, not even Dom. Clearly, cheating on Roisin was embarrassing in front of his oldest friends; that was something.

But with who? He went back to York reasonably often, but usually with Roisin. Since they got the nice apartment, his parents came up to theirs pretty often. Sustaining an affair looked like difficult work, assuming she was based there, and the probability was that she was.

She supposed Joe could have a secret Tinder profile, setting his location to York city centre and waiting for responses, but she couldn't see it, somehow. When Jasper said only idiots had evidence on their phone, it rang as very Joe-ish.

Oh God . . . what if he *paid for it*? This notion was so startling that Roisin hadn't thought of it until now, and still couldn't allow it. There was something not at all Joe-like about that, either. He'd want to think his partner wanted to be there. He liked power over people. If you were making a financial transaction, that was a blunt instrument available to anyone. With him, there'd be a psychological dimension. It'd be a mindfuck, as well as a bodily one.

Roisin googled central hotels in York. She'd heard Joe discussing accommodation preferences in London, New York and L.A. often enough. Looking at the options available, she felt pretty sure that if he wasn't in a private residence – and that was a big if – he'd have been at The Royal, an Edwardian railway building with five stars. They'd stayed there after weddings.

Joe liked grandeur and pomp; he scorned 'the trendy ones with the *nudge nudge wink wink* marketing materials next to your Figgy Pudding flavour shower gel'. And Roisin judged that, if you were having some illicit boot-knocking, you'd prefer the anonymity of a chain to a tiny place where you might be asked, *Special occasion? What brings you to York?*

Roisin couldn't resist an investigation. It was the longest of long shots, but still a shot.

She weighed up how to do this, bypassing data protection, and decided her best bet was: 1. Claim to have been a guest, not asking about one, thus not triggering spying suspicions, and 2. Querying something financial, which would encourage them to prioritise investigation and resolution over privacy.

It had one drawback – they might ask for a card number that Roisin didn't have, or not without subterfuges she'd rather not undertake. She and Joe had separate bank accounts, went paperless for statements, and even if she could somehow access his online banking, he could've paid cash. Proving he was there was the thing.

Deep breath. She looked up the hotel online, typed the number into her phone, listened to the automated response. She pressed 5 to Speak To A Member Of The Reception Team.

'Hello, The Royal York, how can I help you?'

'Hi! I stayed at your hotel last Sunday, the fifteenth. I've had my credit card statement. I've been charged a ton, and I think it's the wrong bill? I should've noticed at the time, but I was so hungover I paid it without checking, haha! Would it be possible for you to pull up my original reservation and see what room I was in, in the original booking?'

'What name was the reservation under, please?'

'Roisin Walters. R–O–I–S–I–N. Walters with an S.'

She figured the faster this went, the better it'd go for her, but a woman calling to ask about a man's bill was too risky in sounding snooping alarm bells. This was necessary scene setting.

There was off stage tap-tapping at a keyboard.

'I don't have anything in that name on the system, sorry?'

'Oh? Oh, wait . . . of course – it was booked by my boyfriend. Try "Joe Powell"? P–O–W–E–DOUBLE–L. Same date, obviously.'

Only at this moment did it occur to her Joe might've used a false name. He'd have had to use his real bank cards though, and that might've been too conspicuously *wedding ring in the glove box* for his tastes. The tap-tapping, silences and breathing on the other end of the line were agony.

'Ah, yes. Found you. It was a suite? In the extras, our records don't have anything from the minibar, only a bottle of champagne on arrival in the room?'

Roisin's veins pumped pure adrenaline.

'Oh, I forgot the champagne!' she said, improvising at a hundred miles per hour. 'Haha! I've obviously been in denial about my massive Visa statement, apologies. Thanks for your help.'

She rang off, heart thundering. FUCKIN' GOTCHA. No one, but surely no one, ordered champagne to a suite to sit and drink alone in contemplation. No one gilded a night of solitude to that extent: a suite was either someone on work expenses for travel, which Joe wasn't, or someone showing a second someone a good time.

She had the smoking gun, and yet no fingerprints on it.

It's not unfaithful to drink a bottle of Möet in a spacious room with a trouser press, last I checked.

One thing Roisin was sure of: this time she'd not tell anyone, or involve anyone.

She paced the room, mobile in a grip so tight her knuckles were white.

What did Joe call himself? A 'dull serial monogamist'? A dull serial monogamist with . . . a mistress in York? Something about it being his birthplace made her feel this would be more than a one-off.

And what did Joe teach her about writing? Apart from the fact it apparently legitimised a lot of shit behaviour? *Good plot comes from character.* Ergo, Joe being a hopeful beggar on an app, cosplaying single, with a profile that could be screen-shot – *nah.* He'd think that was for absolute morons. Joe paying for it – *nope.* He'd say it was not for men of his calibre, for sure. Joe, in the years of penury when it was definitely impossible to book suites, and then the years of being kinetically busy, having time to start and maintain an extra-curricular in another city? Implausible.

Joe had been a light-to-now-non-existent user of social media, so he'd not picked up Side Lady there, either.

Back to character. He believed himself to be a serial monogamist and self-image mattered to Joe, however much he warped the Ts and Cs.

Who could he sleep with, and maintain his own fictions? Who was a somehow more ethical, less traitorous shag for Mr One Woman Guy?

Who did he somehow have a head start, an 'in' with? A friend of Dom and Victoria, hence not wanting Dom to know? Didn't Dom have a futile crush on a siren called Amber, who inspired the Gina-alike, Gwen? Was Amber's admirer in fact, Joe? Joe was a daredevil, but if so, voluntarily naming her to Roisin stretched credulity. It *could* be her? With no surname, Roisin was up a gumtree in ever identifying her.

Wait. No.

The answer came to Roisin like magic, in that inner voice, from nowhere. Or, perhaps, a 'nowhere' that involved ten years of close study.

65

The Last Woman, of course. Beatrice.

When they went to his schoolfriend Jim's wedding, a year ago – the one of the beautiful candid photograph – Joe had assiduously avoided his ex. He had pecked at Roisin to leave the reception early, spent the evening stuck to a far wall.

'Remember when' is the lowest form of conversation.

'I have absolutely no interest in small talk, and Beatrice will probably be quite curious about you,' Joe had said. 'If she smashes down the rosé and buttonholes us, we should make a sharp exit.'

Roisin had probed this aversion to their contact, to check it wasn't his lingering feelings.

'God no! It's the exact opposite: it's such old news and I barely remember that time. She's sent me chatty messages down the years I've left on Read, because who wants to get into that? I'm wary Bea will get hammered and make a beeline for us, that's all. No pun.'

Roisin had never questioned the terms of their break-up very closely: she didn't even know how long they'd been seeing each other. She was responsible and it was too uncomfortable. No one aged twenty-three and falling in love wants to ponder the collateral too hard.

They'd had a grand total of one conversation about it, fizzing with nerves and novelty on their first date in a tapas bar.

I was dreading telling her, but it was pretty civilised, once she got over the shock, Joe had said. *She was very Live and Die in York, York Forever, if you know what I mean. She'd already declined to move to Manchester – she'll barely visit. I didn't want to stay there, and we'd reached a crossroads anyway. I mean, she wasn't OVERJOYED to discover you exist. I don't wanna pretend. But I think she knew the end was nigh. She wants to stay friends, and I'll stay friendly, but not friends.*

Who knew if any of that had been true.

That night at the wedding, Beatrice had given Roisin at least one long, enigmatic, borderline resentful look across the room, when the table wine was flowing. You were fully entitled to resent, and inspect, the woman he left you for. Roisin only hoped Beatrice knew that nothing had happened until she and Joe were post fact.

Bea had very straight, platinum-blonde hair, with a swept to the side long fringe, a style cut short enough she could tuck it behind her ear. She was hip and slender, in an over-sized tortoiseshell necklace in the shape of an autumn leaf, a tropical-patterned pant suit and platform heels. She was cool, Roisin thought, and confident.

Roisin remembered thinking she didn't look like the nervous, parochial girl that Joe had painted, blaming that on her own stereotypes or the passage of time, rather than any fault in his original account.

Meanwhile, Joe played his discomfort off as advanced boredom. Yet looking back, Roisin could see it was more like fronting nerves.

What if his reluctance to be at that event, and his unwillingness to be around Bea specifically, wasn't because she didn't matter any more, but because she *did*?

What if the 'she's never got over me' hints were some really plucky 'foreshadowing', as Joe would term it? Insurance, if Bea slurred, *you don't know the half of it* in the Ladies?

For the first time, Roisin realised she'd conflated two separate things after seeing *Hunter*.

There was having sex with someone other than your partner, repeatedly. Then there was having that sex with a merry-go-round of near-strangers. Joe being cunning, fearless, and adept at the latter was always improbable, and her friends rightly called out that it didn't sound like him. That part felt like what it was: the sort of high-wire antics that sustain a TV series but don't happen much in life. *I'm no Rufus Tate, and I don't have any cinematic licence to clear a restaurant.*

The high stakes Sesso encounter didn't stack up as Joe.

But that didn't mean Joe couldn't still be guilty of the former crime? That could still be the spark that lit the flame?

Roisin asked herself: what if it wasn't tons of women, and not younger waitresses he had fifteen minutes flat to seduce? But one, ongoing affair? Joe had used his times with Beatrice as inspiration, and embellished.

Roisin settled on a firm conviction: if it was anyone, it was her. He was at that hotel with Beatrice.

Roisin had been fatally incurious about he and Bea's

beginning and their ending, and in such areas of ambiguity, Joe thrived.

There was one huge impossible challenge facing Roisin, and it stood in the way of some kind of truth at last about Joe Powell.

Getting Beatrice to admit it.

66

Your Destination Is Two Hundred Yards Ahead On Your Right.
You Have Reached Your Destination.

The tinny voice of the satnav didn't know how true she spoke. It had been a long winding road since the screening room in a stately home. Literally as well as figuratively, for the last two hours. Yet Roisin felt she might finally be in sight of some closure.

She'd had two minor miracles come her way; now she needed a third. The first miracle was Dominic unintentionally contradicting Joe. The second was that Beatrice McMahon, according to her online research, ran a florists in central York called *Blooms By Bea*.

Roisin calculated that most florists were independent and didn't make extraordinary profits, giving her a decent chance of finding the owner behind the counter before closing. It was preferable to sitting outside her house in a stake-out.

She'd picked up her car in Webberley and set off, full of trepidation and butterflies, but no anger, not even indignance. Why *was* she devoid of wrath at the woman who likely had had intimate encounters with her other half? After all, it was virtually certain that Beatrice knew about her, and not vice versa.

The obvious explanation was because she wasn't in love with Joe any more and she was in love with someone else. The deeper one was that she felt sure Beatrice had been contracted into it with deceptions.

The conundrum of coaxing Beatrice into a disclosure with her was similar to the Sesso waitress: *what was in it for her?* How did Roisin leapfrog the greater loyalty Bea would naturally feel she owed to the man she'd been having intermittent liaisons with for a decade?

After all, to have done it, she must either be a moral-less jackal or pretty terminal-smitten, and Roisin heavily betted on the latter.

Having thought and thought and *thought* about this, Roisin figured she had one card to play – only one. If it didn't work, if Beatrice wasn't brought onside, she was done. She felt a curious peace and satisfaction with this, rather than desperation. Beatrice telling her to do one couldn't send Roisin into a tailspin of *what next*, as there was no *what next*.

Roisin knew something for sure, anyway. She'd confirmed to herself that Joe had lied, and she had no doubt Joe had cheated. If Beatrice chose not to corroborate that, then OK. A shame, but it wouldn't change her mind.

Plus, if Roisin was wrong on specifics, if it wasn't Beatrice at The Royal, then she'd made a tit of herself, but nothing more. The good thing about not going in guns blazing was that she had nothing to apologise for, except wasting her time.

The only part she regretted in this plan was the necessity

of doorstepping Beatrice, which was, if not an aggressive act, then at least without Beatrice's consent.

There was no other way. Messaging Beatrice came with such an incredibly high chance of Beatrice reading and rereading her typed words, trying to assess if Roisin was for real. And inevitably, even if she later came to regret it, snatching up the phone and calling Joe in a panic. Roisin couldn't bear for Joe to get the jump on her, yet again. Next time, if there was one, he needed to be completely ambushed.

Roisin had a case to make to Beatrice, and some promises could only be made in person.

She parked up in the city car park she knew from her girlfriend visits. God, what if she ran into her former in-laws? She'd be having a day out, or something.

Roisin's heart rate increased the closer she got to the location she'd looked at dozens of times on Google Maps. She walked past a dry cleaners and a vape shop and the windows of empty premises, scoured with whorls of white paint. She caught an amazing waft of dough and sugar and saw a fashionable bakery. On fidgety impulse, she darted inside and bought some dough-nuts, straight out of the fryer.

Then, resuming her walk, there it was: buttercream-coloured signage with the name in curly green script, a doorway crowded with wooden pots of pansies and a chalk A-board, promising many more plants inside.

Roisin could feel her heartbeat in her neck as she wrenched open a heavy door that sounded a loud jangle of old-fashioned shop bell.

Inside, the floor was artificial grass, the ceiling a cluster of creepers like an invading alien force, and it smelled characteristically of a florists: damp soil and floral musk.

Beyond the counter there was a slight, fair woman with glasses on her head, wearing gloves, snipping long rose stems with secateurs. She looked up at Roisin, and froze. It was as if she'd seen a ghost, and Roisin supposed she was one. The Prying Lady.

It was about three quarters of all the confirmation that Roisin would ever need. She glanced to her left and saw a teenage girl with a septum piercing observing Roisin and her lightly steaming brown paper bag.

'Hi. Is It Bea?' Roisin said, to a still-frozen Beatrice.

She nodded, in mute horror.

'I wondered if I could have a quick word, in private?'

A moment passed. Roisin could barely have got more of a reaction if she'd flapped a coat open to reveal a holstered gun.

'Er . . . Yeah. Upstairs,' Beatrice said, in a quavering voice. She came out from behind the counter, laying down her tool and peeling off her gloves, and led Roisin up a short flight of very deep steps to a tiny, low-ceilinged office-cum-storeroom. It had an overflowing desk and nowhere much to sit, so Roisin stood.

'Sorry to barge in like this. I guess you know who I am: Roisin. Until very recently, I was Joe Powell's girlfriend. You need to know that I come in total peace. I've brought these as an offering.' She held aloft her doughnuts to a bewildered Bea, as if brandishing a dog poop-scoop sack. 'Nothing you can say will make me upset at you. I'm only here to put my mind at rest.'

She placed the bag on her desk.

'If you tell me to piss off, I will piss off at once. This is emphatically *not* girl-on-girl violence. The only person I want to expose or get into trouble here is Joe. I don't care or mind what you did. I only want to prove for my own sake that I never got the truth from Joe.'

Beatrice looked, understandably, stupefied. As Roisin had predicted, this announcement alone didn't tip the scales into Bea reflexively unburdening about her sex life to a stranger who'd breezed into her place of work at five o'clock with sweet pastry goods (two jam and two ring).

'OK, so. When I was twenty-three, I worked with a guy from York at Waterstone's Deansgate. Joe, who had a girl-friend back home, here. You. He flirted. *We* flirted, I should say. Only for about a month, six weeks. I'm not without guilt. It was never going to go any further, as far as I was concerned, as I knew about you. I should've kept a more respectful distance though.'

Roisin smiled awkwardly and drew breath. It was impossible to tell how this was going across.

'Then one day, he came up to me and said he was ending it with you in order to ask me out. He told me afterwards you two were pretty much on the rocks at the time, you wanted different things. You didn't want to move to Manchester. The break-up was very amicable. You wanted to stay friends, but he didn't. I didn't feel fully comfortable about you being dumped so fast for me, and nor should I. But he made it easy not to think about it.'

Beatrice, albeit not having many options in the matter, was listening so intently her forehead was furrowed.

'If that was true, and you are completely fine with how Joe represented your situation, and . . . possibly have other reasons for doing what I think you did at The Royal hotel a few weeks ago, then that's that. But I have this intuition that I got told what I needed to hear when you split up. And that, perhaps, you've never had a true account either. That although by rights we should be enemies, we might have some common ground.'

Beatrice was perfectly silent, totally still.

'Or alternatively, some woman has marched in here, dragged up very old news for you and mentioned hotel stays that mean nothing to you. In which case, feel free to pity me.' Roisin smiled. 'But I hope you don't feel attacked. I'm just trying to put the puzzle pieces together, having shared my life with someone who was hiding half the jigsaw from me.'

'Uhm,' Beatrice cleared her throat.

Everything hung in the balance. Roisin thought the very fact Beatrice hadn't said, *what the hell, get out,* indicated a willingness to discuss this.

'I . . . I have no idea what this is about, sorry. I've not seen Joe in years.'

Roisin felt sadness, but not surprise. 'Ah, OK. Absolutely fair enough. Apologies for the strangeness of my approach. Please enjoy the doughnuts, at least.'

Beatrice nodded.

Roisin smiled a hearty stoic's smile, turned and descended carefully down the stairs, and saw herself out of the shop, avoiding acknowledging the curiosity of Beatrice's assistant.

She closed the door behind her with a jangle, walked down the street, inhaling the early evening air in deep gulps as the adrenaline receded.

Well, that *was* that. Did she believe her? She was unsure. Not really. That wasn't the demeanour of someone genuinely perplexed, more cornered.

As Roisin reached the car park and blipped the key fob to open her car door, she felt a hand on her arm.

She turned to see Beatrice, slightly out of breath from having chased her, wind blowing her hair across her face.

'Roisin. I'm sorry. When you said you'd walk away if I said I didn't know what you were talking about, I had to know you meant it, and it wasn't a trap. Would you have time for a glass of wine?'

67

'I can have one if I'm driving, right?' Roisin said, smiling at Beatrice, who, despite proposing this drink, looked stricken.

She'd taken her to a tiny nook of a hipster bar with copper surfaces, Pet Nat wine and uncomfortable folding seats, and got herself a large white, small for Roisin.

'First of all. Oh God.' Beatrice pressed at her eyebrows with her fingertips. She was very attractive in a delicate, unmade-up, continental sort of way. She had a small gap between her front teeth and looked like the smart and mysterious love interest in the lecture hall in an indie movie. '*First of all*, I was told you asked Joe out. You seduced him, threatened to tell me, and threw down a gauntlet. Said it was me or you. You burned every photo of us together, so he had no pictures of his early twenties. You were a force of nature and Joe got devoured by you, he said. A rampaging succubus in Agent Provocateur lingerie – no man was safe.' Beatrice rolled her eyes.

'Fuck off!' Roisin said, inelegantly, mouth hanging open, then hooting with laughter so loud the barman looked up. 'Seriously?

I was the girl in *The Muppets* t-shirt with major insecurities and an overdraft.'

She'd pretty much expected this sort of thing, and yet it was still incredible.

'It was what I needed to hear, of course. Some massively hot slut had stolen him, just because she could, as the song goes. *Ro-sheen, Rooo-sheeen*. I used to call you "Rolene". I feel so ashamed and embarrassed . . .' Beatrice said. 'Carrying on seeing Joe, on and off, knowing he was with you – it's the worst thing I've ever done. Today you walked in, and it was my nightmare coming true.'

'That's me,' Roisin said, grinning. 'A vision from hell.'

'Why are you not throwing that over me?' Bea nodded at the wine Roisin was sipping. 'I don't understand.'

'Because while it was wrong, you never told me any lies or made any promises to me. Joe did. I was the woman who stole your bloke, and you owed me nothing.'

'It was still shit, Roisin. I knew you lived together. I can't blame it all on his inventions and my trauma.'

Roisin realised she'd something powerful to offer Beatrice she'd not considered or factored in, whatsoever. Absolution.

'Trauma?' Roisin said, carefully.

Beatrice swiped her fringe to one side. 'Joe and I got together in sixth form . . .'

Roisin sucked in breath even at this, and Beatrice noticed.

'Oh yeah. Joe was my first everything. You didn't know that?'

'No. I got "post-university casual thing became comfy, both of you know it's a starter relationship" vibe.'

'Hah, no. We'd have been going out six years, when you met. We were seventeen.'

'Wow.'

'I was nervous when he moved to Manchester. I couldn't go too, for various reasons. My floristry course was here, and I needed to save money by living with my parents for a while. I got suspicious when he wouldn't take me on your work nights out. I only ever went on one, and I twigged much later he'd picked a time when you were away.'

Roisin nodded.

'Then' – she twiddled her wine glass stem – 'he said he'd met someone, and we were over. I was absolutely in pieces. It was a side of him I'd not seen before. Merciless and brisk. Like he was restructuring his company. He never cried. No tears at all.' Beatrice looked down at the table. 'Or not in front of me,' she added.

'I'm so sorry,' Roisin said.

Beatrice shook her head. 'You hardly need to apologise to me! The thing is . . . this is no excuse. But to give you context that I'm absolutely sure you don't have. We'd had an accident. Six weeks before Joe told me it was over. I had a termination. We thought we were far too young, and it was never in doubt that we'd decide what we did, but still. It was an ordeal when we were long-distance, and I wasn't prepared for how I'd feel. I couldn't believe that so soon after he was finishing with me for a girl he'd clearly been falling for, for a while. It screwed me up, wondering at the timeline between dashing back to hold my hand at the clinic, and getting off with you.'

'Fucking hell,' Roisin said. She'd blithely thought Joe was no longer capable of shocking her. She was wrong.

She wasn't going to lie to herself: had Joe told her all this, and that he and Bea were still through, and he wanted her instead, they likely would've gotten together eventually anyway.

But seeing how he treated his ex, in these circumstances – it would've been instructive about him.

'I became obsessed with you. The way you always are with your *rival*, in those situations, I suppose. Read everything I could see online, ransacked Joe's Facebook for details. I was so jealous of you, Roisin, it was like a disorder. I lost a stone and a half,' Beatrice smiled. 'It would've helped if you weren't beautiful, but of course you bloody are.'

'Hah. I think years at the frontline in a comp has aged me,' Roisin said. 'But thank you.'

Roisin felt a swell of genuine, heart-lifting female solidarity at pooling their resources like this.

'Eventually you weren't another woman to me, who might have your own story – you were a mythical creature. Joe came back, that first Christmas, without you. I was in a group of friends with him who went to the pub. I was shaking at seeing him. I was in such a mess, mentally, that I believed that the fact that you weren't there signified that you and him wouldn't last. We ended up getting drunk and doing it in the pub loo.' Beatrice covered her eyes with a palm.

Roisin thought of Joe's brash dismissal of the Petra at Sesso accusation, his moral outrage. All the while knowing he *had* done that, just not with Petra.

'I thought it was a victory. I thought if he still wanted me, he'd come back to me. Those early days, I didn't feel guilty at all. It was like warfare and I was taking back my territory or something. I was so in love with him. And very broken.'

'Yes,' Roisin said. 'Except Joe wasn't broken – he was exploiting you.'

Beatrice nodded, looking at Roisin with pure wonder. That Joe's girlfriend would ever see it her way, was understandably not a thing she had ever anticipated.

'The trouble was, having done it that Christmas, when I saw him the following Easter, it happened again. Once you've done it already, your conscience is already dirty. It became a thing. A glitch. Joe was back in town, on his own, and we'd end up in bed. Sometimes I was in a relationship, too, to my utter shame. He got off on that.'

'How many times did it happen?' Roisin said. 'I don't know why that matters . . .'

'No, I get it. Probably about a dozen? Once a year or so.'

Roisin exhaled. Every year.

'At first, as I said, I wanted him back. Obviously at some point I let go of that and Joe was more like a poison I couldn't get out of my system. I thought we were fucking Emma and Dexter in *One Day,* and we were in fact *Groundhog Day* with fucking.' She looked at Roisin. 'How on earth am I treating you as an agony aunt?!'

'Because I'm in fact your agony sister,' Roisin said.

68

'Watching his series, *Hunter*, I knew in my bones that it had come from somewhere in Joe's life. He gaslit me and fumed at me. Our mutual friends thought I was crazy; that's how good a liar he is,' Roisin said. 'But the thrills in it were based on your meet-ups, right?'

Beatrice said, unable to look at her directly, 'Yes. I recognised lots of it. Somehow, in his head, I didn't count as being unfaithful. That should've told me I was worthless, but . . .' Beatrice made a 'rotating finger to side of head' gesture.

'This is a minor thing, but I have a thirst for knowledge,' Roisin said, and Beatrice grimaced. 'Oh God, no, not about *that*. How did you communicate? I'm certain Joe wouldn't leave any trail. So much so, I've never once thought of checking his phone.'

'Oh, he was very into that, you're right,' Beatrice said. 'Very strict about it. When he finally put me into his phone it was under his agent's name, as their second mobile. He said we had to use "London" instead of York or home and to couch it all in work-speak. You know, "are you free for

meeting on X, I need to go over this latest draft with you",
etc. Utterly tacky.'

*Sneaking around is rather exciting and becomes a bit of an art.
It was very much part of what made it electrifying.*

'I finally stopped it after Jim and Liddy's wedding,' Beatrice
said. 'When I saw you in person. I'd bought into so much
about how you and Joe had this loveless relationship, and
you were a fragile, volatile person he couldn't risk leaving
because you'd blow his friendships apart as revenge.'

Roisin struggled to absorb the extent of the treachery from
someone she had loved, whom she'd thought had loved her.
Joe was multiple people, and she lived with only one version
of him. Bea knew another.

'I'd known deep down they were excuses for a while, but
I'd made a mess that felt too big to clean up,' Beatrice said.
'Then I could see with my own eyes none of it was true.
When I saw you as a couple, you being lovely to everyone,
I could tell it wasn't an act. I realised you were his Significant
Other and I was his Insignificant Other. He leaned on me
hard not to go that day, and the penny dropped as to why.
I'd been really, really stupid.'

'Hmmm, Joe's been off with me for around a year,' Roisin
said. 'I wonder if that was the trigger.'

'I think he hates losing control of people. Control is what
he calls love,' Beatrice said, and Roisin had to abruptly clash
her wine glass to hers to emphasise the nail being hit on the
head.

'If it was over, what was the five-star hotel stay about?'
Roisin said.

'He said he wanted a deadly serious discussion. I thought maybe a parent was ill or something. I turned up, saw the fizz in the ice bucket and never even took my coat off. It was the ol' razzle dazzle. The fabulous offer to get back together at last. I said no.'

Roisin thought about how, in different circumstances, they'd have been friends. 'You said no?'

'I did. The attraction had been dimming for a long time. When he said that, I knew for sure I didn't want what I wanted when we were twenty-three any more. Plus, I knew who he was. Why would he commit to me if he'd done that to you? My friends pointed that out, endlessly.'

Roisin nodded. 'He'd offered me a fresh start, relationship counselling, and we were hanging in the balance at the time,' Roisin said. 'I guess he decided to ask both of us and see who said yes? If we both did, he'd choose, or worry about that later?'

'I guess?' Beatrice said, aghast. 'I knew what he did with me was weak and wrong, but it's pathological, isn't it?'

'The thing with Joe I've learned,' Roisin said, 'is that when you catch him in a lie, there's a new lie to cover for the old lie. There's layers of it. It's like scraping away old gloss and wallpaper. Together, we've found at least a patch of original bricks and mortar, I reckon.' She clinked her glass to Bea's again.

Beatrice twitched a smile, looked down at the table. 'What I did to you is unforgivable. I'm so glad to have your forgiveness, but I don't deserve it.'

'I needed to know for sure who Joe is,' Roisin said. 'You could've said nothing and protected yourself. Most people would. That's exactly what Joe relied on. Instead, you've been decent enough to tell me the truth. That took guts. *That* deserves forgiveness.'

'You're a pretty extraordinary person to see it this way,' Beatrice said, welling up. She laughed. 'The irony . . .'

'What?' Roisin said.

'All these years, Joe built you up to be intimidating. It turns out, you are. Brilliantly so.'

Back at her car, Roisin turned to Beatrice.

'Do you mind me telling Joe what I know, and saying you told me? I don't have to.'

Beatrice exhaled. '. . . God, sure. Having nothing to hide any more is such a good feeling. If you know, then he has nothing to threaten me with. Give him hell.'

Beatrice looked like she was momentarily assessing whether she dared, then pulled Roisin into a hard, wine-fuelled hug.

69

The formality of a forwarding address for mail now provided her with drone-strike coordinates. Roisin checked her WhatsApp from Joe, bashed the flat's postcode into her satnav and drove straight from York to his new place in Chorlton.

She pulled up at gone eight p.m. and thought he might well be out, on a Friday night. Yet when Roisin got out of the car she saw he was walking down the street, holding two pizza boxes, chatting with Dominic. It was unfortunate for Joe that Dom was there, yet not unfortunate enough to change Roisin's plans.

It might even be useful for him to bear witness. Women would come and go, but his best friend would always have an eye on Joe. Or so you'd think.

'Hi, Joe! Hi, Dominic,' Roisin said, nodding to them as they drew near.

They both looked discomposed.

'I've come from York. Had a drink with your ex, Beatrice,' she said to Joe. In a moment Roisin mentally filed away for many future replays, he looked like he was going to drop the pizzas.

'I say "ex". I should say, "other girlfriend". I think when you carry on having sex with someone who loves you for ten years, they deserve the same status title. Don't you?'

Joe was frozen still. Dominic had eyes like saucers. By rights he should leave them to it, yet Roisin could tell that the tea was simply too piping hot for him to resist.

'I begged you to tell me if *Hunter* was based on your life, and you not only said it wasn't, but that I was paranoid and nasty for contemplating it. Thanks to Beatrice's stories of sex in pub bogs, and even behind the glühwein tent at a Christmas market – your willy must've been freezing – my curiosity is finally satisfied. Amazing scenes. On television, and off.'

Joe was still incapable of speech. Dominic wordlessly relieved him of the pizzas, perhaps thinking as Roisin had that his Pepperoni Extra Cheese might hit the pavement.

'Bea is a great woman, by the way, and deserved infinitely better than you abusing her devotion and using her as your plaything.'

'Yeah, the thing is,' Joe said, sounding weedy, a poor facsimile of his usual glib self, 'you ended our relationship, Roisin. We're not a couple. Now you're sleeping with one of our closest friends. I'd rate your right to throw accusations around and get judgmental as absolutely nil.'

'A very key thing about the sex I am having with Matt . . .'

She let that bomb land, and crater. Joe, who had declared himself certain of this anyway, clearly hadn't been, as he looked like he wanted to be sick.

'. . . is that it started *after* you and I had ended. You and

390

Beatrice were doing it behind our back from our first Christmas. There has, in fact, never been a time you were faithful to me.'

A beat passed. Roisin was grateful Dominic was here, as Joe didn't quite dare issue a fully callous dismissal.

'I'm not saying I've been an angel, but you don't know the context,' he said, in a low, terse voice.

'Some of it involves you supporting her through an abortion and leaving her for me, shortly after. Don't worry. I didn't come to you for answers. The next layer of lies have no value to me. I just wanted to tell you that the power trip you get from lying – from people believing things you've just pulled out of a hat in order to mess with them, to get them to do what you want – it's abusive, and it damages lives. You need to stop.'

Dominic opened his mouth and Roisin said, 'Don't bother to talk across me unless you have a *phenomenally* good insight, Dominic.'

Dominic closed his mouth again.

'I'm not a liar,' Joe said. 'I lied about this, because being in love with two people at once isn't something you can get help for. It's what happened, and it was wrong.'

'*In love with two people at once*, haha. Inside your head must be a very strange, cold place. I would talk to someone professional if I were you. But thank God I'm not. Lastly, I'd never have been with you if I knew about Beatrice, and you knew that. You stole consent from me. You stole ten years of my life from me. Our whole time together was a form of fraud.'

Joe could barely meet her eyes. Dominic no longer looked

like he wanted to say anything. He no longer looked like someone who'd take Joe's side. He was staring sidelong at him.

'So yeah, I will take your half of our property, Joe – thanks for that. It doesn't come close to what you owe me. Which is my freedom, from your mendacious shit, back when I was twenty-three. Goodbye.'

She turned to walk back to her car.

'Hey. There might be an unexpected plot twist in this, for you,' Joe called.

'Try me,' Roisin said, still walking.

'Out of all our friends, one of them knew about Beatrice and me. Imagine if that one person had agreed not to tell and keep my secret for me. I imagine you'd feel pretty betrayed by that friend, right? Choosing me, over you?'

Roisin made a shrug gesture and produced her car key fob, while her heart raced.

'Go ask Matt McKenzie why you didn't deserve to know. I'm sure he'll keep his white knight credentials intact through that.'

Roisin betrayed no emotion, despite her queasy shock. 'You are one spiteful bastard, aren't you.'

'Just introducing some balance to the narrative. Inconvenient to your world view, but there we go. One thing I'd like to know, in return,' Joe said, as she unlocked the car door. 'How did you find out? I know Bea wouldn't have told you.'

'I turned detective again. I'll let you work it out. You write the stories, don't you? Thing is, Joe, if you play the odds, sooner or later, you win.' She hesitated. A last roll of the dice. A neat way of showing his best mate that no one was sacred. 'Oh, and Dominic, can I ask you something? What's Victoria's closest friend called?'

'Er. Closest friend? My wife's? . . . Jess.'

'Not Amber? You don't know an Amber?'

Dominic frowned. 'Er. No? Amber? Should I? Who's that?'

'I think I will take it that your character "Gwen" was based on Gina, then,' Roisin addressed a glowering Joe. 'But shouldn't Vic have a best friend called Amber, who Dominic's got a secret obsession with?'

'What?!' Dominic said.

'I'll let you make something else up to cover for that one, Joe. Enjoy your pizzas.'

70

Roisin let herself in with the key that, only hours ago, had felt like such a lasting pledge. She placed it on the coffee table instead of back in her bag, in a tiny act of pessimism and defeat.

'There you are, I left you a voicemail. I was going to ask if— Are you OK?' Matt said, seeing Roisin's murderous countenance.

He snapped the hob ring off, pointed his phone to turn the music down.

'I found out who Joe was going behind my back with. His long-term ex, who he originally left me for, Beatrice. In York. I met up with her, heard all about it and had a showdown with Joe, just now. Which felt like closing the door on it, on my terms.'

She left a pause, let Matt nod. She could see he was apprehensive.

'. . . Except right at the last minute, he told me a really awful thing. He said you knew all along. Tell me it isn't true, Matt.' Tears started to slide down Roisin's face, and she wiped them away. 'I've prayed all the way here you're going to tell me it's not true. You're going to say it *is* true, aren't you?'

She knew it had to be. It made no sense for Joe to use it unless he knew it'd pay off.

'That total bastard,' Matt said.

'Don't do that!' Roisin shrieked, emotion breaking free. She'd had to stay in character with Joe; she couldn't manage that now. 'Don't turn it into a You Versus Him! The whole point is you're better than him, Matt.'

'I knew about one incident. When we'd be about twenty-six. Not through choice.'

Roisin slumped against the wall. She should've known this, the two of them together, was too perfect to be true. Her life never worked out that way.

The flat was quiet and the city noises, a long way down.

'One evening, I got a pocket dial from him. I answered the call. I didn't hear much, but enough to get the gist it was not meant to be overheard. He was calling her Bea.'

'You heard him actually having sex?' *Hunter*. He'd used this in *Hunter*. Of course Joe had. The whole thing was a crime scene with those number markers next to each exhibit.

'No,' Matt said, 'but as good as. I could tell it was a possibility in the near future, put it that way. I messaged him and asked what was going on. He scrambled to meet me for a pint and did the whole number about how it was a mistake, he was knocking it on the head immediately. *Don't ruin what I have with Roisin, she's the love of my life. My future kids are erasing from the* Back to the Future *family photo as we speak*. Heaped all the responsibility onto me if I told you. Pleaded and begged and leaned as hard as he

395

could on our friendship, which existed a little more back then.'

'You knew she was his ex?'

'Yeah, he told me that much. Ex going through a rough time, who he really felt for. He had stupidly let himself be dragged back into her orbit. A one-off etc. You know what a fast and plausible talker he is.'

'Did you believe him?'

Matt paused. '. . . For the reasons it happened? No. I didn't. I'd heard how he was speaking to her. I thought Joe was the same guy who'd screwed me over, so of course he was doing it to you, too. I hoped being caught and realising what he was risking would shake him to his senses. I believed he was desperate not to lose you.'

'I meant, did you believe him that he'd stop?'

Matt inhaled, heavily. 'I hoped he'd value the second chance. I wasn't sure.'

'The second chance, that you gave him. *You* knew who Joe was, but left me in the dark?'

'Roisin, what was my track record on successfully interfering in other people's business, at this point? If you'd stayed with Joe, would either of you want to keep the guy who blew the whistle in your lives? Yes, it was selfish, but I cared about you too much to lose you over something he did.'

'Why does it follow that you would? I wouldn't have held it against you for telling me the truth, whatever I decided.'

'It's not that simple, is it? Joe would've wheedled his way out of it and you two would've patched it up. I'd have been your guy's mortal enemy. You'd have phased me out, dropped me off invites, because it was too tricky not to. There's no way I stayed in your life as a couple after getting embroiled in that. Joe would've made sure of it.'

'It's irrelevant anyway, as I can tell you I wouldn't have stayed with him!'

'You say that now – Joe could talk himself out of a Russian prison.'

Roisin thought of what Matt said about her liking Mean Boys. Underneath this perhaps was the tyranny of low expectations. Maybe she deserved those low expectations after a decade of failing to see Joe for who he was. But she could've had this wake-up call six years ago, if Matt had been the honourable person she thought he was.

'In short, you didn't think, *does Roisin deserve to know, does Roisin need to know?* You thought, *what are my interests here and how are they best served?*'

'If I could go back and change it, older and wiser, I would do it in a heartbeat. At the time, I was freaked out and just thought no one prospers from getting involved in other people's relationships. Not when they have fights, and not when they make up. It's between the couple.'

'I don't understand: Joe goaded you and insulted you, endlessly. Didn't he worry you'd say, *yeah well, I'll tell your girlfriend what I know?* How was Joe so sure you wouldn't?'

'Hah. As you may have gathered, Joe is a fucking great liar. World class. It was such a bold move, antagonising me and portraying me as the cad. He can read people very closely. Once we were years out from my discovery, he knew that I knew I'd lose you as a friend if I told you. Imagine it?

"Oh, by the way, now he's wound me up sufficiently I feel motivated to blow your life up to get even"? You'd have *maybe* dumped him, but *definitely* told me to get to fuck. He knew I wasn't going to risk that. He was safe. There was a time limit on my telling you.'

'You know what I can't tolerate, Matt? If I'd found this out some other way, some other time, I'd hear you out on Joe putting you in an impossible position. But earlier this summer I came to you, as a friend, in confidence, my mind all over the place and said, "I think Joe might be cheating on me." You were an ally. Someone I could confide in. You offered to help me. Have you got any idea how stupid and betrayed I feel that the whole time, you were merely playing along? Humouring me?'

'I saw that as atonement, not playing along! I did what I could to find out the truth for you. I wanted you to find out, for yourself.'

'But you could've told me right then!' Roisin said. 'That was your second chance! You're saying it didn't occur to you? While you were strolling my village, pretending to think it over, saying, *ah well, yeah that sounds suss as fuck, Rosh, but who can say.*'

'That's true,' Matt said, 'I should've rethought. Instead, I thought helping you was the right way for it to come out.'

'What if I'd said to you, "I was wrong: Joe didn't cheat, I've grovelled my apologies to him, and we're back together and engaged"? Would you have said, *woah there*?'

Matt raised and dropped his shoulders. 'I'd have been gutted, but that would've been your choice, presumably for all sorts of reasons. How could I have interfered?'

'You washed your hands of me.'

'Does it look like my feelings towards you have ever been getting shot and walking away?'

'Do you know what I think? I think you were perfectly aware you could tell me,' Roisin said. 'I think, once again, you put your interests first. There was no glory in telling me at that point, only difficulty for you. Much more kudos in going to Sesso.'

'*Glory*?' Matt said, recoiling. 'You think I wanted rewards from helping you? That's a pretty grim thing to accuse me of. Do you share Joe's opinion of me?'

'Honestly? I don't know,' Roisin said. 'An hour ago, I'd have said it was impossible you could find out he was shagging around on me and agree with him that you'd keep it from me.'

'Do you know what? You're essentially angry with me for not telling you who your ex was,' Matt said, angry himself now. 'You only had to pay attention. Joe wasn't nice, Roisin. Not then, not now. It wasn't someone else's job to tell you that.'

This was a sharp jab at Roisin's weakest point. The one thing about Joe Powell she'd never resolve: how she'd missed it. She felt deep confusion and shame.

'So I'm a stupid girl for not spotting it? It's the victim's fault? It's the *woman's* fault?'

'That's not what I said, and you know it wasn't. Don't play his games.'

'*His* games?!'

Matt shook his head, folded his arms and stared at the couch. 'I don't know how you're making someone who received an unwanted phone call, and Joe, the same person. One of these things is not like the other.'

'I thought you were the one who told me the truth. I'm done with men who lie to me and rationalise it afterwards. No matter how eloquent the excuses are. No matter how good they are at turning it back onto me in the analysis. Your spare key's over there.'

She saw herself out, and he didn't stop her.

71

BRIAN CLUB

Dev
New message

ping

New message

ping

New message

ping

Roisin put down her roller. She was wearing pyjamas inside out and her hair bundled up into a Sainsbury's bag to keep it from paint flecks.

She'd tried headscarves in the past; they looked more appealing and yet didn't keep her puce hairline safe enough.

The thing about being single was, there was no one to see her looking like a *Mars Attacks* alien with a plastic shopper on her head.

Roisin wiped her hands on a cloth and picked her phone up. She best not switch to video call by accident.

She was in the process of turning the chapel-shaped open-plan reception room 'Lamp Black' by Little Greene. It was a dramatic shade that Joe had once upon a time, refused to sign off on, making it feel like a definitive break with the past. It was also a definitive break with good taste. Three-quarters of the way through the project, she had to admit it might've been the one thing Joe was right about. It had recreated a shop where they'd burn incense and try to sell you Himalayan salt candles that looked like lumps of ear wax. She could imagine Matt saying *surely there are easier ways to open a portal for The Wicked One.*

Matt.

Being busy helped banish Matt McKenzie from her mind. When masking-taping edges, swapping her brush sizes for the corners, she didn't think about the contours of his face as much. Or his hands on her body, or how it felt when he kissed her, or any intimate moment that they'd shared that was unhelpful to the decision she'd regretfully made that they were no more.

It was the walks she couldn't forgive, she thought, hand wavering while she was dragging bristles along the skirting board. At a bleak time in her life, those rambles through the woods had saved her sanity. Yet the whole time, Matt was a double agent. He could, as she'd said, have ended her doubts over Joe there and then. But he held it back, made a fool of her.

God, she'd even told him about her short-lived bout of misery-promiscuity in her teens. *That* was how much she'd trusted McKenzie.

What did Gina say? *I feel naked around him anyway, so once he'd literally seen me naked, it was more than I could tolerate.*

Yes, that. Her port in a storm had turned out to be more storm.

She opened the messages on Brian Club.

Dev
GUESS WHO DIDN'T GO TO SOLLER

PLEASE SAY CONGRATS TO THE NEW MR & MRS DOSHI!

There followed two photos of Dev and Anita, one a selfie of them holding up their ring fingers to the camera, another outside the Little White Wedding Chapel in Las Vegas.

While Roisin was marvelling at this, another message arrived.

Dev
Forgive the surprise, we decided to go for it. If we weren't waiting, then why wait. HOWEVER. If you think you've dodged celebrating with us you'd be wrong ☺ <3

*Got a cancellation slot at the Midland Hotel **next Friday** GET YOUR GLAD RAGS ON FOR OUR WEDDING RECEPTION!*

Meredith
MANIACS

I am laughing out loud at my desk.

However sadly next Friday I have cinema tickets. Have fun xx

Gina
Me too, same film. It stars The Rock and Sir Ian McKellen.
What a shame. Congrats guys! Xx

Roisin
DEV & ANITA – THIS IS AMAZING! Mr & Mrs! Wonderful
news <3

However, I need to be in for E.on to read the meter on Friday
night. Gutted. Xx

Anita
BAD BAD BITCHES

Dev
Snakes everywhere, Mrs Doshi. Just u and me now hun xoxo

Joe
(Assuming the girls are joking) but I genuinely have to fly to
the States on the Wednesday prior. So sorry ☹ Have a great
day, guys, congrats and see you soon Xx

Roisin couldn't deny she was relieved at not sharing a ball-room with Joe's seething discontent. Nor did she want him intuiting he'd succeeded at blowing her and McKenzie apart. Hmmm.

She'd tried not to think about how, in not forgiving Matt, she was dancing to Joe's tune.

Dev
No worries mate, we know we're chancing it here – we figured that if anyone can't make it, we'll have a separate celebration with them. Safe travel Xx

Once she'd finished painting, Roisin messaged Meredith and Gina separately.

Has anyone told Dev & Anita about me and Joe? I think he'd call me straight away, so guessing not?

Meredith
No!

Roisin
Given Joe's not going to be there, easier to leave that now until after his knees up?

Meredith
Good thinking

Gina

Also I rang Matt as soon as I got the message from Dev, and had a REALLY good chat. He'll definitely be coming to the reception. He doesn't want to rejoin the WhatsApp group for now because of the heat with Joe, but he's basically back on board for events without him. Feels really good to have made up. ☺

Roisin wished her fulsome, positive response to this wasn't so false. It was clear Matt hadn't told Gina what had happened between them, and nor had she. She and Matt were over before they'd begun, so what was the point? She'd tell the girls one day, but couldn't face it right now. Having felt the need to disclose a kiss, she was far more resigned about neglecting to mention their having done much more. Life moves pretty fast.

Nor had she told her friends about Joe and Beatrice; that could wait, too.

Irony upon irony: Gina was overjoyed that Matt was free to come back to the Brians, but Roisin knew now he never would.

This was where Roisin and Matt would be forever, then: decoding information passed between third parties. *Oof* – while she'd accepted there'd probably be occasions she'd have to socialise with Joe and New Mrs Joe (God help her), Matt and New Mrs Matt was going to be torment.

Roisin inspected the quantity of Goth paint left in her tin and sighed heavily.

'I'm going to need a good dress,' she said aloud, to a mostly soot-coloured room.

72

Roisin picked up a black satin court shoe from the box with tissue paper, examining it with resentful suspicion. The heel was like a chopstick. She pushed her foot into it and noticed how awkward and less comfortable she was, and how nice the silhouette of her leg looked with her calf muscle tensed.

Bloody women's fashion.

She'd booked a room at The Midland to get ready for/ crash out after the Doshi nuptials, and if she was honest, have a place of retreat from the party if it got too much. The electrics at the apartment were playing up – she couldn't bring herself to call Cormac – and the whole place smelled of paint.

She didn't know if Matt was bringing a date. It would be a bit much, a fortnight after they parted ways, but equally she didn't expect his dating patterns to follow earthbound rituals and he didn't owe her not to.

Roisin had completely failed to find a dress for tonight, which was unsurprising, given she was looking for a magical suit of armour for £150–200 max. She wanted the beholder to see a stylish, confident, yet not tits-forward woman who could rise to the occasion without actually trying, because she was too cool for that.

After approximately seventeen online options were returned, Roisin went with a black sequin minidress she'd had since forever, teamed with black opaques, which would have Lorraine saying, *I do wish you'd try a pop of colour instead of this Worst Witch thing.*

The new footwear, at least, was a way of announcing she was still battle ready.

Roisin appreciated the irony that she'd never once worried about what Matt McKenzie thought she looked like in clothes, until after he'd seen her out of them.

Sharing a ballroom with him was what Wendy Copeland would, again, call NFI. That she quivered at the thought of locking eyes with him was ethically and practically irrelevant, however!

Roisin couldn't expect her attraction to him to vaporise overnight, so she'd simply have to wait for it to catch up with her intellect. She was likely to find exceptional forgiveness for someone beautiful she'd spent the best night of her life with. Who could say.

I don't know how you're making someone who received an unwanted phone call, and Joe, the same person. One of these things is not like the other.

She increasingly found it hard to deny the truth of this.

Was she disappointed? Yes. But . . . did Matt have rights to be disappointed in her, for not seeing through Joe for so long?

As Roisin checked her eye make-up for the fifth time in

the unstinting magnification of the circular, barber's shop mirror in the hotel bathroom, an inner voice whispered that now the anger with Matt had largely gone, what remained, might not be disappointment, so much as fear.

Her head knew that Joe Powell was a rare aberration, her heart wasn't so ready to accept it. The thought that Matt might hide things from her . . . ? Trying not to flinch when his phone rippled with messages from admirers? Forcing herself to never ever check he'd deleted the dating apps?

So . . . you won't give him another chance because you like him too much? said the inner voice. Roisin told it to shut up.

Her phone pinged. Meredith, Gina and Aaron were here and waiting for her in the lobby.

As she descended in the lift, gibbering terror took over. What if Matt HAD brought a date? What if it was High Ponytail Ivy Legs from festa?

Roisin, she said to herself sternly. In the words of Lorraine, *a grip should be fucking gotten.*

Downstairs, she greeted the group and could quickly see that Aaron was a delight: a slim, curly haired lad in a navy suit who smiled broadly at everyone. *He must adore Gina, to walk the plank of meeting all her friends this soon,* Roisin thought.

'Wow. You'd never know that Dev and Anita had days to prepare this?!' Gina said, as they entered a hotel ballroom full of white balloons, white flowers and two huge lightbulb-illuminated letter initials.

Meredith whispered, 'That'd be a thing called money,' to them.

'WOMEN. Notice, A&D, not D&A, very important to me,'

said Anita, seizing hold of them. She was in a sapphire-coloured gown with a waterfall cape attached to it and looked like the benevolent queen in a science fiction film. Screaming with delight at the sight of her ensued.

'Come see this,' Anita said, beckoning them over to a corner display of photographs of her and Dev as kids, on their first date, foreign holidays. Roughly in the centre was the one of the Brian Club, ten years ago, and the one at Benbarrow Hall.

Roisin gazed at it and thought about the distance between those two images for her. She looked at Joe, hiding his face, and Matt, both pushed out and keeping a distance, and thought, *it was always all there from the start, if you looked for it.*

The riddle of Joe Powell wasn't Then Joe turning into Now Joe. He didn't change; their circumstances did.

Meredith found her hand, without anyone noticing, and squeezed it.

'Fancy finding a drink, Miss Walters?' Meredith said, and Roisin said, 'Fuck, yes.'

An hour after the do started, Roisin saw him from a distance. He looked fashionable as always in a fawn, needlecord suit that would have had Terence remembering why he hated coming into Manchester. The room was large enough for them to keep a respectful distance and Roisin gathered they'd do that, rather than speak.

At one point, chatting with a good-looking cousin, she caught Matt's eye across the room and they shared a look that Roisin couldn't really decipher beyond a hard, mutual *ouch.*

★

As the night entered its later hours, she sensed Matt had gone. Occasional little heart-stopping glimpses of him dwindled to none.

Sod these shoes, Roisin thought, she was going to switch to the flats she had in her room. Her inner voice said, *he's not here, nobody to impress, huh?* and she internally thundered, *SHUDDUP.*

As she stood by the lifts and fumbled for her key card in her bag, she heard, 'Can I have a quick word?'

She looked up to see Matt. Being booze-worn didn't make it easier: she had no idea what to say.

He led her through the foyer, beyond the revolving door, onto the hotel's front step by the Hackney rank. She rubbed her arms in the nocturnal chill. Autumn was coming. Other than that, she had no idea what was coming.

'I won't keep you a minute,' Matt said, hands in suit trouser pockets. 'OK, so – I'm telling you this not because I expect it to change anything, or because I think it casts me in a better light. It's honesty for honesty's sake. I asked myself why I didn't tell you. You know, the reason behind the reasons I'd told myself at the time. I don't think I really, deep down, thought you'd ditch me as a friend. You were right to call bullshit on that. It's not in your nature. It was because I didn't trust my motives.'

'I see,' Roisin said, not yet seeing.

'. . . I'd wanted you to leave Joe from day one, so here I was, being handed a way to make that happen. I couldn't be sure what to do because it was so clouded by my own interests. I told myself therefore that stepping back was the pure and noblest route.' Matt drew breath. 'You're absolutely right that my decision making was all about me, not you. Once again, my ego and self-image were running the show. I should have put you first, asked myself what *you'd* want me to do, and I didn't. And I should've told you what I knew when you finally said you had your fears. I wanted to look better in your eyes, as you said. I'll always regret that.'

Roisin nodded.

'. . . But it wasn't in hope of any reward. You can hate me for everything else, but don't hate me for that. I was a long way past thinking you'd ever see me as anything but a friend. That's the truth.'

Roisin had nothing prepared in reply. 'OK. Thank you,' she said. 'I believe you.'

In the ensuing silence, Matt added, 'Night, Roisin.' He turned and walked away without Roisin knowing what to say to stop him, or if she should.

She went back into The Midland, forgetting she was going to change her shoes or even that they'd pinched as she wandered back into the ballroom.

'Hey, there she is!' Dev said, at sight of Roisin at the door. 'Can I have this dance, Miss Walters?' he said. Even in the melee at his own wedding, Dev was displaying his extraordinary emotional sonar that could detect someone feeling a little lost. Roisin had never been so grateful to be wrapped in a Dev hug and spun around.

After a few turns to Joe Cocker's 'You Are So Beautiful', Dev said, 'Listen,' leaning in. He checked behind them to be sure they weren't being overheard. 'I know I'm not supposed to know about this. I'm not going to tell anyone else; I've not even told Anita. He didn't intend to tell me – your name came up and he got upset. Feel free to tell me to piss off out of your business for saying this much, Rosh. But I met up for a drink with him and we had a massive heart to heart. He's absolutely head over heels in love with you and so sorry he hurt you. He's a very good person, you know. I know I tend to see the positives about people, but he really is. If you gave him another chance, I can't see you regretting it. That's all.'

'That's so nice of you, Dev,' Roisin said. 'But the thing about Joe is, he's really skilful at being the person that the situation demands. I promise you that whatever he's told you, it's tons more complicated and more ugly in reality. I don't want you to feel you have to take sides, but trust me, we're better off apart.'

Dev smiled. 'I'm talking about Matt.'

Someone else cut in, and Dev left Roisin standing on the dancefloor, looking comically stunned.

73

Roisin was roused from deep sleep by caterwauling. She opened her eyes and gazed at the drum-shaped lampshade in the gloaming. She didn't know if it had happened in her dream or in the waking world. By mutual agreement, this Sunday was her last night at The Mallory before she settled back in to West Didsbury and faced a new school term.

'ROISIIIIIIIIN! Roisiiiiiiin?'

Roisin sat bolt upright, sweat forming at the nape of her neck. She grasped for the hair bobble she always kept on the bedside table.

'*ROISIN!*'

She leaped out of bed and padded down the corridor, almost letting go of a scream at the sight of her mother, in her silk nightdress, slumped in a heap in the hallway.

'What's wrong?'

'I'm in quite a lot of pain,' Lorraine said, clutching her abdomen, as Roisin pulled her hair into the band to get it out of her pale, half-slept face. 'It's my stomach.'

She took in her mother's lemon-coloured, damp complexion and, to real fright, what looked like a pile of vomit nearby.

'I'll call an ambulance,' Roisin said.

'I don't know if we need to go that far. I'll be alright . . . Call the other number where they tell you what to do,' Lorraine said.

She tried to move and involuntarily made a noise which tipped Roisin from 'extremely agitated' to 'actually very scared'.

'DON'T – stay there,' Roisin said, running to her room, grabbing her mobile, yanking it from the charger and tapping the 999 which, at the age of thirty-two, felt surreal to finally use.

Someone else's daughter had called the ambulance for her dad.

'Operator. Which emergency service do you require?'

'Ambulance – it's for my mum – we're at The Mallory pub in Webberley, just off the high street . . .'

She gabbled the address twice and things about stomach pain, confirming that her mum was conscious.

'The ambulance is coming, stay still,' Roisin said, running back down the hall.

'Thank you,' Lorraine said. That she didn't object frightened Roisin out of her wits.

'When did the pain start?' she said.

A pause.

'. . . You're going to be angry with me.'

'*Angry* with you? Why?'

'I've been having pain in my guts for a while.'

'How long?'

'Months. I've gobbled ibuprofen like it's going out of

fashion and soldiered on. You know me. It's like Liz Taylor said. "Pour yourself a drink, get your lipstick on and pull yourself together."'

'MUM! What?! So you didn't go to the doctor?'

'No.'

'But your biopsy? The breast lump?'

'I told a few white lies. I *was* feeling poorly.'

'None of that happened? You invented a cancer scare?'

'I knew you'd never come back here if you didn't think I was ill! I wanted to see you. I told you it was clear; I didn't worry you!'

Roisin was speechless.

Only Lorraine Walters could say, *sorry I invented a possible cancer and an investigation that never happened, but please be appreciative I also invented an all clear that never happened. PS: I am seriously unwell anyway.*

'But you *were* ill! You just weren't doing anything about it!'

'I don't want to be an old sick person or have a bald head, Roisin! I'd rather be me or not at all.'

Lorraine's face contorted as a wave of pain rolled over her, and a wave of panic in Roisin's stomach followed its trajectory.

'Are you seriously saying you'd rather be dead than bald?!' Roisin said.

Lorraine tried to adjust herself on the carpet and winced. 'Like I say. I didn't want fuss. I only wanted to see you.'

'Wanted the bar shifts from me, more like,' Roisin said, rolling her eyes and trying to lighten a mood that was hardly likely to be lightened.

'I had calls to return to Amy and Ernest ages ago. I thought it'd be nice to spend some time together.'

'Did you not think Ryan deserved to know?' Roisin said.

Lorraine raised her shoulders a centimetre, all she could muster by way of a shrug. 'Further to travel, isn't it. Mothers want their daughters at times like this.'

What times they were remained to be seen.

Roisin tried to absorb this. Her mother had feared she might be dying, she was in so much agony, this whole time? She'd sought no treatment. She'd hoodwinked Roisin. An awful realisation dawned: her mum would rather do all this, risk all this, than tell Roisin she loved her, and she needed her. She'd rather do this than risk Roisin rejecting her.

There was the additional inhibition that Roisin would've forced her to the GP. But it was also obvious that Lorraine had no language to bridge this gap between them, and make believe had been used to fill it.

'Now. I need you to put my lipstick on before the para-medics get here,' Lorraine said. 'The Charlotte Tilbury in the navy quilted bag with the flowers on the top of the cabinet in my bathroom. Walk Of No Shame or Lost Cherry, please.'

'You HAVE to be kidding,' Roisin said.

'This might be my last request!' Lorraine screeched and Roisin extravagantly tutted and huffed, as much to mask her terror as anything. Of course her mother wasn't sparing her, in spelling out the threat. *Lorraine gonna Lorraine.*

She ran to her room and shuddered at the glass of water

spilled on the floor. Her mum had crawled on hands and knees to her position in the hallway. Roisin raked through the contents of the toiletries bag, squinting at the base of each lipstick to see the name. She felt sure Lorraine would spot the wrong shade, even when crippled by a seven to nine on the official pain scale.

Walk Of No Shame hit her as gruesomely apt. The arc of history was long, and it bent towards sick humour. She went for Lost Cherry.

Don't think about lying to Joe. Don't think about what he made you swear your life upon. Don't think about it, don't think about it.

She returned to her side, kneeling down and twisting the lipstick out of its case.

'I can't believe I'm doing this. Pout your mouth out then.'

Lorraine, who was clearly conserving energy due to the unbearable agony, pushed her lips towards it as Roisin dabbed the colour on.

The process was utterly ridiculous and felt unbearably tender, at the same time. Roisin couldn't think about anything that was happening too hard, or she'd lose it.

'Can probably do without the lip liner,' Lorraine said, smacking her lips together, and Roisin barked, 'YA RECKON,' to cover her emotion.

'Listen. There's something I want to talk to you about,' Lorraine said as Roisin re-capped the Lost Cherry, as if they were having a natter over their passing trolleys in Sainsbury's. 'In case I don't get the chance again.'

'Mum, please don't say things like that.'

'I know how this works. They put a mask over your face and then that's it.'

'*Mum!*'

'I watched Joe's series. The one about the policeman having lots of how's your father.'

Roisin's blood temperature dropped to freezing.

'Did Joe do that? Play away on you?'

Bloody hell. Her mother had got there faster than anyone. *To catch a thief.*

'Yeah,' Roisin said. 'With the girlfriend before me. Turns out they were never really over.'

'You were right to finish it. It's what I should've done with your dad. I let him say what went, and I wish I hadn't.'

She gave Roisin a look and Roisin perfectly understood what she was referring to. 'Don't worry, I know.'

'I know you adored your dad and there was never a way to raise what . . . well, you know.'

Roisin didn't know what to say.

'Now, about Matthew. What's the state of play there? You know he's in love with you, don't you?'

Roisin laughed weakly. 'How do you know that?'

'I have eyes and a brain, darling. For now.'

'. . . Yes. We were together briefly, but I found out he knew about Joe's cheating years ago and didn't tell me. Which made me quite mad. So we are currently apart.'

'That's a damned if you do, damned if you don't, isn't it. I suspect, Rosie, he might've got nothing but grief if . . .' Her voice squeaked as she fought through her suffering. '. . . he'd told you.'

No one else in the whole world called her Rosie. Why do the tiny things become suddenly gigantic? Roisin checked her watch.

'Where ARE they?!' Roisin said, not wanting to panic her mum but not being able to contain it. It already felt like hours. Eighteen minutes. That was long enough, surely?

Roisin heard a hammering at the front door and got down the stairs and through the bar, faster than she'd ever moved in her life. People in green uniforms with flashes of high-vis were waiting on the other side and she garbled about her mum and her pain and *she's up here.*

She had to stand behind them as they attended to Lorraine at the top of the stairs, asking questions in upbeat voices, grabbing equipment, moving with practised efficiency.

Roisin didn't know what to do with herself, where to stand, what to do, other than crane her neck.

She'd hoped they'd tut and say this was nothing, not that a stretcher would emerge from the back of the vehicle with the flashing lights.

Then an oxygen mask appeared, and Roisin felt instantly frantic.

'I don't want you to go!' she cried, looking at Lorraine, no longer a patient but her mother. She didn't mean the hospital; she meant anywhere, ever. It was a childlike plea of pure terror at separation, at possibly permanent separation. Roisin burst into a flood of hot tears. Lorraine grabbed clumsily for Roisin's arm and kissed the back of her hand, as she was pulled away.

The blue-lights journey to hospital was overwhelming, Roisin's vision blurred by her partially suppressed crying. On the one hand, professional people had taken over and she could gratefully relinquish responsibility. On the other, the beeping machines, sirens and concentrated attention of third parties tore away any pretence that this wasn't as bad as Roisin feared.

'We'll give you an update when we can – take a seat,' said the paramedic, as her mum disappeared on a gurney through the doors of Macclesfield District, to pass into the hands of strangers. Roisin was left to wander A&E like a ghost.

She was awash with fight-or-flight. The concept of sitting still in one of those plastic bucket seats under this light, for an unspecified but protracted length of time, was like being told she should start Morris dancing.

She checked her phone. No bars of coverage, and it was just gone three a.m.

The time difference in Toronto was five hours: Ryan might pick up, but it seemed smarter to wait until she had something to tell him, rather than taking a night's sleep from him when he might need those energy reserves.

Oh God.

She had to go outside to get reception. She scrolled her phone and rang the number. Selfish, unfair, outrageous, even. She couldn't help it. His was the only voice she wanted to hear.

This experience was an emotional X-ray. The superfluous had disappeared; she was only essentials, bones and organs. She could see what mattered.

Hi, this is Matt! I can't answer right now – leave a message, if you don't hate leaving messages.

'Matt,' she choked into the receiver, after the beep. 'It's me. I'm at hospital. In Macclesfield. It's Mum. They don't know what's wrong yet . . .' She let out a sob and stifled it. 'I found her on the floor, in extreme pain, about an hour ago. The doctors are with her now. I don't know what the hell she's been playing at, 'cos she told me she'd had a clear biopsy before I came back this summer. In true Lorraine fashion, that was bullshit. She's been ignoring pain for ages, using over-the-counter meds to control it . . .' Roisin realised she was spiralling. She paused and gulped.

'. . . Remember you once said that thing about not having many people in your life? I've never missed my dad and my brother like I do now. Anyway. You don't need to reply to this or call me back, or anything. You don't owe me anything at all. I just needed to talk to someone. Not someone. I wanted to talk to *you*. Leaving this message has helped, stupid as it sounds. Anyway. OK. Thanks for listening, even though I didn't give you much choice in the matter. Bye.'

When she walked back into the hospital, a consultant was craning his neck, looking for her.

'Miss Walters? I need to speak to you about your mother.'

She looked at the back of her hand, which bore the smudged imprint of Lost Cherry.

Roisin listened to the soft hiss of medical machinery, the rustling of the ward beyond the thin curtain, as the day began.

Outside the window, the sky had started to lighten in a

sickly tangerine-grey. It was the most beautiful sunrise Roisin had ever seen, because it was the first one she feared her mum would never see.

It turned out this emergency wasn't anything more than a turbulent, yet brief and fully survivable, episode, one she could leave Lorraine to sit up in bed and recount to Ryan later on her mobile.

Roisin was still scrabbling to catch up, retrieving her imagination from the dark places it had roamed to during the crisis. Part of her was still travelling the alternative time-line.

What she'd discovered was that her mother needed her. And Roisin needed Lorraine, too. Not in trivial, mercenary ways, but profound ones that neither of them had articulated. Roisin had been so preoccupied with her mother's indulgent tolerance of her father and brother that she'd absorbed a deep sense she didn't matter. That wasn't ever true, she realised.

Lorraine knew Roisin was angry with her, for things they could never discuss without it provoking scorn and disgust, more damage. It had created a barrier between them.

Roisin needed to stop punishing the people available to be punished, who might've made mistakes but sincerely loved her back.

She would be back later with a bag packed with her mother's favourite perfume, her Kindle, her pyjamas. She leaned in and kissed her sleeping face.

74

She was heading to the door of the A&E department when she saw him. Arms folded in that dark denim jacket, sitting on one of the plastic seats, head to one side, eyes closed, boot resting on opposite knee.

Roisin stared and stared at him. She took in every detail and committed it to memory as her heart tripled in size. It was almost six a.m. and Roisin was lightheaded. She wondered how long he'd been here: she'd spent two hours by her mum's bedside, so he must have arrived then.

She reached out and put a hand on Matt's shoulder.

He started awake and focused on her, rubbing his eyes as he made sense of his surroundings.

'Morning,' he said, blearily standing up.

'Morning. You came all this way?' she said.

'I left as soon as I got your message. How are you? How's Lorraine?'

'She's . . .' Roisin bit hard into her bottom lip to maintain a semblance of composure. Seeing Matt, after the outcome of such a sleepless and turbulent night, could be like a dam breaking. 'She's fine. It was a burst appendix. It can be life-threatening, but they caught it in time. Most of their patients don't ignore the signs of appendicitis for as long as my mother did.' Roisin made a face.

'Oh, thank God,' Matt said.

'They'll keep her in for a few days and she'll feel like she's been run over for weeks, but such a relief.'

'You'll know she's truly recovered when she's pressing the bed alarm for a Kir Royale.'

'You know her too well,' Roisin said, her voice thick. She was broken with gratitude at the sight of him. The love was like a physical weight on her chest.

'Fresh air?' Matt said, after a loaded pause, and Roisin nodded as he pushed the door open.

Under the bricked shelter of the A&E entrance, they took in the view of hospital grounds at dawn, breathed in and out, looked at each other and shook their heads. Sudden illness was like being torn from the normal world and hurled into an alternative universe.

'I'm so glad you're here,' Roisin said.

Matt turned to face her fully. 'Listen, Rosh. I want to make it clear, I'm not here with any expectation of—'

Roisin grabbed him by the lapels, buried her face in his chest and howled. He put his arms around her and held her tightly.

'You're OK,' he shushed her. 'She's going to be alright. You're going to be alright.'

'I know, I know. It's just . . .'

When Roisin had shed enough tears to have the power of speech back, she said, 'My mum lied to get me to spend this summer working at the pub. She didn't feel she could tell me she wanted me there, in case that was all the time she had left. Absolutely insane.'

'Why didn't she go to the doctor? It's a bit of a leap to say, "I've got stomach pains, oh maybe it's terminal?"'

'I know. I think she has to be *this* Lorraine. Glamorous, confident, youthful Lorraine, who runs the show. The thought of even being prescribed treatment that might make her anything other than that was utterly petrifying to her. Scarier than dying when she didn't have to . . . ?'

She looked at Matt in bewilderment. 'She thinks those are the conditions for being loved, I guess. Partly because my dad was a shallow bastard in that regard. My brother's long since fled the scene. He takes after my dad like that. And she wouldn't tell her own daughter, "I'm scared, I need your support."'

Roisin looked at Matt in the grey early light. 'I'm not going to make the same mistake. I called you because you're the one person in the world I wanted to see.' Roisin smiled. 'I'm not going to pretend to be more resilient than I am. I need you.'

Matt smiled back. 'Well, this morning there's nowhere I'd rather be than here. I'm glad you called me. I was actually over the moon you called me, and how often can you say that about three a.m. voicemails?'

'I've been far too hard on you, McKenzie, and you've dealt with it with your typical generosity. Do you want to give that "being a nauseating couple" thing another try?' Roisin said. 'I decided I was going to ask you this over what

426

they call *dressy drinks* on a nice evening out. Instead, here we are, outside Macclesfield Hospital, me having forced you to do a mercy dash. Near a pigeon with a manky foot, pecking at a Ginster's pasty.'

She pointed behind them, and Matt brushed her tears away. 'More than ever, oddly enough.'

They stared into one another's eyes and silently, mutually acknowledged the point they'd arrived at. This was the understanding you always hoped you'd find.

Roisin rubbed her brow. 'God's sake, I've been here half the night. I must look like a haunted turnip.'

'Love isn't dependent on looking glamorous, remember.'

'Oh yes, haha. Just as well.'

Roisin hesitated as Matt got his phone out to check for taxis. She was raw, like she was in emotional High Definition. She felt certain there was a moment here that should be used before normality, with all its virtues and vices, crept back in.

'Whatever happens between us, Matt . . .'

He looked up at her.

'I promise you, we can always tell each other the truth, with no fear of shame. Secrets end up poisoning the person keeping them, I think.'

'What if my final poisonous secret is that I once wrote a poem about the first time I saw you. You were walking down Deansgate in the driving rain, fearlessly head high, with no coat on. You later told me you'd had a row with your mum and stormed out like that. The poem was so bad that the last time I unearthed it, I both wept with laughter and wanted to physically die. I rhyme Roisin with GLEAM. But I STILL couldn't destroy it, because it reminded me of you.'

'Oh my God! Even that! Can I read it?'

'Fuck no.'

75

'Welcome back!' Roisin said, leaning against her desk, watching 10E, who were now 11E, file into the room.

It was either God's sick sense of humour, or Wendy Copeland's front-footed HR strategy, that had given her this class as her first lesson of the autumn term.

Some of them scrutinised her in a pointed way, and Roisin returned the curious looks with a beaming smile.

'Nice holiday, Caitlin?' she said to Caitlin Merry, who wrinkled her nose.

'Alright, I guess. Too soon to be back in this hole, lol.'

'True,' Roisin said, laughing.

'Feeling better, Miss?' sing-songed Logan Hughes, with clear reference to last term and a signal to others.

'Really good, Logan. Thanks for asking.'

If pupils could smell fear, they could equally sense its complete and total absence. Confidence created an almost tangible forcefield; it was very strange. It had deserted Roisin; now she had it back. It obviously came from a mystical well-spring inside and was index linked to your happiness, given how it radiated from her.

MHAIRI MCFARLANE

Roisin could feel their teenaged hopes of further disturbances perishing and shrivelling, second by second. Miss was Miss again.

'Is your husband's sex show gonna be on again? Next year? Miss?' Logan persisted, clearly feeling the loss of any spectacle more than everyone else.

Roisin moved a strand of hair out of her face, tucking it behind her ear, and let a beat of silence pass that increased the attention upon her. It was designed to deliberately up the ante, so they would better appreciate her composure in answering.

'Television drama is fiction. And the only work of fiction I want to talk about is Charles Dickens's *Great Expectations*,' she said, picking up a copy and grinning, to a ripple of groans.

She grabbed a marker and squeaky-penned on the white board.

THE TWO ENDINGS

'SAD' VS 'HAPPY'

She turned back to the room. Roisin was her old self. Actually, no, that wasn't true. She was her *present* self, this self. She liked this self.

'Now, what we're going to look at in today's lesson are the competing endings of the book. Charles Dickens originally wrote different last chapters, where Pip is single and Estella remarries. The one we have in the final version was suggested after his friend, another writer called Wilkie Collins, objected to it being too bleak. He insisted he lighten it.'

430

'Why didn't he say, "It's my book, Wilkie, you wasteman!"' Amir said.

'Yeah, if I'd written the whole-ass thing, slaving away for hours and hours, I'd be like, "Write your own, man,"' Pauly agreed.

'Good point. Literary debate continues to this day over whether Dickens should've yielded to the complaint, and whether it improves or damages the text.' Roisin pointed at the board. 'Do you think the story is better served by the ending you read over the summer on your print outs, where Pip is single and Estella remarries? Or the one in the book we studied, that hints that Pip and Estella will marry? Who fancies answering?'

'Pip should be single at the end,' said Logan Hughes. 'She's cucked him already, right? And you don't want to be married at . . . what is he? Thirty? He should call himself Philip, too. Or Phil. Pip is not a grown-ass man's name, you know.'

'This is olden times though,' Pauly said. 'Thirties was well old. They died at like, forty-one or forty-two.'

'Very specific, Pauly,' Roisin said.

'What do you think, Miss?' Amir said. 'Do you like happy endings?'

Pauly slid off his chair, honking.

'No, I mean! For real! I want to know? Aren't happy endings a bunch of lies, Miss? To make us feel better? Everyone dies in the end, so life doesn't have a happy ending. It's writers telling lies.'

'What if happy endings can be happy beginnings?'

'Like . . . you don't know what happens next?' Amir said.

'Yes. If Pip and Estella marry, that's a beginning. It's where we leave them, but it's not their *ending*, as such.'

'You're saying it's a happy *start*,' Amir said. 'I get it.'

'Yes, a happy start. Or, in one word: hope,' Roisin said, smiling.

'Who wants to read from the last chapter for us?'

'I do, Miss!' said Amir. 'I'm good at it.'

This caused a light outbreak of guffawing and cussing from his peers, which he revelled in. She remembered the handshake through the car window. He was a sweet kid, Amir.

'I agree. Go ahead.'

He cleared his throat and began speaking. Roisin surveyed rows of reasonably docile pupils with satisfaction.

As he said, '*I have been bent and broken but − I hope − into a better shape . . .*' out of the corner of her eye, Roisin noticed an envelope in her bag that she was sure hadn't been there when she packed it last night. She slyly fished it out to look at the single word written on it.

Her name, in his handwriting.

Acknowledgements

Firstly, thanks to my charming, unflappable and wise publisher, Lynne Drew, ably assisted by the lovely editor Lucy Stewart, who both always managed to make work a pleasure. Well at my end, I apologise if it wasn't at yours, heh heh.

The whole HarperCollins family are a delight to deal with, thank you for your support, with a high five to Holly Macdonald for the wonderful artwork. This is how Roisin and Matt looked when they lived inside my head.

Much gratitude to Doug Kean, my wonderful agent, my work husband, the man with the best laugh (not always laughing at me).

Research-wise, thank you to the brilliant Sarah Ellison for walking me through the challenges of teaching in a secondary school in the 21st century (however, any mistakes and all ripe swears regarding pupils are my inventions).

Once again thanks to Manchester resident and expert in all things stylish, Julia Mitchell, for keeping me up to date with one of the world's best cities.

Cheers to my screen agent, Mark Casarotto, for naming *SEEN*! I still think this series idea is solid, you know.

Bryan Ferry wrote 'Slave to Love', not me, and I thank him for my little borrow of its opening line.

Furthermore, I am devastated to be forced to recognise the contribution of the Stoke Newington flâneur, my friend Leo Barker. Incredibly, some passages in this work of complete fiction are directly inspired by his lurid antics. We'll draw a veil.

I nicked a joke from one Olly Richards and had an observation in this novel generously donated by Justin Myers, thank you both for graciously allowing my thefts.

Thank you to my loyal band of first-draft readers: on this go round, Tara, Katie, Kristy, Sean. Couldn't do it without you, or not without ending up completely off my chanks, as they say.

Thank you to my readers out in the world – the privilege of having your time is a thrill that's never worn off and I strive to earn it.

And thank you, as ever, to Alex. To quote your favourite Coldplay (ARF), nobody said it was easy, nobody ever said it would be this hard. My process is a journey, thank you for taking over the driving when I'm busy looking at the map.

If you enjoyed *Between Us*, you'll love

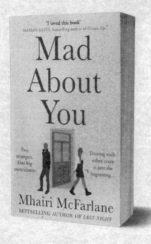

Harriet Hatley is running away from everything.

A dream house-share seems like the perfect place to hide,
but her unlikely housemate has some secrets of his own . . .

'She writes with a singular wit,
charm, and emotional complexity,
every word just right'
EMILY HENRY

Two best friends.
One missed chance.
And a night that changes everything.

'Gorgeously romantic, as well as a
story about friendship and grief and loss;
I never wanted it to end'
BETH O'LEARY

Laurie and Jamie have the perfect office romance.
(They set the rules via email)

Everyone can see they're head over heels.
(They staged the photos)

This must be true love.
(They're faking it)

You can't break your heart in
a fake relationship – can you?

'Hilarious, warm and life-affirming'
JENNY COLGAN

It began with four words. 'I love your laugh. X'
But that was twelve years ago.

When Georgina's new boss, Lucas McCarthy, turns out to
be the boy who wrote those words to her all that time ago,
it feels like the start of something.

There's only one problem:
he doesn't seem to
remember Georgina at all . . .